"Highly entertaining, refreshing, and ⸻ ⸻ ⸻ ⸻ ⸻ enjoy the banter between the wallflower and her captain in this beautifully written, delightful, and faith-filled romance of two endearing hearts."

GRACE HITCHCOCK, award-winning author of *My Dear Miss Dupré*, *Her Darling Mr. Day*, and *His Delightful Lady Delia*

"A heartwarming tale that's sure to inspire and delight readers. Theodosia's determination to protect her friend's daughter makes her an admirable heroine and a worthy intended for Captain Daniel Balfour. They share delightful banter, and Carolyn's descriptions bring the era and Northumberland setting to life, making this a memorable story to savor."

CARRIE TURANSKY, award-winning author of *No Ocean Too Wide* and *No Journey Too Far*

"*Dawn's Untrodden Green* is a sweetly woven romance, with threads of family, faith, and Heyer-esque humor. Carolyn Miller writes with warmth and authenticity, making Theodosia and Daniel's love story a pleasure to read. I thoroughly enjoyed it!"

MIMI MATTHEWS, *USA Today* best-selling author

PRAISE FOR
REGENCY WALLFLOWERS
◇◇◇◇◇◇◇◇◇◇◇◇◇◇◇◇◇◇◇◇◇◇◇◇

"Best-selling author Carolyn Miller is back with a fresh series that will not only thrill readers eager for more of her work, but bring in new fans looking for beautiful writing, fascinating research, deftly woven love stories, and real faith lived out in the Regency period."

Midwest Book Review

"The Regency Wallflowers series has a message of redemption and forgiveness which is sure to resonate with readers of inspirational romance."

ALISSA BAXTER, author of *The Earl's Lady Geologist*

"Fans of Julie Klassen and Abigail Wilson will delight in this newest offering from Regency-favorite Carolyn Miller."

JOANNA DAVIDSON POLITANO, author of *A Midnight Dance*

"Carolyn Miller's authentic portrayal of real-life struggles, raw pain, and faith in the midst of difficult circumstances will resonate with readers. Heartfelt and satisfying . . . sure to captivate fans of inspirational Regency romance."

AMANDA BARRATT, author of *My Dearest Dietrich*, *The White Rose Resists*, and *Within These Walls of Sorrow*

"[Miller] brings Regency England to life with a charming and inspiring romance that is sure to warm readers' hearts."

CARRIE TURANSKY, best-selling author of *No Ocean Too Wide* and *No Journey Too Far*

"Miller's latest captivating romance is rooted beautifully by the threads of redemption and hope."

ABIGAIL WILSON, author of *Twilight at Moorington Cross*

Dawn's
Untrodden Green

REGENCY WALLFLOWERS

Dawn's Untrodden Green

Carolyn Miller

KREGEL
PUBLICATIONS

Dawn's Untrodden Green
© 2023 by Carolyn Miller

Published by Kregel Publications, a division of Kregel Inc., 2450 Oak Industrial Dr. NE, Grand Rapids, MI 49505. www.kregel.com.

Scripture quotations are from the King James Version.

Library of Congress Cataloging-in-Publication Data
Names: Miller, Carolyn, 1974- author.
Title: Dawn's untrodden green / Carolyn Miller.
Description: Grand Rapids, MI : Kregel Publications, [2023] | Series: Regency Wallflowers
Identifiers: LCCN 2022049120 (print) | LCCN 2022049121 (ebook) | ISBN 9780825446559 (print) | ISBN 9780825468513 (Kindle) | ISBN 9780825476853 (epub)
Classification: LCC PR9619.4.M565 D39 2023 (print) | LCC PR9619.4.M565 (ebook) | DDC 823/.92--dc23
LC record available at https://lccn.loc.gov/2022049120
LC ebook record available at https://lccn.loc.gov/2022049121

ISBN 978-0-8254-4665-9, print
ISBN 978-0-8254-7685-3, epub
ISBN 978-0-8254-6851-3, Kindle

Printed in the United States of America
23 24 25 26 27 28 29 30 31 32 / 5 4 3 2 1

To all those who dare to dream.

. . . on the shores of darkness there is light,
And precipices show untrodden green,
There is a budding morrow in midnight,
There is a triple sight in blindness keen.

John Keats, "To Homer"

Chapter 1

Stapleton Court of Wooler had, in its day, oft been described as a monument to quiet pretension. The Elizabethan farmhouse boasted more chimneys and mullioned windows than humble people thought it ought and was nestled behind antique stone-pillared gates within a picturesque landscape that included the hilly backdrop of the Cheviots. These days, however, the buildings and gardens held an air of weary resignation, or perhaps that was merely evoked by the occupants within.

Theodosia Stapleton eyed a stubborn string of cobwebs as she made her way down Stapleton's grand staircase to the dining room, which was, like everything in this house, presided over by her grandfather, General Theodore Henry Stapleton. The decorated war hero, whose only son had died before Theo could grow of an age to remember him, had surprised the county by showing his largesse in allowing his daughter-in-law, Letitia Stapleton, and her wee children to live with him.

"So kind, so very kind," Letitia had always insisted to her daughters in broken, tear-filled whispers whenever the general's gout was playing up and his manners were less than pleasant. Theo suspected most of the villagers believed his cantankerous ways were the norm rather than the exception. Not for nothing had she overheard comments about "General Contrary" and his parsimonious ways. But Theo knew better, and it was proven in his agreement to take in the orphaned child of their neighbor . . . even if it was a temporary thing.

Theo drew inside the oak-panelled dining room, nodding to the room's two occupants, and resumed her place at the mahogany dining table, at the right hand of her grandfather, opposite her mother, the table seating she had always known.

"Has the Mannering lass stopped her infernal crying yet?" the general asked, eyes glinting, bushy grey brows lowered, a piece of beef suspended on his fork.

"Yes." Theo sipped from her glass. "She's asleep now. Annie made poor Rebecca some warm milk, and I stayed with her until she drank it and dropped off to sleep." But only after Theo held her hand, whispering prayers of comfort, as the last of winter's winds shrieked and moaned.

"The poor little dear, losing both parents within a year." Mama's faded blue eyes shone with tears. "How dreadful she must feel."

"Indeed." Sorrow twisted within, pressing fresh fingers of pain through her chest, up her throat, to the back of her eyes. Theo blinked, swallowed the hard ball of emotion, and sought to remember Clara Mannering was in a better place now, with her Lord and Savior, and one day Theo would see her neighbor again.

"Such a silly nonsense, carrying on so." The general rested his elbows on the starched tablecloth. "I have never heard the like, caterwauling in that way."

"Not everyone deals with grief in the same manner." Theo's gaze lifted to eye her grandfather squarely. "I think it shows a tremendous deal of heart that she would mourn her mother so. I'm sure it will take many days before she will not feel like weeping, and until then, we should remember she is in many ways a child."

"I dare say you would never have acted in such a way," he muttered, with a sharp, quick look that, if she was in vain frame of mind, she might even consider possessed a trace of pride.

"I'm afraid I cannot remember my papa, so have not known what depths of emotion the loss of a parent might lead to."

Her mother's bottom lip quivered, a sure sign that poor Rebecca would soon not be the only one weeping.

Theo sighed within, ruing her o'er hasty words. But she could not allow the evening to get maudlin, so turned to her grandfather and forced brightness into her tone. "I do think your agreeing to have her stay with us is quite the most charitable thing you could have done. Thank you."

"Yes, well." As if embarrassed by her words, he plunged his fork into his beef, avoiding eye contact and mumbling incomprehensibly into his gravy-stained beard.

"We couldn't let such a waif of a thing live at Mannering House alone." Mama dabbed at her eyes with her napkin.

"Indeed we could not." Not dear Clara's only child. Not their nearest neighbor. And especially not with the house in such a state of disrepair.

"Those dreadful peacocks Mannering insisted on keeping." Mama shuddered. "They always sound like a woman is crying, or dying, or some such thing. Poor child. Can you imagine growing up listening to that every waking hour?"

Theo was glad she need not. "I'm hopeful that in time we shall be able to distract poor Becky with reminders that not everything in this world is so very sad and sorry. But as for us, we should give further thought as to her future."

Grandfather grunted agreement, echoed by her mother's soft affirmative. "Has she given word yet as to who is the next of kin?"

Theo nodded, refraining from pointing out she'd mentioned this before. "Clara had a brother. He is in the army."

His countenance brightened. "And what's his name?"

"A Captain Balfour, I believe."

"Balfour, Balfour." His brow knit in concentration, his fork hovering in the air, as time expanded into a length that would distress more impatient people.

Theo exchanged glances with her mother, then refocused on her meal. Grandfather's recollections of army colleagues and events had often formed the substance of their mealtime conversations. Attempts to redirect discussion to other topics sometimes met with derisive snorts as he struggled to remember exactly which battlefield or London soldiers' club he'd encountered the man or situation.

She sliced her beef, the sputtering candlelight reminding her to speak to Annie about checking the supply of candles. They might have but recently escaped the drear of wintry darkness, but the weather in this part of England could never be relied upon to recall the relentless turn of the calendar.

"My dear," Mama said, as the general's silent cogitations continued, "do you think we should make over those drapes in dear Rebecca's room? I'm afraid it must seem so outdated for her, poor pet. It has been so long since we've had a young girl in the place," she added with a wistful sigh.

Becky Mannering might, at sixteen, be considered more a young lady than a girl, but she was far more youthful than Theo's own advanced age of one and thirty.

"Perhaps we should wait until we know what her uncle wishes to do." And what the general—and their meagre household allowance—would permit. "But I agree, it would be good to do what we can to make her feel as comfortable as possible."

"Speaking of visitors, do you think Seraphina might be persuaded to a visit?"

She might if her sister's nipcheese solicitor husband wanted to prove solicitous to his wife's family for once. Theo kept such thoughts behind her teeth and murmured a noncommittal "Perhaps."

"I simply long to see her." Mama sighed plaintively. "It has been such an age, and—"

"Are you sure it wasn't Captain Daniel Balfour?" Grandfather interrupted. "Did something heroic. His decisiveness saved a hundred men or some such deed."

Theo's lips tweaked in rueful apology as she shifted attention to her grandfather. She had been too filled with cares and responsibilities to remember every whispered word that Clara had uttered. "I think that was his name, but I'm afraid I cannot recall his exploits."

"You cannot recall?" he asked incredulously, as if he himself had not struggled to do so these past minutes. "You cannot remember that it was his quick wits that shielded his men from enemy fire while on the Peninsular?"

"There are so many stories of heroic exploits—"

"None like his!" the general insisted. "I can never understand why you don't pay attention to what truly matters," he said gruffly. But from the way his moustache lifted, a smile lurked beneath his beard, hinting of the fondness she had always known behind his oft-brusque exterior.

She swallowed a wry smile—open emotion was never welcomed at the table—and said carefully, "I think what truly matters is that Becky's uncle is informed about his sister's death as soon as possible."

"You will write?"

"Yes. He will be too late for the funeral, of course, but I'll write to him again tonight." Clara's whispered request had led Theo to write, informing him of his sister's illness not so long ago. Her heart sorrowed. How much harder would it be to pen—and read—the newest state of affairs.

"I'll see it gets franked and sent off tomorrow."

"Thank you."

The general shook his head. "A bad business, this."

"Poor little mite. Two parents gone in a matter of months. It is so sad, so very, very sad." Mama's voice wavered again.

"We must do all we can to make her time here as easy and pleasant as possible." Theo eyed her grandfather. "Even if she is inclined at times to be weepy."

"That's enough sauce from you, little puss."

A smile escaped—"little" she had not been these past eighteen years—and she turned her attention to her meal while her heart continued to pray for the poor girl upstairs who had wept herself to sleep.

Dear Lord, send Your comfort to poor Becky. Be with her uncle. Lord, be with us all.

Becky's tears of the first week eased into a general melancholy, something Theo attempted to alleviate by offering the girl distractions. But the delights of puppies and spring lambs and what tired treasures Wooler's small shops offered only boosted Becky's spirits for a short while before the sadness settled again.

As for herself, Theo was at a loss as to know what to do. Until Captain Balfour replied, she was responsible for Becky's welfare, and it seemed society in general was at once torn between astonishment at her grand-father's willingness for Theo to assume such a role and relief that they need not assume the task themselves.

"But my dear!" Lady Bellingham exclaimed during one of her near-daily visits to Stapleton. "I understand you were close to the girl's mother, and of course, here at Stapleton you are Mannering's nearest neighbors, but how can one expect a young lady of one and thirty to know how to care for a young girl?"

Theo smiled, shrugging off the sting of the thinly veiled advice from the squire's wife. "I may not be the best qualified, but I was young once myself."

"Oh, I know you were—I mean, are! Oh, you cannot try to pretend to not understand what I mean, passing yourself off as if in your decline, wearing the cap like you're an old maid, when every young man in the village would pick up the handkerchief should one be thrown."

Theo's smile grew wry, and she resisted the temptation to touch her marred cheek. "Please spare my blushes, Lady Bellingham."

"Blushes, indeed. You know it is so. And *I* know it is most commend-able for you to wish to care for the child. But what does it mean for your future?"

"I do not see this as a burden, nor as something I will do forever. Cap-tain Balfour will return one day, and then we shall know what to do."

"Oh, but what if he is killed?"

"Then Rebecca shall remain with us until she is married," Theo responded calmly.

That's what Mr. Cleever, the Mannering solicitor, had approved and said was most appropriate when he had called to inform them that Rebecca Mannering was a young lady of independent means—or would be when the house was sold and she reached her majority. Such news they and Mr. Cleever had determined to keep to themselves, sure this infor-mation would only prove food for those of a mind to fortune hunting and those idle tongues that already wagged too quickly over the poor girl with her famous uncle.

For famous he had turned out to be. Action had seen his name grace dispatches from the front, reported in newspapers the length and breadth of Britain. The general had, unsurprisingly, been the first to point it out. His unguarded conversation around Lady Bellingham had been enough to prick that lady's ears and cause a gush of high-pitched emotion that had soon propelled him to scowl and mutter about the indecency of visitors whose shrieks drove a man from the comfort of his room.

Not that the squire's wife seemed to notice. Or care. "Truly? Such a hero is our dear sweet Rebecca's only living relative? Oh, how wonderful!"

"One can hardly think either of them feel such a thing at this moment," Theo gently reproved.

"Oh, yes, yes, of *course*. But imagine! We will likely soon be visited by such a man! Oh, I'm sure he must be handsome—all heroes are, are they not, Miss Stapleton?"

"In books, perhaps," she murmured.

Lady Bellingham tittered. "Oh, how very droll you are."

How very levelheaded. She could count on one finger the number of truly handsome men she had met, or at least that matched the image conjured up in forlorn dreams. The men of her village—save for her grandfather—were for the most part farmers, and their bluff manners and weatherworn looks were hardly those of a charming prince. Not that one could always trust a handsome face . . . Her heart twisted.

Enough of the past.

"Regardless of his outward appearance, I think it's most important for dear Becky to feel like she is loved. She is such a sweet, tender-hearted girl, and we are doing all we can to help her through this difficult time."

"I'm sure you are. You and your mother have always been softhearted that way. And after your own poor papa's demise, well, I can imagine you understand something of her pain."

There seemed little point in mentioning that Theo's memories of her father were at naught. "If you would, continue to hold Becky in your prayers, Lady Bellingham."

"Oh, of course. And if there's anything I can do, please let me know."

Theo held her tongue, sure that telling her ladyship that the best thing she could do would be to refrain from further speculation would meet with deaf or, worse, offended ears.

Not long after the squire's wife had departed, Becky crept in, accepting Theo's invitation to sit beside her on the sofa and rest her fair head on Theo's shoulder. "I heard what you said before," she whispered.

"Which part, dearest? I'm afraid I say so many things sometimes it is hard to recall." Her lips curved. "Or perhaps that's just the effect of listening to Lady Bellingham."

"She talks such a lot, doesn't she?"

"She has a good heart. Now, what thing in particular did I say that you took exception to?"

"No, no! I could never take exception to anything you might say, dear Miss Stapleton."

"I think you could if you knew me better, but as you don't, I shan't tease you anymore. What did I say that concerns you, my dear?"

"About my being sweet." Becky's dark eyes glistened. "I'm not sweet. Not at all. You know how much I loved Mama, but sometimes I can't help but feel so very angry with her. Why couldn't she fight harder against the illness? Why did she have to leave me?"

How to explain that the sordid legacy of one's father had led his wife to contract a disease more commonly associated with those ladies who plied their trade at night, a disease that had seemingly eluded him while ravaging poor Clara's body and mind.

Poor Clara. Poor Becky. She smoothed the girl's golden hair. "Oh, darling, you know she loved you very much and had no wish to depart this world. I know it doesn't seem fair."

"No." Becky burrowed into Theo's shoulder. "It *isn't* fair."

As Becky wept Theo prayed for peace to fill Becky's mind and heart, for the weight of grief to lift, for these savage tugs of sorrow to recede.

A shuddery breath, two, and the tears eased. "I'm so sorry, Miss Stapleton. I have made your sleeve damp."

"It is no matter. I have another."

A chuckle pushed through the sniffles. "You are so good to me, Miss Stapleton."

"Theo. Have we not agreed that you are to call me 'Theo'? Theodosia is such a mouthful of a name, is it not? And Miss Stapleton makes me sound far too much like a maidenly aunt that I'm afraid I can never subscribe to such a thing—and not just because my dear sister has yet to produce any progeny."

"Well, yes." Becky's broken smile quickly faded. "But I do not like to hear of my uncle as being some kind of hero. He is not."

"I'm afraid nearly all of England would disagree with you, my dear," Theo said gently. "I'm assured by my grandfather that his actions were such that he saved hundreds of lives."

"Perhaps he did. But my father could never stand him. Did you ever meet him when he visited when I was a little girl?"

"I do not believe that I did."

"He and Father had the most awful row. Father said he was a bully, someone who insisted on getting his own way, and would not let a man take care of his own family."

Theo nodded but kept her lips fastened. From the way Becky talked, he seemed a fearsome monster indeed. But unlike one bound by cords of filial affection, she could imagine the former owner of Mannering would take exception to his own bullying tactics being brought to task. As for the irony of Francis Mannering declaring his interest in family responsibility . . .

"Oh, Miss Stapleton—I mean, Theo—please don't make me go and stay with him. I could not bear it."

"To be frank, I do not think it would quite suit him at this time. You are a *little* young, perhaps, to be forced to follow the drum."

Another sniffly giggle. "But when he writes, he might insist I leave, and I could not bear to leave you."

"One day you will have to." Theo drew her own handkerchief from her sleeve and offered it to Becky, who accepted it with alacrity. "Take heart, my dear. One's memories of a person are rarely borne out as true. You will likely find your uncle much more personable than you recall."

"I doubt it."

"Regardless, until your uncle writes, you may rest assured that you are safe and protected here."

But Theo's chest tensed, as if protesting her words. It had been weeks now, and still he had not written, which lent weight to Becky's doubts about the true honor of the supposed hero.

Theo's grandfather had assured her that enough time had passed for her letter to arrive and an answer to be penned and returned. So where was his reply? What had he to say?

She stifled her worries, reminding herself that God was in control. They would find out soon, she was sure.

Her smile faltered. Well, she hoped.

The next week saw the arrival of a letter. The scrawl was very blunt:

Mr. Stapleton,

Thank you for your care and concern for my sister and niece. I intend to send my man of business to visit shortly, as soon as duties permit. Such future plans will be discussed then.

Yours etc.,
D. Balfour

Theo frowned over the opening appellation. Had she been so careless in her previous letter that *Theodosia* could appear as *Theodore*? Mama had always decried her penmanship, as if she blamed that for Theo's unwedded state. Not that it mattered. What mattered was that she had the implied consent of Becky's remaining relative to care for her until such matters may be otherwise arranged.

A sound at the morning room's door drew her head up, and she offered Becky a greeting.

Becky glanced at the paper. "Mr. Siddons said the post had come."

"Indeed it has. And there's something that affects you."

"Is that from my uncle at last?"

"Yes."

"May I see it?"

"Of course." Theo handed over the short missive.

"Hmph." Becky frowned as she read it, then glanced up. "See? I told you. He doesn't even wish to see me! He is rude and inconsiderate."

"Because he wrote a letter in a style so matter-of-fact? Come now, you can't hold a man's inferior letter writing skills as indicative of his general character."

"You'd be surprised," Becky said darkly.

Theo suppressed a smile. "I would hope that I not be judged simply because I might not be so flowery in my descriptions as some prefer. In fact," she added thoughtfully, "I feel quite certain my sister is not impressed by my lack of detailing of the gowns I wear or the arrangement of my hair. I am sure my correspondence is forever a sad disappointment to her."

"You could never be, Miss—Theo."

"Very good. You will remember to call me as such one day, I hope."

The wavering smile settled into lines of petulance. "I wish *you* were my aunt."

"But as that cannot be, we best turn our attention to something more apropos. I know! You might teach me something about your trick with arranging your hair like so. It really is most becoming and suits you so very well." Theo admired the glossy blonde curls spilling sweetly from Becky's topknot. "I'm afraid that I have never quite mastered how to make one's ringlets last longer than an hour. Mine always fall flat within minutes."

"That's because your hair is so thick."

"Only too true, I'm afraid." Theo sighed. "Sometimes I fear for my comb, that it will get lost forever in my mane. I'm sure there are some pins lost in there for years."

Becky giggled before protesting, "But it is such a pretty color."

"It is kind of you to say so, but I'm afraid many would disagree with you."

"How silly! As if one can be responsible for the color of one's hair. You cannot be responsible for it being red."

"No. Though I am assured by my sister that its hue could be diminished by the careful application of lemon juice. She is such a believer in the power of lemon juice, she believes it might even make my freckles disappear."

"I think your freckles hardly signify."

"They do to my sister," Theo said with wryness. She'd once overheard Seraphina's pithy description of Theo's person. *Sadly bran-faced.*

"Forgive me, but I think your sister is very wrong to say such things." Indignation colored Becky's words.

"I happen to agree with you. But as I prefer to not think on such misery, let us turn our minds to other things. Perhaps our spirits would benefit from a walk."

A walk in the fresh air over hills might blow away some of the dusty cobwebs of the soul.

⸎

As the carriage clattered over the causeway, Captain Daniel Balfour settled back against the squabs, smiling a little as he thought on his friends, one older, one more new. His visit to Langley House—although the moniker *castle* would be more apt—had proved a chance to get to know James and Sarah Langley far more than he'd anticipated, with all kinds of drama proving that the battlefield was not the only place where danger lurked.

He'd enjoyed meeting James's wife. Had marveled at the transformation of his friend. How wonderful that such a sinner could see salvation, that God could choose to reform a rake. But that same impulse that had propelled Daniel to hasten his arrival at Langley House, thus witnessing the doctor's unfortunate fall and protecting his friend from the noose, now also urged him further north. He withdrew the crumpled paper, flattening it against his thigh. The handwriting and direction in the upper left corner were unfamiliar, but the scrawled words inside he could almost recite.

It is with profound regret that I write on behalf of your sister, Clara Mannering, to inform you that she has recently fallen extremely ill. Whilst all is being done for her, I would strongly encourage you to visit

Wooler at your earliest convenience. Please be assured that both Clara and your niece, Rebecca, are being cared for at Stapleton Court.

Yours truly,
Theodore Stapleton

Clara.

Regret crossed his heart. He should have tried harder to stay in touch over the years, but with war and his career, and after that last visit when he'd been told in no uncertain terms just how poorly his brother-in-law, Francis, thought of Daniel's low connections, he had made little effort over the years, save to answer the rare letter from his sister.

Of course, that might have been as much about protecting his sister and niece from another unfortunate scene. During their last encounter, Daniel had not held back from succinct observations about his brother-in-law's commitment to his marriage vows, a fact Francis had not appreciated. Still, Daniel should have made more of an effort. Especially after Francis's death. He could only hope he wasn't too late now.

Glimpses of countryside flashed by, and his mind turned to his recent time in London. He was a military man, and not cut out for the parties and social intercourse his awards apparently demanded he participate in. Friends like Lieutenant Musgrave excelled in societal discourse, but Daniel's overly developed sense of irony kept him from drawing quite so much pleasure.

He had simply been doing his duty, after all. There was no need for phrases like those uttered by his superiors and repeated by the King about "invincible bravery" and "determined devotion to the honor of His Majesty's arms." After the King's commendation at St. James, he had been hounded by people, inundated with invitations to parties galore.

Duty had forced attendance at a few such functions, but he'd been sickened by the show. Those claiming an acquaintanceship, those offering extravagant dinners that would feed his men for a week, he had little wish for. He'd grown only too aware of those that had much and those who did not. Few, if any, of these people would give him a moment's thought if it wasn't for King George's medal glinting on his chest.

"But everyone wants to meet the great hero," Lieutenant Jeremy Musgrave had entreated during one particularly loathsome London event when Daniel had protested and made his feelings known. "The young ladies are all agog with excitement. You need only throw the handkerchief and take your pick."

"What a coxcomb such a picture suggests."

"I did not mean you were, only that you could."

"I could be a coxcomb? Why, thank you. I think."

Musgrave chuckled. "Always so quick to take a miff, aren't you? That must be how you have got on so well these past years."

"A secret I am loath to share."

His subordinate grinned. "But in all seriousness, may I ask how long you plan to remain in London? I know you can hardly bear to tear yourself away from such joys as these festivities, as well as the young ladies wishing to know the famous captain and perhaps be considered Mrs. Balfour."

Daniel cut him a look.

Musgrave's amusement sounded again. "But I should very much like to show you off to my family back in Leicestershire. And come to think of it, I do have a younger sister who is dying to meet you."

"While I appreciate your interest in my matrimonial prospects, I assure you I have no immediate plans to embark on such a pleasant task. I have family matters to attend to in Northumberland."

"That great distance?"

"That great distance." He'd written at first to say his man of business would attend but, after sending the missive, had realized the callousness of such an action, and thus he'd determined to visit, a decision affirmed when he'd received the legal summons to speak on James Langley's behalf in Northumberland. Wooler was only a day or so's carriage drive away from Langley House. He would visit, see his sister and niece, attend to whatever needed doing, and within a week return south to London.

"Better you than me." The lieutenant's blue eyes had lit. "Perhaps on your return from your visit to the north, you will find need to stop in and see us at Thorpe Acre. We are not so very far from the North Road."

"Perhaps I will. But only if you promise not to have your sister thrown at my head."

Musgrave raised his brows. "Mariah? It isn't likely. She's only fourteen after all. You need a wife of greater years and sense than that."

Daniel acquiesced, but inside his heart protested. He was wedded to the military and had no desire to marry. Felicitations to friends like James Langley and Adam Edgerton, who had found wives and settled down, but such was not for him.

The moor and treeless landscape beyond the window spoke clearly that he wasn't in the tamed pastoral setting of his youth. The area here possessed a kind of wildness, something remote, something that seemed to call to him, much like Spain and Portugal had done, drawing him into adventure, into territory unexplored.

He was a loner, someone whose quick wits and sense of duty meant a quiet domestic life held no charm. He wanted to be doing, not wooing, and was happy in his life.

Such thoughts proved he did not need a wife at all.

Chapter 2

Theo guided Becky down the aisle to shake the rector's hand. She complimented Mr. Crouch on his sermon—under half an hour today—and moved outside under heavy grey skies, where the servants of Mannering beckoned them nearer.

Janet Drake, Mannering's housekeeper-cook, and her groundsman husband, Ian, stood chatting quietly with Annie and Robert Brigham, who held similar roles at Stapleton. Unfortunately, Janet's propensity for dithering had led to meals served at Mannering House always arriving far later than Francis Mannering had liked, and the sluggish efforts of her husband had led to the near ruin of the house they were paid to care for. Still, stubborn loyalty to the family meant that the Drakes knew how to hold their tongue, a quality many could learn from.

"Oh, Miss Becky, Miss Stapleton," Janet said in a loud whisper. "Did you hear?"

"Hear what, Janet?" Becky adroitly avoided a large mud puddle as they drew nearer.

"He's coming!"

"Who is?"

"Why, the captain hisself!"

Becky's shoulders slumped, her face a mask of disconsolation such that Theo abandoned her code of restraint.

"Forgive me, Janet, but I understood that it was his man of business who would attend. That is what his latest correspondence suggested."

"Oh! P'raps it is. I do not rightly know."

Theo exchanged a look with Becky. Mr. Cleever had advised that Janet and Ian retain their positions at Mannering and maintain the property as best they could until its future—and that of its young mistress—could be determined, but neither servant had ever been known for their wits. "Muttonheaded" was one of Grandfather's many epithets for Mannering's servants. "As bird-witted as Francis Mannering was close-fisted, and a churl." Indeed, Francis Mannering had never been shy about tossing around his own descriptions about his servants. Of course, he did not attend to household matters unless they directly affected him, and such selfishness curtailed the Drakes' ability to manage their other duties. Be that as it may, the Drakes' loyalty could never be questioned. In fact, they had faithfully nursed Clara until Theo had encouraged Clara's and Becky's removal to be cared for at Stapleton Court during Clara's last weeks.

Lady Bellingham sailed into their knot of conversation. "Ah, my dears. Has there been any more word about your uncle's return, Rebecca?"

"Actually—" Ian began.

At Becky's indrawn breath, Theo judged it best to not upset her further. "We cannot say for certain."

"When you do know, you must be sure to inform us. I was thinking, during Mr. Crouch's sermon, how wonderful it would be to host a turtle dinner for the conquering hero."

"Indeed."

"Yes! Don't you think that would be a most marvelous treat?"

At the expectant look, Theo could only murmur, "I must confess such a treat has not come my way before."

"I'm not surprised." Lady Bellingham patted her arm. "Such treats are not inexpensive, and thus are reserved for the most important personages, after all. But just think—how wonderful it would be to honor such a distinguished visitor to our part of the world. Oh! And what say you to a Venetian breakfast?"

"A what, madam?"

"A special afternoon garden party. Or perhaps we should have a ball. Yes, a masquerade could be the very thing, wouldn't you agree?"

"I am not certain that this occasion would see a masquerade as being considered quite the thing," Theo said cautiously.

"Oh, that's right. I was forgetting. You poor dear." Lady Bellingham gave Becky a look of sympathy. "How dreadful all of this must be for you."

Becky's pleading eyes drew certainty that they should effect their departure quickly. But just as Theo began to make their excuses, Frederick Bellingham moved closer and was quickly pulled by his mother into the conversation.

"Ah, Frederick. You would not say no to a ball for our hero, would you?"

"Our hero?"

"Why, Captain Balfour, of course! We were discussing this just last night, were we not? That it would be good to honor his arrival with all manner of functions and activities such that I'm positive he's not had the chance to enjoy for some time. How could one, after all, when one has been so very busy fighting for so long? And a ball would give you a chance to dance with dear Miss Stapleton here."

Frederick blushed, and Theo's heart pinched in sympathy for him. The poor fellow was a worthy soul, and his holding a candle for Theo had not gone unnoticed this many a year. But even if he wasn't several years younger, she could never seriously entertain him as a matrimonial candidate no matter how she liked him. Only one man had ever piqued her interest, but he'd made it very clear she had not piqued his.

"W-would you do me the honor of standing up with me for the first two dances, Miss Stapleton?"

His embarrassment made her agree, an acquiescence she instantly regretted as his eyes lit. Oh dear. She had no wish to encourage the boy. "But only if such a thing should indeed take place," she reminded softly. "And I feel it wise to caution you that Captain Balfour may feel it somewhat inappropriate to be dancing when he would still be mourning the loss of his sister."

"Of course, my dear," said Lady Bellingham. "One always wishes to observe the proprieties, and we would not be so heartless in planning a large entertainment when people are still so sad." She patted Becky's shoulder, before her attention was diverted. "Oh, Mrs. Cleever," she called across the church grounds, "I wonder, what say you to a Venetian breakfast when dear Captain Balfour arrives? Excuse me, my dears."

Theo's lips curved in wryness, and she was not unhappy when the heavy moisture in the air resolved into a light shower of rain. She made their excuses to Frederick and beckoned for Becky to join her in the carriage.

"I cannot understand why people are so insensitive." Becky slumped in her seat. "Don't they know my uncle is a villain?"

"He can hardly be considered a villain," Theo objected gently. "Not when he has saved so many people's lives and been awarded a medal from the King. And please, dear Becky, remember, he was your mother's brother, and therefore must be afforded some measure of respect."

"I cannot believe he would only send a man of business to look in on me," she grumbled. "You would think he would have a care at least."

"I'm sure he does," Theo said, as her mother and the general finally drew near the carriage.

"Detestable popinjay," muttered her grandfather. He waited for Theo's mother to sit next to Becky, then hefted his way inside and to his seat. "Dares to sermonize for goodness knows how long, then has the temerity to tell me I should not disagree when he says that an eye for an eye is not a precedent that we should follow. Have you ever heard such nonsense?"

"Very bold-faced indeed." Theo lowered her gaze and bit her bottom lip to stop an indiscreet smile.

"Where would we be if we simply turned the other cheek all the time?"

"I wonder."

He harrumphed. "I might remind you, young lady, that the fifth commandment reminds us to honor our father and mother."

"Indeed it does," she agreed, meeting his gaze innocently. "Who was it you feel did not honor you sufficiently today?"

"You, at the moment." Another noisy clearing of the throat, and he glanced out the window, further mutterings lost behind his moustache.

"Theodosia, dear, you know it is imprudent to speak to your grandfather in such a way," her mother remonstrated. "Why, when he has always been so very kind as to permit us to live at Stapleton—"

"Oh, stop your fussing, Letitia," he snapped. "The girl knows I mean nothing by it."

"Forgive me, Grandfather," Theo said, ruefully aware of her quick tongue.

"Saucy puss," he muttered, but not before she glimpsed his smile, and knew herself forgiven.

The carriage grew quiet and Theo caught Becky's look of alarm. Poor dear. She was still learning the ways of the general and the dynamics of their household.

Theo patted Becky's arm. "After luncheon, it might be of benefit to have some quiet rest and reflection."

"Indeed it would," her grandfather growled.

Theo mouthed an "I'm sorry" to her mother and refrained from more conversation. Perhaps, if this rain let up, a moment of quiet reflection could be followed by a walk. Such activity could help bring appreciation of the countryside, with its offerings of spring, as well as help clear this restlessness induced by the conversation of the squire's wife and son. Yes. A walk might prove the very thing.

Daniel's plan to arrive by Sunday had been thwarted by an obstreperous carriage wheel. Given the lack of the cheering light of a house, and his disinclination to send the coachman to search for one in the wet and dark, Daniel had spent a long and cold night huddled inside the broken vehicle, wearing as many of his clothes as could be found. He and the driver made the best of it, having a picnic of sorts with the leftovers Sarah Langley had insisted he take for the journey. He'd demurred at first, but as the rain pattered on the roof and the wind rocked the unstable carriage, he'd been extremely thankful for the generosity that supplied their meagre evening meal.

The following rain-soaked morning had revealed a glimpse of a nearby farmhouse, which Daniel visited, and though he'd had no wish to disturb their Sabbath rest, had found shelter and strong backs which insisted on attending to the wheel. It proved to be much later on Monday morning when he finally made his way into Wooler and stopped at the small inn, whereupon he ordered a hearty meal for the coachman and himself.

A blessedly hot meal and cold drink later, he made enquiries about the hiring of a gig, paid off the coachman, and transferred his luggage to the gig. He hadn't brought an excess—the life of a soldier demanded that he not own an excess of anything. And this visit would hopefully prove of short duration, enough time to see Clara and her daughter, and determine if he could do anything for them before he returned south and resumed his armed-forces career.

A slap of the reins and he began to follow the road past the village shops to Mannering, if his memory served, when a window display snagged his attention. Perhaps . . . yes, perhaps that would be best. He stopped and tied up the horse outside the small shop he'd spied. Last time he'd visited, he couldn't help but notice the sad lack of fineries he'd assumed his sister would be accustomed to, especially married to someone like Francis Mannering, who so often was dressed in the expensive clothes of an aspiring dandy. Not that his brother-in-law's manners had ever been polished, though he must have had some measure of address to persuade both Clara and their parents that he was not simply a loose fish. Perhaps the promise of inheritance of Mannering had blinded them to his less savory qualities. Or perhaps he'd genuinely once loved Daniel's sister and had grown out of it. Regardless, Clara—and little Rebecca—might appreciate a small gift in addition to the doll he'd purchased in London, especially seeing as Daniel had neither opportunity nor finances to bestow such things until now.

So he entered the small shop, a kind of haberdashery, with a sign advertising woolen draper, linen draper, hosiery, and gloves, "the shop first in size and fashion." He stifled a smile. It seemed this was the *only* shop in this village selling such wares.

"May I help you, sir?" a colorless woman of uncertain years asked.

Oh. He realized how out of place he must appear, the only man in such a store. "I am just looking," he hedged, moving swiftly behind an assortment of ribbons hanging from a display.

The hushed murmur at his entrance swiftly rose in volume again, prompting an infernal desire to flee. Brave man that he was, able to face cannon fire yet afraid of a few village women's tongues.

". . . heard that he'll be here any day!"

"Yes. Dear Lady Bellingham was telling me just yesterday that she plans to welcome him with all kinds of gaieties."

"She is inclined to make rather a fuss, isn't she, Mrs. Cleever?" said a woman of nasal inflection.

Cleever. His ears latched onto the name. The solicitor his sister used was named Cleever. How many people in this town would possess that name?

"I think it only right that such a hero be feted in this way," countered the woman who might be the solicitor's wife. "It's not every day a man is given a medal from a king."

His breath hitched.

"I quite agree with you," said the first, apparently fickle-minded, woman. "One can only wish to see a man honored in such a way. Why, I overheard Lady Bellingham the other day talking about a Venetian breakfast. Now, have you ever heard of such a thing?"

Why yes, he had. One of the more outlandish entertainments provided for his amusement back in London. He had no desire to repeat the experience. Pretending he was more of a gentleman than he was, well-versed in the art of conversation when every young woman he'd talked to had uttered nothing of sense or interest. How was he supposed to know the first thing about a lady's reticule? He was not even completely sure he knew what one was, having never held an interest in women's fashions of the day.

"And a ball! It's been so long since we had a ball."

"Elvira Bellingham is the only one with a room large enough for such a thing—"

Good heavens. What would they say next?

"—to be a masquerade!"

He shuddered.

"How wonderful!"

"Captain Balfour will feel truly honored, I'm sure."

Oh no, he wouldn't. Balls? Masquerades? His entire body itched.

"Sir?"

He jumped, blindly snatched at two ribbons, and thrust them at the shop assistant. "I'll take these, thank you."

"Certainly, sir."

He followed her to the serving counter and paid, pretending interest in the floor-to-ceiling shelves crammed full of merchandise, all the while only too aware of the women whose conversation had ceased again.

What would they say if they knew he was the man they'd been talking of? Another shudder trembled up his back. Heaven help him should they find out.

"There you are, Mr. . . . ." The shop assistant's brows rose in enquiry as she held out the package.

"Thank you." He stuffed the small paper-wrapped parcel under his arm. He had no intention of satisfying her curiosity nor wasting further time with those inclined to gossip and speculation. He needed to see his sister. Which meant travelling to Mannering to dispose of his luggage, dressing more appropriately than in dirt-specked travel clothes, then making his way to the place mentioned in the letter.

And discovering just what interest this Theodore Stapleton person had in his unfortunate sister and his poor niece.

Chapter 3

Becky had not accompanied Theo on her walk today. Mama's invitation to help her with some sewing proved of greater interest than Theo's expressed inclination to traverse muddied fields and byways. But the last days of enforced confinement had meant Theo needed to escape; there was only so much domestic triviality she could bear, and the smell of fields after rain was one akin to bliss.

The vanilla-and-almond scent of the nearby yellow gorse begged her to pause, so she stopped under a willow tree, closing her eyes to take a deep breath. How heavenly. Some might dismiss these most northerly parts of England as dull, but there was always something to appreciate should one care to look and really see. She savored another inhalation, the moisture in the air drawing her to open her eyes. Ahead, the mist-shrouded breadth of Humbleton Hill rose before her like a mystical castle of ancient times, worthy of the romance woven by Walter Scott and other poets of his ilk. She'd often wondered about the remains of the hilltop fort, whether any descendants remained of those long-ago legends of folklore. This part of the north was said to boast the most castles and forts to be found anywhere in England, even if many of them were in ruins. Clearly this was a land where people wished to claim their dominance, tried to prove themselves as kings and conquerors.

Her thoughts slid back to Lady Bellingham's comments from the other day. What would a modern-day hero look like? Clearly the vast majority of the village expected him to appear strong and possess a handsome countenance. But she couldn't help wonder at such sentiment. Couldn't a plain man hold as much capacity for courage as a man of fine looks? More, perhaps, for he could never rely on his natural advantages to get ahead.

A sharp chirruping and sudden ascent of birds drew attention to a thin stranger driving a muddied gig. He wasn't one of the gypsies of nearby Kirk Yetholm, who travelled the county with their wagons of wares. This was a man she had never seen before, his gaze upon the hills as hers had been but moments before.

As he approached the willow tree, it became clear the man was not very tall, and with his plain features, tanned complexion, and slightly receding hairline, certainly would not be held by many of the female population to accord with notions of handsomeness. But still, for all that, there was a quality about him which drew her attention. Was there sadness in his features, a weariness in the shake of head? Was he lost? Curiosity overcame her reticence and concern about being a single woman out of doors, and she moved from her spot under the tree.

Her appearance seemed to startle him, as he drew his horse to a sharp halt. "Forgive me, madam, I did not see you there."

She nodded in politeness, reluctant to own her earlier concealment.

"If you'll excuse me, could you please tell me if this is the way to Stapleton Court?"

"Yes, it is." Interest piqued—Grandfather had not mentioned he was expecting any visitors today—and she studied him more closely.

The man's cheeks were thin, and his face held creases, as if he either squinted or smiled a great deal. And yet there was that look of sadness in his dark-grey eyes.

For some nonsensical reason, this last thought lodged deep and softened her heart toward him, stranger though he may be. "I have just come from there."

"This is most propitious. Tell me, is the master of the house a kind man?"

Grandfather? "Some would say so, others might not be so inclined." That was perhaps charitable, but she need not speak too openly with a stranger about the neighborhood's fixed belief in the general's contrary nature.

"Ah. And the lady of the house?"

"Mrs. Stapleton?"

"Yes. I believe she is caring for a young lady?"

Who was he? Why was he asking such questions? "I'm afraid I do not understand your interest in such things, but I can assure you that Mrs. Stapleton is all that is good and kind."

He straightened in the gig. "Oh, I beg your pardon, I meant no disrespect. I have had a tiring journey and just learned some hard news, and simply wanted to ascertain if Miss Mannering was being cared for appropriately. I understood the gentleman to have quite a keen interest in the case."

All feelings of goodwill disappeared as the man's meaning became plain. He thought her grandfather had an unwholesome interest in poor Becky? Her chin rose. "I can assure you that he ensures Miss Mannering is receiving the best of care." She frowned. "Who are you to ask such impertinent questions, if you please?"

"Madam, I meant no—"

"Have you been sent by her uncle? Are you his man of business? Or perhaps some kind of enquiry agent sent to spy out the land?" She eyed his attire. "That might account for your less-than-genteel attire."

He flushed. "Forgive me, I certainly did not intend to incite such hostilities today."

"I am glad to hear it. If you had, that would make you the veriest scoundrel."

Much to her astonishment, the weariness of his features lifted as he laughed.

Her indignation faded, chased with chagrin as she realized just what she had said. Surely someone who could laugh as richly as that could not be all bad. "Please, I feel that I must beg your forgiveness for being so rude. We are not used to strangers here, and Miss Mannering's situation is quite challenging."

"How so?"

She wondered at herself. She was not usually such a prattlebox, especially with strangers. But this man's interest drew her from the bounds of propriety. Perhaps it was the way he looked at her, gravely yet with respect,

CAROLYN MILLER

that gave the oddest sense that with him she was safe. Perhaps it was the way he'd asked, with an earnestness that tugged at the emotion she'd had little chance to express and which now threatened her composure.

"Her mother's recent passing"—she swallowed, forced strength to her suddenly wobbling voice—"has proved most trying."

"You knew Mrs. Mannering?"

"She was my dearest friend."

His regard deepened, his grey eyes holding her gaze in a moment of sympathetic accord that seemed to subtly shift him from stranger to acquaintance. Like a page turned in a book, his features, which had seemed so nondescript before, now owned a new understated appeal. Such a revelation happened so quickly, and proved so surprising, that she was disconcerted and rushed to add, "Becky is such a sweet little thing, and holds her uncle in the greatest of trepidation."

"Really?"

"I'm afraid I should not be saying such things. Especially to a stranger."

"Thank you, madam. I promise I shall not pass on such things to him."

"So you *are* here on his behalf?"

He inclined his head. "You could say that, I suppose."

"Then please forgive me for being indiscreet. I did not mean to cast aspersions about a man I've never met."

"It is far better, I agree, to cast aspersions against someone one has met."

That tweak of his lips dissolved her protest. Or maybe it disappeared due to a horrifying desire to laugh.

"May I ask as to why Miss Mannering fears her uncle's return?"

"She is simply in such a quake at the thought of being taken away. But truly, I should not speak so honestly to a stranger."

"No, it is far more appropriate to speak dishonestly to a stranger, it is true."

Conscious she should not be exchanging frivolities with a man she had yet to be introduced to, she straightened and moved to depart.

His voice stopped her again. "Tell me, do you find me so very strange?"

"I beg your pardon, sir?"

"It is I who should be begging yours, madam. I forgot myself."

"You have indeed. I do not know of any other man who would stop to speak and engage in such conversation with a woman to whom they have not been introduced."

"I know few ladies who would do the same."

Her eyes widened. "Are you saying I am unladylike?"

"Not at all. You present a most charming picture."

Her face warmed, and she had a sudden desire to cover her mottled cheek and snatch the stupid lace cap from her head. Such foolishness indeed! "I should leave—"

"Forgive me. I have no wish to upset you." He sighed, his features resuming their earlier gravity. "It would seem from the way in which you speak that you are quite close to Miss Mannering."

"Why yes. Since her mother and I were so close, I have known Miss Mannering since they moved here twelve years ago."

"But you can scarcely be her age. She was older than me."

"Does age always predicate one's friends?"

His lips pulled to one side. "I should think one's wit might hold greater predication to be your friend, Miss . . . ?" He raised a brow.

"Miss Stapleton."

An arrested look came into his eye, and he inclined his head. "I gather then that my comments earlier were taken more from a personal affront than merely that of a friend."

"You gather correctly, sir. Although at the risk of seeming as one permanently offended, I must take exception to your accusation of personal affront."

"You were not offended?"

"No!" The lift of his eyebrow drew heat and belated amusement at how she must appear. "I merely did not expect to be bandying words with a stranger today. Miss Mannering is staying at Stapleton Court, where I also reside."

"Ah. Then perhaps you might permit me to escort you there."

The sound of a carriage drawing close begged attention. Her heart sank in recognition. "Thank you, sir, but such things are unnecessary."

"But as it is Miss Mannering I have come to see," he murmured, shifting the reins as his horse moved restlessly.

"Of course. You are here on her uncle's behest, after all."

"Actually—"

"Oh, my dear Miss Stapleton!" called Lady Bellingham's voice. "How fortuitous to meet you. We had such hopes of seeing you before the day is out, didn't we, Frederick?" Mother and son cast inquisitive eyes at the gentleman in the gig beside Theo.

"And now you have found me." She summoned a smile she hoped would hide the impatience in her voice.

"We should have arrived earlier, but Sir Giles took longer to leave than I'd expected, it being such a way to travel to Newcastle after all."

"I trust he will have a safe journey," Theo offered.

"Yes, well, I hope that too, of course. But I didn't come to speak with you on that. I have heard from those gossips that like to call themselves postmasters that he is here!"

"Who is here?"

"Why, the captain, of course! Really, I do not know why you are not more excited about such things, not when everyone else is so agog to meet him. Why, to think he is to visit our little part of the world, well, it's beyond everything! I cannot wait to write to dear Amelia about such things."

"You have met him, then?"

"Well, no. But I hope to before too many more days pass." Her perusal of the man in the gig became fixed, the slight furrow in her brow making Theo sure she would soon be expected to perform the introductions. Which would prove less challenging if she knew the man's name.

"Well . . ." Theo summoned what she hoped appeared a pleasant smile. "I hope you get the chance to meet him soon, Lady Bellingham."

The man in the gig straightened.

"Excuse me, sir, but have we met?" Frederick's eyes hardened, as he gave the stranger a frowning glance. "You appear a trifle familiar."

"I do not believe so."

"May I enquire as to your name?" Frederick, perhaps aware of the forthrightness of his comment, hurried on. "Only I am interested to learn if you are here on his behalf."

The man tilted his head. "Of whom do you speak?"

"Captain Balfour," Theo said, eyeing him thoughtfully.

He turned quickly at the name. Met her gaze in a look that seemed to transform from chagrin to conspiracy.

She blinked. Surely not.

"Well, sir? You did not answer my son's question." Lady Bellingham intruded again. "Are you here on the captain's behalf?"

"You could say that—"

"Oh, by all that is wonderful! You cannot know just how excited we are to have such a great man visit our part of the world. They say he is very grand, and *most* divinely handsome, and has spoken with the King himself! I simply cannot wait to meet him. He will be invited to dine at all the best establishments and be the guest of honor at parties the likes we have never seen! I have great plans for a turtle dinner, and a ball, *and* a Venetian breakfast."

Theo thought she detected a slight shudder from the man, which elicited the strangest surge of protectiveness and hastened her to say, "Such things sound quite spectacular, Lady Bellingham, but I do not think we need to regale strangers with every plan for local entertainments." She glanced at him. "Such things might be better left as a surprise."

His slate-colored eyes held a twinkle that caused the oddest disturbance within her heart. She glanced resolutely back to the squire's wife as Lady Bellingham spoke again.

"Perhaps you are right, dear Theodosia. In that case, sir, I hope you will pass on to him the wonderful offices dear Miss Stapleton here has performed for poor Miss Mannering. So good she has been, so kind."

Conscious of the heat filling her cheeks, Theo nodded to Lady Bellingham. "Forgive me, Lady Bellingham, but I must return home."

"I could offer you a ride, if you wish," Frederick said eagerly.

"Thank you, but I am quite used to walking by myself."

"Now, now, Miss Stapleton. That might be so, but we all know young ladies should not walk unescorted," admonished Lady Bellingham.

"Especially with strangers about," added Frederick, with another hard look at the man.

"Thank you, but I have been assured that not all strangers can be considered strange. And I am attended already. Captain Balfour—"

"—is sure to attend to his niece soon," the man in the gig interrupted.

Theo shot him a quick look, then turned to Lady Bellingham. "And won't that be wonderful? I know poor Rebecca is longing for her family. She misses her poor mama so. And while it will be good to have the captain in our neighborhood, I cannot think how keen he would be for turtle dinners and the like, not when he must be grieving the loss of his sister."

"Oh, yes. I keep forgetting. I suppose we should wait a while before we can issue such invitations." Lady Bellingham's brow puckered. "Do you think waiting a week would suffice?"

"That I cannot say. Forgive me. I am needed back home and must return."

Frederick cleared his throat. "May I call on you tomorrow, Theodosia?"

"Thank you, but no. I suspect I will be fully engaged with matters concerning Miss Mannering tomorrow."

"You do, do you?" murmured the thin man.

"Yes." She said in a louder voice to the pair still peering from the chaise. "I will keep an eye out for the captain. Being a hero, he will likely be very easy to spot. Such a hero is sure to be over six feet tall—"

"Quite the giant," the man agreed.

"And likely has a great, booming voice."

"Indeed, at times that is so," the man murmured.

"And I should think that he might share the family propensity for fair hair."

"Are you sure it is not red?" the dark-haired man suggested, studying her tresses. "Such a vibrant color would suit a man—or woman— renowned for quick wits."

Again her cheeks burned.

"Well, given such details it would seem that the captain should not be difficult at all to spot." Lady Bellingham patted her son's arm. "Good day, Theodosia, sir."

Theo nodded, waited until the carriage pulled away, then turned to the man in the gig studying her with his lips curled to one side. Her midsection twisted disconcertingly.

"Theodosia?" the man said. "Not Theodore?"

"Do I look like a Theodore, sir?"

"Not at all."

The way he looked at her—with warm interest, as if they were not the merest of acquaintances—renewed heat to her cheeks, and a breathlessness that urged her to leave. "Good day, sir. I must return."

"But am I not supposed to offer you a ride?"

"You offered already, and I already declined. I suspect you know why I said what I did."

"Because you might be good and kind and have quite the loveliest hair color I have ever seen, but you are also given to dissembling."

"I am not the liar, sir." She tilted her head. "Or should I say *Captain*?"

Chapter 4

Daniel couldn't help it. He chuckled. "I dared not introduce myself to such a lady destined to look so disappointed when she realized just how far short I fall from her exalted ideal."

"So you *are* Captain Balfour."

"At your service." He dipped his chin.

When her green eyes met his again, they had sobered. "You must pardon my earlier levity, sir. I wish you to know how very sorry I am for your loss."

"Thank you." The sorrow in her eyes tugged at his chest and made him swallow. "I admit I was taken aback when I arrived at Mannering House to see the hatchment on the door and to learn from the servants of poor Clara's demise. She had long been in my prayers."

"Mine too." She sighed. "I'm so sorry. I wrote to you to let you know."

"I have been travelling and received your note about Clara's illness but nothing more."

"I'm sorry this was such a shock."

That was not the only unpleasant surprise. "I had not expected the place to look as poor as it did. Had Clara and her daughter truly been living in such squalor?"

She pressed her lips together.

"Miss Stapleton? Surely someone who can be so free with a stranger can own truth when it concerns a woman dear to the both of us."

"You must forgive my candor, sir, when I say your brother-in-law did not leave Clara and Becky situated in the manner in which they deserved."

Truer words were rarely spoken. "Such candor is no crime. I will be the first to own that Francis Mannering was a bully and a skinflint and had little liking to be called to account for his crimes." As Daniel's last visit ten years ago had proved.

"Becky seems to have forgotten that."

"It is natural she would want her parents to remain in high regard."

"Indeed."

She peeked at him, then instantly glanced away when she noticed his gaze. "May I offer you a ride back to Stapleton Court, ma'am?"

"You wish to see Becky now?"

"Yes. I think it only best. Even if she has no wish to see me." He held out a hand.

She glanced at it uncertainly.

"Please, Miss Stapleton, do me the honor. A true gentleman could not abandon a lady to walk alone."

"I am prepared to overlook such things if you will."

"But I cannot. Please."

After another moment's hesitation, she assented, accepting his hand as she climbed onto the gig beside him, and thanking him for the courtesy.

He snapped the reins. "You must forgive my curiosity, but is it common for young ladies to walk these parts unescorted?"

"Very common. I'm surprised you feel the need to mention it, as it is so common that you must have encountered many such sights today."

His lips twitched, and he wondered at himself not for the first time in the past half hour. How could he jest on the day when he'd learned of his sister's death?

Perhaps it was the travel-induced weariness that banished proper emotions and self-control.

"You are sure my niece has little wish to see me?"

"I'm afraid so."

"Hmm. I must own to a degree of apprehension at seeing her once more as well."

"Do not fear, sir. Rebecca may be young, but she does not bite."

"I am most relieved."

The gig dipped into a large, muddied hole, bumping her shoulder against his.

"Please forgive my clumsy driving. It's been a while, I must confess."

The gig gave another alarming creak.

"Tell me, Miss Stapleton, why does my niece hold me in aversion?"

She sighed. "I cannot be rightly sure, but I suspect her father poisoned her against you."

"I never could understand what Clara saw in him," he muttered.

"Nor I."

He glanced at her.

She hurried on. "Forgive me for speaking on what must be private family matters, but it is something the local community has often discussed. Dear Clara was such a sweet and gentle thing."

"Too good for the likes of him."

"Yes."

He felt her gaze glide along his skin. "What is it, Miss Stapleton?"

"Forgive my boldness—"

"Of course. Say what you will."

"I admit to a degree of surprise that a man generally held as possessing so much courage would quail before the squire's wife."

He again felt that disquieting sense of amusement. "It is a mystery, that is true."

"Or refuse to own up to who he truly was."

"That, I'm afraid, was not my finest hour." Conviction panged within. He cleared his throat. "I know our Lord does not look kindly on deception, and such I find abhorrent too. But if I may throw myself on your mercy, it was the talk of turtle dinners that did it."

Her mouth twitched. "You do not like turtle dinners, sir?"

"I confess to feeling a great deal of compassion for the poor turtle."

"As do I."

The gig dipped into another hole, and her shoulder knocked his again.

"Miss Stapleton, apologies once more. I have long been out of the practice of driving such things."

"I suspect wars do not lend themselves to driving carriages."

"Very true."

She straightened her skirts. "I feel it only fair to warn you that the general will most likely want to chew your ear off about matters pertaining to your campaigns in the Peninsular."

"The general?"

"My grandfather, General Stapleton."

"Of course! I should have realized. But things have been so busy lately . . ." He frowned. "He fought bravely in the action at Camden, did he not?"

"That was my father, Major Stapleton. He returned home and later died of his wounds."

"I am sorry."

She gestured for him to turn at the stone pillars and rusting gates marking a drive. They passed under low overhanging branches that doubtless would appear to best advantage in the autumn.

"Miss Stapleton, even with the very grave risk of sounding like a coxcomb, for Lady Bellingham's words have filled me with fear, but is all the neighborhood so enamored of the exploits of Captain Balfour?"

"Nearly all," she affirmed. "Such bravery is most remarkable. You will be quite the toast of the neighborhood."

Perish the thought. He had no desire to be so feted. "I wonder . . ."

"Whether the truth of your name should be broadcast?"

"I see I was not mistaken about your quick wits. Yes. I have no desire to be lauded in such a way. I saw enough of it in London and cannot stand the thought of being toad-eaten anymore."

"Poor man."

He gave a rueful smile. "I suppose I deserve that."

"What you *deserve* is a turtle supper at Lady Bellingham's, where you can regale the local notables with your exploits for the hundredth time, all the while endeavoring to look humbled at the thought of being so celebrated throughout the land of England, including here, in what some might consider the veriest wilderness."

Amusement sparked again, threaded with appreciation. "Now that's a setdown."

"Oh, sir! My unruly tongue. I did not mean—"

"No, no. Don't spoil it with apology. Tell me, Miss Stapleton, what would you advise—should I own up to all that my name involves, or could I pretend to be the steward Lady Bellingham apparently assumes me to be?"

"Pretense tends to have a way of being found out."

He sighed. "And I suppose neither the general nor my niece will be likely to keep such a thing a secret." He drove the gig around the circular drive and pulled up outside the weathered stone of a gracious two-storied house.

After he helped her down, she looked at him thoughtfully. "If you truly are desperate to remain incognito, perhaps you could see if they could be persuaded to keep such matters secret. It is not as though you are to be here for any great time, is it?"

"I intended to return to London as soon as possible, but matters here suggest it may need be longer."

"The longer you remain, the more likely your secret will be revealed."

He inclined his head, as an officious looking personage drew open the front doors.

"Miss Stapleton, you are back."

"Hello, Mr. Siddons." She turned to him, her smile holding mischief. "This is Mister . . . ?"

"Daniel," he supplied.

She nodded, lips curled to one side, and they entered inside a dim hall. The butler eyed Daniel askance, then opened another door.

Following Miss Stapleton's lead, Daniel passed into a well-proportioned room lined with windows and shelves of books. Three sofas were positioned in front of a roaring fireplace, which made the room feel insufferably warm. A cat eyed him, then turned its black back, as Miss Stapleton guided him to where an elderly man with an alarming beard squinted up at her, then at him.

"Well?"

"Grandfather, may I present Mister, er, Daniel."

"Who?"

Daniel stepped forward and bowed. "Good afternoon, sir. My name is Captain Daniel Balfour. I am the uncle of Miss Rebecca Mannering."

"Oho, so you've come at last! Well, it's about time."

"Indeed, it is," Daniel agreed. "I have come to extend my apologies for my delay and offer my appreciation for your care for my niece in these past weeks."

"Past weeks? Past months, more like it."

Daniel shot a look at Miss Stapleton, but she was watching her grandfather, as if worried at his response. Was she worried for Daniel? "Such tardiness is unfortunate, I know. But I have been unable to come before now," Daniel explained.

"Captain Balfour has been in Spain, Grandfather."

"Eh? What's that? Spain, you say? What fool thing have you been doing there, lad?"

Miss Stapleton's mobile lips tweaked as if smothering a smile. "He is a captain in His Majesty's Army, sir."

"What?"

"Remember? You have been speaking of his exploits these past few months."

Daniel swallowed amusement. The older man reminded him of his own father, a man whose denial of ever-diminishing hearing and ever-progressing memory loss had been matched by his increasingly brusque reckonings with his family members.

A sound denoted the door opening, and Daniel glanced behind him to see a faded woman of middling years enter, followed by a short, fair-haired lass possessing a heart-shaped face.

"Uncle!"

He bit back a smile at her look of shock, glad that he had owned the truth of his name. "Hello, Rebecca." He stepped toward her, then paused. Was he supposed to embrace her? Was affection something she expected, or needed? He shot Miss Stapleton a quick look.

She nodded slightly.

He continued his walk to the young blonde and held out his hand. "Forgive me for taking so long to see you."

She clasped his hand, doubt writ in her brow and eyes.

"How good it is to see you," he said.

"And y-you."

He drew nearer, folding her into a hug unlike that which he would offer his fellow officers. "You are the very picture of your mother," he murmured in her ear.

"Uncle, I . . ."

He felt a shuddering, then she was weeping on his shoulder, soaking through his coat with her tears. His throat grew tight, and he gently stroked her hair. Another glance stolen at Miss Stapleton revealed her talking quietly with the older woman and her grandfather, as if encouraging them to leave. He cast Miss Stapleton a look of entreaty. He appreciated her thoughtfulness but would prefer instead to have guidance as to what to do with a weeping girl. His experience of such things was naught.

"Rebecca?" he said softly. "Please, do not cry. Clara is with the Lord now, and we must take comfort that those of us who believe in God, as she did, will see her in heaven one day."

"Come, Becky," Miss Stapleton murmured, drawing near, rubbing the girl's upper arm. "You do not want to give your uncle the idea that you are a watering pot, do you? He wishes to get to know you, but you will give him a very odd sense of who you are if all he hears are your tears."

These words, hard as they appeared, seemed to have the desired effect, as the tears subsided into a series of juddering sighs. Rebecca pulled away, wiping her eyes. "I'm sorry."

"There is nothing to be sorry for," he said. "Not on your part, anyway. I wish I had opportunity to come sooner. I imagine the past few years have been very difficult."

"Oh, yes. But dear Theo has been so very kind."

"Theo?"

"Miss Stapleton, I mean. She cared for Mama after poor Father's passing, then when Mama sickened, she nursed her every day. I could not have coped if it had not been for her."

He glanced up, saw Miss Stapleton had now also left the room. "It appears we continue to be in her debt."

"Oh, she is everything good, but not so good that it makes one feel small and worthless, if you know what I mean."

"Indeed. There can be something rather nauseating about the overly virtuous."

She laughed, a sound that seemed strangled by tears, then studied him shyly. "You do not seem like what I imagined, but so Theo said."

"Miss Stapleton said what?"

"She said you were sure to be different from what I remembered as a young girl, that Father had been perhaps a little unjust in his reckonings with you."

He smiled. "Surely I did not feature as some kind of ogre in your memories?"

"It does not matter now. You are here." She bit her bottom lip.

"What is it?" His words were gentle.

"I suppose you want to take me away."

"It was what I had thought best." But to where he still did not know. Was she too old for boarding school or a seminary somewhere?

"Oh, please, Uncle, if you don't mind, I would so much prefer to remain here! Miss Stapleton would not think it a bother, for she often says how much she wishes for my company and will mourn the day of my departure."

"Were you not but a minute ago outlining all the services she has already rendered you? We cannot intrude further on her good nature, nor that of the other inhabitants of this house. I'm afraid I shall need to take you back to London with me as soon as I have closed up the house."

"Mannering House is to be closed?"

"Yes." From his brief visit earlier, the place seemed hardly habitable for mice, let alone his only niece. It would most likely need to be sold, but this he couldn't admit. Too many shocks would not be wise on one day.

"Oh, but . . ."

"I know it is your home, and we can make a new home in London."

"Are you going to live there?"

"When my duties permit."

Her countenance fell. "Will I have to live with an elderly relation I have never met?"

Like his aunt Louisa, whom he had tentatively sounded out about moving to London to care for his sister and his young niece. "Better that than abusing the hospitality of those who might be excellent neighbors but are not our kin."

She nodded, eyes refusing to meet his, and he knew a twist of regret that his plans were so vague and obviously did not meet with her approval.

The door opened, and Miss Stapleton returned, her kind smile a balm to the churn of his emotions burning within. "I trust I am not intruding, but Captain Balfour, I hope you will do us the honor of sharing our meal tonight. Alas, it will not be a turtle dinner, but I hope our meagre offerings will suffice."

"What? No turtles?" Warmth lit his chest at her soft chuckle, while Rebecca glanced between them as if unsure what to think. "I gladly accept, thank you. If you can promise me there will be no Venetian breakfast either."

"I can safely assure you there will be none."

"Then I best return to Mannering so I can finally wash off some of the travel dirt and grime. After the news I felt to come here immediately."

"Oh, we do not stand on ceremony here, sir."

"You may not, but I suspect General Stapleton may, and I have no desire to incur the wrath of that man."

Her smile grew knowing as she looked at his niece. "It is a hard thing, is it not, Becky? Here we were assured of his heroism, of his immense courage, only to be so sadly let down. Ah well. It would seem life is full of disappointments."

He grinned. "Thank you, madam. I am quite content to live below heroic status."

Her gaze met his and they shared a smile, one that seemed full of understanding.

"We shall eat at six," she said. "I trust you will remember the way home?"

Home. A concept he had never really known, at least not since the age of sixteen, when he had left his parents' small cottage in Wiltshire, at the opposite end of England, and joined the army.

Becky quietly excused herself, Miss Stapleton's tease apparently only wringing the smallest distraction from her moroseness.

"I fear my niece is not happy with me," he said, once the door was safely closed.

"No, and yet that is hardly a surprise. She has had a lot to come to terms with in recent weeks and months, and the thought of yet more change will likely be even more daunting. But if I may encourage you, sir, she seems far more accepting of you and more kindly disposed toward you than what has previously been expressed."

"That is something, I suppose. I shall continue to trust God that He will soften her heart."

"As will I. Now, before she returns, I wanted to ask you what your plans were regarding Mannering's servants." Miss Stapleton clasped her hands as she stood before the crackling flames of the fireplace. "Mr. Cleever advised they should remain, at least for the interim. Janet and Ian are good sorts, loyal, if inclined to idleness at times. They can be trusted to keep their mouths closed, but should you encounter anyone else, you may want to consider whether you will be ready for invitations to dinners and parties galore."

"Those turtle dinners?"

Her lips lifted, and he was privileged to see the appearance of two small dimples. "I confess that I have never tasted one. Obviously I don't associate in the same hallowed circles as do you, sir."

"I have eaten turtle once and must plead my low standards—I thought it tasted like chicken."

"Another sad disappointment, then."

"Exactly so." Another moment lit with accord seemed to pass between them. "So, you are advising me to maintain my non-captaincy persona?"

"Unless you feel ready for the onslaught of invitations destined to come your way, then perhaps yes, that would be best. Especially if you only plan a short stay in these parts. Although it will be considered quite cruel of you to have visited and the villagers discover later you had been here without a word of recognition." She studied him with her head tilted on one side.

"Cruel?"

"Oh, yes. People do pride themselves here on being a tad more distinguished than those of neighboring villages, and to know one of our own is related to England's hero, well, I hope you shall forgive our tendency to gloat."

He laughed, bowed slightly, and effected his farewell and exit. Once in the gig, he turned the horses toward Mannering, the house of his sister, from where he'd once been banished.

Chapter 5

Dinner that night was an interesting affair, made all the more so by the unnerving experience of having a man such as Captain Balfour seated opposite her at the table.

She was unused to conversing with men whose ready wit matched hers. For too long, conversation at this table had been dominated by the general's grunts and sporadic references to long-ago battles that forever left Mama and Theo struggling in their wake. Such slowness had led to accusations of disinterest, which though partly true, did not engender participation from her mother to answer the general's barked questions.

To have a man, sober as he might be—and made more so by the visit to Mannering that had also left Becky even quieter than before—enquire about the girl's life in such a kind and courteous way engendered warmth toward him. Though she might not have known him long, it became increasingly apparent that all Francis Mannering had said about his brother-in-law was patently false. Daniel Balfour was patient, generous, and kind.

Theo slid a glance at Becky. How curious that she had almost instantly recognized her uncle was not the monster her father had made him out to be. Theo's attention returned to their other guest.

He nodded and looked away.

Had he been watching her? She'd felt the weight of his gaze on her a number of times today and had fought the urge to cover her cheek. Yet she sensed no focus on her blemish. Rather, their easy discourse suggested this new acquaintanceship could fast ripen into friendship. But he was here for only a short while, until matters at Mannering could be best sorted. It was folly to think someone who'd known the breadth of England might consider pursuing friendship with her. Her lips twitched. How self-interested was she?

"Miss Stapleton? Was there something you wished to say?" Captain Balfour asked.

Her stomach tensed. Heaven forbid her thoughts be made plain. She shook her head and refocused on her food.

"I must thank you all, once again, for your hospitality." The captain's clear voice echoed in the wood-panelled room. "I certainly did not expect to be met and accepted on such easy terms."

"We could not have you dine at the inn," Mama fluttered. "I'm afraid The White Hare's cook is not known for his care with meat, and it would have proved most trying dining there. One has to think of one's teeth, after all."

"Indeed one does," he agreed kindly.

"I'm sure caring for one's teeth was one of your top priorities on the battlefield," Theo said as seriously as she could.

"On the front, one might trust a surgeon to dig out a bullet but not one's tooth," he said, with the faintest glimmer of a smile.

"What?" The general stirred himself from an unusual taciturn lethargy, where he had stayed ever since the captain's arrival. "What are you talking about?"

"Dentistry on the battlefront, Grandfather," Theo said.

"What?" He frowned. "Back in my day, we simply let our teeth rot out. There was none of this namby-pamby business of caring about teeth."

Into the silence that met this statement, Mama ventured, "It's always been my experience that an aching tooth can have a most marked effect on one's sense of well-being."

"You talk the most utter nonsense, Letitia," Grandfather barked.

Theo shot her mother a quick look, unsurprised to see her quivering lip, but was saved from the need to intervene by the captain's gentle voice.

"Mrs. Stapleton, I find I must agree with you. It surprises me how

CAROLYN MILLER

often a seemingly insignificant ailment can have a proportionately inverse effect on one's sense of comfort."

"Comfort, my foot," Grandfather said with an inelegant snort.

"I have to concur with you, Captain Balfour," Theo rushed to say. "It is similar to how a midge, or a mosquito, can be so small yet hold such power to disturb one's sleep. One doesn't like to think of oneself as being at the mercy of a small insect, but there it is."

"Exactly so." His lips lifted as he studied her.

Her pulse quickened and she quickly glanced at the head of the table. "Grandfather, I hesitate to contradict you, but we all know that Mama is a most sensible woman. And really, the one who talks the most utter nonsense would be poor Willie Dillikins."

A smothered chuckle came from the man across the table.

"Who is 'poor Willie Dillikins'?" asked Becky.

"Poor Willie Dillikins is something of a local legend." Theo rested her fork on the side of her plate.

"I've never heard of him," Grandfather said suspiciously.

"I don't recall the name," Mama said. "There used to be a Billy Gale who lived in the area, but never a Willie Dillikins, not that I can remember."

"That does not surprise me." Theo turned her full attention to Becky. "He was considered a simple man, a man who enjoyed walks and trees and flowers. He was apt to say whatever popped into his head, which proved most disconcerting for some people."

"Disconcerting indeed," murmured Captain Balfour.

"But now I think on it," she said determinedly, "one shouldn't say what he spoke was nonsense, when I am sure it made perfect sense to him. For really, who are we to judge how another person sees the world?"

"Nonsense. There be right and wrong, black and white, truth or false. There's nothing in between," Grandfather objected.

"Do you really believe so?" Theo mused, sipping her lemonade. "Do you recall just last week when you declared that Mr. Brannock should not sell old fish and were inclined to tell him exactly what you thought of such a practice? Not a day later, we learned it was actually his nephew who had sold the fish that was slightly off."

"Yes, well . . ." The rest of her grandfather's response was lost within his beard.

"It's easy to make judgments, but things aren't always as they seem."

"That fish did have a most peculiar flavor," Mama said absently. "I can't say that I would ever choose to have the same sort again."

"And poor Willie Dillikins?" the captain asked Theo, one eyebrow aloft. "Whatever happened to him?"

"He is no more."

"How unfortunate."

"Indeed it was."

"I should have liked to have met him. People who say whatever pops into their head are people I tend to find most intriguing."

Her heart scampered as she worked to keep a straight face. "Speaking of things not always being what they seem, Captain Balfour, I wonder when you expect your man of business to arrive."

He met her gaze with a rueful glance.

"What? What man of business?" demanded Grandfather. "Why would you need a man of business if you are here yourself?"

Theo's head tilted as she sent the captain her own raised brow look of enquiry.

"You are correct," he said slowly. "I am in somewhat of a quandary regarding that."

"But if your stay is not so very long, then it need not be a concern," Theo reminded him.

"We shall have to see." He glanced at Becky. "I cannot like the idea of pretending to be—"

"That fool of a Bellingham woman was here yesterday, jawing off about you," the general interrupted, studying the captain. "You should have heard her, going on as if you'd hung the moon or some such nonsense."

"Grandfather," Theo protested.

"I can't imagine the fuss when they learn you are here, nor all the visitors and the like that will demand to see you. The way that woman carries on." He snorted. "She talks even more nonsense than poor Letitia here."

Mama carried on eating her soup, as if she had heard nothing.

"Dinners, and balls, and all manner of things." Grandfather shook his head. "We'd never get a moment's peace, and neither would you."

"It is not something I wish for," the captain admitted.

"Then who needs to know you are here?" Her grandfather huffed. "Janet and Ian might have the sense of a peahen between them, but they know enough to keep their mouths shut. Same goes for our servants here. And if you have no wish to advertise your presence, then I don't see why you should."

"Ah, but I have been reliably informed that the delay of such information might prove problematic in days to come," the captain countered, slanting a glance at Theo.

"Oho! Scared, are you?" Grandfather jeered.

"No sir. Simply aware of a need to be cautious."

"A little subterfuge is sometimes necessary in times of war."

"Grandfather, this is hardly war," Theo remonstrated.

"Quiet girl. I wasn't talking to you." He turned to the captain again. "How long are you in the neighborhood for?"

"Again, I cannot say. At least until I speak with Mr. Cleever and matters are settled with the house and Rebecca here."

"But I don't want to leave," Becky protested softly.

"She's a good girl," Grandfather said. "Never gets in the way of anyone here. Inclined to be blue-devilled and sniffle a little too much sometimes, though."

"Which is only to be expected when one has undergone so much hardship and change." Theo reassured a startled-looking Becky with a smile of sympathy.

"I quite like having a young girl around the place," Mama said. "It's been so long, after all."

"Oh, please. I'd do anything to stay," Becky implored.

Theo exchanged glances with the captain, and he offered a helpless shrug. Poor man. Faced with such domestic challenges, it was little wonder a man of action might wish to effect a speedy exit from their area.

Why this thought caused a twinge in her breast, she did not care to explore.

"Captain Balfour, do you really wish to stay at Mannering tonight?"

enquired Mother. "I am sure that a bed can be made up here, if you so wished," she added falteringly, with a quick look at her father-in-law.

But the general seemed disinclined to participate in any more conversation, his attention now firmly fixed on his plate as he carved his mutton.

"Thank you, Mrs. Stapleton," the captain said pleasantly. "But I would not wish to inconvenience you any more than I have already."

"It would be no trouble," Theo reiterated. "Becky will forgive me when I say that conditions at Mannering are not necessarily conducive to a good night's rest."

"Thank you, but I feel it would be best for all concerned if I was not known to have lodged here, charming as the company may be."

Oh. Her cheeks grew hot, and she glanced down. She was a fool to take his words and manner to heart. He meant nothing by it. She could see that he was tired and would likely be emotionally spent. She must spend some time in prayer and quiet reflection and remind herself what God said, that His love would never leave her, that she should focus on her blessings, and thus find contentment. And hope that such ruminations might help calm these recalcitrant feelings.

⁂

Many a night he had spent under canvas, within earshot of cannon fire or gun. But rare had been the night within four walls and under a roof where he had experienced such little sleep, wondering if plaster would again drop from the ceiling, when he might hear the next eerie cry of the peacocks, or whether the scurrying creatures he could hear along the floors would make their way into the bedclothes.

Miss Theodosia Stapleton had not exaggerated when she had warned him about the sleeping conditions here. He was glad that the previous few days' travel and all the challenges of yesterday's reception in the village and at Stapleton meant he'd finally reached a state of utter exhaustion, and he'd managed to snatch a few hours of dreamless sleep. But such rest had been bookended by restless wonderings, where he watched cobwebs dance in the draughts as his heart foolishly dared wonder about Miss

Stapleton. It was a good thing he was leaving soon, else a miss like her might be dangerous for his peace of mind. He liked so much about her, from her calm voice and steady green eyes to the concern and compassion he could see in how she'd cared for Becky, to that mischievous sparkle of fun. Willie Dillikins, indeed.

But he couldn't afford distractions. He needed to manage this situation with Becky, speak to the solicitor about what would become of Mannering, then return to London and his regiment as quickly as he was able. Anything else was impossible, and quite out of the question.

Finally, when the window shutter had clattered against the wall for the tenth time and the peacock's persistent cry suggested seeking future rest was pointless, he pushed up . . . and pushed his foot through a worn sheet.

At least he had sheets, he thought ruefully as he dressed and gingerly made his way down the creaking stairs. Good heavens. How long would it be until the stairway gave way? He might hate to be indebted to the Stapleton family, but he couldn't help but be thankful to know his niece would be far safer in that establishment than she would be here.

"Mrs. Drake?" he called up the dusty hallway. "Hello?"

Really, the place could do with a dozen more servants in order to get it up to snuff. He eyed a particularly large spiderweb lurking in the corner under a glass lamp that appeared to have the coatings of a dozen years of dust. Regret knotted afresh that his poor sister had been forced to endure such conditions in her last months, when the burden that had lifted at her miserly husband's death should have brought a new lease of life.

"Janet?" he called again.

There came a trudging of feet, then a door peeled open, and a harried Mrs. Drake clapped floured hands together, releasing a fresh layer of white powder through the room. "Oh, Captain Balfour, sir. Oh, I didn't expect you to be up as yet!"

"I'm afraid I've never been accustomed to sleeping in," he said apologetically.

"Oh, of course not, sir. I can't imagine war allows for much in the way of sleeping in."

Try any.

"Now, would you be wanting your breakfast, sir? Mr. Drake, my Ian, as is, is just getting some eggs from our best hen—a regular good layer, that she is, although unlike you, sir, she's not overfond of being disturbed in the morning, and is rather inclined to peck at one, should one be over-familiar, if you know what I mean, sir."

He nodded as if he knew, but truthfully had found her accent and manners of speech rather hard to follow at times. "I am not especially hungry, so I need no breakfast at the present."

"Oh, but sir, we should fatten you up! A man of your occupation must be strong and hearty, and I won't have the likes of Annie Brigham saying we don't feed you enough here."

He swallowed a smile. "And who is Annie Brigham?"

"The cook over at Stapleton Court. Always thinks she can look down on me because she is employed by a general, not a mere mister, like it was when Mr. Mannering—God rest his soul—was in charge here. But I don't mind telling her the next time I see her that *I'll* be the one serving one of England's heroes, and then we'll see what she has to say about that!"

"I did not realize such things were so serious. I assure you I have no desire to be the cause of, or to get into the middle of, any trouble for you."

"Oh, but you could never cause no trouble for me, sir."

He smiled. "I believe you are being most generous when you say that, when it is most apparent that I have caused you no end of extra work."

"Whether I be troubled or no' is for me to decide, if you don't mind me saying so, sir, and I am of the opinion that it is no trouble," she said firmly. "Now, what can I be getting for you for breakfast, sir?"

"A piece of bread should suffice for now, Mrs. Drake."

"At once, sir. If you'd like to attend to the dining room, then?"

"Forgive me. Which room is that?"

She hastened to a door in the corner and opened it—well, shoved the door with her shoulder—and invited him with a gasp that he be pleased to sit.

He obeyed, but as soon as she left, pushed to his feet again and moved around, studying the room's dusty furnishings. Clearly some attempt to clean had been made here. The silver was not all tarnished, and there was a vase of faded flowers. Perhaps it was simply the guest bedchambers that had seen so little attention in recent years, and those rooms more likely to see public notice had been cared for.

He shifted to the frayed curtains and looked out on a side garden that was clearly overgrown. He might not know much about gardens, but he could spy what looked like roses and the yellow heads of daffodils, currently being trod over by a peacock displaying his feathers to advantage. Daniel could barely recall the state of the gardens from his previous visit, but he was sure things hadn't seemed so unkempt. Perhaps this was another instance of preserving energy to attend to those more public spaces that would be seen by visitors. His lips tweaked. Much like some people he knew, all handsome peacock show but hiding attitudes and circumstances they wanted none to see. People like James Langley, who for many years had owned the manners of a rakehell but was hiding the brokenness of a misunderstood family. How blessed his friend James was to have found a real family and love with someone like Sarah.

Daniel shook himself from such musings—how his fellow officers would laugh to know the battle-hardened bachelor was thinking on such things—and moved back to his seat just as Mrs. Drake opened the door carrying a tray. A moment later, a plate of buttered bread and a hot cup of coffee was deposited in front of him.

"I'll be fixing the rest of your meal now, sir."

"Please"—he held up a hand—"I have no wish to be a bother."

"Oh, 'tis no bother at all, sir. I be that glad to serve one who has seen the King hisself. Did you speak with him? What did he say? What was he like? Is it true he be a tad totty-headed?"

He smiled at the expression. "He was all that was pleasant." And officious. And grand. Much too grand for the likes of a boy raised in the small Wiltshire village of Melksham. "I will confess that I found it all a little overwhelming."

"Did you really? And you so brave and all! Well, I never." She collected the tray and moved to the door before pausing. "Are you sure that be all, sir? You don't require nothing else?"

"I'm perfectly satisfied," he declared, before memories from earlier made him add, "Although I'm afraid the sheet in my bed now has a slight tear in it. Well, more than slight, I'm sorry to say."

"Oh, dear." She shook her head and sighed. "I'm so sorry, sir. That room hasn't been used in an age, and I plumb forgot about the state of the linens. I'll be sure to deal with that immediately."

"There's no hurry, although I wouldn't like to make matters worse."

"You'll be in fresh bed linen tonight, sir," she promised. "Now, is there anything else?"

"Thank you, no."

She bobbed a curtsy and exited.

His plans for the day remained nebulous. Yes, he needed to return to Stapleton and see his niece and begin the task of slow persuasion to return to London. He had little wish to encumber the Stapletons with her care any longer. And he supposed he should make himself known to those in the village who needed to know of his presence, little as he might desire it. But it was only right that the solicitor, the doctor, and the church minister be paid the respect of a call. Especially as he wished to know a little more about how exactly matters stood for the Mannering family, and more particularly, those matters concerning his niece.

But a visit to the squire could currently not be had, given he was on a journey. How long could Daniel forgo making himself known in that particular quarter anyway?

He wasn't proud of not owning his identity yesterday to the squire's wife and son, but in the chaos of emotions, he had found himself quite unable to bear with what one could plainly see would be an overflow of commiseration and adulation the like he'd always abhorred. Much more did he prefer Miss Stapleton's straightforward heartfelt offering of sympathy and the knowledge that Clara's death had grieved her too.

Clara. His heart sank. He supposed his first port of business should be to see what he could learn about his sister's death and matters of legality concerning his niece.

And perhaps a gentle reminder to Mrs. Drake and her husband that he'd appreciate their forgoing any mention of his name.

Chapter 6

"No! I shan't go!"

"But, miss!" Hettie knocked on the door, glancing across as Theo paused in the hallway. "She's refusing to open the door, Miss Stapleton. I think she's jammed it with something."

Theo swallowed a sigh and rapped the varnished wood. "Becky?"

Some days it seemed to Theo that her youth was very far away. Those days tended to coincide with nights when she had slept little due to the greedy winds outside, which only exacerbated feelings of impatience she did not like to own. She would prefer not to concur with her grandfather's assessment of their young guest, but at times she could not help but agree that Becky was far more childish than what Theo remembered herself as ever having the luxury of being. But perhaps that was the effect of Becky growing up with an absent father and a mother whose many illnesses often stole attention from her daughter. Should she have done more to assist her friend and her daughter? Regret gnawed, tempering exasperation into patience.

She knocked on Becky's door again. "Becky, my dear, please open the door."

"Is it only you?"

Theo thanked Hettie and motioned for the maid to leave. "Yes."

There came a sound of furniture being dragged, then the door swung open to a scared face. "Dear Miss Stapleton!" She flung herself into a surprised Theo's arms. "I'm sorry. You don't hate me, do you?"

Her words drew a new thread of compassion. How the girl longed for affection. "Of course I do not hate you. How could I, even if you act a little goose-like at times?" she teased, easing back.

Becky shook her head. "I cannot leave. Please don't let him take me away."

"Now Becky," soothed Theo, "you must be brave. You know this is not at all the way to carry on." She encouraged her to complete her toilette, and Becky slumped into the small chair at the dressing table, eyeing Theo in the looking glass with a mutinous tilt to her chin.

"But I don't want to leave all my friends." Becky slowly dragged a brush through her hair.

"Lydia and Patricia will still be your friends no matter where you are," Theo assured, her voice holding more certainty than her heart. The twin daughters of Mr. Cleever, the local solicitor, had proved stalwart in recent months, but she sometimes wondered if their friendship was based more on the convenience of similar age and location rather than those bonds that truly knit the soul.

"I don't know anyone at all in London," Becky complained, fixing her hair as Theo held the pins.

"Such need not concern you now." Theo patted Becky's shoulder. "It is best not to borrow trouble."

"Sufficient is each day's worries without borrowing more," finished Becky. "See? I was listening to Mr. Crouch's sermon last Sunday."

"And wise advice it is too." Theo handed her another pin. "There. Now you look most presentable for when your uncle comes." She encouraged Becky to gather her book and sewing and go to the downstairs parlor. As Theo passed from the room, she caught her own reflection in the looking glass and lingered a moment.

The morning light was not kind, revealing all her skin's freckles and flaws. She bent closer. Was that a vertical line in her forehead? How wonderful. She turned to study her cheek, the mottled pink color that had forever marked her as different. Her lips twisted. There was little point in trying to make herself more attractive, as no man could see past the fact she'd never meet any of society's expectations of beauty. She straightened. Not that she should care. Vanity was simply an invitation to comparison and dissatisfaction, and she'd worked so hard to learn to be content.

She drew in a deep breath, lifted her chin, and moved down the stairs. It was best to carry on as normal, to simply be her usual unadorned self, and do all she could to dampen the foolish attraction she had felt yesterday. If questioned, she might never have described the captain's looks as that belonging to her ideal. But his character, his wit, and the faith he'd shown with his surety of Clara's being in heaven seemed to have knocked all other considerations from her mind. Hence the need to banish such foolish fancies, sure as they were to be disappointed.

"Ah, my dears." Mama stretched out a hand at the breakfast table, accepting Theo's kiss on her softly perfumed cheek. "How are you both today? I trust you slept well, dear Rebecca?"

"Yes, thank you, ma'am," Becky said with a small curtsy, before accepting the invitation to help herself to the breakfast items on the sideboard, whereupon she took a seat and focused on the very important task of eating.

"And you, Mama?" Theo asked, having served herself a small portion of eggs and toasted bread. "I hope the wind last night didn't keep you awake too long."

"Oh, I'm rather afraid it did." Mama's large mournful eyes turned to Theo. "I know I have spoken to your grandfather about such matters, but at times it almost seems he has little care beyond that which directly affects his own comfort. I know it is probably most uncharitable for me to mention it—"

Even though it was true.

"—and especially in front of one who I regard as almost but still not *quite* family, but I cannot help but wonder sometimes." Mama sighed. "You must forgive me, Miss Mannering, for being so plainly spoken."

"Oh, Mrs. Stapleton, you need not mind me." Becky took a sip of her tea. "Apparently my father was well known as being the most parsimonious clutchfist in the county."

Theo choked on her bread. "A clutchfist? My dear Becky. From whom have you heard such terms?"

Becky's cheeks pinked. "I'm sorry, Theo, but I heard the general describe him as such just the other day."

"Hmm. I cannot own that your uncle will be impressed to discover that you have learned such a term as *clutchfist* from us here at Stapleton."

A cleared throat at the door drew her attention—and a rush of heat to her own cheeks.

"Learned it from you, did she?" Captain Balfour's small smile arrowed straight to Theo's heart.

"Oh, good morning, Captain," Mama said. "Would you care to join us? I'm afraid we are without the general this morning. He had an attack of gout last night that kept him up far too late."

"Thank you, but I had no wish to intrude. And despite my knocking on the door, it seemed your very proper butler had no wish to answer it. Then when I heard voices from this part of the house, I hoped your good natures would permit me to treat this as my own and venture inside, so I may speak with you." He glanced around the room, offering a nod to each lady, and a murmured good morning, before accepting Mama's repeated invitation to sit.

"Good morning, sir," Theo responded. "May I offer you a cup of tea? Or perhaps you prefer coffee?"

"Thank you, I require nothing."

"You are sure?"

"Well, perhaps a cup of coffee. I'll confess the liquid Mrs. Drake served this morning was a little more bitter and watery than what I like, but such a thing I could not admit there. Apparently, she thinks herself to be in a kind of competition with your cook here and would hate for me to tell you otherwise."

"Ah, yes." Theo poured him a cup of coffee, then took care to note how he preferred his degree of milk. "She is not, perhaps, the most forgiving of ladies, so you were wise indeed."

"Poor Mrs. Drake," Mama said distractedly. "I remember once dear Mrs. Brigham here saying how Janet Adkins—she was an Adkins, then, my dears, before she married Ian Drake—never had quite forgiven her for stealing her sweetheart."

Diverted, Theo asked, "Surely you don't mean to say that Annie stole

Robert from Janet?" Proper Robert and slapdash Janet? No wonder that hadn't lasted.

"Oh no," Mama said. "It was another man entirely. But that did not matter. The iron had entered poor Janet's soul, and forgiveness was not something to entertain. Poor thing."

"Such intrigues one does not expect when one visits the countryside," murmured Captain Balfour.

"Ah, but the countryside can be quite full of interesting things if one cares to take the time to notice," Theo countered.

"Indeed." The captain tilted his head, eyes fixed on her, winsomeness dancing in his upturned lips.

Her chest fluttered, and she rushed to say, "And how did you sleep, sir? I trust the wind did not howl under the gutters and cause too many restless hours for you."

His wry smile and quick glance at Becky told her all she needed to know.

"In that case, I hope you have not too many appointments today."

"Thank you, but I am determined to see those who must be seen."

"And admit your identity to them?"

He sighed. "I still cannot determine quite the best course of action regarding such. I hope I might persuade the reverend, the doctor, and the solicitor to secrecy until matters can be arranged for extracting Rebecca and returning to London, but I am not entirely sure that can be accomplished."

"You need have no worry concerning the Mannering servants," Theo assured. "Mrs. Drake might hold her grudges, but she can also hold her tongue, and just the thought that she is hosting such a hero is enough for her, and she won't noise it abroad."

"I hope so," he admitted. "I truly have no wish for the kinds of entertainments Lady Bellingham spoke of yesterday."

"Must we leave so soon?" Becky finally spoke. "Uncle, I *truly* would prefer to stay."

"I'm sure you would," he said, voice gentle, "but as I said yesterday, we must not trespass on the good natures of those who have been so kind to you already."

"But what is to become of me?" Becky cried, with a sound suspiciously like a sob.

From the startled look the captain threw at Theo, she guessed he had come across few women given to emotional outbursts. Taking pity on him, she said to Becky, "Come now, Becky. Did we not agree just this morning that we should avoid borrowing trouble? Why not see this as an opportunity, rather than something torturous? I should dearly like to visit London and see the wonderful museums and famous places there. Perhaps we should cajole your uncle into describing some of those awe-inspiring sites."

"You have never visited London, Miss Stapleton?" he asked.

"Alas, no. I confess I have not even visited Newcastle, so my knowledge of such grand places is very small. So you see why we must depend upon a well-travelled man such as yourself to describe such places to us."

He studied her a moment, then dipped his chin and described some of the treats London had to offer. The talk of Astley's Amphitheatre and parks and museums drew Mama's wistful reminisces of when she, as a young bride, had seen the city with her new husband, "but I am sure it is very changed now."

"Time has a way of altering places, ma'am," the captain said. "But I'll confess that while London has much to amuse, and I believe would indeed prove most diverting for a young lady, I am not so enamored with it as some. My friend, Lieutenant Musgrave, is rather more fond of the city than I."

Theo's brows rose. No, this was not the way to garner Becky's interest in her future abode.

He ignored her, focused as he was on the small bowl of flowers centering the white tablecloth. "I find that after many years of war, I sometimes quite envy those who live in quietude, yet such is not to be my lot, committed to the army as I am."

"Forgive the impertinence," Mama said, "but have you no young lady you wish to wed?"

"None," he said promptly. "I am wedded to a military career, which is why such fancies must forever remain fancies to me."

"I remember my darling Teddy saying something similar to me once," Mama said dreamily, "then he quite changed his mind."

"Such does not surprise me, madam," he responded gallantly.

"It could happen to you too."

"Perhaps. But sufficient for each day is its troubles without borrowing more."

Becky's mouth parted as she raised her brows at Theo.

"What have I said now?" He glanced between them.

"Nothing of consequence." Theo shook her head slightly at Becky. "Now, would I be correct in assuming you wish to speak to the solicitor?"

He inclined his head. "Yes. And the reverend and doctor too. Provided, of course, they can be persuaded to hold their tongues."

"All have proved to be souls of discretion," Theo answered. "The squire, however, is not a man known for his reserve."

"I wondered. Thankfully, I expect I shall not need to call in there any time soon."

She smiled. "May I enquire whether you have written to these gentlemen yet? If not, you may find a visit to the village leads to more enquiries about your identity."

"You have the right of it. I have not fully thought on how to carry out my visits there."

"If I might be so bold to say, your ability to remain unknown might be better served if you invite them to speak with you at Mannering. Or, if you prefer, we could invite Mr. Cleever and Mr. Crouch here, on the pretext of dinner, if that suits."

"The general would not mind?"

"He cares more for his stomach than conversation, and we are in the habit of Mr. Crouch attending a meal at least once a fortnight."

"Perhaps that might work well. The state of Mannering is hardly conducive to visitors." He shook his head, as a chuckle tumbled from him. "And here am I wishing to relieve you of the burden of my company, and yet so easily do I succumb."

"Oh, but we do enjoy visitors," Mama said. "I find I cannot easily make visits elsewhere these days, so it's lovely to have others come to me. Well, to you, sir, in this case."

"And there is no burden. We are happy to do all we can to help." Theo smiled at Becky. "Your niece is a credit to your sister."

"That she is." He gave Becky a fond glance that warmed Theo.

Further discussion secured the promise of an invitation to be sent to both Mr. Cleever and Mr. Crouch for a meeting at Stapleton Court on the morrow, as it was determined that while the solicitor might be persuaded to hold his tongue, his wife's discretion could not be so readily counted upon, so a dinner would not do.

"And perhaps after you have met Mr. Cleever, you could return to Mannering and point out the state of things there, thus eliminating any need for him to admit he was seeing you or Mannering, which may be the case should Mrs. Cleever learn of an invitation there," Theo suggested.

"I believe you would make a great strategist, Miss Stapleton."

She lowered her gaze, willing her heart to stop its futile patter at his praise.

A visit to the doctor was deemed less essential, especially when Mama explained that the doctor was likely to call in to see the general in the next day or so, and a servant could be sent to Mannering to fetch the captain, if he so wished. The captain assented, then spoke of his determination to look over the Mannering estate and delve into what ledgers and accounts remained on the property to have some idea of what the meeting with Mr. Cleever might involve, and soon made his adieu.

"Oh, Uncle, might I please come back with you?" Becky asked. "Just for a quick visit? I have scarcely returned to Mannering since"—she swallowed—"since Mother died, and I would like to see how Janet and Ian are getting on."

He shot Theo a quick glance.

Theo leaned forward in her chair. "That would be a very good idea. I am sure your uncle will appreciate your showing him various matters around the house and gardens."

"I'll just get my pelisse then." Becky hurried from the room.

"I'm sorry if I was presumptuous," Theo said in a lowered voice, "but I do feel it would be best for her to return, as she's been quite unwilling to visit Mannering until now."

"Of course. It is her home, after all. Well, it was," he added uncertainly.

"I'm sure it will help."

He sighed. "I don't mind admitting that I hope she can see some of the decay and the like, and perhaps realize that living elsewhere will prove to be of benefit rather than a disappointment."

"Mannering has been in sad decline ever since your poor sister's husband inherited," Mama said. "I remember the days long before poor Clara and Francis came, when balls and parties were held there and the gardens were so lovely. It's always puzzled me how one generation can hold such differing personalities to the next. Francis's parents were such kind and generous souls."

"Qualities my brother-in-law was not known for," the captain muttered.

"Quite so." Mama clasped her hands on the table. "It is such a shame to know things are rundown as they are. And I can't help but think his parents would have been so disappointed that it must be sold."

The captain's lips compressed.

"And yet such things must be done. Or so you must see what the solicitor says." Theo pushed to her feet. "Please excuse me, sir. It seems I have some invitations to pen."

"Thank you." Warmth radiated from his words. "I appear to forever be in your debt."

"Nonsense," she said, though his kind words elicited a glow in her chest. "Now, please excuse me."

"Of course." He bowed.

She nodded and escaped to find paper and pen. And to tamp vain imaginings from taking hold.

⁓

The visit from the solicitor to Mannering the subsequent day confirmed what he'd suspected. As the last male of the Mannering line, and according to his last will and testament, Francis Mannering wished for the place to be sold after the death of his wife, with the proceeds supporting his only child, Rebecca Clara Mannering.

"It behooves you, sir, to ensure that such a place is brought into a condition that will enable a most profitable sale," advised Mr. Cleever.

"I have no wish to remain beyond this week," Daniel admitted to the solicitor. "I rather hoped we might come to a quick sale that would permit Miss Mannering to begin her life anew in London."

"You must forgive the question, sir, but do you have a house of your own in which you wish to see Miss Mannering established?"

"My parents are dead," he said quietly, "and my time has been spent abroad. I have had little need for an abode here in England. I have a cottage in Melksham, not far from Bath, which I have rented out this many a year."

"You have no wish to live there yourself?"

"No. It is a pretty market town, but I have no use for it, not with my commitments so often taking me elsewhere. I had thought to set up my father's sister as a chaperone for my niece in a rented house in London, but now I wonder at the wisdom of that."

"And . . . ahem, are you not in the way of seeing connubial bliss yourself?" The solicitor smiled. "It seems from all I've read you need not scruple to find a willing young lady."

Daniel scoffed. "I have no intention of marrying simply to create a home for my niece. I plan to continue with my military career once the matter of my niece is sorted."

"Ah. I see."

Daniel hoped he did. Perhaps, if the solicitor ended up being not as closemouthed as everyone believed him to be and this was to trickle out, it might save Daniel from some of the more obvious local lures and invitations.

Mr. Cleever pressed his fingertips together. "I wonder if a little delay in order to attend to some of the most pressing household repairs at Mannering might prove wise. Prospective buyers will be far more likely to wish to obtain a house that at least offers some degree of charm."

Was that best? As much as Daniel had little wish to stay, the time here in Wooler was about securing Rebecca's future. He was not by any means rich, but he had enough set aside to fund some of Mannering's more basic repairs. A discussion concerning the accounts had shown Francis had set aside nothing, so it was little wonder that the house and grounds had reached such a state of disrepair.

They spent a good half hour discussing the pros and cons of such renovations, what the priority should be, how much the expenditure might cost, and where local laborers could be sourced.

"I apologize if I seem reticent," Daniel said, "but I remain firm in my wish to stay incognito. I have little desire to be forced into entertainments for the masses, such as proved the case in London."

"I quite understand and must reassure you as to my discretion. Now there just remains the matter of funds."

During further discussion, Daniel disclosed he had enough to cover the expenses.

The solicitor nodded. "Then perhaps Mr. Drake's attention can then be focused on the drive and front garden, and Mrs. Drake could be assisted by some local maids to make the main rooms look as they ought." He glanced around the drawing room, with its tattered, peeling papers and dust-lined faded paintings. "I recall the time before Mr. Francis took possession, and it seems such a shame to see it now."

"Indeed." Daniel released an internal breath and resigned himself to a stay for a trifle longer.

Much as he might dislike this place and wish to leave, Rebecca's future seemed to require his capital and energies a little longer. He would simply have to trust God would direct his paths.

Chapter 7

Theo examined the bolts of fabric propped in the corner of Wooler's haberdashery. The captain's unexpected gift of two ribbons that matched nothing in Becky's meagre wardrobe meant some careful thinking about how best to incorporate them into a garment she might use, so he might not think his gifts wasted. She suspected he was embarrassed that his other gift of a doll—far more suitable for a girl of younger years—had not proved the hit he wished with Becky, so if his other gifts might be seen as valued, then this could be a blessing to him.

The task had led to musings over whether she could quickly fashion a reticule, or perhaps persuade Mama to use her excellent needlework skills in creating an elegant spencer, that might incorporate the slender lengths of violet and cornflower-blue satin. She would not bother asking the captain which was his preference, sure he had no interest in such frivolities as ladies' reticules and the like.

A bell above the door signaled the arrival of another customer.

She touched a pretty print, imagining their budget could stretch to a new gown for Mama and herself, while a dancing thought teased her to wonder when they might next see him.

"Oh my dear Miss Stapleton, have you heard the news?" Lady Bellingham bustled up, eyes wide.

Theo stilled. Had the captain's identity been discovered? "You must enlighten me, ma'am. What news do you speak of?"

"I suppose it is quite foolish of me, for I'm persuaded you must know, as it concerns one of your closest neighbors."

"Do you refer to Mannering, ma'am?"

"Exactly so! So you know about the servants, then."

"The servants?" she repeated blankly.

"Aha! I see that I was right, and you have not heard. It seems the captain has employed an army of people to set the place aright."

"The captain? Do you mean Captain Balfour?" Had he not wished to keep his identity secret? She had not seen him these past two days, after the meetings with the solicitor and minister. She'd been dying to know how he had got on, but his visits to his niece had come at times when she'd been out on visits of her own, and not for anything would she stoop to show her interest in his affairs.

"Indeed I do! He's sent word to Mr. Cleever, and it appears he is to get the house set to rights at long last."

"Really?"

"I'm surprised you did not know of this, seeing it is Miss Mannering's home, and she still resides with you. But gentlemen do not always let us into their little schemes."

"It would seem so."

"But do you not see what this means?" Lady Bellingham clutched Theo's arm. "He is coming at long last! Why else would he be spending so much blunt on fixing up the place?"

"Perhaps he has a mind to sell it?" she suggested carefully.

"What tosh and nonsense. Why, with a little work, Mannering could be one of the grand houses of the area again. Admittedly it has been allowed to fall into somewhat parlous condition, but with a little work it might even rival Stapleton Court again."

With a *lot* of work, Theo thought cynically. "Well, that is exciting."

"Isn't it? And I can't help but feel certain that, when he's here, he's going to be keen for all manner of exciting things. Else why ever would he go to so much trouble?"

"Why, indeed?" Theo soon made her excuses, completed her purchases, and hastened home, conscious of a little ping of hurt within. Not that she needed to be in the know about everything that pertained to Becky, but nobody liked to be behind the times in learning news. Especially when it concerned oneself to some degree.

Still, Theo shouldn't be focused on herself. A recent Scripture reading drew to mind: "Let nothing be done through strife or vainglory; but in lowliness of mind let each esteem other better than themselves." Thinking she must know all was folly. Far better to spend her time in thanks and prayers for those around her rather than contemplating hopes that were not to be.

She drew in a breath, admiring the waving heads of crocuses scattered along the road. Things to be thankful for: it was spring, the weather was fine, there was no wind to chase her on her walk, Mama was well, Grandfather's gout had improved, and Becky was enjoying time with friends.

A nicker of a horse drew her glance over her shoulder, and she straightened to a standstill. "Captain Balfour!"

"Ah, Miss Stapleton. I was hoping to run into you." He dismounted and drew the horse to the side of the road. "I trust you are well?"

"Yes, thank you, sir."

"I have missed seeing you these past days and have had no chance to tell you of my schemes."

"It seems your schemes are quite the talk of the village."

"Ah. You have heard, then?"

"That you mean to do up Mannering and host many parties? Forgive me, but I had rather the opposite impression when we last conversed."

"Yes. Well." He rubbed a hand along his jaw. "I wondered if rumors to that effect might occur."

"Rumors are the bread on which many a villager feasts."

He gave a rueful chuckle. "Precisely what I wished to avoid. Miss Stapleton, I—"

The sight of a gig on the next hill drew awareness that Frederick Bellingham had threatened to visit today. She held up a hand and stopped the captain. Heart sinking, she said, "Frederick Bellingham, the squire's son you met the other day, will be passing this way in just a minute."

"Are we to never have a moment's conversation?" he grumbled.

"If you wish to converse, sir, then perhaps you might find a space of quiet in the trees over there." She pointed to a nearby copse of oaks.

"And speak with myself?"

"And not be discovered," she retorted. "Go. I will be finished with Mr. Bellingham shortly."

He shook his head and drew his horse away, and amusement tugged at the sight of the bold hero of England so meekly obeying her and hiding in the woods.

It wasn't many seconds later she heard her name called and paused her walking to turn and lift a hand to shade her eyes.

"Miss Stapleton! Allow me to offer you a ride home."

"Thank you kindly, Mr. Bellingham, but I should not."

"Why shouldn't you? You have done so many times in the past."

She winced internally, sure his voice carried to the man behind the trees. "You have offered many times in the past, but I have rarely accepted."

"I am just trying to be a gentleman."

"And I truly appreciate that. But I enjoy walking."

"So you always say."

"Because it is always true. Now, I must thank you for your kind offer, and wish you a good day."

"But you should not be walking alone here."

"Nor should I accept rides from a young man when I'm unchaperoned."

"Yes, but I'm a gentleman and quite safe. I would never let any harm befall you."

"You are very kind," she said. "I'm sure you will make some young lady a wonderful husband one day."

"Oh, Miss Stapleton, I am so glad to finally hear you say so." He quickly climbed down, moving nearer when she really thought he'd be better off to hold the reins. "It has been my dearest dream for so long—"

Her insides tensed. What might be overheard?

There was only one way to make him stop.

"But that young lady is not me." She stepped back. "Alas, one and thirty is not so young after all."

"The difference in our ages means nothing to me." He shifted in a manner so she was horribly suspicioned that he was about to move to one knee.

"Unfortunately, the disparity means quite a lot to me. Now, please excuse—"

"I do not even mind your cheek!" he added, somewhat desperately.

She stilled, heat surging, begging utterance. How dare he speak so impertinently? She blinked back stupid tears, drew in a breath, tamped down the offense. "You must forgive me, but I have an interview I must attend."

"Are you sure you cannot think of me more kindly than that?"

"I'm sorry, Frederick. You are like the younger brother I never had, and thus I feel you will ever remain to me."

His mouth a tight, flat line, he jerked a nod and climbed back into the gig. Then took an age to turn around on the narrow road.

She wavered between pretending not to notice his troubles and offering to help. But an offer to assist might be construed as interest she did not possess or be regarded as yet further wound to his pride.

"I will not give up, Miss Stapleton," he called, before driving disconsolately away.

"Alas," she muttered.

"Alas," came a voice behind her, drawing her attention to the captain, holding the reins of his horse behind him.

"He is but a child."

"A child capable of great rudeness."

She glanced away, pressing her lips together. He sounded almost angry on her behalf. That thought renewed heat to the back of her eyes, but for a very different reason.

"He seems a spoilt child, whereas you are one and thirty." He eyed her. "I would never have picked that. You hold your age very well, Miss Stapleton."

"I've such an advanced age, after all," she said, glad her voice worked as normal.

"Not nearly as advanced as six and thirty."

"That is true. Six and thirty must be considered very ancient indeed."

He laughed. "You are a minx."

She finally smiled. "Was there something you wished to tell me? Apart from mocking my poor and only suitor?"

"Only? I cannot understand why someone like you might be unsought at your age."

"Hardly unsought, as you just witnessed."

"But unwed. The men here must be blind."

"Nor that, as you just heard."

His gaze held intensity. "I repeat . . . they must be blind."

Her heart fluttered foolishly again. Perhaps she was coming down with something. "It is not to be wondered at, not when I have rarely left the village, and the village contains so few men of marriageable age."

His brow furrowed. What was his purpose in this conversation?

Yet such speculation would prove hazardous to her earlier determination not to think on him. It was best to steer this conversation onto safer grounds.

"Your interest in my matrimonial chances is flattering, but I believe you have come to a decision about Mannering." She submitted to his gestured invitation to continue to walk along the road. "A decision that, according to Lady Bellingham at least, means that you might be casting out lures for your own matrimonial chances, should you indeed be staying."

"I wish people would disabuse themselves of such a notion. I have only the desire to prettify Mannering up to a standard that will make it easier to sell."

"You still wish to leave?"

"I would have preferred to depart by the middle of next week, but it seems the house will delay me a few days more." He led the horse behind him as they strolled.

"Leaving you to skulk through the bushes, praying not to be seen?"

"You have the right of it, ma'am."

A chuckle escaped.

"What is it now? I should not have thought this was a laughing matter."

"Forgive me. But I continue to be amused that a hero should find himself in such a predicament."

"You would not be so amused if you were the one facing all manners of invitations."

"It must be *so* hard." She paused at the turn that signaled Mannering's drive.

"I was right," he said. "You are a minx."

She gave another choke of laughter.

"Do you do that often?"

"Do what often?"

"Make that most delightful sound."

"I think," she said with sternness, "that if you don't wish to be seen and wondered over, then you had best mount your horse and ride away. But wait," she said, as he seemed inclined to obey her immediately. "How exactly do you plan to stay invisible for the hordes of workers bound to come your way?"

"Ah. Yes, well, I had wondered about visiting some friends near Coldstream who also attended the Walcheren campaign with me."

"And thus avoid exposure here." She nodded. "I wish you well, sir."

"Thank you. It should only be for a week or so, as I am told the clearing and cleaning should not take much longer than that."

"Once you see the place readied for sale, you'll return to London?"

"My plan precisely."

She bolstered her smile and willed it not to fall. "You have my good wishes, then."

"And you, Miss Stapleton." He nodded.

And as he mounted and rode away, she couldn't help but wonder wistfully what her life could've been if he'd decided to stay.

Theo predicted the next days would pass immeasurably slowly, counted in the steady ticks of the clock and in the busy nothings of domestic duties. But Becky's request for help with sorting and storing her mother's things soon filled Theo's time, while bringing its own challenges. Clara's possessions held poignant memories: an ivory fan Theo had once given her, a book of poems they'd laughed over, the traipsing through memories proving both bitter and sweet. Still, it was another way she could say goodbye, even though it seemed there were far too many goodbyes to be had in what felt too close a time.

She thought by now she'd been inured to departures, but with the loss of the captain from their neighborhood and the upcoming loss of Becky's company, it seemed Theo faced a future infinitely bleaker than she had known. Talk of London, of travel, of a future that had always seemed too remote to even pay heed to, now seemed a little closer, a little more tantalizing. Sometimes she was half-tempted to ask sweet Becky if she would like Theo's company as a kind of companion. But then the thought of leaving her mother to her grandfather's ever-volatile moods soon damped down such foolish fancies.

Oh, but how wonderful it would be to have a life beyond these four walls. To dare dream that there might exist a man in this world—whose name was not Frederick—who might wish to share his life with her. Over the years, she had worked hard to find contentment, so at night she'd pray and ask God to take such desires away, only to wake up each morning with the thoughts still firmly entrenched.

At least progress at Mannering came steadily, and daily was the wonder at what changes had been wrought. It was a pleasant surprise to see by Tuesday's end that the gardens had been scythed and weeded, and the front door had been scraped and freshly repainted. Apparently the captain's instructions to Mr. Drake had encouraged steady focus for once.

Inside, too, Becky's gasp at seeing the front hall transformed from dust and dirt to clean and bright echoed Theo's surprise. She complimented Mrs. Drake, who had overseen the changes, finally able to spend the money in order to set the house to rights.

"I did not think I would ever see this place shine again as it ought," Mrs. Drake confessed. "And it has done my heart no end of good to see things as they ought be once again. As they should have been in your dear mother's time, Miss Rebecca."

Becky nodded, the quick sheen to her eyes suggesting tears were not too far away. This prompted Theo to wonder aloud what Becky's uncle would say when he returned.

"I hope he will be pleased," Mrs. Drake confided. "I have had a letter from my sister asking that Mr. Drake and I go and live with her. She's in Berwick, you see, and her husband died not so very long ago, and she's in a big house all of her own, and desperately lonely. And when this place sells, well, I don't fancy staying on here forever. It gets so awful cold, you see, and my rheumatism isn't what it was, so if we could live with Sister by the seaside, then I think I should be quite content."

Theo nodded but said nothing, envy lodging words in her throat. Mr. and Mrs. Drake did deserve to spend their twilight years in comfort, but oh, how she wished she might be the one to see the sea. To have any kind of adventure, really.

"My uncle wrote and said he'd return this Thursday and hopes to begin the journey south on Saturday." Becky trailed a hand along the cleaned plasterwork lining the hall.

"You will not get far," Theo said. "Not with having to rest on Sunday."

"He mentioned staying with friends at Langburgh."

"Is that not on the sea?"

At Becky's nod and "I believe so," envy struck again.

"How lucky you will be."

"I wish you would come with me." Becky reached for Theo's hand.

"You are sweet, but it cannot be. My mother cannot fend off the dragon that is my grandfather alone, now can she?"

As hoped, Becky laughed, and Theo shifted the conversation to suggestions for a special dinner to bid farewell to Becky on Friday night before she'd leave.

"Just a quiet affair," Theo said. "It's not as if we could arrange anything on a grand scale, not at this short notice." And not when Becky should still be in mourning. "Perhaps we can invite some of your friends too."

If the truth of Captain Balfour's identity was discovered at such an event, then that could solve several problems. He need not be forced into more entertainments he had no wish for, yet learning of his identity would still prove to the locals that he'd received an honor of sorts. Yes, she nodded, such an event would prove of benefit indeed.

Chapter 8

After discussing matters with her mother and grandfather—who had not been shy in offering his opinion that it would be good to see an end to all this fuss—they had finally decided that yes, a dinner to farewell Becky should occur.

"Just a quiet dinner," Theo proposed. "I'm sure it would help her feel loved and appreciated."

"I do enjoy a good entertainment." Mama straightened, eyes bright. "Do you think we could invite dear Seraphina too?"

"I think it will prove of far too short notice, Mama, but perhaps we could see if she might be persuaded to come in the next few weeks." It might be good to see her sister, despite their at-times-fractious relationship. Having a new focus would be good for them all, especially for Mama. They would all miss Becky, Theo told herself firmly, unwilling to acknowledge that she might miss the company of Becky's uncle too.

She wrote to her sister, then sent out hastily scrawled invitations to Becky's dearest friends plus a few notables who would be most hurt to learn that England's hero had been in their midst incognito all this time. Not that she admitted to his being in attendance at the farewell too. That would prove a surprise sure to surpass any turtle dinner.

The next days passed in a flurry of preparation: cleaning, cooking, running here and there to help the servants, while also assisting Becky in her packing. Becky's things had already been moved to Stapleton, so she hadn't needed to return to Mannering to collect anything. And yet it seemed the selection of gowns, bonnets, shoes, and the little trinkets a girl deemed necessary simply refused to be easily fitted into the trunks and boxes to be taken to London. Added to this was the vacillation over precisely which of Becky's mother's and father's things should be taken and which should be stored or sold or given away. The job had enlarged in significance quite substantially, so the farewell dinner would serve as a fitting reward for all the hard work of the week.

Acceptances for the dinner from Becky's friends demonstrated a mixture of anticipation and grief at this honor before their dearest Miss Mannering quit the neighborhood. The responses from their elders proved to be of a rather more questioning nature.

The likes of Lady Bellingham—whom, despite not being one of Becky's chosen friends, proved impossible to leave out—had teased and tugged to know precisely who the mystery man was who would escort their dear Miss Mannering down to London.

"I cannot conceive how such a hero of England should not want to visit our sweet part of the world and do his duty for his niece. I don't mind confessing to you, my dear Miss Stapleton, that this rather tarnishes the halo I thought he possessed."

Not for anything would Theo admit to the arrival of the man in question a week or so ago. So she hedged and spoke vague murmurings of the person appointed as being trustworthy and sure.

"I suppose it was that rather plain-featured man we saw last week," Lady Bellingham said with the slightest of curled lips. "*Not* the kind of man I should expect to be acquainted with such a handsome hero, but there is no accounting for taste, is there?"

"Indeed not," Theo had said as gravely as she could.

Friday arrived, and the scent of Becky's favorite dinner drifted through the house. The rooms were all placed in order. Theo surveyed the dining room, hands on her hips. Fresh spring blooms spilled daintily from vases galore, echoing the colors of the new gown Mama had quickly fashioned as a parting gift for Becky. It would be several more weeks before she could enter half mourning, but the pelisse trimmed with purple velvet was, according to *La Belle Assemblée* ladies' magazine, quite *en vogue*. All that awaited was for the man himself to finally grace them with his presence.

"Oh, where do you think he is?" Mama whispered, wringing her hands.

"He is probably still on his way," Theo assured. "He likely has many last-minute details claiming his attention."

Captain Balfour's acceptance had arrived this morning courtesy of Mr. Drake, whose visit this morning had also delivered the admission that Mannering was to be closed, and that he and the missus would take off for her sister's place that very day.

"The captain said he would be right in finishing the packing up and the locking up of the place. Mannering looks a hundred times better than it ever did. I never knew the walls of the hall were that color before," Mr. Drake had confessed.

"Then it was a good thing to do."

"Hard work, though. I never worked as hard in my life."

She didn't doubt it.

"Anyway, here is a little note from him to you, miss, and he wanted me to pass on his good wishes."

"Thank you. And I trust you and Mrs. Drake will enjoy your new circumstances."

"Thank you, miss. I can't say that we haven't earned it."

"Indeed you have," she said warmly. "And I know that Rebecca has been most comforted by your careful tending to both her needs and that of the house."

She'd summoned Becky, who was quick to offer her thanks and good-byes before returning to her packing upstairs, which allowed Theo privacy for the reading of Captain Balfour's note.

She'd broken the seal and unfolded the paper.

Dear Miss Stapleton,

Thank you for your kind invitation. You may be sure that I am pleased to accept, although I shall have to plead an early night in order for us to leave by nine the following morning.

Yours etc.,
Daniel Balfour

She'd traced his name, then shook her head at herself.

Well, there had been no word that he was reluctant to own his identity tonight, so she would have to let things occur as they may. And seeing no point in standing and dreaming, she had returned to the myriad of tasks to be completed.

But now she joined her mother in watching the clock, waiting as the hour hand passed from seven to eight with no sign of the man in question.

Their other guests had all arrived, and the dinner would spoil if not served soon. She stole to the drawing room, where she could see the drive and any late arrivals. Becky chatted with her friends as the other guests conversed quietly. No one seemed to notice anything amiss. Perhaps none of them—save Becky—would wonder at the absent final guest.

Not that they'd yet admitted to who exactly he was, simply saying that Becky's uncle had made arrangements for her to be transported on the morrow, much to the horror of Lady Bellingham, whose protests of "But who shall chaperone you, my dear?" creased worry in Theo's heart that she hadn't been as circumspect with arrangements as she ought.

"I think we best serve the meal," she now whispered to her mother.

"But the captain is not here."

"It can't be helped," she said, conscious of a small thread of irritation. He knew the importance of tonight. Why hadn't he worked harder to be on time? She moved to speak to Mrs. Brigham and Mr. Siddons about serving the meal shortly, returning in time to see Becky exclaim over a gift from Lydia and Patricia before wrapping them in a tearful hug.

"Oh, the poor thing." Mama studied Becky with a fond expression.

Becky seemed to vacillate between giddy delight at being the recipient of small gifts that would necessitate repacking much later tonight and tears over the coming departure. Fortunately, she did not seem to waste much thought on her uncle. Perhaps a quiet word about some unfortunate delay would be enough to assuage her concern and not spoil her last night.

This accomplished, Theo encouraged removal to the dining room, where grace was followed by further quiet conversation, as she tried to keep up her end of exchanges while keeping her own concerns in check.

Perhaps he had other matters of business he deemed more important than finally making his triumphant debut into their rural society. But from what she'd learned of his character, he didn't seem so prideful that he'd either want to make such an entrance or be so conceited that he would look down on their village. She was half-tempted to send Mr. Brigham to visit Mannering and discover if some accident had befallen the captain, but the outdoorsman's presence became increasingly necessary as the night wore on, taking on a footman's role of retrieving the hot dishes from the kitchen and helping Mr. Siddons to serve the meal.

Lord, wherever he is, You know. Be with him, keep him safe and well.

"What do you think of that, Miss Stapleton?"

Theo blinked. What was Mr. Crouch asking about?

He smiled. "I suspect you are too busy thinking on all the things that must be done still to pay attention to my conversation."

"Forgive me, sir, but you have the right of it."

"My wife is the same." He cast a fond look across the table at Alicia, a meek woman who possessed a heart of gold. "She always says she wants to entertain, but when the time comes, she is forever busy in making sure every little thing goes to plan that she often forgets to eat." He cast a look at Theo's nearly full plate. "Or take the time to relax and enjoy her guests herself."

"Fortunately for me," she confided, "I have been sure to seat myself next to the *most* understanding member of the community, whom I am confident will know how to extend grace and overlook my momentary abstractions."

"Most fortunate for you," he agreed, with a chuckle.

She smiled and carefully cut into her portion of roasted chicken. As she savored the taste—Annie had outdone herself tonight—Theo shifted her attention to the end of the table, where the general had finally lifted his head from his meal and was speaking to Becky.

"We'll be sorry to see you go," Theo's grandfather said. Though his words were gracious, the gladness washing his features suggested the opposite.

Naturally enough, such comments threw Becky into wrinkled-brow confusion, which only grew as the general spouted further observations, the chief of which seemed to consist of the likelihood of rain, which he strongly believed might make the River Till rise, and thus prevent any departure at all.

"Oh, Grandfather," Theo protested, "you should not tease Becky so."

"I'd much rather stay here," Becky insisted. "I hope it rains for days and days!"

"The poor pet," Mama murmured.

"It's my belief that rain would be a fitting farewell to you, my dear," Lady Bellingham said. "Your family has had a long association with this part of the world for many a year now, so rain to accompany your departure seems only appropriate, dear Rebecca. Tears, you know."

Feeling that Becky would not fully appreciate this point of view, and that Lady Bellingham was not to be persuaded from seeing things from any angle but her own, Theo did what she could to distract and entertain and play the role of the hostess even as her heart grew increasingly sore.

While she knew it was only right and good for the girl to live under the offices of her uncle, Theo could not help but recognize she would miss her young charge. Becky's presence had brought renewed purpose for Theo and had brought joy to the Stapleton household, even though the reason for her stay had been due to the most trying of circumstances. Theo was going to miss having a younger perspective. Once again she must resign herself to the dull certainties of existence at Stapleton Court.

Despite her best efforts to stimulate invigorating conversation, she couldn't help but feel that the dinner itself was falling sadly flat, with no sign of England's hero. Her lips curved wryly at her presumptuousness at wanting to cause a sensation, and she mocked herself for being as quick to self-conceit as anyone else in the village.

Ah, well. Perhaps this was just another lesson in pridefulness, which she had best pay heed to.

Dinner drew to a conclusion and, owing to the early time of Becky's departure the next day, the guests soon made their farewells in a chorus of well-wishes, hugs, and tears.

"I can't believe we see the end of the Mannerings." Lady Bellingham dabbed a lace-edged handkerchief to her eye. "So sad, my dear, so sad."

Frederick Bellingham, who had studiously avoided eye contact with

Theo these past days, offered a short bow and his best wishes for Miss Mannering's future and his hope that her travels would go well.

Theo was not at all sad to see the last of their guests depart, which seemed to relieve Grandfather and her mother also, both appearing so weary that she insisted they leave the clean up to her.

"You too, young lady," she advised Becky. "Your friends have been very kind bestowing such lovely gifts on you, but I'm afraid you will need to repack so you can fit them in your trunk."

"Thank you, Theo." Becky gave her a hug, which made the efforts of the past days all the more worthwhile.

Her lack of mention of her uncle's whereabouts soothed Theo's fears that Becky might have taken his absence as a personal affront, but Theo's questions about him persisted, an undercurrent of speculation accompanying her efforts to assist Annie and Hettie with the rest of the cleaning.

Where was he? Why hadn't he come? He had never struck her as an unfeeling kind of man, and his absence at what was Becky's final meal with friends seemed to suggest a hardness of heart she was loath to believe about him. Perhaps he truly had suffered some misadventure. But this, too, she could not entertain for long, given the man had fought so bravely and so well and, by all accounts, was well able to acquit himself in trying conditions. Which left the other emotion, that mingled with a degree of pique—injured pride at not being able to unveil the great man himself, and annoyance that he would be so uncaring about his niece that he should forgo attendance at what would prove to be her last engagement in the district.

Surely he should have more care for her than that. For *Becky*, she emphasized to herself sternly. Fondness for any other woman was obviously quite out of the question.

Later, having helped the servants clear and clean as best as possible, she moved upstairs to comfort Becky in her tearful reminiscences and assist in the repacking that yet remained. It was past midnight, according to the longcase clock that had sounded twelve triumphantly, when she finally encouraged Becky to get some rest, seeing as the captain was due tomorrow morning.

Theo moved to her own room, drew the curtains closed, and wearily exchanged her gown for a night rail. She blew out the candle and lay in her bed, listening to the familiar creaks and groans of the house. Tonight *had* gone well, despite the absence of the captain. Her heart grew tight. She had no wish to take it personally, but it did feel like a slight. But no. This was probably for the best. In a matter of hours, this brief interlude of interest in her life would be over. He would leave, and she would find solace in God's promises and be content once again. It would be best for her mind to stop its turning and succumb to her exhaustion.

But wishing for rest did not make it so. Unnamed concerns made her toss and turn.

And when the captain did not appear at nine, then made no appearance yet by ten, well past the appointed time for departure, Theo determined to ride her horse, Gracie, to Mannering. Having missed her breakfast, she plucked an apple from the kitchen and, employing Robert Brigham as an escort, she rode through the misting rain prophesied by Grandfather and knocked upon Mannering's freshly painted door.

Really, the place looked very smart, and no one would ever know it had been subject to recent tragedy.

"Perhaps he's had a big night." Robert twisted his cap in his hands.

"Perhaps," she agreed doubtfully. Though Captain Balfour had never struck her as the kind of man to seek comfort or courage in a bottle.

"Want me to see if anyone is around the back?"

"Yes, please." She knocked and called again, then, remembering that Mr. and Mrs. Drake had submitted to Mrs. Drake's sister's pleas to live with her by the sea and wouldn't be here anyway, she bolstered her courage, turned the handle, and pushed it open. "Excuse me, Captain!"

The darkness spooling across the hallway led to a still-darker patch toward which she tentatively inched, calling out his name. A moment later she discovered a large hole of broken floorboards, and Captain Balfour's body lying brokenly in the cellar far below.

Chapter 9

There were sorry plights that one might term a pickle, then there was falling through a floor and breaking one's leg.

Daniel was quite certain it was broken. The angle at which it now rested, as much as anything else—like the relentless throbbing pain—suggested he would be lucky to have only broken one bone.

How it had happened, he still did not know. One minute he'd been marveling at the improved grounds and house, the next he'd heard an ominous crack, and the floor—not the ceiling, as he'd always supposed—had fallen in, and he'd plummeted to the broken bricks below, striking his head on the ground and going out cold.

Such must've been the case, for when he next woke, the shadows and sounds were different. Instead of bright sunlight, he saw dimness and heard the crowing of cockerels and patter of rain.

He heard other things, too, and was fairly certain his eyes had not been playing tricks on him when the small scurrying creature fled when he'd shifted his foot. Ugh. Some might call him a hero, but he'd never been able to overcome his dislike of mice, and that creature had been far too close to his leg for ease of mind.

Since then, he'd drifted in and out of consciousness, vaguely aware there was something he was supposed to be doing, something he was supposed to have done, but for the life of him he could not recall. Still, the belief fueled hope that someone might realize he was not there and do what they could to learn his whereabouts.

He drew in a careful breath, inhaling mustiness and dust. His mouth twisted. If only he hadn't been so magnanimous as to send the Drakes off with his blessing, to enable their visit far sooner than they had anticipated. Even if that had been partly decided upon by his own need to escape the wilds of Northumbria and prevent further distraction, as he was wont to do.

Blast and nonsense. What *was* he to do? A noise, high up, drew his attention to the light. "Lord, help me," he prayed aloud for the hundredth time.

The agitation in his soul eased a mite, and he shifted on the broken bricks, working to alleviate the discomfort. But such efforts drew such a thrust of pain that he fainted again, and lingered in the rest, savoring the blissfulness of sleep.

When next he awoke, it was to hear the faintest sound. Not like his imaginings, but a knocking, a call. He shifted again, tried to speak, but his throat was as dry as his stomach empty. Not that he hadn't been in similar situations before, but few had been the times when his hunger had accompanied such pain.

"Hello?" a voice called.

He tried to wave, but the effort drew so much energy he nearly fainted again.

"Excuse me, Captain—oh!" A gasp.

He forced his eyelids open. Far above moved a blurry figure that seemed vaguely feminine. "Are you an angel?" he called, his voice cracked and rusty.

"No."

"You sound like an angel." His eyes closed once again. "Voice of one, anyway." His thoughts seemed to swim slowly, a heavy lethargy rolling across him in a way that made him care for nothing. He shivered and his teeth chattered as when his unit had been trapped for a winter in the Netherlands, when their beards had grown icicles and too many good men had died for want of a blanket and nourishing food.

"Captain Balfour?"

That voice again.

He forced open his eyes as a dark shape hovered high above him.

"Forgive me, sir, but I daren't come any closer."

"The floor," he mumbled.

"The floor is broken. I'll be back in just a moment."

"Don't leave." He wanted, needed, his angel to return. Trying to negotiate this pain without the angel might be more than he could bear.

Somewhere inside his head, a voice mocked him. How strange that he could endure all he had on the battlefield, but a few months home in England had softened him to such a state. He truly was undeserving of the medal King George had pinned on his breast if he couldn't withstand a little pain.

From far away he heard a low exchange of voices, then there came a sound of creaking, a scattering of rubble, and he opened his eyes to see a dark shape draw near. He forced himself to focus, and as the edges of his vision sharpened, he recognized the person as the pretty miss who had cared for his niece. Not that he could remember either of their names.

"You."

"Hello, Captain Balfour." She drew near. "You seem to have had a tumble."

"Floor."

"Yes, the floor collapsed. I am here, and Robert Brigham too, though he daren't venture down the rickety stairs, as they might give way under his weight."

"You're brave."

"Well, not as brave as some," she countered, with an upward tweak of lips.

Warmth bloomed across his chest. He liked her voice. He liked her smile. It seemed to illuminate her face. Or perhaps that was simply the effect of the lantern she held.

Her gaze left his and ventured down his body, her breath catching as she saw his leg. "Oh my!"

"Hurts like the blazes."

"I'm sure it does." She moved as if to touch his arm, then seemed to think better of it and shifted away.

"Don't go," he begged, stretching his fingers toward her. "Need you."

"The person I think you need is the doctor," she admonished, clasping his hand. "Please, sir, I will do all I can, but you need to be brought out of here, and I dare not try because I fear I have neither the strength nor the manner of doing so that would not provoke you to even greater levels of pain."

"Fetch the doctor," he muttered.

"I will send Robert to do so at once. Please excuse me for a moment."

"You'll return?"

"I assure you I will."

He heard her move away and shut his eyes, wishing he might shut out the pain as well. Heat swept over him in a thousand prickles. Was it a return to the fever which had first struck in Walcheren? He'd been lucky to only suffer a mild case, unlike poor Adam Edgerton, who had suffered far more devastating consequences of the insidious disease.

Noise drew his attention and he opened his eyes again.

Her face was very pale, and her hair, having escaped its chignon and silly cap, clung damply to her skin. From this angle, with the lantern spilling light, he could see her eyes, could see the gold flecks in the dark-green depths. Fairy eyes, his mother used to say.

"You're very pretty," he said, eliciting her wry smile.

"And you've obviously bumped your head to be saying such things."

"Why not? 'Tis true. And better than focusing on my leg."

She bent closer and gently wiped his brow with a white handkerchief. "Do you remember when this happened?"

"Yesterday afternoon, I'm fairly sure."

"I'm so very sorry." She bit her lip. "Are you in pain anywhere else?"

"My head."

"Excuse me." Her cool fingers slid through his hair.

Despite the dull throbbing he reveled in her gentle touch.

Her breath caught. "Oh, sir, you are bleeding." Within a moment she had removed her scarf, folded it, then gently eased his head up and placed the scarf under his wound, cushioning his head. Next she removed her shawl and laid it across him, apologizing for the fact that it was damp. "But at least it should help you be a little warmer."

"It is." He could feel its soothing comfort. Or perhaps that was just the body heat from her. Or the slightest scent of violets that clung to its perfumed folds.

"You must be so thirsty."

He nodded, sucked in a whimper of pain.

"I shall see if I can find a glass."

There came a creaking of bricks, and her soothing presence moved away.

He counted his breaths until she returned.

"Here." She moved beside him, held a glass of water to his lips, and lifted his head.

Soon he felt the sustaining liquid trickle through his lips and down his throat. "Th-thank you."

"I know it's not the drink of preference for most men, but I trust you'll forgive me this once."

"This once," he muttered, lips lifting a little in appreciation of her efforts.

"And—oh! You have missed your meal. Here." She shifted and withdrew an apple from her pocket. "I know it's not much, but it might sustain you a little longer, at least until Dr. Linton arrives."

His stomach growled, drawing her smile as she handed the apple to him. His fingers touched hers ever so slightly, rippling further warmth up his arm. "You truly are an angel." He bit into the apple with a loud crunch.

"What an unusual idea of heaven you have, sir."

His hunger forbade speech until he'd polished off every tangy-sweet mouthful.

She sighed. "I wish it were more but, unfortunately, the eggs and porridge made too much of a mess and did not survive the journey here."

A glimmer of amusement pushed past his weary pain. "You put them in your pocket also?"

"Alas, my sewing skills seem rather less than they ought, and they slipped—or was it dripped?—through, leaving naught for you save one poor piece of fruit."

"It wasn't poor, I assure you."

"I could go upstairs to the kitchen and see if there is something more."

"I don't know if those stairs will bear much more traversing. Besides, I find this has now quite taken the edge off my hunger."

"I am glad, even though I'm sure you're being kind. I cannot imagine such a humble offering even beginning to assuage your hunger."

"You might if you knew what conditions had been like when we were fighting the French."

Her head tilted. "I suspect it best we not think about that now."

"What would you prefer to think about?" He shifted slightly, only to gasp in pain.

"There, do not move. We cannot afford to aggravate that injury."

"Yes, Doctor."

"*Miss Stapleton* will do for now."

Miss Stapleton, yes. And what was her first name? Something outlandish, a name he'd never heard before, but now could never think of her as anything but . . . "Theo."

She blinked. "Sir?"

"Forgive me, I have been trying to remember your name."

"Ah, yes. Theodosia is rather an odd name to give a girl, is it not? But then, you've met my grandfather. The pride that keeps him afloat would demand a namesake of his own. And apparently my mother and father preferred Theodosia to Theodora, which was as close as they could find to match his, without being *too* close, if you know what I mean." She readjusted the shawl so it reached his chin. "I count myself fortunate that at least I am not named as my younger sister."

He blinked. "I thought you an only child."

"Ah, well my sister might act like that is the case, but no. She is married, and lives with her husband in Hexham."

"Do they not visit you?"

"Not often. I don't think Roger is overly fond of my grandfather, and I know the general is not too fond of him."

From what he'd seen of the general, he doubted the old man would make his feelings anything but plain.

"Seraphina might—"

"I beg your pardon?"

"My sister is named Seraphina."

"Another angelic reference?"

"You might think that to look at her, for she is very pretty."

"You're pretty," he insisted.

"And you have hurt your head and are prone to saying nonsensical things."

"Not nonsense."

Her expression held doubt. "Hmm. I'm sure you must think my parents were quite whimsical. Well, my mother was anyway, a fact I'm sure surprises you, naming her daughters as she did. Apparently Theodosia means gift of God, which is—"

"Most appropriate," he murmured.

"Well, 'tis kind of you to say so, but we both know that isn't true."

"But it is. I prayed, and there you were. A gift of God for me."

Her cheeks pinked. "What nonsense you speak, sir."

"Not nonsense." He smiled. "Not like silly Billy Willikins."

"Now, that is not quite right. I believe it was poor Willie Dillikins."

"Forgive me."

"I will, but only because you are in such pain." She patted his arm gently.

"You are all kindness."

"I suppose if you think such things, then it's not to be wondered at you're so willing to believe I might actually live up to my name. Now, it appears to me that you might as well get comfortable—"

The look she gave him drew amusement, despite his pain.

"—and listen as I tell you a story, because indeed your adventure today has put me in mind of it." Her head tilted. "My grandfather delights in telling my mother and myself some of the antics my father got up to when a young boy. It seems he was quite the harum-scarum child, which one day led him to the top of the stairs at Stapleton Court with the fixed belief that he could fly."

His eyes widened. His mouth twitched. "Let me guess—he discovered he could not."

"Now sir, it is quite ungenerous of you to guess the end of the story before I am even halfway there."

"My apologies."

"You are forgiven." She inclined her head.

"So what happened?"

"As you surmised, he discovered the laws of gravity do not permit small boys to fly and was only saved from injury far worse than a broken tooth and arm by the fortuitous passage below of the butler. Of course," she added, "it is debatable whether poor Mr. Siddons thought a small boy landing on his head was fortunate."

He chuckled.

She joined in. "I have often wondered if that is why Mr. Siddons is forever on his dignity. Because he is desperate to forget a time when it would seem he had none."

His chuckles grew to loud laughter, and the cleansing power of it quite drew him to forget his own injuries and attempt to move, thus drawing rippling pain and a sharp gasp.

"Sir, please. Try to stay still."

"It is hard when someone insists on making me laugh."

"Now that is most unfair. I am simply the vessel of communication, not the inciter of laughs."

"You're a bringer of joy." In the echo of his words, he realized it was true. While his experience of young ladies was limited, he was hard-pressed to recall any who shared such a ready wit. He never knew what outrageous thing might next fall from her lips. Her very pretty lips. So quick to turn up in a smile or pucker into tease. He found himself listening, waiting, watching for whatever those pink lips might say next.

"Captain?" those lips now said. "You are looking at me most peculiarly."

"Forgive me. I . . ." Could not explain exactly what foolishness was going through his head. Only that he rather doubted he could communicate any of it to her in a way that would not lead to all kinds of further difficulties. Best to change the topic. "I suspect I was meant to be somewhere, but for the life of me I cannot recall what it was."

"You need not concern yourself, sir."

"But what if my absence disappointed?"

"You were expected to attend a dinner last night, where the grand unveiling of your identity was to occur. Alas, it would appear some people will go to extraordinary lengths to preserve their privacy."

"That was it exactly," he agreed meekly.

"I thought so. And it seems you possessed a secret longing to stay in these parts and not return south after all. Why you couldn't have just stated that plainly, rather than going to all this trouble, I do not know."

"Forgive me."

"Next time, you must simply be honest about your disinclination to leave. Luckily for you, I'm rather certain the doctor will not be inclined to permit you to travel any further than Stapleton Court today."

"I cannot impose—"

"On the contrary, you cannot refuse. Where else can you maintain your privacy, whilst receiving the benefits of comfort, care, and commiseration, as you so choose?"

"I'd rather be in London."

"I hesitate to point out the ungracious nature of your remark, sir, only because I know the pain must have injured your manners."

"I beg pardon."

"And you shall have it," she said promptly. "And my full sympathies as well. But until that moment of departure can be, I'm afraid you must put up with our company a little longer."

His eyelids drifted closed. "Your company I don't mind."

"How kind of you to say so."

This clever, witty woman was one he'd never mind. Or—he tensed— perhaps she was someone that he should.

"Sir?" Her voice now held a note of constraint. "Are you feeling in greater pain?"

He denied it and was thankful to soon hear the sounds of approach.

"Miss Stapleton? Hello?"

"Dr. Linton! We are down here."

The arrival of the doctor refocused attention to extracting him from this predicament. Fortunately the doctor's lighter weight meant he was able to descend the stairs to examine Daniel's leg more closely.

"Captain Balfour. We meet again."

Had they met before? He scarcely remembered. Perhaps they had. Not that it mattered.

The doctor administered a sedative, which numbed the pain, then splinted Daniel's leg, and through an unfortunate amount of jostling, which proved the sedative was not completely effective, the doctor and Miss Stapleton helped him upright. It took much gritting of teeth to complete the torturous ascent of the stairs, but finally, with only a few unmanly whimpers of pain, he escaped from the wretched house to fresh air and freedom.

Sweat trickled down his back at the effort, and he gladly obeyed the doctor's instructions to take Robert's arm and lie down for further examination in greater light, albeit with the attendance of drizzling rain showers.

He drew in deep inhalations, as much to relinquish the dank staleness of before as to combat the pain.

"I do not like the look of this leg." Dr. Linton prodded him, as if intent on seeing whether he could make Daniel cry. "He must be transported to an inn."

"I think he would be better off at Stapleton Court," his fair rescuer objected.

"But your grandfather—forgive me, miss, for speaking so bluntly, but the general is not exactly known for magnanimity."

"Then it's time such things were changed." Miss Stapleton smiled uncertainly down at him. "That is if you have no objection, sir."

"No objection," Daniel admitted feebly.

"Then I really feel this would be the best way to ensure he receives good care and still retains his anonymity."

"If you are sure." The doubt weighting the doctor's voice said he remained uncertain, but Miss Stapleton's quick thinking and determination met no further protest.

It took some time—and much jaw clenching—across rough passage in rain showers until the gig finally turned in at the stone pillars marking Stapleton Court's drive, and it wasn't much longer until he was met with cries of "Oh, Uncle!" and "What in heaven's name has happened?" and "Of course he must stay!"

Daniel was taken upstairs, further attended by the doctor who promised to visit again tomorrow, washed by a tight-lipped Mr. Siddons, and soon ensconced within heavenly fresh sheets. Miss Stapleton arrived with a hearty broth, which he ate while she looked on with sympathetic concern.

"I know this isn't quite what you wished, but perhaps you will find some benefit in your enforced stay here."

"Benefit?" He grimaced, gesturing to his bound leg. "This certainly doesn't feel like it holds much advantage."

"I'm sorry you feel that way, Captain. But as you are the nearest relative of our young charge, I think it a wonderful opportunity for you to get to know Becky more. She, while being most concerned about your health of course, is perhaps a *little* overjoyed at the thought she will not be leaving for London quite as soon as was previously thought."

"Benefit indeed."

"I am glad you can see it that way." She moved as if to leave, then paused. "Is there anything you need, sir? Perhaps, as the doctor advised, you might sleep easier after a few more drops of laudanum."

He agreed, his body aching, wearied, but it seemed his mind was reluctant to rest.

"Would you like me to read to you until you fall asleep?"

He agreed, and she whisked from the room, only to return a minute later with a small volume and seated herself on the chair beside the bed.

She flipped through the pages, then glanced up and blinked, as if startled to see he watched her. "I hope you like Walter Scott's poetry."

The name was familiar, but he wasn't sure he remembered any poetry.

"Scott based the poems on places not too far from here, and this poem was one of your sister's favorites. Indeed, it's said that he has stayed in a nearby farmhouse. Perhaps we should see if he is in the area and invite him to come meet you. I'm sure such a man would be delighted to meet a hero. You could provide more inspiration for his poems."

"Minx." His heart lifted as she uttered a low-throated chuckle.

She began to read and, as he was surrounded by comfort and stories of legends of old, he soon found himself soothed to sleep by the dulcet tones of a voice he was fast starting to love.

Which was ridiculous, his mind told his heart. But could not be helped. Not when she was proving, time and again, to be of great benefit. Indeed, as if she truly was his gift from God.

Chapter 10

"Thank you, Annie." Theo collected the tray and made her way up the stairs.

The installation of Captain Balfour in Stapleton's best guest room had met with grunted consent from Grandfather, flurried murmurs of "Oh, the poor man!" from her mother, and suppressed glee from Becky. The servants had also been sworn to secrecy, and complaint about their extra duties seemed to fall by the wayside when Theo pointed out the honor of caring for so great a hero.

As for herself . . .

She rounded the landing, carefully balancing the tray. She would have to tread carefully. The captain's misadventure and her time alone with him seemed to have bonded them more closely, in a way that both thrilled and terrified. Not that she was happy he was injured, of course. But the captain possessed a charm her heart had instantly responded to and had never encountered before. Perhaps that was why she felt so strongly attracted. In the absence of other young men of his calibre, she had found him to be the epitome of all she held dear. Which was sheer folly, and something she would admit to no one. But it meant she'd need to temper his kindnesses with reality and not allow her feelings to hold sway.

A few last steps before she steadied the tray on one arm and warily knocked on the door.

The door was swiftly opened by Mr. Siddons, who had been pressed into service as required, although she suspected caring for an invalid, even one as famous as the captain, might prove rather lowering for that man's pride.

She nodded to him and carried the tray to a small table beside the bed.

"Miss Stapleton."

"Good morning, Captain. How are you feeling today?"

"I have felt better." He winced as he pushed up against the pillows, his bad leg propped on the bedcovers and slightly raised, strapped in a rigid splint made of wood and leather.

"I'm sure you have." She offered a sympathetic smile. At least six weeks, the doctor had said last Saturday, due to the bad break.

"You are very understanding, Miss Stapleton."

"I try to be."

A reluctant sounding chuckle pushed from him.

"I have brought your breakfast. Porridge and eggs."

"I trust no pockets were involved."

"As you can see." She gestured to the tray.

An enquiry was made about his need for tea, which he accepted, and Mr. Siddons murmured that he would see to that immediately, thus prompting his escape.

"I trust the sustenance will prove sufficient." She moved to the door.

"You are not leaving, are you?" He swallowed. "Forgive me. I'm sure you have many things to attend to which must demand your time, rather than keep me company."

Actually, no. The misty rain of Saturday had strengthened in past days, and the roads were impassable, thus preventing attendance at services two days ago. Her time yesterday had been spent productively completing what odd jobs required attention, so today she had little to do except check in on their injured guest. And certainly nothing that appealed more. She hesitated, conscious of her decision not to engender romantical notions, yet also aware of the entreaty in his eyes.

"Please. Unless, of course, you think by doing so it may harm your reputation."

As if he could do her any harm. "I can spare you a few minutes."

"Thank you." He accepted the bowl of porridge and milk, ate a few mouthfuls, then paused. "I do appreciate your family's hospitality in allowing me to stay. I'm sure your grandfather was not best pleased."

She settled into a nearby chair. "Sometimes it's necessary for us to do what is good and not what is merely expedient."

"A do-gooder, are you?"

"Do you take exception?" She glanced up from adjusting her skirts.

"Well, no."

"I am pleased to hear it, for I should think your heroics qualify you for such an epithet. As for myself, I cannot claim it."

"Bravo." He chuckled again, more wholly this time.

She encouraged him to eat some more.

He obeyed, taking several more mouthfuls. "At least if I am forced to stay, it is with such convivial company."

"We are extremely convivial, it is true."

Again that crack of laughter. "Are you always so witty, madam?"

She paused, her head tilting. "You know, I have never truly considered the matter."

A grin lit his features. "I do appreciate your solicitude and that of your family's. When I think I could have ended up at an inn, forced to endure all sorts of hardship . . . but instead I am here, being fed by someone I suspect might be a descendent of angels."

"It appears you must have hit your head quite badly."

"My head? No."

"You must have, seeing as you appear to be suffering from some form of delusion."

His gaze remained fixed on her. "No delusions, I assure you."

A ripple of unfamiliar emotion crossed her heart. She hid her confusion by busying herself with the medicine bottles and other accoutrements of illness. When she judged her voice could speak normally, she said, "You might consider several other advantages. Your enforced stay will encourage you to rest, which I gather the past few years has not allowed much time for."

"Try the past couple of decades." He winced as he pushed himself higher in the bed then adjusted the sheets. "I joined the army when I was just sixteen."

"Is that not awfully young? I know Grandfather and Father were both eighteen when they joined."

"And eighteen is so much older than sixteen."

"Isn't it?"

He smiled, and her pulse knew another undulation. Oh, it was too easy to banter with him.

"You might consider, too, that staying longer allows more time to consider what you would wish to do with Mannering. It certainly looks better now. Well, except—"

"For the floor in the hallway?"

"Precisely so. It is a wonder that happened as it did, given the number of persons and furniture moving across it in recent days."

"Perhaps that was the problem, and it simply could not withstand the continued weight. I am simply thankful that it happened to me and it was not Rebecca's misfortune to be present when the floor decided to give up."

"Something to be thankful for indeed! Not, I assure you, that I am in any way pleased that you are injured, of course."

"Of course." The look of amusement in his eye provided reassurance before he bent to finish his bowl.

A prickling kind of awareness grew that she should leave. "It seems Mr. Siddons has been waylaid. Shall I go see about your tea?"

"I would prefer your conversation."

At his request, she resettled into the chair, uneasily conscious that by agreeing to do so she would be testing her resolve to remain immune to him. Not wishing to pursue this—or the missing cup of tea—she asked what he intended to do about Mannering's floor and its sad condition.

"I suspect the joists and supports will require major work. A job I had time to contemplate from my position."

"So Mannering requires more of a total overhaul, and a lick of paint and a trimmed garden won't really suffice."

"No, I'm afraid not."

"I am sorry."

"Why? You did not saw the joists, did you?"

Horror curdled. "They were sawn?"

"No! No. I think it was merely old age, and as you say, there seemed to have been a bit of movement, which might have progressed matters somewhat."

"Mannering has always been prone to creaking and the like, so perhaps you are right. Well, you have time to employ builders, should you wish to do so. It would only be right for the future occupants to know the house is well and truly fit for habitation."

"That is so." He dipped his chin.

A noise at the door drew attention to Mr. Siddons, who had finally arrived holding a tray with a teapot and a cup, and a look of disapproval.

She thanked him and smiled inwardly as the butler exited, glancing at her sternly as he propped the door a little wider.

It seemed someone had a care for her reputation, at least.

She poured and passed the captain's cup of tea to him.

"Tell me, Miss Stapleton, what would you do if in my situation?"

"Which situation is that, sir? Being housebound, responsible for a young relative, or being answerable for a broken-down house?"

"I was thinking of the latter." He sipped his tea.

"What to do with Mannering?"

He nodded, eyeing her above the rim of his teacup.

"I'm afraid I cannot offer an opinion."

"Yes, you can. In fact, I suspect you have many opinions that you carefully offer in such a discreet way that you come across as merely being very thoughtful and obliging."

Amusement tweaked her lips. "I cannot be sure if that is a compliment or not, so I shall overlook that remark, sir."

"Oh, it was most definitely a compliment."

His intent look heated her cheeks. Too much more of his flattery and she might—foolish girl that she was!—very soon start believing it. She hurried to say, "I should go."

"I would not have you run away."

"Yet you shall be doomed for disappointment, as I have been here far longer than I intended."

"Before you go, may I ask one thing?"

She waited.

"My staying here won't injure your reputation, I trust?"

"People may think it strange that we harbor someone considered to be the captain's agent."

His brow knit. "I had forgotten that."

She offered another sympathetic smile. "As someone recognized for her deep stratagem, you may want to reconsider your being incognito. Now, I really should go."

"But you have not yet answered my question."

"What question was that, sir?"

"About Mannering, what you think I should do." He finished his tea and placed the empty cup on the table.

"You truly want my opinion?"

"You seem to have no small degree of common sense. I would appreciate the advice of a sensible, clever lady about what to do."

She studied him a moment. He did indeed appear sincere. "I cannot think you mean it to be a ruin."

"Is it worth fixing?"

"Can you afford to leave it? Would not a little expense in fixing a few things allow for greater income if you leased it out? I believe the house would prove quite popular, should it be known it was available to let."

"You think this is what I should do?"

"I do not claim to know your personal situation, sir, but if this is something you can afford to do, and if it is a house that holds sentimental value—"

"It is not."

Very well. "Regardless of whether one intends to sell, I believe that the house could benefit from more than a simple spruce up. If I was in possession of such a house, then I would reverse the rooms so that the main reception rooms looked out across the back and the inhabitants could enjoy views of the river."

"You have thought on this, I see."

"To effect such a change would not be greatly expensive, I should think. It's simply a matter of switching furniture and intention. One can afford to have one's study at the front of a house when that house is more secluded and not prone to many visitors. And can you not imagine how lovely it would be to have the drawing room at the back, where one can see the Cheviots beyond the stream and trees? To be honest, I have never understood why people do not wish to make the most of the natural beauty to be found and arrange their rooms accordingly. I should much prefer to look at the hills rather than a fussy, ordered garden."

"You do not admire artifice?"

"No indeed, sir, I do not."

His gaze trickled over her hair and cheek, and she wondered if she should have powdered her face earlier. Oh, how nonsensical was she!

"It is rare to encounter a woman who does not wish to employ tricks and ploys to garner attention. You are most refreshing, Miss Stapleton."

She was?

"You appear to possess remarkable good sense and sympathetic understanding."

Oh. "I'm afraid I might be known around these parts for such things. However, good sense is not always valued highly, especially from . . ." She bit off her last words. She had almost said *young men*!

His perusal of her lingered, unsettling her.

She moved to the door. "I can furnish you the names of several competent builders, if you so wish. But if you don't wish it, then I shall bid you good day."

"These builders, you could write to them for me?"

"Yes. Although it might prove of greater benefit if you, should you continue to represent yourself as the captain's steward, make such enquiries. Besides"—she offered a saucy look—"it will give you some occupation for the next hour that won't distract me from mine."

He laughed and agreed, and she shut the door, her heart beating foolishly fast.

The next days of Daniel's enforced stay saw a welter of conversations with such people as Rebecca, the minister, Mrs. Stapleton, and the solicitor, with whom he variously explained the situation, sought assurance over reputation, and procured recommendations about which builders could be trusted to attend to Mannering's deep-seated issues. Such conversations were swiftly followed by letters to the appropriate concerned parties, one of which included a missive to Lieutenant Musgrave, explaining the necessary delay to the expected return to London. In much of this, Miss Stapleton proved invaluable, concerned as she was with his health and doling out frequent encouragement not to overexert himself.

"Which must seem strange to you," she said, on one of these occasions, "when it is apparent that one does not achieve heroic status without exerting oneself."

"Truly, I wish people would not hold that against me."

"Hold your courage against you? Never." She smiled.

He'd found himself thinking about that smile on more than one occasion.

She was a good nurse. Quick to notice when he was in pain, quick to offer diversion by way of interesting conversation, which veered from amusing anecdotes of the locals to those which hinted at some of the struggles Clara had faced these past years.

He did not get the sense Miss Stapleton blamed him for staying away. Indeed, her conversations about her father and grandfather showed she quite understood the need for men to serve their country, which necessitated their time away from family. Her graciousness didn't help his renewed regrets, although it did spark fresh determination to help provide for Becky as best he could.

His niece did not seem overly disappointed by the situation. On the contrary, while not precisely pleased about his predicament, she made no effort to hide her pleasure at being able to stay in the district a little longer. "Oh, Uncle, I am indeed sorry that you are in pain—are you in great pain?"

"I find the distraction of conversation with people such as yourself helps keep my mind on other things."

"Would you like some other visitors? I know Mr. Siddons isn't as bright as one might like—Theo says he likely was born without a sense of humor, which must be why he and the general get on so well."

Daniel smiled.

"Oh! I didn't mean to sound so disparaging, because it is indeed kind of the general to let you stay here too."

"I don't know if Miss Stapleton gave him much choice."

"She is quite marvelous, isn't she?" Becky enthused. "I don't think I know anyone quite like her. She's always so kind and positive and can turn the worst situation around with just a smile or a jest."

"A true paragon."

After a beat, Becky asked, "Don't you like her? I thought that the two of you got on."

"Indeed I do," he hurried to assure. "But I find I have no desire to injure her reputation by staying here."

"I don't think she gives a snap about things like that."

"She may not, but I suspect there are others who may."

"You mean her mother? Mrs. Stapleton is such a dear. It's a shame she is not well enough to venture out very often."

"The weather does not make that easy either," he said with a smile. "But no, she was not whom I was thinking of." Mrs. Stapleton had assured him it was their Christian duty to care for him, so he had no misgivings there.

"You mean the likes of Lady Bellingham," Becky guessed. "She is hardly a concern, although I've always thought she wished for her son to marry Theo."

His stomach tensed.

"Oh, don't look at me like that. You can't have been too surprised. Not that they would suit, well, not to my way of thinking anyway. Theo is much too lively and clever for the likes of him."

He silently agreed. But conscious of a certain assessing look in his niece's eye, he hastened to turn the subject. "Have you no suitors, Becky?"

"Me? How could I? I am not quite seventeen."

"Age does not determine whether one has suitors."

"It does here," she said bluntly. "Mama was always encouraging Theo to travel, because there were no young men of her age in the vicinity. But Theo has always said she could never leave her mother to cope with the general alone. He is rather frightening." She shuddered.

"How so?"

"I suppose you have not seen it yet, as he has been behaving rather well. But he's known as General Contrary. He can seem quite pleasant one moment, then quite horrid the next. I have heard him shout and hurl abuse at anyone who dares come near."

His chest grew tight. "At Mrs. Stapleton and her daughter?"

"I think he terrifies Theo's mother," she confessed. "Theo is able to stand up for herself, although I'm sure she does not like it above half."

"I doubt she would," he said dryly.

When Becky left, he found himself wondering about Theodosia Stapleton again, his thoughts steering to admiration. She was quite remarkable, and if he was a young man in the district looking to be leg-shackled, then he would snap her up.

But he was not.

And remembering that assessing look in his niece's eye, he had no plans to be. Really, inscribing another letter to Adam Edgerton would be best to think on right now. Deal with thoughts that held a degree of reality.

Not distractions that could never—*would* never—be.

Chapter 11

The remainder of that first week passed in a constant supply of rain events, so it was well into ten days of the captain's prescribed stay before news of Stapleton's additional guest finally made its way to the village. Theo was not sorry, for the time had allowed the captain to get some much-needed rest without the distractions of visitors, save for some interviews with builders. But the time had also allowed her to see that while he might never complain, the confines of his stay were not a little dull. She sought to amuse him as best she could, in a manner that neither raised questions of impropriety nor raised her feelings beyond what they ought be. She couldn't help feel compassion for him, though, for his enforced stay with those with whom he shared little in common.

One would think the general might be persuaded to talk and exchange reminisces, but her grandfather's gout had flared again, and he was disinclined to partake in matters which alleviated the discomforts of anyone but himself. The solicitor, too, had other pressing matters, and there were few others who could both understand Captain Balfour's past and be trusted to keep his identity a secret.

The lack of disclosure about his name would end badly, but there seemed little point in making his true name known when it would likely result in a trail of constant visitors, which was not to the liking of any of Stapleton Court's inhabitants. Theirs was a place of quietude, and none of them had ever liked the feeling of being at the mercy of whatever person took a notion to drop by.

Pity the poor captain whose work might have led him to prefer to socialize.

She knocked on his door, carefully balancing the tea tray.

"Enter."

With a twist of the doorknob, she entered the room, only to catch a glimpse of a pale scarred chest and muscled shoulders as he exchanged a shirt. She instantly averted her eyes. "Oh, sir! Forgive me! I did not know—"

He put his back to her. "No, forgive me. I thought you were Mr. Siddons."

"He is sick with a cold, otherwise I never would have—oh, I should go." She quickly shifted to place the tray atop the nearest table.

"Please, don't leave."

Sounds of hastily dragged-on clothing reached her ears. She peeked across the room at the mirror, saw he indeed now wore a shirt. And that he was watching her watching him. Her cheeks heated. "I really must—"

"Please, don't. At least, not until you have moved the tea things closer." He smiled apologetically. "I cannot reach them over there."

"Of course."

She placed them on the table beside the bed.

"You are all solicitude. Thank you."

"I'm afraid it isn't me you should thank. It's Mrs. Brigham, our cook. She thought you might find this welcome, especially given the drop in temperature overnight." She poured a cup and handed it to him. "I trust you are keeping warm?"

"Yes, thank you."

"Good. I shall leave you in peace."

"I really wish you would stay. At the risk of sounding ungrateful, the lack of conversation is most dull. Mr. Siddons might be a good servant, but his conversational skills leave a lot to be desired."

"But it would be considered improper."

"Only by those who know. And who are they? Please, Miss Stapleton, you do not strike me as missish. Won't you take pity on a man in pain and allow him to talk with someone who is interesting?"

She hesitated, then finally nodded, and—ignoring the wayward feelings in her breast stirred up because he thought her interesting—asked if he would like the curtains adjusted, whether he'd like the window opened, and finally took the seat farthest from him.

He enquired about her day, and she shared about her duties of mending linen, caring for the chickens and livestock, and organizing the running of the household.

"You do so and not your mother?"

"She has little energy to attend to such matters."

He nodded. "She is a kindhearted woman."

"That she is." How touching he would recognize that quality about her mother. "Some people take advantage of her kindness"—like Grandfather—"but I think her uncomplaining spirit is to be greatly admired."

"You possess that too," he observed.

"'Tis kind of you to say so, but I'm afraid I would never be as considerate as she. For while I may not express my complaints, it does not mean I do not feel them."

He chuckled, and the sound warmed her.

Conscious of her disinclination to permit softer emotions from seeding in her heart, she hurried on. "You must forgive me, sir, I should have asked before. Do you have anyone you may care to have come visit and alleviate this boredom?"

"I'm not bored," he protested.

"Then you are not truthful."

"Miss Stapleton, I must object. What with discussions with builders and your cheering presence, I have not had time to be bored."

"Hmm. Well, if there is someone you should care to invite, then please feel free to do so."

"Thank you." He leaned forward and adjusted the pillow behind him. "Speaking of visitors, I, er, believe I heard a scratching sound last night on the door."

"That was most likely Maisie."

"Maisie?"

"Our supercilious cat. She thinks herself quite above us all but will likely condescend to visit you, especially as you are so famous."

He smiled. "I shall look forward to her company."

"If there is anyone else apart from our cat, please don't hesitate."

"I should not impose upon you further. You already do so much."

"Oh no. I'm afraid you mistake my efforts for those which are done by the servants who are put to *such* troubling lengths as your presence demands," she teased. "But just between us, it would do me a world of good to know their time is being gainfully employed. They are *so* prone to bouts of lethargy, especially now with Grandfather taken to his sickbed. It's as if they scarcely know what to do with themselves."

"A habit picked up from their mistress, perhaps?"

"Mama?" Her chest flared with offense.

"You."

She recognized the jest in his eyes and dropped her gaze. "I am quite the lady of leisure, that is so."

"Nobody could think so," he objected. "You are the one who keeps this household running so smoothly."

"I'm sure you are mistaken, sir. The servants answer to Mama."

"Yet are handled by you. You really are quite the skilled manager, are you not?"

Heat flushed her cheeks. "If you insist on such nonsense, I'm afraid I shall have to leave."

"And run away again? You disappoint me, Miss Stapleton. I thought you possessed more mettle."

"I have enough mettle for what must be done and sometimes precious little more," she said quietly.

"I'm sorry. I didn't mean to—"

"Now, if you'll excuse me, I have other work to do. Unless you require anything more?"

"If it is not too much trouble, I would be most obliged to have ink and paper. If your mother is truly willing for me to entertain a guest, then I would very much like to write to my friend Lieutenant Musgrave and beg him to visit. I was supposed to see him in London, but as I cannot make it to the city, then I might ask London to come to me."

"He would be very welcome, sir."

"Thank you. Can you recommend a good inn? I would not wish to impose another on your household here."

"The White Hare is the best such establishment, but only if you consider Stapleton Court to be too cramped and small."

"You have done so much already."

"Tosh and nonsense. You are Becky's uncle, and as such are to be considered almost like family, as she is. A visitor to you would be of little consequence to the running of things here, and so is not to be wondered at, and will not be wondered at, unlike if the lieutenant stays in town and is forced to explain exactly why he has come to this part of the world."

He frowned, then nodded. "I never realized just how burdensome keeping my identity private would prove."

"You cannot have known just how things would eventuate." She rose and moved to the door. "If you wish to invite the lieutenant, then please assure him he will receive a warm welcome." She smiled. "We cannot have England's hero complaining of being lonely."

A ring on the bell drew her downstairs in time to catch Mr. Siddons opening the door to Lady and Frederick Bellingham. Her heart, which had only moments earlier felt light, seemed to shadow.

How would their most constant visitor respond to the knowledge that their guest was the one man the squire's wife longed to meet?

She placed such concerns to one side as she hurried down the stairs. "Dear Lady Bellingham! How wonderful of you to take pity on us and deign to visit us in this foul weather."

The squire's wife drew off her gloves as they moved to the drawing room. "I was afraid something must have happened to you, what with no sign of hide nor hair of any of Stapleton's inhabitants for over a week."

"You must forgive us. The weather has been most atrocious, and the general has been unwell." She gestured for them to sit.

"Gout, I suppose?" Lady Bellingham asked.

Theo nodded.

"That must account for the doctor's visits."

"He has been most faithful in his attendance." All true. "Although I must confess to some ignorance as to why the movements of the doctor to our door would prove of interest to others."

Lady Bellingham tittered, as if Theo had spoken wittily. But she didn't answer, only slid a look at her son.

Hmm. Had he been the one most interested in the goings-on at Stapleton Court?

He bowed slightly in greeting. "I trust you are not missing Miss Mannering too much."

"Miss Mannering?" she repeated. "Oh, I take it you have not heard the news. Rebecca is with us still. Her, um, escort for the journey south had an accident, and so she remains a little longer."

"I see." But the cloud in his eyes made it clear that he did not like it.

She turned to Lady Bellingham. "Should you wish to speak to my mother? I am sure she is as keen as you to enjoy a comfortable coze."

"That would be very kind."

Theo rose, as did Mr. Bellingham, and she was about to offer to get tea when the door opened and in walked Theo's mother, trailed by Becky.

"My dears!" Lady Bellingham shook hands with them. "How wonderful to see you both, although I am a little surprised to see one of you."

Theo met Becky's quick glance with the slightest shake of her head. "I was just telling dear Lady Bellingham about how glad we are that you have not yet left us."

"Y-yes," Becky said. "I love it here, so I was very glad to learn that I could stay a little longer."

"An accident to your escort, I understand?"

"Most unfortunate, wasn't it, Becky?" Theo willed her face to assume pleasantness. "Especially as it accounted for his absence at Becky's last meal."

"And there you were, teasing us about him, saying it was to be a great surprise."

"But that is the nature of a surprise, is it not? There is a tendency for it to surprise even the most careful of plans, thus surprising the surpriser."

Becky chuckled. "I rather doubt he enjoyed that surprise."

"No."

The look that Lady Bellingham and son exchanged suggested they would be wise to move on from this topic of conversation, but before Theo could return to a focus on the weather, Lady Bellingham addressed

Becky again. "Have you any idea of how long we can be assured of the pleasure of your company, Rebecca, dear?"

"I . . . I believe it is another five weeks or so."

"In that case, perhaps your uncle might be persuaded to come after all. It really was too bad of him not to make a push earlier. We were all so excited."

"Perhaps he learned of it and decided to stay away." Theo raised her eyebrows.

"Oh, Theodosia, you are too cruel! I know you are funning, but really, such things are not to be mocked. I am sure that dear Captain Balfour would be most gratified by our parties here."

"I wonder if a hero used to being feted in London would wish for more of the same here in the north?" Theo mused aloud. "If it were me, I would much prefer to rusticate and go about my business quietly."

"That is because you are a such a modest girl," Lady Bellingham said. "If you were more used to parties and the like, then I daresay you would enjoy those entertainments of a more sociable nature."

Theo bowed her head in an attempt to look as modest as Lady Bellingham seemed to believe her to be.

The two older ladies pulled away into conversation, which left Theo to do her best to balance the surly probing queries of Frederick with the shy responses of Becky. Such a conversation, with Becky's capacity for near misses concerning her uncle, left Theo feeling a little exhausted when their guests finally departed.

"I do not know how much longer we can keep this pretense," Theo said, when they had returned to the drawing room after waving off their visitors.

"Is Uncle Daniel still determined to hide himself?"

"Determined or not, he feels this is the best course for the immediate future. But you may find that things change." She glanced apologetically at her mother. "Forgive me, Mother, for I should have spoken about this to you sooner. I was speaking to the captain earlier and encouraged him to invite a friend to come and stay."

"But of course he would appreciate a visitor! Oh, the poor man. Hiding up here as he is must be *so* hard for a man of action. I hope he agreed."

"Eventually. But I should think he would like your reassurance too. He seems to be under the impression that I run the household, and it would be helpful, perhaps, if he could see that you are the real lady of the manor."

"But we all know that is you, my dear." Her mother caressed Theo's hand with affection. "I could not pretend to do half the things you do, for which I'm so very grateful."

"Did my uncle say whom he wished to invite?" asked Becky.

"Lieutenant Musgrave."

"Oh!"

"Who is he?" asked Theo's mother.

"I recall Mother speaking of him, that he was a man every bit as brave as Uncle Daniel but a number of years younger. He also fought in the Peninsular and is considered to be very handsome."

"If that is the case, then he is sure to be welcomed in the village. Handsome young men generally are." Theo stood, moving to stir up the fire.

"I don't think Mr. Bellingham will like that very much," said Becky, with a most unladylike smirk.

"It is a good thing we need not take his feelings into consideration, then." Theo laughed. "Oh, won't the lieutenant set the villagers on their ears?"

From Daniel's position on the bed, he could almost see the budding of trees. If he inched a little to his right—

There. He smiled with satisfaction. Springtime had certainly arrived, if those blossoms were to be believed. He fought the desire to sigh and wish he had never set foot in Mannering. The past couldn't be changed by regret. Better to focus on what he could be thankful for.

He was still healthy, mending leg notwithstanding.

He was extremely grateful for such accommodations, which seemed the height of luxury to him, especially compared with what he'd been used to in recent years.

He was thankful that this enforced rest did give him time to get to know his niece a little more, and time to consider other things too. Was a return to war the only path that lay ahead? He'd prayed and asked God for direction, and even dared to ask Him to show if a different path might be in his future. His morning's Bible reading in Proverbs drifted back to memory. *A man's heart deviseth his way: but the LORD directeth his steps.*

A man might have plans for his life, but trusting God meant trusting Him with the future, whatever that might hold. Daniel's heart flickered. He tamped it down. Not that he could afford to get carried away and contemplate anything to do with the gentler sex. Between his pay and what little rent the house in Wiltshire brought in, he might have a degree of income but could provide little for someone accustomed to Stapleton Court.

He blinked. Shook his head at himself. Really, the sooner he mended and left, the sooner these strange musings might end.

A knock drew his attention to Mr. Siddons, who held out a paper. "The post has come, sir."

"Thank you."

He accepted the letter and slit the seal. Apart from updates from the builders, wondering whether he'd be fortunate to receive mail was his chief source of entertainment these days, and great was the day when a letter found its way to him.

James Langley's epistle had arrived yesterday, and in it he'd reiterated his wife's invitation to return to Langley House, should Daniel require a stop on his return to London. The generosity and kindness he'd experienced on his brief visit north only showed the depths of God's grace in transforming a heart once so black. James Langley was blessed with a capable and pretty wife, a sizeable home, and what looked to be restoration in his family. But such did not mean similar blessings lay in store for all.

Daniel chewed his lip. Was it faithless to believe so? Or mere pragmatics? The simple fact was that some men did not marry, either from lack of opportunity or inclination. But did that mean he should forever count himself as one of them? What if God had a future Daniel had not envisaged, a path yet untrodden for the future?

Uncertainty gripped him, and he unfolded the page and studied the writing, lips pursing as he read the words.

Dear Sir,

Thank you for your recent letter. I am glad to inform you that my circumstances continue to improve. I have indeed found a most excellent wife, who I am half-persuaded believes she has found a measure of happiness too. I don't doubt that she will add in her own thoughts on the matter, but let me assure you that he who finds a wife finds a good thing.

My Mary is increasing, which has brought my father and mother much joy. Mary herself keeps well and assures me she is eager to meet you at your earliest convenience—which does not seem like it will be soon. But when you are mended, please know you are assured of a bed here in Ambleton, where you can see with your own eyes just how things are.

Gilroy and Conwell continue to thrive. It seems hard to believe that they were not born to farm life, but then, I never expected to take to it as well as I have either. I trust you will give some consideration to what lies in your future, and recall that though we plot our course, sometimes our Lord has other things in mind, which may well prove to be of far greater value.

Daniel paused, rubbed his eyes. Reread the last line, heart tensing. Did God have other things in mind for him? He resumed reading.

I never expected to be able to say I am content, especially with matters developing as they did, but I can now assure you that is truly the case. Our Lord has good plans for us, of that we can be certain.

Please visit when you can. I long for you to meet my dear sweet wife.

Yours etc.,
Adam Edgerton

In a postscript, the same hand had written:

Dear Captain

I trust you will heed what my dear husband has said. He is most eager for your visit and to show the great leaps he has made in his recovery. Please know you are indeed most welcome,

Mary Edgerton

He tapped the paper thoughtfully. Two recent letters from friends— from James and the Edgertons—both of similar subjects and tone. Perhaps when he had mended enough to journey, he could visit one or the other of them. One *or* the other, as they lived on opposite sides—one in Cumbria, one beside the North Sea.

How he'd like to see Adam Edgerton, though the man might never see him again. How marvelous was his progress to normality, that his future seemed secured, despite his most devastating of affliction of blindness. God was good indeed.

But their words also contained a subtle challenge he was hesitant to take. Just because his friends had both found happiness and secured wives did not mean such was the path for all.

It couldn't.

Could it?

For a moment he dared contemplate life without his regiment, without the structure and security of the armed forces. Could he, like Adam Edgerton, turn his hand to something else? But unlike Adam, Daniel had no family farm. Neither was he due to inherit a broken estate that required his attention like James had.

Daniel's legacy, apart from a very small house in a nondescript village in Wiltshire, had been carved out elsewhere. Such was all he now knew. If that were given up, what would he be? *Who* would he be?

A man couldn't just exchange his life and put on another as one might swap coats. A man's life involved the hundreds of decisions that had made him what he was, and Daniel was a soldier. A man of action. A man others looked to in a crisis, whom they counted as a friend. What would he be—who would he be—if that was stripped away?

He frowned and was still frowning when a tap came at the door. At his call of "Enter," Miss Stapleton drew inside.

"Forgive the intrusion, sir, but we were wondering if you might prefer beef or pork for dinner tonight."

He pushed up higher against the headboard. "I declare you have made my stay here very difficult."

"How so?"

"How can I ever be expected to resume normal life when I have been treated like a king?"

"Would you prefer us to ignore you? Abandon you to your own devices?"

A life without her in it? Why did that thought catch him in the heart? "Really, I must thank you—"

Further expressed gratitude was silenced by the raising of her hand. "Sir, I am well aware of your indebtedness. You make that plain every time I visit."

"Is my conversation so very tiresome?"

"I hesitate to agree—"

He laughed.

"Upon reflection, the person you should be thanking is Mrs. Brigham, our cook. You were likely unaware of the grand preparations at what would have been the dinner where your identity was to be revealed. Annie went to so much trouble. Then when you did not show and it had to be delayed a little . . . Well, you should have heard the complaints. We all did, for much of the next day," she said ruefully.

"I confess I had no idea."

"That does not surprise me, seeing as it would be most impolite to bring this to your attention."

"Indeed it would." His smile spread unrestrained.

"If I may be permitted to continue?"

He waved his hand in invitation. "By all means."

"As I was saying, Annie was that upset about that special dinner nearly being spoiled, the fact she deigns to feed you at all these days is entirely miraculous."

He chuckled. "I suppose I should thank her, then."

"You should. She would be most gratified to have a hero stoop to speak with her."

"I shall endeavor to do so at the next opportunity."

"Please. And if you could gratify us all by making a decision about your preference for beef or pork?"

"I'm rather partial to beef."

"Beef it is, then. Thank you. Now I shall leave you to your letters." She glanced at the paper on his bed. "Good news, I hope?"

"The best." He explained a little about Adam Edgerton, his loss of prospects, then his regaining new life after losing his sight.

"He sounds quite the intrepid," she said with a warm smile.

"His wife even more so. There would not be many women courageous enough to take on a man who cannot see."

Her head tilted, and she glanced out the window. "I think you do women an injustice there, sir. If the right woman meets the right man, who is to say they cannot make things work, especially if they love each other and are both determined to succeed?"

He bowed his head. "Forgive me. I did not mean to cast aspersions on your sex."

"And I did not mean to seem quick to take offense. Only that I think the ways of such relationships are most wonderful and almost mysterious. It's definitely miraculous how God can bring two people together and blend them into a healthy, happy union."

"Miraculous?"

"Oh, yes. Would you not agree it is rare for two such differing personalities to encounter one another, then to have the time to grow and develop sympathetic understandings with each other, even to the point where they can be considered one?"

"It is not something I have seen often, that is true."

"And yet your friends seem to have achieved it, which is most marvelous." Her gaze found his again.

He drank in the sight of her, fresh and vibrant and pretty.

Then she blinked, blushed, and murmured how she really ought to see to the dinner.

What had suddenly occurred to her?

As the faint scent of violets trailed after her departure, another thought teased.

Would a miracle be possible for him one day too?

Chapter 12

Theo hesitated on the upper landing, as the memory of the last conversation with Captain Balfour rippled to awareness. She winced, remembering her all-too-eager sounding words about relationships—to an unattached young man, no less. Mama would've gasped. Lady Bellingham would have had an attack of the vapors and many asides: *How could she be so careless with her words? Did Theo mean to be setting her cap at him?*

Another shudder crossed her soul. Just because the man possessed a voice and smile and scent that plucked at her heartstrings didn't mean she couldn't also temper these feelings into mere friendliness. She'd done it before and eventually learned contentment. She could do it again. She would simply need to capture every squirrelly thought and bend it to her will—that is, to God's will—and count her blessings.

She tapped on the door, relief filling her as he called to enter. "Excuse me, sir, but I wondered if you might prefer something to read."

"More poetry?" Apprehension shaded his eyes.

She tucked that book at the bottom of the stack and drew out the next. "Actually, I wondered if you were partial to Shakespeare."

He blinked.

"I thought you being a military man might enjoy reading *Henry IV,* especially seeing as it is set nearby."

He folded the newssheet. "Really?"

She nodded. "It is one of Grandfather's favorite plays, that and *Henry V.*

I think it's all the references to war that he appreciates, or that he thinks he would devise military stratagem more effectively." She held out the book. "I have marked the play. This volume contains the histories, you see."

He grasped the hardcover and flicked it open, ruffling pages until he found where she had placed the bookmark.

"I hope you enjoy." She offered a smile and moved to the door.

"Wait."

She arched a brow.

"How do you know this play is set nearby?"

Surely a moment longer would not hurt. She accepted his unspoken invitation and sat in the wooden chair next to his bed. "You permit me?"

"Of course."

She retrieved the book and turned to the first scene of the first act, tracing down the printed lines until she read aloud.

"'For more uneven and unwelcome news
Came from the north, and thus it did import:
On Holy-rood Day the gallant Hotspur there,
Young Harry Percy, and brave Archibald,
That ever valiant and approved Scot,
At Holmedon met, where they did spend
A sad and bloody hour—'"

She looked at him. "Holmedon is another name for Humbleton Hill, which is not five miles from here."

"Really?" He leaned forward, eyes brighter than before.

"Really." She turned back to the book, pointed out lines a little further down. "Again, we see it here—

'Betwixt that Holmedon and this seat of ours,
And he hath brought us smooth and welcomes news.
The Earl of Douglas is discomfited;
Ten thousand bold Scots, two-and-twenty knights,
Balked in their own blood, did Sir Walter see
On Holmedon's plains.'"

His gaze was locked on her, but his expression was unchanged.

Perhaps this held no interest for him. "I'm sorry if this is dull. I thought it might prove of interest—"

"It's most interesting. Forgive me. I was enjoying listening to you speak."

"Ah, but I do not need to read Shakespeare for you to hear me speak."

"That is true, but you read so well. I confess I have not studied the Bard overly, but I vaguely knew something of this story and that it was set in the north."

"One day before you leave, you may wish to see the stone that commemorates the battle."

"Thank you for your thoughtfulness, Miss Stapleton."

She dipped her head as pleasure swelled within.

"I wonder . . . but I'm sure that you are busy."

"I can make time."

He rubbed his jaw, speckled with dark bristles. "Would you be so kind as to read some more to me?"

"Read more Shakespeare?"

"More of *Henry IV*. I should like to know more, especially if I am to see this commemoration stone one day."

"Truly?"

A nod.

"Very well. You may wish to make yourself comfortable. This will take some time." She read through the list of characters, then began.

> "'So shaken as we are, so wan with care,
> Find we a time for frighted peace to pant,
> And breathe short-winded accents of new broils
> To be commenced in strands afar remote.'"

She read on, looking up every so often to either catch his eyes on her or his gaze fixed on the ceiling, as if he imagined the scenes depicted. How odd that for him so many of these scenes were not those of a romantic past but were lived battles, battles like those from which he wore scars. She'd seen those scars on his chest.

"Miss Stapleton?"

His deep voice drew her to herself. "Forgive me."

"You need not continue if you do not wish."

"I am happy to continue, sir."

"As long as it does not deprive you of your duties elsewhere."

She leaned forward conspiratorially. "To be quite honest with you, I much prefer to read Shakespeare than attend to my duties elsewhere."

"In that case, carry on."

And so she did.

She read, he listened, and they chuckled over Falstaff's quips, raged at Hotspur's treatment of his lady, applauded Prince Hal finally owning his princely heritage.

He seemed to truly enjoy it, and when she'd finished reading, they discussed the play as if it was normal to enter into so fully comprehending another's feelings and emotions.

At services, Theo spoke to the doctor and asked if he could visit on the morrow. The captain seemed to be improving, and she'd wondered if perhaps the captain might be well enough to take a different room. "I fear he is getting dreadfully bored in there. It's not the largest room, and our company cannot be very entertaining, I fear. A different view might prove diverting."

"I'm afraid it's still rather too soon for him to be moved," the doctor advised. "But I don't see any harm in his having visitors."

"We have made enquiries for his friend to come and stay. A Lieutenant Musgrave."

"Ah, another young man to tease and disconcert our neighborhood?"

"Only if it is found out that he knows Captain Balfour."

"Who knows Captain Balfour?"

Theo turned to encounter Mrs. Cleever's inquisitive expression. Her mind raced. What to admit, what to say . . .

"If you'll excuse me, ladies." The doctor tipped his hat, offering Theo a private grin.

"I still cannot believe the captain has made no appearance," the solicitor's wife complained.

"It is a mystery to the town, that is true," Theo said with care.

"He seems to be in regular communication with my husband. All Mr. Cleever does is talk of Mannering this or Mannering that."

"I'm sure there is a lot to consider, especially with its being sold and all."

"Why doesn't Captain Balfour wish to keep it? From what Betty has shared, it's looking far nicer these days. Perhaps once he sees it . . ."

Ah. Betty who had recently been employed as one of Mannering's cleaners and was also the daughter of Mrs. Cleever's cook. "I'm given to understand that there may still be a few issues."

"If he should happen to choose to marry someone of an eligible age"—her gaze swept Theo up and down, ensuring Theo knew who she did *not* consider eligible—"he might reverse his decision."

Theo's smile stiffened.

"My young daughters are happy not to have to forgo the company of Miss Rebecca, though I wonder if she has any idea as to when her uncle may finally appear?"

"I'm sure she knows as much—or as little—as I do." A guilty laugh filled Theo's throat. "If you'll please excuse me." She hastened away and advised Becky in hurried whispers of the imminent threat of questions from Mrs. Cleever, reminding of the need to be circumspect.

This conversation was in itself interrupted by an invitation to visit the solicitor's family, which immediately prompted Becky's pleas to attend.

Theo, as Becky's chief guardian, could find no reason to refuse. "I'm sure you would enjoy such an outing. It has been a while since you have had opportunity to mix with your friends."

"You are so good to me." Becky gently squeezed Theo's hand.

"Just remember to take care." She raised her brows in a silent prompt to recall their interrupted conversation.

"Always."

Somehow her mother had managed to invite the Bellinghams, now that the squire had returned, to partake of a dinner for the morrow, which would likely prove an interesting challenge to their desire to preserve the secrecy of their guest. She volunteered to pass on the news to her grandfather upon their return home. Visits to the general largely proved not such a pleasant task. Though his temper was exacerbated by his bouts with indigestion and gout, for some reason he never took kindly to being told he should refrain from imbibing quite so much in the way of rich foods and spirits.

Once home, she knocked on the library's door and entered at the grunt she'd always taken as a sign that she might go in.

"I came to see if you should like some company."

"I can think of nothing worse," her grandfather grumbled.

"Then I shall be sure to tell the squire his visit is unwelcome on the morrow."

"Giles is coming here? Well, I suppose I could do the pretty and be civil."

"Mama and I would be most grateful. I know that Sir Giles enjoys speaking with you."

"Because he's surrounded by a bumptious wife and dunce of a son. He coming too?"

"Frederick? I imagine so."

He snorted. "No need to look so woebegone, my dear. I can have a word with him if you don't want him hanging around."

"And send him off with a flea in his ear? I thank you, but no. Besides, I have no desire to make things uncomfortable for poor Mama."

"She and Elvira have always been thick as thieves." His brow lowered. "Elvira Bellingham is a gossip. You'll want to stay well clear of her while Balfour is here."

"That, unfortunately, cannot always be, as tomorrow night proves."

"That woman has a way of ferreting things out," he warned.

"And yet she is still to learn the truth of his identity, for which we remain grateful."

He huffed. "Methinks it will prove only a matter of time."

"I'm sure you are correct. But until then, we shall make the most of our little subterfuge."

"Minx."

His epithet drew a sparkling recollection of the way the captain had so referred to her, and she drew in a sharp breath to press down the emotion. "May I do anything for you?"

"Nothing."

"Then I trust you shall have a refreshing rest this afternoon."

"Resting is about all I'm good for these days," he grumbled.

"You might wish to converse with the captain," she suggested. "I am sure he would enjoy seeing a different face than mine and Mr. Siddons."

"Siddons I don't doubt, but your face I am sure he does not mind."

"'Tis kind of you to say so."

He eyed her. "You be careful, young lady, what you're about. He'll be headed back to war soon."

"Yes. And we shall wish him well. When he *is* well, I should say."

"You have no interest there?"

"How could I?" she said as blithely as she could. "Not when I have you and Mama to keep me company, and when he is heading off to battle."

His stern gaze quite unsettled her, so after enquiring a final time about his well-being, she escaped, closing the door and leaning against it with a sigh. She could not afford to care, that was true. So it would behoove her to ignore the other pain-ridden soldier resting in the room directly above.

The doctor arrived later the next afternoon. Mr. Siddons conducted him straight to Grandfather, where the doctor pronounced himself satisfied— albeit warning him, not for the first time, to avoid wine—then headed upstairs to the captain's room. Not half an hour after his arrival saw that of the Bellinghams, whom Theo conducted straight into the drawing room, before wheeling her grandfather out to meet them.

"Ah, Giles, Elvira. Good to see you." He nodded, his brow lowering as he glanced at Frederick, who wore his own frown whenever he looked at Theo.

"It is lovely to be at Stapleton Court once again," Lady Bellingham trilled. "I have quite missed my comfortable chats with Letitia and dear Theodosia."

"It is a shame this weather has proved so disagreeable," Mama said.

Conversation centered on the rising levels of the Till and the scandalous price of sheep. As such conversation required little input from the youngest members of the party, Theo was unsurprised when Frederick turned to her, looking for all intents and purposes as if he wished to conduct a private conversation of his own.

"I trust you are well, Miss Bellingham."

"Thank you, yes. I rarely get sick."

"I know." He gazed at her with a soft look that filled her with misgiving. Would he return to his declarations of several weeks before? She hastened her attention back to the others.

"I hope no other members of your household are unwell."

Her gaze snapped back to him. "I beg your pardon?"

"The servants. I trust they are not suffering from a disease of a communicable nature."

"Thank you, but they are well, and you really need not concern yourself with the state of our servants' health."

He gestured to where the doctor's gig could still be seen. "Dr. Linton is here."

"Yes. He has been visiting somewhat regularly to check on Grandfather's health."

"I see." His brow creased. "And yet the general is here with us, and the doctor does not appear to be leaving. So if he's not visiting him now, or any of the servants, then what keeps him here?"

Perhaps she had underestimated Frederick's wits. For a long moment, she struggled with what to say. Utter a lie she would not, but admit to the real identity of their mystery guest she was loath to do. She battled for a moment longer before saying slowly, "That is a good question."

She glanced at Becky, who immediately pushed to her feet, as if glad for the excuse, and drew near. "Was there something I could help you with, Miss Stapleton?"

"I wondered if you might be a dear and discover what keeps the good doctor here. I believe he has already seen Grandfather."

"Oh, yes. He's probably here to see—"

Theo shook her head, and Becky stuttered to a halt, casting wide eyes between Theo and Frederick.

"See who?" He leaned forward.

"Oh, no one of any great importance. Excuse me." Becky hurried from the room, leaving Theo to rue her gaucherie in expecting a young girl of barely tempered tongue to withhold their secret.

Frederick scratched his whiskerless chin. "No one of any great importance? So there *is* someone."

"You must forgive me, Mr. Bellingham. I do not understand the desire to pry into other people's affairs."

"Pray excuse me. My interest was simply that of a friend."

"And such is appreciated," she said, before forcibly inserting herself into the other conversation, as she determined to steer the ship far from the rocky shores of truth.

"I'm afraid it is as I told Miss Stapleton just yesterday. You would be best to remain here a trifle longer," Dr. Linton advised.

"As I suspected," Daniel admitted, unable to restrain a sigh.

"I believe she is concerned you tire of being shut-in, sir."

"She is thoughtful that way."

"Mmm." The doctor glanced at him under heavy brows. "You still wish to persist with this subterfuge and not own your name?"

"It seems I have entered a situation that is not easy to extricate oneself from."

"At least you are well looked after here."

"That is certainly true."

A tap came at the door, which then pushed open wider to reveal his niece.

"Hello, Becky."

"Ah, Miss Mannering," the doctor said. "Do you require my services?"

"Thank you, sir, but no." She turned to Daniel. "I came because, well"—she glanced at the doctor, who was collecting his medical instruments—"Miss Stapleton wanted me to. She's downstairs, being visited by Mr. Bellingham."

"Oho, her persistent suitor." The doctor chuckled. "One day he may wear her down."

Daniel's insides twisted.

"He is not at all who I think she should marry," confided Becky.

"I sometimes wonder if she ever will." The doctor's expression sobered before he glanced at Daniel. "Forgive my idle musings."

"You need not apologize to me," Daniel assured.

The doctor offered his farewell, then made his way from the room, and they could soon hear his tread creak on the stairs.

"There are visitors downstairs?" he asked his niece.

Becky nodded and took the seat beside him. "I should probably be there, but the conversation was so dull I did not think anyone would miss me."

"I don't find Miss Stapleton prone to dull conversation."

"Oh, I did not mean her. She is usually ever so lively, but Mr. Bellingham seemed to want to speak to her privately, and I couldn't help but wonder . . ."

"Wonder what?" How he loathed himself for stooping to gossip like an old woman. Perhaps being bedridden was turning him into one. But his ears itched for news of her, especially as she had not visited for several days. Not since that time when he had lain here listening to her melodic voice as she read tales from years ago. He hadn't expected to be mesmerized, but whether it was her animated voice or the story shaped by a great poet, he hadn't wanted her to stop reading, his disappointment at her finishing only leavened by the thought that he could ask her to read the second volume of *Henry IV*. Then perhaps read *Henry V*.

"Uncle?"

He told himself to focus. "Forgive me."

"You seemed most distracted. We were speaking about Miss Stapleton and Mr. Bellingham, then a faraway look came into your eye."

What had he been thinking on? Oh. Miss Stapleton. He frowned. Surely she wasn't enamored of this young man, despite what others might say. And yet why else would she permit herself to be closeted in this way?

"I can't help but wonder about her. She usually looks so vivacious, but she seems quite drained tonight."

Concern knotted within. "Perhaps she is ailing."

"No, she directly told Mr. Bellingham she is well."

"She has been rather busy."

"That cannot be it, for she is always so." She stood and fluffed out her skirts. "I suppose I shall have to return. Wish me luck."

"You don't need luck," he admonished. "Just be your sweet and charming self."

A beautiful smile lit her face at his praise.

Good thing she was sequestered here. The girl was fast becoming a young lady, and it would fall to his domain, no doubt, to fend off eager suitors.

The evening passed, and he found his ears straining for the slightest tinkle of laughter, the sounds of joy. How he wished he could be downstairs, joining in on the evening's entertainment.

A plate of the meal prepared for downstairs was brought to him as well, so he was informed by Robert Brigham, who advised that Mr. Siddons was busy attending to duties downstairs and could not attend the captain up here tonight. "But Annie—that is, Cook—wanted you to have this mutton pie especially," he said, as if reciting from memory.

"Tell her I am most appreciative." Daniel cut into the crust and inhaled the meaty aroma.

"Yes, sir."

He ate the pie and vegetables, again wondering at the lack of recent visits from Miss Stapleton. He had not precisely been lonely, but he had missed her way of brightening each day with smiles and laughter. Which wouldn't do, he told himself sternly. She was not for him. He would leave, she would stay, and that would be that.

But another part, a deeper part, wondered again if it could ever be possible to have a wife and a home where such things as dinner parties were the norm, where he could exchange private conversation with a handsome woman, and share the jokes and joys that added cream to one's day. Was such a thing possible? What would happen when he was old and grey?

He glanced out the dark window, frowning. What *would* happen when he was too old for the battlefield? Would he be packed off to some home for old soldiers? Would Becky find it in her heart to take him in? Did he want a home full of paid servants to care for him, without the softer bonds of love and affection?

The general's rattling laugh travelled up the stairs. Even the general had married, had a family. While this family unit was not quite the norm, Daniel had seen the love between its members. Was such a thing possible for him too?

Lord?

Chapter 13

Candlelight flickered off glassware, the silver epergne spilling with nuts and sweetmeats to enjoy after the second course had been removed. Theo offered a smile to Lady Bellingham, seated opposite her. The servants' hard work had created such a feast from what had seemed a larder more fit for famine. God was good, and so faithful.

"This is such a lovely meal," Lady Bellingham complimented Mama.

"It is dear Theo who should be praised," Mama demurred. "She gave Annie all the instructions, and all I have to do is turn up and receive the accolades."

"In that case, Mama, it is only fair that Annie be the one to receive the praise, especially seeing as she is the one whose idea it was to dress the pheasant this way."

"You must learn to accept your share of compliments, Theodosia," the squire said from next to her.

Theo bobbed her head in acquiescence and glanced in Frederick's direction. Mama had insisted on seating him next to Becky, and Theo couldn't help but wonder at the arrangement. Could Becky be trusted to hold her tongue? Extricating herself from Frederick's persistent attempts to resume the previous conversation had made Theo dangerously aware that her avoidance earlier had only fueled his curiosity. She would have to satisfy him somehow. But what drove his interest? Was he suspicious after she had turned him down? She hardly thought his attempt at an offer of matrimony so genuine that he should take a miff. Had whispers leaked that there was a stranger residing here?

Regardless, she wished this dinner over, so she might speak to him and offer what reassurance she could.

But after the syllabub was consumed, and the ladies moved to the drawing room to wait for the men, her agitation increased. How could she apply herself to the entertainment of the others? She had no interest in playing cards, and everyone knew the squire and his wife were most partial to a game of whist. Could she perhaps steal Frederick's attention while the others played—for only four players would be needed, and the general held little interest in it—and somehow persuade the young man to drop his enquiry?

Oh, to not have to play this game anymore.

Her mother gently fanned herself beside the painted fire screen. "My dear, would you care to play the piano?"

"Of course, Mama." Theo moved to the small pianoforte, which saw rare use now Mama was often given to feeling poorly. A run of the scales and she commenced to play a sonata by Haydn. She did not play well, nothing to Mama's standard anyway, but she muddled through as best she could.

The door opened, and in came the gentlemen, with the squire applauding her. "Very pretty, my dear. Very pretty. I wonder if you might encourage Miss Mannering to sing. I'm told she has a most charming voice."

Theo turned to Becky, seated on an embroidered chair. "Rebecca, would you wish to sing?" Theo asked.

Becky cast the squire a look before lowering her voice. "I am not sure it is very proper."

Of course. "I'm afraid it is not. I'm sorry, Sir Giles," Theo said in a louder voice, "but as Miss Mannering is still in mourning, it's best she does not."

"A shame. Well, perhaps you will entertain us."

"Of course, sir." She moved to play one of the easier pieces and made it through without obvious mistakes. It was well received, and she accepted their praise, begging young Mr. Bellingham to take his turn. He did have a fine singing voice, and she was not averse to play and accompany him.

When this request was followed by another, she pleaded tiredness, which was true. "Perhaps you might enjoy a game of whist, Sir Giles."

"Oho! Indeed I would."

To encourage this, she immediately obtained the cards and arranged the table and chairs to encourage a four-handed round. Grandfather—as she suspected—soon murmured of his disinclination to stay up much longer, insisting he was exhausted. Long had Theo and her mother known this was simply an excuse for him to get Mr. Siddons to wait on him in the library with the good port he refused to share with guests, even those as well-liked as Sir Giles. But selfishness at his age was not to be wondered at, so they let his ruse slide and concentrated on their guests instead.

"I would wish you for my team," Sir Giles said to Theo.

"Forgive me, sir," she said, "but I have little inclination to play."

"Ah. You'd rather be on my boy's side, would you?"

Conscious of the unwelcome connotations of this, she murmured, "I'm afraid I could not maintain my concentration, no matter who I played with tonight. But perhaps you might find Miss Mannering a more favorable companion. She is still learning the rules of the game, you see, and would likely appreciate the benefits of such an expert player."

"Would you really?" the squire said, turning to Becky. "Come and sit here, and we'll take on the two matrons, and watch them squirm as we win."

"Oh, sir," Becky bit her lip, looking at Theo as if she wanted an escape.

"With Sir Giles as your partner, you are sure to succeed." Theo turned to Frederick. "I wonder if you might be willing to continue our conversation from before."

His eyes lit. "I most certainly would."

"Mother, Lady Bellingham, you have no objections if I should take Frederick to the library. We all know it is rather hard to hold a conversation when Sir Giles is bent on winning."

The squire laughed at this but didn't dispute it, for his reputation as a particularly enthusiastic and vocal whist player was known throughout the village and beyond.

"You may be excused, of course," her mother said, as they shifted to the card table, their chatter and excitement such that Theo knew she would not be missed.

"Come, Frederick. There is a book I think you'd like to read, and you might even be able to persuade the general to let you borrow it." She led him out into hall and to the next room, where, sure enough, Grandfather was sipping his port while reading his book before the fire. He looked up with a start. "Theodosia? Oh, and it's you, young Bellingham."

"The others are playing whist in the other room, and it's rather hard to concentrate," explained Theo. "But we can return there if you are busy."

He arched a heavy brow at her and glanced between her and Frederick with a wrinkled forehead, doubtless wondering what she was doing. "I suppose you know what you are playing at," he grumbled.

"Just some quiet conversation," assured Frederick.

"As long as that is all," growled Grandfather, in his best General tone and look, which blanched Fredrick's cheeks to an undignified shade.

Theo sat on the single chair in a small alcove, within earshot of her grandfather, and arranged her skirts after gesturing for Frederick to take a seat opposite. "Now, Mr. Bellingham, you were enquiring about the doctor's visit earlier. And seemed most keen to learn of the reason for it too."

Beyond Frederick's shoulder, she saw her grandfather's head jerk up, his eyes narrowing as he blatantly listened.

"You must forgive me if I seemed impertinent," Frederick said. "I did not mean to give offense."

"Oh, I am not offended, just a little puzzled. Then I realized that my refusal to give a direct answer might be construed in other ways. So I determined to share with you what has been happening here but must beg your indulgence to keep our secret for a little while longer."

Grandfather's eyebrows almost met the crown of his head. He'd given up all pretense of reading his book, his arms crossed as he scowled and waited for her to continue.

"Miss Stapleton, I can assure you anything you tell me will be in the strictest confidence and shall never pass my lips."

"Truly, I hope you shall prove to be a man of honor and a gentleman of your word."

"Oh, Miss Stapleton, you must know you can always trust me."

"It may seem a little peculiar, but we all know how gossip can thrive in this district, and I cannot help but wish such an explanation would not prove necessary."

His hesitation suggested Frederick was torn between decrying his interest and wishing to know the truth. Eventually honor won out. "Please, do not feel you must share such things with me if you would rather not."

"But that is the thing. I feel somewhat uncomfortable now, and it seems anything I say will prove a sad disappointment."

"Nothing you could say could ever disappoint me, Miss Stapleton."

Now that was patently untrue, as had been proved, but she would overlook it. "You see, I fear you will think it much greater than it is, when really, the great secret is . . ."

"Yes?"

She exhaled heavily. "It's simply that the man who was to fetch Miss Mannering and take her to London met with an accident, which I believe you already know."

"Yes, yes," he said impatiently.

"Well, that man is here."

He blinked. "Here?"

"Here. Upstairs." She sat back and watched his fresh struggle between propriety and his wish to know more.

"Is that all? You're telling me the doctor was here to see a servant?"

Not exactly a servant, although the captain was in service of the King, so that might suffice. She avoided answering the question with a small laugh. "You can see now why I didn't feel like such an inconsequential matter needed to be elaborated on."

"Yes." But the crease in his forehead suggested he did not. "So the man who is upstairs was here to collect Becky."

"Exactly so."

"Can I meet him?"

The bold-faced question made her blink. "I, er . . ."

"Indeed not," Grandfather interrupted from his corner. "The captain needs his rest,"

"The captain?" Frederick quickly turned to face the general.

Alarm sped up Theo's spine, and she frowned at her grandfather, but swiftly found a gritted-teeth smile when Frederick looked back at her. "Why yes! The captain arranged for Miss Mannering's return"—all true—"and I'm sure he is enjoying his time away from the fighting. It must be so arduous. Can you imagine trying to sleep in the midst of a battlefield?"

Frederick scoffed. "I'm sure they do not try to sleep on a battlefield."

"No, I imagine you are right," she said meekly. "I'm sure any quiet place as can be found in England must prove a wonderful respite."

From Frederick's frown it was apparent her efforts to distract and dissuade were not working. "Miss Stapleton, sir." He bowed slightly to her grandfather. "I do not wish to appear intrusive—"

Then perhaps he should leave. She bit back a small smile.

"But I cannot help but be a trifle concerned about your guest."

Why was he so persistent? She shot her grandfather a look.

He coughed and studied Frederick with narrowed eyes. "If young Bellingham holds some misgivings about our guest, then I don't see why you should not take him, my dear."

Her stomach tensed.

What was Grandfather playing at? Surely no good could come of this. Frederick was hardly the sort to draw back when presented with a sliver of opportunity. He was like his mother in that. Would the general's contrary nature prove to be their undoing?

But at the raised brows Grandfather cast her, she propelled to her feet. "Very well. Mr. Bellingham, if you would like to come this way. We shall see if he remains awake, or if the doctor has given him something to help him sleep. I would not have you doubt our word, after all." She tilted her chin.

"Miss Stapleton, I did not mean to upset you. It's simply that there are people out there who cannot be entirely trusted, and I would hate for you to be taken in by someone of unsavory character."

"Your thoughtfulness does you much credit," she said. "But your assumption that we are not up to snuff with such things gives me pause. Would you have my grandfather think you suspect he is unable to distinguish a fraud from a genuine article?"

"Absolutely not." Frederick's eyes rounded, then he glanced to where the general surveyed them with a look of frank suspicion. "He looks displeased."

"As one must suppose, seeing as his intelligence has been called into question. But never mind that now. What damage has been done is done."

"Oh, but Miss Stapleton—"

"Would you care to step this way?" She ignored his further protests and moved up the stairs. How had she tumbled into this plight? And what might happen next?

Daniel's ruminations about who had been singing and playing the pianoforte were cut off by the creak of the stairs. Probably Mr. Siddons. But the tap on the door didn't sound like the butler's usual ponderous knock, and as he pushed himself upright—and checked his attire and hair were as they ought be—he grew aware of a tightening in his middle that had nothing to do with the food he'd just consumed.

And when Theodosia Stapleton walked into the room—smiling, offering apologies—he barely heard her remarks as that tight feeling immediately moved to his chest. How lovely she looked, in that fancy gown, with the candlelight dancing in her beautiful hair.

"Miss Stapleton. How good it is to see you. It seems like such an age."

She pressed a finger to her lips, then turned to a man Daniel hadn't noticed until now, standing half-hidden in the hall. "Mr. Bellingham insisted on seeing you, sir. Which is why it's such a good thing that you are awake to be seen. I rather believe he would think there was something amiss if you had been asleep and unable to entertain visitors."

Daniel's breath held, as much from the tautness in her voice as the clearly unwanted guest. So, the first real test of his identity had begun.

"Miss Stapleton," the man's hushed voice sounded from the doorway. "I beg of you to forgive me. I truly meant to give no offense."

"Why should I be offended when my word is doubted? But doubt no more, Mr. Bellingham. Here is Miss Mannering's escort, injured, as you no doubt can see. I hope that will suffice."

Daniel swallowed a smile at her look of coolness, the raised brows and flashing eyes holding more than a hint of contempt. But amusement would not fit his role here, and he endeavored to cough and appear sicker than he was.

"Why, it's you." The man pushed into the room.

The same whippersnapper whom he'd met weeks ago on the road. Daniel's stomach dipped. "Have we met?" he asked, feigning forgetfulness.

"Indeed we have, sir," Bellingham said promptly, before glancing at Miss Stapleton with a puzzled frown. "Has he been staying here all that time?"

"No, he was residing at Mannering for some time."

The man's frown deepened as his attention returned to Daniel. "It is strange that no one mentioned you."

Daniel sighed weakly. "I'm afraid I cannot help it if people are inclined to ignore me."

"Your name, sir?"

He stifled annoyance at the officious tone and glanced at Miss Stapleton, whose bottom lip was tucked in under teeth of pearl, whether in apprehension or restrained amusement, he could not tell. "Daniel."

"Well, Mr. Daniel, I don't mind telling you I think it most peculiar that you are here and not still there."

"You might be less inclined to wonder should you see the state of Mannering." Daniel coughed again, drawing the blanket higher.

"Yes, yes, I understand it needs some work done to it. But still, you could stay elsewhere, could you not? Miss Stapleton is somewhat innocent to the mischief wrought by idle minds and loose tongues."

"Not entirely innocent," she murmured, eyes dancing in a way that bade Daniel to bite the inside of his cheek.

"Do not distress yourself, Miss Stapleton." Bellingham crossed his arms. "This is something that a gentleman should have realized."

"It would perhaps be better if I were to stay at an inn," Daniel agreed humbly.

"Exactly so. Although I'm sure the attentions you receive from the staff here are preferable and of better quality than what one might expect to receive at an inn."

"The staff here have been most kind." His gaze took in his hostess. "And Miss Stapleton has been an angel."

Her cheeks pinked as she excused herself to tend to the fire.

The younger man's confusion was obvious as his gaze swung between them.

Feeling he had ventured into treacherous waters, Daniel dared to continue. "Miss Stapleton was most heroic in my time of need."

"Truly?" Bellingham's brow wrinkled as he glanced at her.

"Please don't mind him." She frowned at Daniel slightly. "Mister, er, Daniel has proved himself prone to bouts of great exaggeration, but I strongly suspect that is due to the blow to the head."

"Blow to the head?" Bellingham's eyes rounded.

"Or perhaps that is just the effect of the company," Daniel dared.

"If you mean to imply, sir, that Miss Stapleton ever speaks anything less than the truth, then I assure you that you will have me to answer to," Bellingham snapped, hands moving to his hips.

"Now, now," Daniel said in a soothing tone. "I meant no such thing. Miss Stapleton is all that is good and true."

"Indeed."

"'While you live, tell truth and shame the devil.'" He quoted the line from the play emblazoned in his heart.

"Sir! I must object to your use of such language in front of a lady."

"Forgive me." Daniel caught another flash of amusement in her eyes. Yes, she'd recognized the quotation.

Mr. Bellingham's frown returned, and he swung back to Miss Stapleton. "Really, I don't understand why he is being housed in one of these rooms as if he is a guest."

"Again, such a reason need not concern you. But if you feel it important, perhaps you can enquire of the general."

Mr. Bellingham's shoulders fell. "Oh. Well, that won't be necessary. But still, he is just a servant."

"A man who was kind enough to assist our dear Miss Mannering in her time of need cannot be relegated to the servants' quarters. Now, I really must insist we leave him in peace." She turned to Daniel, her smile holding conspiracy and relief.

He once more felt that quickening in his chest.

"Please forgive the intrusion, sir. I trust you will sleep well."

He nodded, her parting smile ensuring he'd have the sweetest dreams imaginable.

Even if they might also be populated by a scowling youth and questions over impropriety. And questions about how long it would take before the full truth was finally told, and just what that might mean for his future.

Chapter 14

"Whatever made you do such a thing?" Mama said, when the household—save for their injured guest—had gathered the next morning in the drawing room.

"You had me in such a quake," confessed Becky. "I was never so surprised as when you told me to play whist. I do not like that game. And I fear Sir Giles will never want to play with me as his partner again."

"It can be so difficult to remember the rules," Mama said with sympathy. "I remember the first time I played—"

"Why couldn't you have left things alone?" Her grandfather snapped his book closed. "Young Bellingham is hardly the sharpest of men."

Theo kept her eyes on her embroidery hoop. "I thought it best to allay his concerns."

Grandfather sniffed. "We need not explain ourselves to the likes of him."

Thus saith the man who had insisted she take Frederick upstairs to see their guest. Alas, General Contrary was also prone to general bouts of forgetfulness.

"You were not such a ninnyhammer as to tell young Bellingham the truth now, were you?" her grandfather demanded.

"Of course not, sir. I simply explained he was Becky's escort, and if Frederick made assumptions based on that, well . . ." She shrugged.

Becky glanced up from where she was poring over pictures from *La Belle Assemblée* with Theo's mother. "How did you manage to introduce him?"

She explained about the captain's owning his name as Daniel, which caused Becky to giggle, and her mother to say, in an uncertain manner, "Well, I suppose that *is* his name."

"And it has to be of help when his friend arrives."

"Is the lieutenant coming?" enquired Becky, all pensiveness gone from her face.

"I believe your uncle received a letter from him earlier this morning, according to what Mr. Siddons said. As to the contents, well, we shall perhaps learn them if Mr. Daniel chooses to share."

"Mr. Daniel, indeed," the general growled. "Such nonsense."

Daniel. A strong, manly, biblical name. She'd always had a fondness for the hero in the Bible named such, with his own heroic nature, standing up for what was right, even in the face of jealous kings and lions' mouths.

She'd spent far too long last night thinking on the situation, thinking on him. It would serve herself right if he was miraculously healed and spirited away. But such a future was not one she dared envisage. Not yet, anyway.

It wasn't until later, after she had complimented Annie about last night's meal and consulted with her about tonight's menu, that she finally had a chance to venture up the stairs and tap on his door.

"Enter."

She obeyed and saw his face light even as he closed his book and laid it on the table beside the bed. The novel rested next to two letters, one opened, one untouched.

"Good morning, Miss Stapleton."

"Good morning, Mr. Daniel," she teased.

"Ah, yes." His smile grew rueful.

"I trust you slept well?"

"Well enough, thank you."

"Would you like this window opened?"

"I do appreciate the fresh air, yes. Although Mr. Siddons assures me it is not healthful at all."

"It pains me to observe that Mr. Siddons is not always in the right about things. And I cannot help but think that fresh air, cool though it may be, must be of greater benefit than the stifling heat that always seems to come from shut-up rooms. The air is too stuffy and close for one to breathe. So, let's invite the morning air in." She suited the action to the words and hefted up the small window.

"Thank you, Miss Stapleton."

"You are most welcome. Now, I wanted to beg your pardon for that horrid intrusion last night. Mr. Bellingham asked nonstop questions about the doctor's visit, and it occurred to me that our hiding of you without any explanation at all would surely only further increase speculation about who you truly are."

"No harm occurred, I assure you."

"It also struck me last night that perhaps the knowledge you are here will be in our favor, for when your friend comes. Then there will be less questions about who he is and why he has come. That is, if he can be persuaded to hold his tongue."

"Musgrave is a good chap, and trustworthy. And yes, you were prescient in smoothing his path." He held up the missive. "I have here a letter from the man himself, and he hopes to arrive in the not-too-distant future."

"How good it will be for you to have a friend."

He placed the letter on the table nearby. "I confess it will be nice to swap stories with someone whom I need not scruple to own my identity."

"And he will keep your secret?"

"I rather think he will consider it a good jest. Though he might prefer to see me called Billy Willikins," he mused.

She chuckled. "You mistake, sir. It is Willie Dillikins. Although the odds of two such men being called that in this area are extremely unlikely."

"I would certainly hope so."

She bit her lip to stop her smile.

His gaze, which a moment ago had seemed so alive with amusement, now seemed to have softened into regret.

"What is it, sir?"

"Miss Stapleton, truly I did not mean to get you into such a mess. I would have owned the truth last night save for the fact he seemed so eager for me to be but a servant."

Guilt wove within. "That might have been encouraged a little by myself. I might have implied you were."

"So you do dissemble, then."

"Sometimes, Mr. Daniel, we must do what we must."

He laughed. "Still, I cannot like it. I shall have to one day soon own to the truth of who I am."

"Why?"

"'To tell truth and shame the devil'?" he suggested.

Her lips lifted in appreciation. "By that remark, do you mean we should satisfy the scruples of Mr. Bellingham? I do not think such things are necessary, do you?"

"But your reputation—"

"My reputation has long been that of an honest, God-fearing woman with an unfortunate propensity to common sense. If people choose to sully their minds with idle speculation that suggests otherwise, then, frankly, I have no inclination to alter my actions to pander to such narrow-minded morality."

"While such a view is noble, I cannot dislike feeling I will be responsible for impairing your marital prospects once the truth is known."

Her laughter rippled.

He stared at her. "How have I amused?"

"Oh, it is not you, sir. I simply appreciate that you think I still have any marital prospects at all." Her gaze grew wry. "This is not London. And even if I were still young, it is not as though we live surrounded by eligible gentlemen wishing to toss the handkerchief."

"I fear you do yourself much disservice, Miss Stapleton."

Did he really think her a fine catch? "And I fear you might be a trifle addled in your wits, sir, to think otherwise. However that's probably a reaction to the medication," she added kindly.

He studied her for a long moment, until she grew uncomfortable and wondered what he was thinking.

No. Enough of this foolishness. She needed to get back to work. To attend to the household and the garden and to busy herself with good deeds. He disconcerted her, this man, with his too-discerning eyes and his too-quick and charming smile. She found herself far too easily succumbing to his charm, charm that lived in his jovial nature and ready wits, charm that made her feel younger and prettier than she could ever recall before. Charm that suggested her days as one destined to be over-looked were over, and perhaps she need not think of herself as a wall-flower any longer.

Daniel's smile lingered after she gently closed the door, though the room seemed to at once hold less of the morning light. He was not used to encountering a lady who made him wonder about the exact color of her eyes, or how many freckles adorned her nose, or what secrets quirked her soft, sweet lips. Most young ladies he'd met were all too eager to divulge their every thought, many of which would have been better left unsaid. For what could a man of war have in common with a lady whose idea of conversation was about the color of a shawl? His life in the army had hardened him to female concerns. His time in London had inured him to feminine wiles, and rare was the social encounter that didn't leave him at the edge of utter boredom. Yet this young lady . . .

But no. He had no time for such contemplations, especially not if the remaining letter contained the news he hoped it would.

He drew it near, slit the seal, and studied the contents.

Despite his recent letter informing his superiors of his enforced delay, he was being released from the upcoming tour and would remain in England until such time as his services were required again, etc., etc.

His heart sank. Truly? They wished to forgo his willingness, simply because he'd been hindered from appearing due to a broken leg? He tossed the letter to one side.

It fluttered off the bed, the broken red seal staring up at him like skin scored with a bullet hole.

"Lord?"

What would he do now? He'd been counting down the days until his return, and now he'd been judged wanting. His lips curved with-out amusement. Oh, how people would stare if they knew the hero of England could be so meekly cast away.

There was little point in speeding back to London, little point in insisting on employment with those who would have it otherwise. He'd likely get stuck working in an office, the idea of which held as much appeal as eating a live eel.

What *would* he do now? *Lord?* His mind spun, turning over the possibilities. Perhaps this time of enforced rest would help him see new directions in which his future could lie. His might not need to be a solitary path, after all.

Another knock, and the tentative nature of this one suggested it might be his niece. He shook his head at himself. Oh, how far his life had fallen when his entertainment was reduced to playing guessing games about who might be on the other side of the door. "Enter."

The door opened to reveal Becky's timid expression. "Good morning, Uncle."

"Good morning, niece."

She giggled, but in such a different way to Miss Stapleton's rich vibrato. "What is it I can do for you?"

"It's just that Theo—I mean, Miss Stapleton—said I might ask something of you, and . . ."

"And what is that?" He forced interested cheer to his voice. "Your wish is my command."

"Well, it is not something I should precisely command, it's just that, well, I was wondering . . ."

"Out with it, lass. I can feel what hair remains on my head growing grey as I wait here, breath held in anticipation."

Another giggle.

He smiled ruefully. Would that all young ladies had Miss Stapleton's directness of speech.

"It's just that my birthday is soon, you see, and I was hoping—"

"For a kitten?"

She blinked. "Er, no."

"A pony? I believe that is what all young ladies desire."

"I had a pony once." She stared at her clasped fingers. "Then Papa had to sell him."

Probably to settle his gambling debts. Resentment flared at his brother-in-law's carelessness. If Daniel was ever so blessed with a family, he'd make sure to provide in a way that would permit no regrets. Of course, that meant he'd have to find a way to provide . . . He cleared his throat. "I am sorry."

"It is not so very bad. Theo said I can ride her horse Gracie. She doesn't have a chance to exercise her as much as she'd like these days."

Probably because she was busy tending to a myriad of other tasks. Like caring for an invalid.

"Uncle?"

"Forgive me. You wish for a different type of doll?"

"I am not a young girl!"

"No, indeed. You are turning, what, fifteen, sixteen?"

She sighed. "Seventeen, thank you."

"And seventeen is too old for a doll? I recall being in a French château with a soldier friend of mine, a Captain Stamford—did you know his father is the Earl of Hawkesbury? He was quite the soldier, nonetheless. Born to the role, even if he was born to a family of noble birth. But I digress. There we were in the château, caring for the sick and the maimed, when one of the orderlies entered the room holding a china doll that seemed most lifelike. To be frank, I found it a little unsettling, this babyish creature whose eyes never closed stuck in the corner. It was as if she was always watching us."

"Oh, stop it!" She shuddered, rubbing her upper arms. "You give me chills."

"So I take it a doll is not what you wish for."

"Indeed not. I would much prefer, well, that is, if it has your blessing, to have a little gathering with my friends."

He shifted on the bed, drew the blanket higher. "I don't see why that would be a problem."

Breath released in a loud gush. "Oh, I knew you'd be understanding. Theo—that is, Miss Stapleton—thought it best I check with you, as some might think a gathering of the sort might be seen to be indecorous, seeing as I am still in mourning. But I quite like her way of thinking about it."

His pulse pattered faster. Why he had this infernal desire to know her thoughts on any and everything, he did not know. But there it was. "And what are Miss Stapleton's views on the matter?"

"She thinks it unlikely that anyone would be so miserly minded, but if they were, well, they were obviously not true friends, and therefore their opinions should not matter."

"Very sensible. I find myself in complete sympathy with her."

Becky nodded. "She also said that a small celebration on the day would be what Mama would have wanted, and I agree. These past few years Mama and I often had a little dinner, always very small, with but one or two guests. Theo always came."

"She has been very good to you and your mama."

"Yes." She fiddled with the pleat in her skirt, as if wishing for further speech but clearly troubled with what she wished to say.

"What is it, lass?"

She shook her head.

"Out with it."

She sighed. Glanced up at him. Sighed again. "They say she is something of an eccentric," she finally burst out.

"Who says?"

"Some of the villagers. I have heard the likes of Mrs. Cleever and Betty Holland say Theo is never going to marry because she is far too nice in her requirements."

"I see." Except he didn't. Why were they now talking about Miss Stapleton's matrimonial prospects?

She peeked at him from under her lashes, and he experienced a premonition of foreboding.

"What is it now?"

"You could marry her, Uncle."

He laughed more harshly than he intended. "Me? I think you quite mistake the matter."

"I am not so sure. She is kind and pretty, and you are not the sort of person to care about a birthmark, are you?"

"I would be offended if you thought I was."

"See?"

His chest twinged. Is that why no man had ever offered for her? Memory clanged of what young Bellingham had said. Truly? Men were that superficial? "Yes, I agree with you that she is quite wonderful, but I have my career, which I fully intend to resume as soon as I am fit and able."

"But don't you want—?"

"Never speak of this again." His words were clipped. What if Theodosia were to walk by and overhear? "I am sure Miss Stapleton would be mortified if she knew her affairs were being spoken over in this way."

Becky's gaze lowered. "I am sorry for upsetting you."

"I am not upset, lass. But I believe such conversation would upset Miss Stapleton were she to learn we had spoken about her, so let's speak nothing more of it."

"Yes, Uncle," she whispered, cheeks pink.

Regret pressed inside. Perhaps he'd spoken too baldly. She was his young niece, not a recruit on the battlefield. He worked to soften his tone. "Now, enough of the doldrums. Tell me if there is something you wish for your birthday. Apparently, a pony or a doll will not do. Is there something else you prefer?"

He managed to inveigle her into owning she had seen the most delightful material in the haberdashery store. Mrs. Stapleton had promised to help her make a pretty evening dress, "should her health permit," Becky quoted. After a moment's pause, her shoulders lifted. "She has really seemed so much brighter in recent weeks. More than before. Mama used to say Mrs. Stapleton often fancied herself ill, which meant poor Theo had to spend so much of her time caring for her. But repeating such a thing could be considered uncharitable, and it would be best not to say it, wouldn't it?"

He inclined his head, glad for her awareness, and that it appeared she was no longer out of charity with him. She was a funny, taking thing.

She thanked him again for his permission for a small dinner on her birthday. Indeed, she looked as though she might wish to hug him when he gave his blessing for the fabric to be purchased, an errand he'd trust to the Stapleton ladies, and one in which he'd ensure they were reimbursed. She did not hug him, though, simply curtsying with a broad grin, and making her excuses that she must take her leave and tell Miss Stapleton she had permission for both the dinner and the gown. "If we can purchase it in the next day or so, it might even be ready for my birthday dinner!"

The encounter, following that of the letter, provided much food for thought. For once, he was almost glad to have the chance to lie in rest and quietude. Was that really the reason Miss Stapleton had not wed? Had she been unsought these many years because the gentlemen of her acquaintance could not see her admirable qualities beyond a mark on her skin? His own looks were oft considered to be less than fine, and it was the glamour of his perceived heroism that endowed him with supposed handsomeness. But witness the reactions of those who knew him not, those people like the Bellinghams, who did not see anyone but an ordinary man. It was hard to believe people were so shallow, but time and again life had proved that to be the case.

Thank God that He did not regard men and women so. Thank God that He could see past skin and into people's hearts. What a blessing to know that his looks mattered not, nor his "heroic" actions. His relationship with God was based on what God had done, not what people might regard as important or good.

Daniel's lips twisted. It amused him when people assumed goodness of those who were beautiful. But did it naturally have to presuppose that, just because someone did not hold the same elements of beauty, they were not still worthy of noble qualities?

His thoughts turned to an overheard conversation about the tinkers, one of whom had tried to visit in recent days and sell his wares. The way Mr. Siddons had carried on, one would think the poor man carried the plague simply because he was so unfortunate as to possess a swarthy complexion and an ancestry that had not been inscribed for generations in the ledgers of the local village church. People were so quick to judge, so quick to dismiss and ignore.

Back to the question Becky had posed, and his summary dismissal of it. No, he was not so blind with prejudice—neither was he so committed to his career—that he'd dismiss matrimony out of hand. It was simply that he lacked provision and could see no way of supporting a wife or family.

That was all.

Chapter 15

Theo studied herself critically in the looking glass. The colored mark stretching across her cheek wasn't as noticeable as some she'd heard about. Dear Clara had once told her about one of the princesses who had fallen in love with a man whose birthmark stretched across his face and over an eye. Her face wasn't nearly as marred. But the overheard words of the captain—and silly, foolish Becky—had made her leave her task of pruning rosehips from below his window and hasten to a mirror to inspect what others could see, and what she'd long thought she'd grown reconciled to.

The pale pink-purple stain looked like spilled wine, stretching from her lip, along her nose, and up into the corner of her left eye. If she stood a certain way, with the light coming in from the window, some days it seemed to not exist. Other days it seemed most prominent indeed. She'd heard comments throughout her life and had been unable to ignore the way visitors to their village and church would glance at her, eyes widening, then quickly look away, almost as if they were afraid her stain would mar them too. She had soon learned to differentiate between those who judged—literally skin deep—and those who saw past her imperfections, as God did. Thank goodness for those who did not think, as some of the more superstitious folk did, that her birthmark and hair color resulted from a witch's curse.

Her eyes lowered as she remembered other words she had been called. The fact the captain now knew some of them stung. She didn't blame him for quickly ending the conversation, though the knowledge he pitied her carved a new hollowness in her heart.

Poor misguided Becky. How Theo would face her or the captain, she did not yet know. But face them—she wrinkled her nose at her reflection— she would. Vanity had never been a problem for her, and she wouldn't let pride stop her from doing what ought to be done. Even if it meant she was now self-conscious, whereas before she had seen no reason to mind.

"Theodosia?"

At her mother's call, she descended the stairs to see Becky excitedly sharing with Mama about the captain's approval for the birthday treat.

"Oh, isn't it exciting?" Becky said, eyes like cloudless skies.

Theo wouldn't begrudge her. Not when this was the most exhilarated she had seen Becky in weeks. "Very exciting. This shall be on two Thursdays from now?"

"If it's suitable, then yes, I'd love to celebrate on the actual day of my birthday."

"Then we shall mark the occasion." Birthdays were not usually grand occasions, unless one was a king or queen. But with this being Becky's first as an orphan, and in these trying years betwixt child and woman, then anything Theo could do to alleviate the ordeal, she would do. The first name day without a mother would be hard, no matter how old one would be. "Have you thought which friends you might wish to come?"

Lydia and Patricia were suggested as guests, and Theo encouraged Becky to write the invitations. "Heaven forbid the society of this place should mean you forgo their company, if they don't hear immediately. We cannot have them accept an invitation to a ball instead."

Becky grinned.

Theo's heart panged. How sad it was that Clara could not be here to see her only child grow into such beauty.

"And apparently we are to make up a new gown." Mama's eyes brightened with delight. Her mother always reveled in employing her dressmaking skills.

"Yes! I forgot to mention to you. Uncle said he would be very glad to purchase the material we saw at the haberdashery the other day." Becky clapped her hands.

"I did not realize he had been to the shop," Theo teased.

"Oh no, I meant—"

"I know what you meant. Well, you have a most kindhearted uncle, have you not?"

"Indeed he is." Warmth lit Becky's words and face.

"Not quite the ogre you once presumed?"

"Not at all." Her smile faded as her brow puckered.

Theo moved to collect the basket of flowers she had been tending to before, and Becky followed her outside to the roses. Too often she seemed to prod Becky into careless speech, when perhaps the girl could benefit from more times of contemplation and reflection.

Busying herself with stripping off the leaves, Theo said, "We could perhaps go into the village later and see about purchasing the fabric, if you would like."

The pucker smoothed, and Becky nodded. "Truly, you are so good to me."

"That I am," Theo said wryly. "But pray don't advertise the fact. I should not want to lose my badge as eccentric any time soon."

Remorse filled her at the stricken look Becky shot her. "Did . . . did you hear what I said before?"

"I've heard many things."

"To the captain?"

Theo bit her lip. Lie she would not do. "I heard some of your conversation from here, and yes, I heard you mention that some of the villagers regard me as an eccentric. Which is true, we both know, so I do not judge you for that."

"But you think I should not have spoken."

She scattered the discarded leaves on the garden beds. "I did not hear the entirety of your conversation, but I will own it is not pleasant to be discussed, especially concerning matters of one's appearance."

"I'm sorry, Miss Stapleton. You have been so good to me, and I spoke heedlessly."

"Well, perhaps if you are aware of this, you shall take heed the next time. Now, I am quite prepared to focus on other things, aren't you?" Theo held out her hand, which Becky clasped.

"If you say that you'll forgive me, then yes."

"Oh, what a silly girl you are. Of course I forgive you." She gently squeezed her hand. "Now, let us think of this no more, and focus instead on what will be. You preferred the violet? You are approaching half mourning, so that should be thought quite proper."

Theo carried on in this vein for quite some time, doing her best to push the unpleasantness from her mind—and from the mind of her young charge—as they moved back inside to plan with Mama and Cook just what would prove an elegant repast, before seeking out the village shop.

In the village, she accompanied Becky to the haberdashery and requested the fabric be cut for transporting home. Wooler was not large enough to boast a modiste, but Mama's talents meant she would ever be considered one of the more stylishly dressed of their acquaintance, and Theo had never seen the need to send out for their clothes to be made, not like others in the village.

Mrs. Crouch, the minister's wife, entered, offering all and sundry a nod and smile.

After greeting her, Theo encouraged Becky to look at the feathers and ribbons, determining to purchase some so she could help refurbish one of Clara's bonnets into something more appropriate for a young lady, and thus provide a birthday gift to her.

They were deep in discussions with the shop attendant about which color most exactly matched the chosen fabric when the sound of a carriage drew their attention to the window. Theo's heart dipped.

Mrs. Cleever was descending, chin lifted and shoulders squared, as if readying for battle.

Perhaps if they hurried their purchases, they might escape her notice. Theo wasn't sure if she would be quite ready to meet rapier thrust with the battered shield of her emotions.

"Becky, dearest, if we are to drop in the notes of invitation, then we should aim to do so before much more time passes," she encouraged.

The door opened behind her, and the shop attendant's "Ah, Mrs. Cleever, how good to see you again" made it apparent they were too late.

Theo nodded, offered a smile when she saw the solicitor's wife's head turn their way, then lowered her eyes to pretend interest in Becky's conundrum about feathers.

To no avail.

"Miss Stapleton, Miss Mannering."

Theo straightened. "Hello, Mrs. Cleever."

"Those are rather pretty feathers."

"We are trimming some bonnets," Becky explained.

Theo waited. Mrs. Cleever never spoke to Theo without having something to say.

"I have just come from a visit with Lady Bellingham." Mrs. Cleever drew a gloved hand down a particularly fine length of silk.

"I trust she is well." Theo caught Mrs. Crouch's look of sympathy in the background.

"Very well," Mrs. Cleever said. "Although a trifle perturbed."

Judging from the look being cast her way, Theo knew it had to do with her. "I hope it is nothing too serious, ma'am. Now, if you'll excuse me."

"Miss Stapleton," Mrs. Cleever held up a hand. "I must beg for a moment longer of your time."

Why did those words never fill her with joy? "Of course. What can I do for you?"

"What you can do is to explain precisely who the young man residing in your house is."

Theo froze, her mind racing through a dozen possible explanations before she settled on playing the woman's game. "I'm afraid I don't take your meaning."

"It is most plain. Frederick Bellingham told his mother there is a strange man residing at Stapleton Court."

"Did he indeed?" Theo said, with a warning look at Becky.

"Yes."

Conscious there were other ears around and that whatever she now said would set a precedent for future interactions and conversations, she spoke with care. "It seems odd that Frederick would mention such a thing."

"How so?"

"I did not think he would say anything. In fact, he expressly told me he would not share the news."

Mrs. Cleever blinked. "Are you telling me that there is indeed a young man residing in your house?"

"I am."

The older woman gasped. "How scandalous!"

"I would think the greater scandal would be to let an injured man fend for himself."

Over near the counter, Mrs. Crouch nodded, as if agreeing.

"Do you not even know who this young man is?"

Oh, her family knew very well. But something prompted her to tease. "I should think the minister's wife would agree that it is important to take in strangers. Is there not a verse in the Bible, Mrs. Crouch, that speaks about entertaining angels?"

The minister's wife glanced between them, her wise eyes seeming to take in the situation. "That verse is quite an inspiration to be hospitable, is it not?" She moved to Theo's side, offering a smile to Mrs. Cleever. "Good afternoon, Mrs. Cleever."

"Er, yes. Good afternoon."

"I'm sure you remember Mr. Crouch's sermon the other day. I should think that our Lord's encouragement to tend to the Samaritan should be example enough," she said, her tone mild.

"And not merely the Samaritan," Theo said, "but all those who we can so quickly dismiss. Including strangers."

"Such is the role of a Christian." Mrs. Crouch patted her arm and, with a small smile that hinted she knew more than she let on, moved past several village women to the other side of the establishment.

Mrs. Cleever's look of disconcert drew Theo's ill-timed amusement. The solicitor's wife had never been able to fence appropriately with the mild-mannered woman with a social pedigree that ranked higher than hers. Not that Mrs. Crouch ever spoke about her connections. She didn't need to. It was evident in her poise and grace and kindly treatment to all.

Mrs. Cleever seemed to take offense at Theo's smile, her brows drawing together like curtains closed against the end of day. "Yes, well, be that as it may, one can be a Christian without doing such outlandish things."

"Outlandish things like caring for the poor, or feeding the hungry, or helping those without a home?"

Mrs. Cleever gasped. "You have taken in a vagrant?"

Theo's chest grew tight, and she was half-tempted to search the nearest highways and byways to find someone who truly fit that description.

"Do you not mean to furnish me with a name?"

"Why?" Her fingers clenched. "Did Frederick forget to mention it?"

Mrs. Cleever drew herself up. "Miss Stapleton, your manner to me is not displaying the respect to which I am accustomed."

"Am I being disrespectful in wishing to keep private matters private?" How dare Frederick break his word? How dare this woman pry and gossip and insinuate in ways guaranteed to leave a stain? "I must inform you, Mrs. Cleever, that your manner toward me in wishing to pry into our affairs shows no respect and little courtesy."

She gasped. "You are being most insolent."

"That is not my intention." She drew in a breath, told herself to calm down. While she was glad to combat idle speculation, Mrs. Cleever was not worth losing her temper. "I simply do not comprehend why you are so interested in the identity of a man who is merely to escort poor Miss Mannering here back to London."

"Frederick claims the man is a servant."

"Aren't we all?" Theo said, pasting on pleasantness as anger rippled inside. "If not serving God, then one would hope serving the King. And of course, a wife must be supposed to serve her husband, or so the sermons I hear seem to suggest, is that not right, Mrs. Crouch?" she called, as the minister's wife completed her purchases.

"We are all to serve God and each other, as best we can." She moved to Theo. "Please give my good wishes to your dear mama. I hope to visit her soon." She gently squeezed Theo's arm.

"She will be most grateful."

"Take care," she murmured, inclining her head to the others present as she made her exit with her wrapped purchases.

Mrs. Cleever seemed impervious, inching closer, her scowl now etched as in stone. "Miss Stapleton, I do not understand why you are being so obstreperous. Surely you can see it is but natural to be concerned when a vagrant takes up residence with two unprotected ladies."

Unprotected? The captain a vagrant? Torn between tears and temper, Theo settled for speaking in a low voice. "I can assure you that you are utterly mistaken."

"But—"

"Was there anything else, Mrs. Cleever?" Theo armed herself with a tight smile. "Perhaps you'd like to know what we ate for dinner last night. For that I'm sure you can apply to Miss Mannering here. She has a most excellent memory, whereas I, it seems, fail to recall what should be made known to the village at large, as it is clearly in their best interests to be informed."

"I did not mean—"

"As I said to Frederick Bellingham, who no doubt will be *most* gratified to learn a conversation I believed was private is now being discussed in the marketplace, if there is anything else you wish to know, you could speak to the general. I'm sure he would be able to tell you what you need to know in a manner that will not be completely disagreeable."

"Well!"

Theo turned from the outraged matron and clasped Becky's arm with a shaking hand. "I believe we are late for our appointment, my dear. Shall we pay for this and be on our way?"

"Yes, please," Becky whispered.

And after a nod to the villagers who watched them still, Theo paid for their goods and led Becky outside to their gig. Emotions still raged inside, begging her to dissolve into either tears or tantrum. But no. She must keep a tight rein on herself. It wasn't fair to Becky otherwise.

Poor girl. She looked as shaken as Theo felt. She placed a hand on the girl's arm. "You must forgive me, my dear. That was not at all seemly."

Becky blinked rapidly and shook her head.

Sorrow panged. "I truly am sorry. I have always had some trouble with my temper, but that is no excuse. And I'm afraid Mrs. Cleever won't be in a frame of mind to want her girls to visit us now."

"After the way she spoke to you, I don't think I'd want them there anyway." Becky tore up the invitation and stuffed the pieces back in her reticule. "I'd be worried they'd be spies."

"I hate to admit it, but I think you might be right." Theo placed the fabric in the gig. "Perhaps someone else might prove amenable."

Becky shook her head. "I prefer to not worry about anyone else. Perhaps Uncle might be well enough by then to come downstairs. Then we need not worry about what anyone else might think."

"Think on it some more, and you can give the invitation at services if you wish."

Becky nodded, and they soon made their way back home.

Some days it seemed he existed for the sound of a certain voice, for the light tread or tap that would admit sunshine to his room and heart. Her visits brought a joy he hadn't known he'd missed until now. Of course, that might have something to do with their conversations, with the plays and poems she read to him. And on those days when she'd yet to make an appearance it seemed his nerves grew tight, waiting, waiting. And if, by some mischance, she did not appear, then it was a day without sunshine, regardless of what happened outside.

He'd heard the gig leave earlier. Had learned from Mr. Siddons she and Becky had gone into the village. And now the gig had returned, he hoped she would return, and they'd read and converse and laugh.

Minutes ticked by, his nerves stretching, straining. Would she come?

But no. That heavy tread outside was definitely not hers. Neither was that ponderous knock.

"Enter." His heart dipped. "Ah. And how are you, Mr. Siddons?"

"Very well, sir." The older man jerked his head. "If you don't mind, General Stapleton would like to have a word."

"In here?"

"Yes."

"Well, of course." Daniel pushed up against the bedhead, and checked he was as presentable as could be. The conversations he'd had with the general he could likely count on one hand, and he'd never gained the impression the man liked him very much. This lying in bed, day after day, with nothing but the occasional chance to have Mr. Brigham's help as he bathed with a sponge, meant he never felt as neat and fresh as he would like. He hoped General Stapleton understood these matters and did not hold that against him.

When he judged himself acceptable, he called for the door to be opened.

The general stalked in, his salt-and-pepper hair seeming to bristle with sparks, his brow full of thunder.

What had happened just now? "Good afternoon, sir."

"It might be for you, but it ain't for everyone," he growled, tugging the chair out from beside the bed and easing into it with all the grace of a stiff-limbed badger.

"Forgive me, sir, but I do not know what you mean."

"I just had a conversation with my granddaughter."

"I trust she is still well," Daniel offered.

"She's not," he said bluntly. "She is, in fact, quite put out."

"What do you mean?"

"She just had the misfortune to encounter that weasel-faced solicitor's wife in the village. Apparently she harangued Theodosia about you, wanting to ferret out all your secrets."

Regret poked sharp and sure. "I'm very sorry that Miss Stapleton was bothered."

"You should be. I cannot recall the last time I saw my granddaughter quite like this. Of course she was distressed when your sister died, as we all were, I might add, but Theodosia never shook because of it."

Daniel's heart tensed. "She is shaking?" *Lord, be with her.*

"I know people think I don't have eyes that see beyond my papers, but I know when my granddaughter tries to hide things with a smile or a laugh, and I certainly know Theo well enough to know when she's most upset."

"Again, I am truly very sorry to hear of it."

"I don't care if you are sorry. I *do* care to know how long we shall have you under our roof!"

Daniel's lips pressed together and he swallowed hard. "I have never intended to put anyone, especially Miss Stapleton, under any burden. I will remove as soon as the doctor permits it."

"Waiting on a doctor's permission never used to get medals awarded," the old man jeered. "Not back in my day, anyway."

"One can afford to be a man of action when one has two legs that work." Daniel pointed at his splinted leg.

The general straightened, as if prepared to scale a high horse.

"But I assure you, sir, I give you my word I shall leave as soon as it is at all possible."

"Hmph." General Stapleton eyed him, with a look likely designed to quell insolence.

But having met Lord Wellesley and the pompous men who served the King, Daniel had learned the best defense was to offer the blandest look possible, all the while unafraid to meet his challenger in the eye.

"I suppose that will have to do."

"I truly am grieved that my actions have led to Miss Stapleton's distress."

"She is not the sort to weep, nor mouth off about her upset, none of Maudlin Meg about her, which is why I felt to warn you." His eyes narrowed. "Never known her like that before."

The man was thinking deeply about something, obviously, but for the life of him, Daniel couldn't tell what it might be.

The general finally nodded, his gaze turning to the letters now neatly arrayed on the bedside table. "Got something from the War Office?"

Daniel offered the paper to him, but the older man shook his head.

"I don't need to know your business."

"I felt, given our conversation, that I should share it anyway. My unfortunate injury means I no longer have any great urgency to return to London. My regiment is shipping out without me."

"What? Give me that." He snatched the paper and perused it quickly.

Daniel had served under a few superiors whose support and interest could be considered kindly. But it had been a long time since he'd come across a man whose biting words and sharp eyes made him long for his father's support. Da's death, so closely following that of his mother's, when Daniel had just turned sixteen, had precipitated his desire to find purpose and a life beyond his small village. But while General Stapleton might wish for Daniel's absence from his home, his frown suggested that Daniel might have his support in other ways.

"Fools. This can't be right." He handed Daniel back the missive.

"I'm afraid it seems that way to me."

"Blockheads, all of 'em. How many times do these chuckleheads make decisions about business they have no experience in?"

"I share your sentiments entirely, sir."

He grunted again, the lines of his face settling deeper into discontent. "So, what'll you do?"

"I confess I do not know."

"If it were me, I'd be writing back and demanding an interview and explanation."

The idea held merit. Inaction had never been his forte. "I'll pen a response today."

The general nodded. "And then?"

"Mr. Cleever and I both thought it would be best to sell Mannering and take Becky away. I have a widowed aunt who could care for her, should I set her up in a small house near London. I suppose Becky is too old for boarding school."

"If you're asking my advice, I wouldn't know. Ask Theo if you must. Although she never went to one of those wretched places, so I don't know how much help she'd be."

"I've noticed she possesses a great deal of common sense."

"Have you now?" His eyes probed Daniel. "What more have you seen?"

Why did this feel like a test? For all his bluff and bluster, the man had a shrewdness Daniel should've recognized. One rarely attained his rank without it. "I, er, have observed that she is possessed of a sparkling sense of humor."

"Too giddy by half at times, but she's not shy of crossing swords. I cannot blame her. Not with hair she inherited from my side." His brow lowered. "Just a shame she lacked the wits to recognize Griselda Cleever is not one to cross swords with."

Daniel's guts tightened with guilt.

"Well? What else about my Theo?"

"She . . . she is refreshing, like the morning air, making one feel more alive. She does much good, but rarely seems to notice when she goes without."

"Goes without? Theodosia has never lacked for anything!"

"Except a father. And the opportunity to participate in the world beyond this village."

The general sent him a sharp look. "She told you this?"

"My niece did."

"Hmph." The man fell into heavy-browed abstraction, his body still, his eyelids half-closed so that Daniel wasn't sure if he was asleep or not.

Should he say something?

Finally the general stirred and cleared his throat with a loud har-rumph. "Her face."

"I beg pardon?"

"What do you think of her face?"

He swallowed. "She is pretty. A man would have to be blind not to notice that."

The general's brows shot up. "That's it? No comment about the mark?" The general motioned to his left cheek.

"I confess I hardly notice it." How could one pay attention to such things, when one could not look away from the sparkling depths of her eyes, save when one's attention stole to her glorious tresses, or her comely lips?

"Hmm." After another long moment where Daniel found himself growing itchy under the man's intense scrutiny, the general finally stood. "If you give me assurance you will leave as soon as that fool Linton says you can, then I will be much obliged."

"Of course, sir." Daniel swallowed. "And if there is anything I can do to alleviate Miss Stapleton's distress, then please tell me what I can do."

The general eyed him again with that unnerving stare, then gave a sharp nod.

Chapter 16

Theo had known attending services that Sunday would be a challenge, but she had not anticipated just what a sad trial it would prove. The walk down the aisle to the Stapleton pew across from the squire's, in prime position underneath the reverend's nose, saw heads shift to watch, then when she made eye contact, they turned away. It seemed Frederick Bellingham's loose lips had caused more than a few people to speculate about the goings-on at Stapleton Court. Or perhaps—her heart twisted with remorse—that was due to the scene at the haberdashery the other day.

Theo herself was long used to the looks and stares and had, for the most part, grown accustomed to such things. But she whimpered inside about what this meant for poor Mama and Becky, neither of whom were hardened in the way she'd needed to be since she was a small girl and the first tittering laughs and pointed fingers had made her realize she was different.

A glance at the Cleever pew, just behind the Bellinghams, made Mrs. Cleever glance away, and redoubled Theo's efforts to act as though nothing was amiss. Surely words were being bandied about Theo's visit, judging from the way the haberdashery's shop assistant eyed her, then bent her head to whisper to her neighbor.

Theo suppressed a sigh. She only had herself to blame. And maybe her hair.

The liturgy was one she'd heard countless times before, but the sermon today seemed to hold a special entreaty she hadn't heard Mr. Crouch share before.

"Friends, the Bible says not to judge, and I beg of you to recall our Lord's words: 'He that is without sin among you, let him cast the first stone.' Not, of course, that our Lord is encouraging the act of stoning today," he paused and smiled. "But it would behoove us all to recall that none of us are perfect, we can all fall, and we see in this world but dimly. Unlike our omniscient God, we cannot see all circumstances to judge with perfect understanding."

Hmm. She eyed him and caught his slight nod. But of course. He knew the truth of the situation. And while it seemed he had not shared Captain Balfour's identity with his wife, his wife had well and truly shared the scene in the haberdashery with him.

Conviction stole across her as she once again rued her quick temper. *Lord, forgive me. Help me remember that You are in control, and that I can trust You with all things.*

The service continued with prayers, the recessional hymn, and the awkwardness of Theo's exit marked by the glancing away of congregants.

Outside, the response from the villagers held as much warmth as the stiff, cool breeze.

Lady Bellingham was the only one brave enough to venture to the Stapleton gig, her tsk-tsks grating on Theo's nerves. "My dears, I do not wish to keep you, but a most alarming report has reached my ears."

Theo glanced at Mama and Becky, the regret from earlier hastening her to encourage them to seek shelter from the cold air inside Stapleton's ancient carriage. "I'm sure that I can help Lady Bellingham with what she wishes to know."

"Indeed, I believe you can." Lady Bellingham frowned, although she waved to Mama and Becky.

Theo tugged her shawl more tightly against her. If only the squire's wife had felt it necessary to make one of her regularly unscheduled visits to Stapleton Court rather than bail her up in this brisk weather in front of the eyes of almost the entire village. She drew herself up, meeting Lady Bellingham's eyes. Sometimes attack was the best form of defense. "Is this to do with Mrs. Cleever?"

"Well, yes."

"I see. She passed on some of what Frederick had shared with her, so I can only assume you want to apologize for this news leaking to others in the village."

"Apologize? Why, my dear Theodosia—"

"Lady Bellingham, I would have thought a person raised in a gentlemen's establishment would at the very least know how to conduct himself in a gentlemanly manner." Her gaze fell on him.

He glanced away.

"You speak of my Frederick?"

"I am *most* displeased that what I shared with him in confidence, which he promised to keep, he then felt necessary to share."

"Oh! Well . . ." The squire's wife's gloved hands fluttered at her side. "That was because I asked him."

"So Frederick did not himself share the information with Mrs. Cleever?"

Lady Bellingham's brow rumpled. "Well, no."

"I see." Theo eyed her, waiting, waiting . . .

"My dear, I am truly most sorry." The older woman's fat cheeks pinked. "I confess I do not know quite how the news happened to be said."

Theo arched a brow.

"My dear Miss Stapleton, please. I do not like to be on the outs with you."

Still Theo said nothing.

Lady Bellingham's hand flew to her chest. "Oh, what can I do to make it up to you?"

"Perhaps you can persuade the likes of Mrs. Cleever to not be so hasty to judge. As I tried to explain the other day, our looking after the man was simply an act of charity, which is why it is so distressing to have an act of kindness sullied by whispers and innuendo. It speaks very poorly of those who utter gossip."

"Oh, I *quite* agree," Lady Bellingham said hastily, apparently unconscious of the irony. "Charitable works should be commended, should they not?"

"That was my understanding, but unfortunately not the view of all."

Lady Bellingham's lips pursed, as she cast Mrs. Cleever a look of significance. "Some people have never been known for their charitable nature."

Theo inclined her head. "I am sure we can all be predisposed to such things. I did appreciate what the reverend shared just now, how we should be careful not to judge. I trust the sermon will provide some stimulating conversations over the next few days."

"Oh, I'm sure it will." The squire's wife beckoned her son to come closer, which he did. "Frederick, you must explain to Miss Stapleton and offer your apologies."

He reddened, and Theo almost felt sorry for him as he was led, rather like a bull with a ring in its nose, around the topics of culpability and remorse. Eventually Frederick was released and he scuttled off to stand with his father, casting only the briefest glances at Theo as she stood trapped by his mother whose hand now pressed Theo's arm.

"My dear, I could not say so in front of him. It is unnatural as a parent to admit one is almost ashamed of one's own son, but I do want you to be assured of our deepest regrets about this situation."

"Thank you," Theo said. "I appreciate that. Now if you'll excuse—"

"Before you go"—she squeezed Theo's arm gently—"I do hope you'll take care of yourself. A woman of fine repute cannot be too careful with unknown men."

"I have it on excellent authority, ma'am, that my reputation is hardly to suffer damage, seeing as I'm considered something of an eccentric. I did not realize that being unmarried at my age would lend itself to such an epithet, but there you have it."

"My dear, who can be so cruel as to utter such things in your hearing?"

No denial, which meant it truly was a known thing. The thought that these people, whom she had long regarded as friends, could be so faithless, sent a sharp pain through her chest. But not for nothing did she have Stapleton blood running though her veins. She tossed her head back. "Is it better they speak such things behind my back?"

Lady Bellingham's eyes fell. "Of course not, no."

No. Of course not.

"My dear, let me just say, for all that you are not a green girl, you are still a friend."

It seemed so hard to stomach the claim, when Mama's friend had been the one to betray them. Theo kept her smile stiff and pushed up her brows, waiting for whatever pearl of wisdom Lady Bellingham seemed desperate to impart, judging from her pressing Theo's arm.

"A lady must always take heed to her reputation, regardless of her age. And while you may not think it so very necessary for yourself, at least consider the young lady who is under the protection of your roof."

"How ironic, as it is all for Becky's sake that his injury even came to be."

"I beg your pardon?"

For a reckless moment, Theo desperately wanted to share the true identity of their lodger. But then memories of Lady Bellingham's fuss, the way she had always inserted herself into every function and party of note, came to mind, and Theo drew back.

"Theodosia? What is it you wish to say?"

"Nothing, ma'am. Forgive me. I suspect this wind might give me a touch of a headache, and I must beg your leave to return to the carriage. I would not have Mama stay out in the cold any longer than what is absolutely necessary. She is so prone to take ill, as you know."

"But of course. I should hate for our little conversation to lead to such a thing. Your mama is rather more delicate than some."

Theo said the Bellinghams would be welcome to visit during the week, although not Thursday, as the household was taking that day to ensure Becky's natal day could be remembered well, especially given her mother's passing.

"Oh, of course. I cannot conceive how poor Amelia would cope if I was to pass on."

A woman with an increasing family of her own, who lived miles away, would likely find the death of her mother rather different to a newly orphaned girl of more tender years. This she did not say, instead finally making her farewell, only to be captured by Mrs. Crouch, who echoed Lady Bellingham's words about taking care to her reputation, albeit in much kinder tones.

"Thank you, but I assure you there is nothing to be concerned about." She mustered a wobbly smile. "The man has a broken leg after all."

"A broken leg matters little to the minds of some here."

Her fingers clenched. "Why must people be so miserly minded?" she cried.

Mrs. Crouch held sympathy in her eyes. "You are likely very tired, Theodosia, and I hope you may get some rest and relax. Life always seems more challenging when we are not refreshed sufficiently."

Relax? What a wonderful idea. If only she could. "Thank you. I will do my best to rest this afternoon."

"That is what the Sabbath is for, is it not?"

Theo nodded, said goodbye, and finally made her escape to the carriage, where she did her best to fend off the concerns and questions of both ladies. Thank God this day of rest meant she could find solitude, once they reached the hallowed halls of Stapleton Court.

But when they reached the house it was to see an unexpected carriage and two figures waiting at the door.

"Who is that?" Becky asked.

Theo's heart sank, while her mother exclaimed with glee. "Oh, how wonderful!"

"Who is it, ma'am?"

"It is dearest Seraphina. My other daughter, you may recall." Her face shone with a brightness Theo had not seen in years. "Oh, Theo, is this not wonderful?"

She forced a smile. "Most wonderful." Apparently her day of rest would not happen after all.

The carriage slowed.

As it stopped, Theo begged a moment of Mama's time. "Before we go in, we should discuss being careful and not admitting the captain's identity."

"Is he really all you think about?" Mama asked. "Your sister, whom we have not seen in many a year, is finally visiting, and you are more concerned about the captain and his secret?"

Regret kneaded within, as her mother exited the carriage, Becky assisting her with a worried look over her shoulder.

Theo tried to offer a reassuring smile, but the years of growing up had proved there was nothing sure about Seraphina. Her younger sister blew hot and cold—one minute sad, the next filled with gaiety—contrary as her grandfather. As for trusting Seraphina with things . . .

Theo's lips tightened, remembering the many instances when she had cried herself to sleep as she endured the lifelong legacy of Seraphina's breaking of things. Her word. Theo's confidence. Friendships. Trust.

Theo knew Jesus Christ's commandment to forgive seventy times seven, but hadn't she exceeded that long ago? Love her sister, she would do. But like or trust her? No.

She joined the others in making her way inside, unsurprised at the squeals that suggested her younger sister was in a good mood. Following the sounds, Theo found her mother clasping Seraphina in her arms, while Becky stood uncertainly and a tall man nodded to her mother before gazing out the drawing room window.

Her heart squeezed. *He* was here.

He turned. Faced her. Looked her up and down without a smile. "Theodosia."

"Roger."

"Still the same as ever."

"As are you." Lean. Handsome. But perhaps a little too pretty.

"Theo, dearest." Seraphina drew toward her, hands outstretched. "How are you?"

Before she gave time to answer, her sister kissed the air either side of her cheeks—she hadn't dared to actually touch Theo's marred cheek since she was a child, scared, she'd once admitted, that the condition might be contagious—and demanded to be introduced to the young lady.

"Why, this is little Becky Mannering." Mama trilled a laugh.

"Look who is all grown up!" Seraphina offered a smile that did not seem entirely genuine. But then, she'd never found it easy to admire anyone she could regard as competition, as the self-inflicted rivalry between Seraphina and Amelia Bellingham witnessed. And Becky was a pretty girl, owning a fair beauty not unlike what Seraphina had known.

Perhaps that was one advantage of being plain all one's life. There was never any pedestal from which to fall.

Enough of such musings. She forced brightness into her voice. "This is a pleasant surprise, sister."

"Is it?" Seraphina cocked her head.

"Pleasant?" Hadn't she hidden her dismay well enough?

"A surprise." Her sister's eyes narrowed for a moment. "I declare, Theodosia, if I was less contented with my lot, I might almost wonder if you were not happy to have us here."

She willed her smile—and what pleasantness her features could find—not to waver.

"Have you forgotten the invitation?" Seraphina tilted her head, the blonde curls dancing merrily. "By the looks of you, it seems you have."

Oh. *That* invitation—issued weeks ago when they'd thought Becky and the captain would be gone. "I do not recall seeing a response," she said apologetically. "Perhaps Mama—"

"I did not think I would need to respond, not for a visit to my family home." Seraphina stripped off her gloves and took the most comfortable chair. "Is Siddons still around? He did not answer the door when we came."

"He was in church." Theo took the chair nearest the fire. "With the rest of us."

"But not Grandfather. The general hasn't been to church more than a dozen times in his entire life. Surely you would not leave him without an attendant."

"We do not expect company on Sundays, as a rule," Theo said. "It is the servants' day off, and—"

"Do you mean there is no one to help us take our luggage to our room?"

Such selfishness. Theo rolled her lips inward to keep the observation inside.

Mama cast Theo a swift look, before lifting her hands helplessly. "My dear. We were not expecting you, and it seems there may be some trouble, as, well, dear Becky is in your room—"

"Oh!" Seraphina exclaimed, petulance twisting her mouth. "Very well, then. The spare room will work, I suppose."

"But—" Mama's hands wrung as her eyes pleaded with Theo.

"But we have a guest installed in there already," Theo interposed.

"Well! Move them on. I am back, and my husband and I need a room to stay in."

"The other guest chamber is available." Mama glanced over to where Roger stood motionless at the window. "It will need to air, as it hasn't been used in some time, and—"

"The one that faces the east and has that horrid slanting roof? No, I thank you. We shall manage quite well in the real guest chamber." Seraphina settled back in her chair.

Becky inched toward Theo and murmured, "I could move, if that would help."

"Aha! The very thing."

How unfortunate that her sister still possessed the hearing of a hawk.

Seraphina unpinned her hat and tossed it on the sofa beside her. "That would suit us perfectly."

"No," Theo said. "Becky has all her luggage there and should not be disturbed."

"I truly don't mind—"

"See? Why do you always think you know best, Theodosia? Besides, you are not the mistress of this house. Mama is. And I'm sure Mama would agree I should be in my former room."

"My dear, the other guest room will be perfectly adequate, I assure you," Mama said, her eyes anxious behind her fluttering fan.

"It most certainly will not," Seraphina snapped. "If I cannot stay in my room, as I really ought, then I at least shall not be relegated to some second-best chamber. Do you know how insulting that is?"

They were sure to be told soon in no uncertain terms.

Seraphina's blue eyes narrowed. "Just who else is staying here, Mama?"

Mama tossed Theo another helpless look, which her sister seemed to notice, as she pivoted to face Theo.

"Who? Who is it?"

Oh, how tired she was of this. "An injured man. He came to escort Becky back to London but was injured in a fall and has been laid up in the guest room for several weeks."

"Truly?"

Theo nodded wearily, as a gentle thump beat behind her eyes.

"And you choose a stranger over kin!"

Had her sister heard nothing of what she'd said? "He is injured,

Seraphina. The doctor has advised he can't be moved due to his broken leg."

"I don't believe you. You have never liked me getting what I want—"

Only because Theo did not always approve of Seraphina's way of getting what she desired.

"—and I don't think you're speaking the truth now."

Theo lifted her chin but said nothing. What was the point in explaining to a person who saw nothing but her own self-interest?

"So . . ." Seraphina straightened. "Who will get our bags?"

Nobody moved.

Not even Roger.

"There must be a servant around. What about Annie? I suppose you're going to tell me she doesn't cook for you on Sundays."

"We have a cold collation, so they can have a day of rest."

"So not only do we have to make do with a second-rate guest chamber, now you're saying there will be no hot meal?" Her sister's voice ended on a shriek.

"Seraphina, my dear daughter—"

"This is not what I expected." Seraphina pushed to her feet, her skirts and hands atremble. "I do not care who is up there. They are leaving. We are staying. And I will tell them so."

Before Theo realized her sister's intention, Seraphina had quit the room and moved up the stairs, ignoring the general when he called to her.

Theo exhaled, unsurprised when Seraphina's husband made no move to stop her. He'd never managed to exert the slightest influence over her headstrong little sister, instead wafting behind her like a malodorous breeze.

She lifted her hands at Mama and Becky, then hastened after her outraged sister before she could intrude into the captain's room. Oh, how wonderful it was to have Seraphina in Stapleton Court again.

Chapter 17

The sound of a carriage arriving far earlier than he expected from services had first garnered Daniel's interest, interest stimulated further at the sounds of complaint when the heavy rap on the door met with no answer. Perhaps the persons—the voices suggested at least two—were unaware a certain resident was at home, might have his windows open, and could hear all they might be so careless to say.

"I should have known they would not be here!" came a petulant young woman's voice.

"You were a fool to think anything else," a man complained.

"Where are they?" Another heavy rap of the door knocker, with enough force that could wake a deaf man from his sleep.

A lower-voiced murmur.

Then the woman's voice again. "What are we supposed to do? We have nowhere else to go."

The familiar clatter on stones signaled another vehicle approached, suggesting the ladies had returned from services, confirmed when the woman said, "They are finally come!"

This had been followed by sounds of joy chased by those of upset, before the stomp on the stairs indicated the visitors were fast approaching. He shifted up, put his Bible to one side, and wondered if he'd be so blessed as to discover their identities. Poor Miss Stapleton. He did not imagine these guests would be as easygoing as some.

The door propelled open with a slam against the wooden sideboard, and one of the prettiest young ladies he'd ever seen stalked into the room. Well, she would have been pretty if it weren't for the scowl darkening her features.

"Who on earth are you?" she demanded.

He raised his brows. How best to treat this intrusion? Ignore her rudeness or point it out? He had a feeling that ignoring this young madam's rudeness was what had allowed it to reach this stage. "Did you use up all your energy knocking on the door downstairs that you had none for this room?"

"What?" She squinted at him. "I asked you a question, sir!"

"And I asked you one."

She blinked. "You are very rude! Who are you? I demand to know!"

Before he could return the question, Miss Stapleton entered the room, her face holding such a plea that it damped further protest. "Sir, you must excuse my sister. She has had a long journey and is a little tired."

"She is your sister?" Incredulity lined his voice.

Miss Stapleton's gaze met his then fell. "May I introduce Mrs. Seraphina Riley."

Her sister, the hellion, placed a hand on her hip and said smugly, "We are not much alike, are we?"

No. One was all humble charm and consideration, the other like well-dressed trouble.

"Who *is* this man, Theo?"

Theodosia raised one brow as if inviting him to speak.

He nodded. Glanced at the blonde whose hauteur reminded him too much of the kinds of ladies he'd met in London, ladies only too quick to show consideration for a person they'd ignore if not for the medal he'd been awarded. "My name is Daniel."

"As I said before, *Mr.* Daniel came to escort Miss Mannering to London. He has broken his leg and has been unable to move from this room for several weeks now. He *cannot* be moved—" Theodosia cut off a sound of protest from her sister. "Not until the doctor gives consent, which is unlikely to be for a while longer."

"But who is he?" Mrs. Riley complained.

He peeked at Theodosia, but she gave little clue as to what to do.

Should he own his true name to her sister? How could he not? "I . . . I am a relative of Miss Mannering's."

"A relative of some distance," Theodosia hastened to clarify, lips lifting to one side, green eyes seeming to plead with him. "You have come quite a way, have you not, sir?"

"Yes, that is so." Amusement tweaked his own lips. Now this game he could play. "Hundreds of miles, in fact."

"You have even sailed seas, I believe."

"Many times."

"Are you a sailor, Mr. Daniel?" the sister asked.

"Not by choice," he admitted. Heaven forbid. "I much prefer land to the sea."

"Hmph. Well, I really don't know why a sailor has been charged with such a task, or why you have broken your leg, but I find your sense of timing most inconvenient."

"It was most inconvenient timing to break my leg," he admitted meekly.

"Agreed," she snapped.

"I should have written of my intention to come." He watched her from under hooded lids. "Writing is the polite thing to do, is it not?"

"Surely."

"But Mr. Daniel," interposed Theodosia. "You must have forgotten. *You* certainly did write to let us know of your planned visit."

He caught the sidelong look the sisters exchanged and the way the blonde's cheeks pinked. The glitter in her blue eyes suggested he'd best take a care to himself.

And that he might need to have a care for what her defeat today might mean for her sister on the morrow.

When he next encountered Theodosia on the following afternoon, Daniel was shocked by the change in her countenance. Gone was the light and life and sparkle, replaced by a dreary weariness he expected resulted chiefly from the woman who'd hurtled back into her family's lives so recently.

He shouldn't have been surprised. Last night, while helping Daniel wash, Robert Brigham had admitted some more details about the force that was Miss Seraphina, "though I s'pose I best rightly call her Mrs. Riley now."

"She seems most determined," he'd said carefully, not wishing to offend the sensibilities of loyal servants.

"Pigheaded also works," the man muttered. "The day that girl was married was the day half the storms left this house."

No prizes for guessing who was responsible for the other half.

"I don't mind saying, sir, it was a blessing for all concerned. Well, not Miss Theo, of course."

"She missed her sister?"

He had shaken his grizzled head, then shrugged. "It was a bad business, the young lass stealing the elder's choice. But—" He raised startled eyes to Daniel. "Don't mind me, sir. I keep forgetting you're not from these parts and don't know all our past." He waggled his head. "Must be that you fit in, while *he* never has."

Such scorn smeared that word. Who exactly was the man downstairs? Sleepless wonderings about what this meant for the elder sister swirled in his mind all night.

And now the elder sister, who stood before him, looked wan and so weary.

"Hello, Miss Stapleton."

Her lips lifted a fraction. "Good afternoon, sir."

"I would ask how you are, but I suspect I know the answer."

She lifted a hand to her hair. "Is it that obvious?"

"Your hair is lovely as ever."

"Ah, it seems your strange sense of humor is still at play."

Why did she not believe him? Memories floated of what had been said yesterday, and that hurt look when he'd all too blatantly admitted he saw little resemblance between the sisters. His stomach tightened. Did she compare herself to her rude and bumptious sister and find herself lacking? "Please, sit down." He patted the chair by his bedside. "You look tired."

"Why, thank you. One always appreciates being told such a thing." She obeyed him nonetheless, shoulders slumping, her expression holding melancholy.

For all her care for others, she rarely seemed to be the focus of others' concern and attention. The thought sparked protectiveness, a wish to help.

"Captain?"

He refocused. "Despite my limitations, is there anything I can do to be of assistance?"

"Can you spirit me away from here?" Her smile appeared, but without corresponding light in her eyes or her dimples. "Forgive me. There has been much to do with my sister's arrival. We were not expecting her, you see."

"How long will she stay?"

"I do not know. Mama is naturally overjoyed to have her here, and I am very glad for her sake."

"Not for your own?" he dared.

"You think it strange that I am not more pleased to have her here. I *am* happy," she insisted, sounding as though she was trying to convince herself, "but our relationship has always been strained."

"I cannot judge at all. You know I loved my sister but should have made more of an effort to stay in touch."

"Yes, but you were away fighting. And from all that Clara told me, your relationship with your brother-in-law was not convivial."

"And your relationship with your brother-in-law?" he probed softly.

She glanced away, lips pressed together and blinks rapid.

Oh no. His chest tightened. He had no wish to ever upset her. "Miss Stapleton, please pardon my insensitivity."

She shook her head. "He and I do not get on, that is all."

What had this man done to hurt her? For hurt her he most certainly had. That wounded expression that wrenched his heart possessed a similar look to one Clara had worn. One of defeat, one of betrayal. Just what *had* this man done?

"Miss Stapleton, truly, I am sorry that I have put you in an awkward position."

She shrugged. "It is not awkward. Well, not yet anyway." A smile pushed past the melancholy. "When Lieutenant Musgrave arrives, that is when it may become awkward. You have not had more word from him?"

"Not as yet, but when I do, I promise you'll be the first to know."

"Thank you."

She seemed disinclined to move, and he was disinclined to let her, so he dared ask for something more. "I wonder . . ."

"Yes?"

"Would it be too much of an imposition to ask if you might let me read to you?"

"If it's another play of Shakespeare's, then I'm afraid I don't have hours to spare." She studied the floor.

"Why not?" he pressed.

"Because I am needed."

"By whom?"

"By my mother."

"Does she not have her younger daughter to pay her heed?"

Her chuckle held no amusement. "Seraphina's presence does not mean she pays my mother heed."

"She has Becky too, don't forget."

A wince crossed her features. "I forgot. We hoped to have a small dinner for Becky's birthday later this week, with hopes you might attend too, but with Seraphina and Roger here . . ."

"That could be problematic," he guessed.

She nodded, pleating the skirt of her gown with restless fingers. "I'm sure Becky will understand."

"She finds my sister a little intimidating, I'm afraid. I suppose it will be good for her when you take her away soon."

He wasn't ready to think on their departure just yet.

"What was it you wished to read?" she asked.

"*Henry V.* I read the second part of *Henry IV*, but it was not the same as having you read it to me."

"I thought you offered to read to me."

"And if you'll hand me *Henry V*, then I most certainly will."

"Do you read plays as well as you tease, sir?" she asked with a half smile.

"You be the judge of that."

As he'd hoped, she gave a small gurgle of amusement and agreed to stay. "But only for one scene."

"One scene?" he protested. "One act, at least."

"One act, then, sir. But you best read it well, else I shall find an excuse to leave."

"Such a hard taskmaster."

She smiled more fully as she passed him the volume.

He found the page, checked she was comfortable, and began to read.

Two acts later, she suddenly straightened. "Oh, sir! You read too well, but it is much later than I dreamed. I had best return downstairs else they will all be wondering what has happened to me."

He bookmarked the page. "I would not wish for you to be troubled."

"I have truly enjoyed this. Listening to you, getting caught up in England's history from centuries ago, is enough to feel I have escaped my troubles. For that, I thank you. You are kind. Much kinder than I deserve."

"I do not have a monopoly on kindness, Miss Stapleton."

She blushed and murmured a goodbye.

His heart grew sore. Just how little kindness did she believe she was worth?

Theo pushed her dinner around her plate. One day of her sister's company and already she was exhausted and nearly at her wit's end. Or perhaps that was the effect of having to guard her heart from the man who had betrayed it. The man who had scorned Theo as Seraphina laughingly agreed and enticed him to woo her instead.

The high point of Theo's day had been the time spent with the captain, but even then duty had ultimately won over pleasure, and she'd forced herself to attend to those tasks sure to be overlooked by others. Not that she would want Mama to give up her joy in reuniting with her daughter. And not that she could expect Seraphina to notice. Or to care. Tasks like ensuring dinner would be ready, and that a plate could be sent to the captain. Tasks like checking that the clothes Seraphina had unceremoniously dumped at Theo's door had been washed and hung to dry. Hettie had worked most of the day to complete the chores, and Theo's exhaustion could not begin to compare. But hers was more an inner weariness, the years of slights and slurs not easily put right by a good night's sleep.

"Theo!"

That peevish note drew up her head to see those around the table staring at her.

Save for Roger. He never looked her way.

"I beg your pardon. What were you saying?"

"I do not understand why you would wish to treat Mr. Daniel as if he was a guest," Seraphina complained.

She swallowed. Glanced at Becky, noting the hurt look in her eye. "But—"

"But he *is* a guest," the general said. "This is my house, Seraphina, and I say who comes and stays, and who goes. I don't recall your informing us you planned to stay."

"Oh, Grandfather." Seraphina tossed him a smile and a girlish giggle. "I did not think you would stand on ceremony where family is concerned."

Did she think her attempt at cajolery would win him over? It had been some years since her sister had lived here, so it seemed she had forgotten with whom she dealt.

"I still find it odd Theo would listen as a servant staying here read her a play." Seraphina took a sip of her wine, glancing at Theo with overly innocent eyes.

"Were you reading a play, Theo?" Mama asked worriedly. "I do not think that quite the thing, my dear."

"I did not realize reading Shakespeare was a crime." Theo sliced into her potato.

"Well, it all depends on the Shakespearean play in question, does it not?" Seraphina set her glass back on the table. "Some have most scandalous subjects, I'm afraid. Quite unsuitable for an unwed lady. Especially in the company of a single man." She signaled for Mr. Siddons to top up her wine. "Is Mr. Daniel unmarried?"

For some reason this question turned Roger's gaze toward Theo.

She kept her gaze fixed on her sister and said as blandly as she could, "I believe so," before taking her own sip of watered wine.

"A hint, sister dear. Some might consider it most improper for you to entertain a young man whilst alone in his bedroom."

Theo's mouth fell open, as her mother fanned herself and said, "Oh my dear!"

"Which play were you reading?" Grandfather asked, eyes narrowing at her.

"The Henry plays. *Henry IV*, and today he was reading *Henry V*."

The old man chuckled. "Not surprised he likes the ones about a soldier."

Seraphina crooked a finger in the air. "I thought he was a sailor?"

Theo's breath suspended. Oh, someone change the subject quickly!

"I wonder," Mama said rather desperately, "about Becky's birthday dinner. Do you think we should see if it should be put off? I'm sorry, dear Rebecca, but we may need to reconsider, given things are, ahem, a little different to what we had once planned."

Becky glanced at Theo, then back at Mama, her disappointment palpable even as she said politely, "Of course, ma'am. I understand."

"We shall do something special," Theo assured.

"Girls in mourning shouldn't hold parties of any significance," Seraphina said to no one in particular. "But it seems certain things are done differently in such rural locations."

This was said with a pointed look that Theo knew precisely what she referred to, Seraphina's earlier comment about Theo's impropriety still burning in her chest. Perhaps she had erred. Perhaps it would behoove her to forgo his company as much as she might like—oh, she could *never* have his company for as long as she liked! But it was not to be. It should not be. Even as she had to endure another's. "How long will we have the pleasure of your visit, sister dear?"

"I do not know what business it is of yours," Seraphina said, bristling.

"But it does concern me." Grandfather's fork clattered on the table. "Well? What is the answer?"

"I, that is, we"—Seraphina gave another foolish giggle as she slanted a glance at her silent husband—"have not decided quite yet."

"Hmph. You come here and expect me to put you up indefinitely?"

"Oh no, sir, it is not like that," Seraphina said quickly.

"Then what is it like?" He glanced at Roger, whose complacent—or was it bored?—expression had barely changed the entire meal. "What have you got to say for yourself?"

Roger placed his fork down and wiped his mouth.

Why had she never noticed how fastidious and particular he was? Had he always been that way?

"Well?" Grandfather demanded. "Are you going to speak or let your wife do all your talking?"

Roger cleared his throat. "We had hoped to stay for a few weeks."

"At my expense? You expect me to put you up and feed you?"

Roger's lips thinned, his expression souring as he glanced across the table at his wife. Almost as if he blamed her for being here.

To be fair, he wouldn't be if it weren't for Seraphina's machinations.

"Whatever happened to your job, Roger dear?" Mama asked, her handkerchief quivering like a restless bird. "You were working at a bank, were you not?"

His features tightened. "A solicitor's office."

"And they do not want you?" Grandfather's voice held an edge.

Roger shot him a quick look, before saying slowly, "My time there has come to an end."

Why? How? These questions burned. And why did he keep casting his wife resentful glances?

Perhaps there was more to this sudden reappearance than what Theo had realized after all.

Chapter 18

"Well, my dears. I am so pleased to see things are being settled as they ought here at Stapleton." Lady Bellingham offered an approving smile. "I shall write to Amelia the moment I am home."

News Amelia would likely little care for, but such was Lady Bellingham's way. Her call upon Mama had consisted mostly of exclamations about delight at Seraphina's return, strong hints the event should be celebrated with a special dinner or a ball, and reiteration of the veiled warnings about entertaining strangers and how one's reputation must be preserved above all else, which met with Mama's usual vacillations of fluster and complaisance.

Theo had held her breath half the visit. Would the squire's wife have the effrontery to demand to see their guest? The other half she had spent praying when it seemed the conversation would steer that way. Fortunately, such an audacious request as to wish to see the supposed servant lying in the best guest chamber was not made, and the distraction of a curricle passing the window—when few such grand vehicles deigned to venture down their drive—soon brought the prior conversation to a halt.

"I wonder who that can be?" uttered Lady Bellingham, with a glance at Theo.

Seraphina put aside Mama's old copy of a periodical and moved to peer out the window, lacking the decorum one might expect. "It's a young man. He . . ." She drew back the curtain a little more. "He is dressed in regimentals! Is he here to see Grandfather, do you think?"

"Oh my goodness!" Lady Bellingham turned to Becky with wide eyes. "Do you think he is your uncle, child? Oh, do take a closer look. You would surely recognize him if that were the case, would you not?"

Becky worried her lip but performed the task obediently. "I, er, I am afraid I do not recognize him, ma'am."

Lady Bellingham sank back against the cushions. "Are we never to see that man? I declare it is almost as if he had no wish to see you, the way he avoids the place. Not," she said quickly, with a wide-eyed glance of apology at Becky, "that I'm not certain but that he *will* come. Because a man as heroic as that must surely know his duty."

Would the guarded talk of Becky's uncle raise any of her sister's suspicions about the man abed upstairs?

The heavy knocker on the front door sounded, and the women kept silent, everyone still, as if their ears strained for the slightest whisper of who the visitor might be, regardless of the etiquette of such a thing.

Theo smiled internally. How funny that what was deemed proper could always be altered to suit one's whims and fancies.

"Theodosia, perhaps you could see if Mr. Siddons needs some assistance," Mama implored, her thin hand grasping the carved wooden armrest.

"Of course." She smoothed her gown and moved to the door, swallowing another smile at Mama's plea. Mr. Siddons possessed a manner of dealing with visitors, whether invited or unwanted, that had never left her in any doubt that he could dampen pretensions. He would never require any assistance whatsoever. Still, the graceful request with which she could learn the visitor's identity showed that Mama was just as eager to know too.

Theo entered the hall just as Mr. Siddons turned, spied her, and announced in a grand voice. "Ah, here is Miss Stapleton now."

"Miss Stapleton." The stranger ignored Mr. Siddons and stepped forward, offering a slight bow. "I am—"

"This is Lieutenant Musgrave," interrupted Mr. Siddons, with a tight smile that said he most certainly did not welcome having his moment of theatre stolen.

"Pleased to make your acquaintance," the lieutenant said. A gleam of amusement in his eye said he appreciated the irony of having the pretensions squashed.

How like herself, and also put her firmly in mind of the man upstairs who owned a similar enjoyment for the ridiculous. "Lieutenant, how wonderful that you could come all this way. I know your presence will be most valued by one who lingers in his sickbed."

"A malingerer, that describes Balfour most certainly."

She recognized his tease and instructed Mr. Siddons to see to the man's bags, then drew the lieutenant to a small alcove and spoke quietly. "I am truly glad you are here, but I must warn you we are not without some other visitors at this moment, one of whom is most eager to learn about the whereabouts of the captain and is quite offended on Becky's behalf as much as her own that he is yet to make an appearance. So if you would be so good—"

"As to maintain the subterfuge? Of course, ma'am. You can trust me."

"Thank you."

He smiled, his handsome features probably far more in keeping with Lady Bellingham's idea of what a truly heroic hero should look like compared with the poor man with the broken leg upstairs.

"Our wisest course of action is to take you to the drawing room, where I can make you known to my mother, sister, Lady Bellingham, and Miss Mannering, Captain Balfour's niece. They are most eager to make your acquaintance. But again I warn you to do your best to hide his true identity, if at all possible, without telling a falsehood."

"Of course, ma'am."

How good it was to be so easily obeyed. "This way, if you please." She led the way into the drawing room and performed the introductions.

Faces lit, proving the women were just as favorably impressed with their guest as she was.

Not that a handsome face counted for much. Witness the husband of her sister, whose words and actions had never matched the goodness of his appearance. She couldn't help but be glad he'd chosen to go riding today.

Another flare of resentment revealed she'd benefit from yet further prayer and quiet reflection.

But the fact of the lieutenant's handsomeness could not be denied.

He was taller than the captain, with eyes of blue. The thick blond hair apparent once he had removed his hat owned nothing of the thinning hairline the captain possessed. Lieutenant Musgrave owned a degree of charm, too, and the effect of such a personable manner was seen in the way Mama and Lady Bellingham's voices had risen rather higher than normal, Seraphina had lost all interest in *La Belle Assemblée*, and Becky kept staring at him as if she'd seen a Greek god turned into flesh.

"Oh, dear Lieutenant Musgrave," Lady Bellingham was now saying. "I wonder, are you related at all to a Mrs. Louisa Musgrave, by any chance?"

"My cousin, ma'am," he said from his position standing near the fireplace. "I am from the Leicestershire branch of Musgraves."

"Please be seated," Mama's softer voice intoned.

He gave a strong shake of his head. "I would not dream of staining your furniture with my mud, but I do appreciate a chance to warm up near the fire. It is so blessedly cold here in the north." He rubbed his hands together and reached them nearer the flame.

"May I get you something hot to eat or drink, sir?" Theo offered from her position near the door.

"Thank you, but I had a light repast in a village not too far from here."

"And was your journey extremely uncomfortable?" Lady Bellingham asked, her tone and tilted head holding sympathy and an expectation he'd agree.

"Not at all," he said. "Two hundred miles of good road these days makes the journey far quicker than one might think. Of course, it would have proved quicker if I had not stopped off at Langley House, which is more of a castle really, to see an army acquaintance."

Seraphina's eyes rounded. "You know a gentleman who lives in a castle?"

"Major James Langley. Lives in a castle by the North Sea. Of course, he's sold out, so not a major now, but rather nicely settled and married. I shouldn't be surprised to hear that his little family will be increasing in the not-too-distant future."

From the startled responses that met this last comment, he might have realized the impropriety of speaking as such to near perfect strangers, as he begged their pardon.

Theo grew uneasily aware that, for all his affable charm, the lieutenant was a talker. Concern threaded through her at his ability to hold his tongue.

Lady Bellingham's gaze narrowed. "You are a friend of Captain Balfour's, I understand."

"Yes."

Theo's heart froze.

"Which is why he sent for me to look in on the situation." He turned to Becky. "Apparently he wants me to keep an eye on you."

She blushed and giggled, dimpling up at him in a way that drew a fresh pang of misgiving. Oh dear. The lieutenant might hold swags of charm, but he was at least ten years Becky's senior. No good could come of a poor girl's infatuation. Theo knew only too well how badly that could turn.

But further thought could not be applied to this, as Lady Bellingham's brow had pleated. "The captain sent for you? Do you mean he is here?"

Theo's breath sucked in, and she could only look between her mother and the captain's friend, her ready wits for once not quick to the fore.

Becky's cheeks flushed. "If he were here, then wouldn't we all know?"

"Exactly so." Theo smiled warmly at her charge. "One couldn't expect such a man to come into the neighborhood without great fuss and fanfare." She shifted to check on the fire, whose welcome warmth the lieutenant still enjoyed. "I trust, sir, that you'd be willing to stay here with us at Stapleton Court. We are rather blessed with company, so I'm afraid it is our third guest bedchamber that would be yours, but I assure you it is most comfortable, though some might think it small."

"My dear Miss Stapleton!" protested Lady Bellingham turning to Theo's mother. "Surely, Letitia, you would not wish to open your daughter up to a charge of impropriety."

Mama concurred.

The man shot an uneasy look at Lady Bellingham. "I rather thought I'd stay at Mannering. I believe that was what the captain said."

"That is a much better idea," approved the squire's wife.

"It would be," Theo said smoothly, "if the house was still able to be used. But as it remains at the mercy of builders, I think you would prefer to stay elsewhere, where you can be assured you will not come to grief."

The lieutenant scratched his cheek. "I could make arrangements at the local inn."

"Nonsense." Theo refused to look in the squire's wife's direction. "If you have been directed to keep an eye on Captain Balfour's niece, how can you be expected to do so when you are all the way across in the village? Did you know it is nearly two miles from Stapleton Court to Wooler? Quite too far to be traipsing back and forth every day, especially when I am sure it is going to rain yet more."

"Exactly so," Mama interposed. "I said as much to dear Theodosia just the other day. I always feel the oncoming rains because my sciatica flares."

Theo readjusted her mother's shawl, her mother thanking her with patted hand. "More rain, I'm afraid, will make the roads impassable, so staying at an inn would be unwise." And if the lieutenant was safely ensconced here at Stapleton, it might mean he'd have less opportunity to allow his tongue to run away. Although, there was the added pressure of Seraphina and Roger's presence. "Now, I must make you known to the general."

"General Stapleton? Yes, Balfour mentioned him."

Oh dear. Theo clasped her hands tightly and smiled at their visitor. "Lady Bellingham, please excuse me while I show our newest guest to his room so he can wash off his dirt and be presented to the general. Come, sir."

Lieutenant Musgrave made his adieus and they exited to the sound of Lady Bellingham asking if Letitia had plans to turn Stapleton Court into a hostelry, as dear Theodosia seemed determined to insist on all and sundry being invited to stay here.

"You seem to have landed on your feet."

Daniel looked up from his book at that welcome voice as Jeremy Musgrave entered the guest room, Miss Stapleton hanging back just behind him.

Musgrave took in the view on all sides then broke into a laugh, as he motioned to Daniel's splint-bound leg. "Except not."

Daniel placed the book to one side. "I am thankful it was on my feet I did land and not my arms or my head." They gripped hands, and he insisted on Musgrave taking a seat.

"So, how goes things?" Musgrave glanced at the stack of books with a wrinkled nose.

Theodosia quietly made her exit.

As he watched her leave, a trace of disappointment crept through his gut that she barely spared him a glance.

"Balfour?"

"Forgive me." Daniel returned his attention to his friend.

"Who would've thought the great Balfour would have his head turned at last?" Musgrave laughed. "She's not unattractive, though cannot hold a candle to her sister, of course. Still, she'd be quite a picture if it weren't for that mark on her face."

"I do not notice it." He noticed other things, like the velvety caress of her voice and the way her laughter tinkled like a mountain stream. Although—he frowned—he had heard neither as much as he would like recently. Was her sister's presence still draining?

"She is Major Stapleton's daughter?"

"Yes."

"I recall talk about him. They say he was a brave 'un."

"I rather think courage runs in her veins too." The look of enquiry shown him made him elaborate. "Have you met the general?"

"General Contrary. Indeed, I have, just now."

Daniel smiled wryly. "I'm given to understand most people in these parts stand in awe or fear of the master of the house."

"That does not surprise me. You know what he said to me when I said it a pleasure to meet him? He told me no, it wasn't. That my foisting myself upon you was a matter of infernal impudence and inconvenience, and that any introduction between us was a matter of social obligation, not anything else."

Oh no.

"When I tried to plead the opposite, he cut me off. If it hadn't been for Miss Stapleton's intervention, and assurance that matters being what they were I simply had to stay here at Stapleton, then I would have departed right then and there. Indeed, I'm in half a mind to do so still."

"If anyone can make him see reason, it's Miss Stapleton. My interactions with her grandfather show he requires tact and sense, qualities Miss Stapleton seems to possess in abundance."

Perhaps he'd spoken more warmly than he meant, for he surprised a look of calculation in his friend's eye. "She seems a veritable paragon."

"She is."

His friend released a low whistle. "I certainly did not expect a lass from this part of England to be the one to steal your heart."

"Steal my—? Really, Musgrave. I did not suspect you to lack such finesse."

"So, there isn't interest in that quarter?" The lieutenant studied Daniel's splinted leg with pursed lip and puckered brow.

"I cannot afford for there to be."

"Hmm." Again, that look of speculation. "Well, I met a dragon in the drawing room. Some Bellingham woman. A local nabob's wife, it seems. Appeared rather interested in you."

"It seems most strange, when she deigned to not recognize me upon our first and only meeting."

"You met her?"

"Many weeks ago now, it appears. Before this." Daniel gestured to his leg. "She did not seem to hold the opinion that a supposed hero could possess looks like mine."

"Such vanity," murmured Musgrave.

Daniel chuckled. "I could not crush her expectations that a man more befitting your appearance should be welcomed into the area with a hundred turtle dinners and the like."

"A hundred turtle dinners? Can you imagine?" Musgrave shuddered.

"It's precisely what I am trying not to."

A quick grin lifted Musgrave's lips. "But come man. You must stop with this ridiculous *supposed hero* thing. One cannot but be supposed a hero when he is directly responsible for dragging one hundred men to safety."

"That was not all me, as you very well know. Edgerton was there, as was Langley, and Stamford too. You all helped."

"We all were quaking in our boots, wondering what course to take when you took charge."

"You exaggerate."

"Says the one commended by the King himself." Musgrave stretched out his long legs. "What were the words he used? Conduct most valiant and honorable?"

"Your hearing is not at fault, at least."

"Nor your understanding. Although it beggars me to comprehend why a man of such valor should remain incognito."

Daniel offered a wry smile. "You do recall London?"

"Why, yes. Oh. I see."

Another memory sparked. "Remember what you once said there? How you would like to be me? Well, here is your opportunity."

"That is extremely obliging of you, but—"

"I would consider myself indebted to you, as I have no desire to be toad-eaten."

"And you think I have?"

Daniel raised his brows and dipped his chin.

Musgrave gave a crack of laughter. "I cannot believe you think so lowly of me."

"I don't. You are loyal and ever supportive of your friends in their hour of need."

"Does nobody know the truth?"

"Miss Stapleton guessed it at once." Daniel adjusted the blankets. "Her mother, grandfather, and the servants here and at Mannering know too. And you did not think I could hide such a thing from my niece, did you?"

His friend studied him with something akin to fascination in his eye. "I find I don't quite know what to think anymore. Who have you been purporting to be?"

"I haven't purported to be anyone. I was only here a short time when the blighted event happened. Since then, I've been ensconced at Stapleton Court, not seeing anyone really, save the doctor, the reverend, and

Mr. Cleever, the solicitor. I had to let them know, but they've been sworn to secrecy."

"The solicitor and reverend I understand, but why did you tell the doctor?"

"I'm afraid that was more Miss Stapleton's doing than mine. After my injury, she convinced him that I should go to her home rather than an inn, and it was deemed proper only because of my relationship to my niece."

"She did, did she?"

His friend's misgivings drew heat to his chest and his protest. "Do not misjudge her," he said quietly, but with firmness. "She is as honorable and excellent a creature as I have ever met."

Musgrave's brows pushed up.

Daniel had to change the subject. Quickly. "But in answer to your question, most people in these parts believe I am Captain Balfour's steward, as suggested by my initial note. Lady Bellingham and Mrs. Riley know me as Mr. Daniel."

"Hmm. That is your name. Half of it, anyway." Musgrave picked up a bottle of laudanum the doctor had prescribed, then set it down.

"I do not like the pretense but had no plans to stay here long enough for it to matter."

"Well, as much as one might wish to be known as heroic, I'm afraid my name is already known to Lady Bellingham and the sister, so that plan will not fadge."

"A pity. I have no wish to deceive, and less wish to socialize. Once I'm recovered, I have no intention to stay beyond fixing things to a certainty with my niece."

"Your niece, you say?" Musgrave eyed him with a gleam of interest in his eyes.

"My niece." Anything—anyone—more was quite out of the question. "Then we shall return to London and pretend this sorry episode never happened. I'd be home yesterday if I hadn't hurt my leg."

"Yes, about that." Musgrave stretched out his hands. "You never really told me how you managed to escape from that situation."

Daniel told him.

Musgrave whistled. "Miss Stapleton rescued you? She's quite the heroine for our hero, isn't she?"

"Musgrave," he growled.

"No, don't snap off my nose. If you wish for me to maintain your subterfuge, then do not deny me what pleasure I can extract from the part."

"Thank you." He eased up in the bed, wincing. "Truly it should not be above a week or two, until I can settle things to a certainty with Mannering."

"But what about your Miss Stapleton?"

His heart thumped. He ignored it. "She is not my Miss Stapleton. She is simply a friend who has proved to be most sympathetic in her understanding."

"I bet she has."

Daniel chose to ignore the glint in Musgrave's eyes.

"Given your experiences in London, I can understand your desire to lay low. It is considered rather bad form to puff off one's consequence, after all." Musgrave screened a yawn with a hand. "Such a thing is hardly considered a sign of humility."

"Quite so."

"Although, forgive me for mentioning it, but such a plan seems to hold the appearance you are afraid of a certain sharp-tongued squire's wife."

"You sound like Miss Stapleton now."

"Oho! What does our fair hostess have to say about the matter?"

"She is of a mind with you."

Musgrave nodded, his grin stretching wide. "I need to have further conversation with that lady."

Daniel's guts twisted disconcertingly. Did his friend have an interest in that quarter?

"I must say, your little niece is a taking thing."

The abrupt change of subject caused a mental blink. "Becky? She has her mother's fairness and features."

"Yes, she will be a beauty, I believe. I could not see much resemblance between you and she," he teased.

"Lucky for her."

"Indeed." Musgrave crossed one booted leg over the other and clasped his hands behind his head. "Now, tell me more about your Miss Stapleton. I want to know about the way of things here."

They settled into a comfortable coze and exchanged stories about the past months. Musgrave offered further opinions of his initial impressions of the general—"most pugnacious, rather like a terrifying old bull terrier we have down at the house in Thorpe Acre"; and Mrs. Stapleton—"a kindly soul"; and Mrs. Riley—"reminds me of a Persian cat."

Daniel shared about his letters from colleagues and the War Office, the latter meeting with Musgrave's shock.

"I have replied," Daniel assured, "demanding an interview, and now await their response."

Musgrave's indignation soon faded, his conversation returning to the previous topic, thus fueling Daniel's misgivings. For it seemed the man Daniel had begged to come and visit was most certainly a ladies' man.

Chapter 19

Daniel's concerns about his friend's reputation were further tested two days later, when Rebecca's birthday dinner resulted in his first removal from his bedchamber in weeks. He despised his weakness that required Musgrave's assistance for his slow passage down the stairs, but the doctor had earlier relented and permitted such a venture, given the occasion.

Becky's party had fortunately coincided with the removal of the younger daughter and her husband—whom he still was yet to meet—on a visit to nearby Bamburgh, or so Miss Stapleton had said. "Apparently the lieutenant's talk of a castle by the sea reminded Seraphina of the need to visit an old friend for a few days. I think she wishes to see if the castle permits tours."

Interesting timing, given the exchange of sharp words between the younger sister and her husband he'd overheard through the guest rooms' walls last night.

Still, it seemed as though a cloud had lifted, and judging from the way Becky smiled and chattered and made up to everyone at the dinner table, she seemed very well pleased indeed.

The Stapletons had been kind enough to issue his niece with a charming bonnet and gloves, which she had shown him that morning when she'd visited his room. Musgrave, too, had picked a little posy of wildflowers, which had drawn her blush and made Daniel determine to speak to his friend about unnecessarily inviting warmer feelings from an impressionable young lady.

Becky wore his gift of a skillfully wrought gown, for which he'd thanked Mrs. Stapleton despite the disconcerting knowledge that it made his niece look older than her newly minted seventeen years. And while she looked sweet and pretty, he couldn't help but notice Miss Stapleton, seated opposite him at the table. Next to the general, Daniel's positioning was necessitated by his leg, which required propping on a low stool. The advantage of this? His view of Theodosia was unencumbered by the overlarge vase centering the table, with its profusion of flowers.

She wore a gown he'd not seen before, in a blue color that drew out the fairness of her skin while also drawing attention to the fiery color of her hair. Neither was her birthmark obvious, perhaps because the candlelight was rather muted. He wished he might speak to her—she had not visited his room since Musgrave's arrival—but had to content himself with observation.

She seemed happier without her sister, less careworn, more at ease. He couldn't help but notice the way she laughed with his friend, and the way her gaze did not linger on Daniel as it did on Musgrave, though her words to Daniel remained polite. He shouldn't be surprised. Ladies had always preferred his friend to him. Mouth twisting, he shredded his meat carefully with a fork.

"Not a fan of beef?" the general asked Daniel with suspicion, as if he questioned his very Englishness.

Daniel noticed Theodosia looking at him with concern now and, knowing she had arranged the meal—Becky had told him—he rushed to reassure. "I am enjoying this very much." He smiled at her, but his heart-kick at her returned look of pleasure faded as she turned to Musgrave again.

"I hope you find this to your liking, sir. I cannot imagine what it must be like to encounter various inns and their meals along the way."

"I can assure you this meal far surpasses anything one might have on the road." Musgrave suited his words with appropriate action, and a blissful look filled his face. "Have you never travelled, Miss Stapleton?"

"I have not."

"Not even to the border?" He glanced at Daniel. "Coldstream is not far from here, is it?"

"It is but fourteen miles." He devoured a bite of creamed potato. "So near."

"If one has reason to go there," Theodosia said, before her gaze returned to Daniel. "I'm pleased to see the potatoes meet with your approval, Captain."

He swallowed a morsel. "The entire meal is most delicious."

She nodded, her attention once again veering away to focus on his niece. "I hope Miss Mannering approves."

"Oh, Theo, it is all so wonderful. Thank you so very much."

Theodosia's head tilted slightly to the end of the table.

Becky followed the movement and quickly exclaimed, "Oh, and Mrs. Stapleton, and General Stapleton too! Thank you for giving me such a treat."

Both parties responded with reassurance that it was no trouble, and Daniel was sure it had not been. Not for the general at least, whose awareness of domestic matters here seemed as remote as Daniel's own.

Miss Theodosia Stapleton was the one responsible for this. She was the one responsible for nearly all that was good in Becky's world, actually. A fresh rush of gratitude toward her filled him. How could he ever show the depths of his appreciation?

But how to show gratitude to someone who suddenly seemed to wish to keep him at arm's length? He would have to ponder this. And pray whatever had caused her to fall from that easy way they'd shared before would soon be put right again.

The drawing room hummed with conversation and good humor. Theo smiled at her mother, then refocused on her embroidery, as across from them the others continued their conversation. The arrival of the lieutenant—and the temporary absence of Seraphina and Roger—had drawn new energy to their days, so much that Stapleton Court seemed to have found a new lease of life. To have someone new to talk to, someone eager and interesting to laugh with, someone to teach her more about the world and experiences she would never know helped assuage some of the sadness that accompanied her renewed determination to draw back from Captain Balfour. How galling for it to be Seraphina's comment that had ignited fresh realization at the impropriety of Theo's visits to the captain's room. How could she have been so heedless, spending hours reading with him, treating him as if he was an old friend with whom she could relax and just be?

She should not. He was leaving. His attention she would not seek. And the only way to lessen the feeling of pain when she caught him looking at her and wanted to hold his gaze was to concentrate on his friend.

Lieutenant Musgrave proved, as she had initially suspected, an inveterate talker. Soon they knew all about his family, who lived in a rather rambling old manor at Thorpe Acre, "passed down to my father when his brother took a tumble while hunting with the Quorn. Goes to show those foxes can be cunning devils—beg pardon, ma'am."

Just this morning, Dr. Linton had visited and pronounced a change in the captain's restrictions. "Seeing as there is another strong back to help move him, he would benefit from a different locale. Accordingly, the occasional visit downstairs might be in order."

Her enquiry about if he meant a place other than Stapleton was forestalled by Mama asking the very question, which the doctor had negated. "It's far too soon to travel, and I must insist he remains a while longer. You may just need to pray that this incessant rain might keep visitors away. If, however, the rain lets up and he finds the crutch to his benefit, perhaps a visit to church might work in another week or so. Then we may consider whether he's fit to return to Mannering."

Another week. Another week of his company, and—God forgive her hopes this rain continued to make roads difficult to traverse—without Seraphina and Roger. One more week.

She bent her head to her stitching, wishing her ears did not so quickly prick to hear the captain's low voice or laughter.

The sound of her name drew her head up.

"Forgive me. I did not hear."

"Miss Stapleton," Lieutenant Musgrave said. "Balfour assures me there is a billiard room, and the general has given permission that a game might be sought and had."

He had? How magnanimous. She inadvertently glanced at the captain and saw his nod. Well, then. She returned her attention to the lieutenant. "I have played against my grandfather several times."

"Aha! Balfour wondered if you were so practicable as to know the game."

Her pulse mounted. She did *not* want to think on what else the captain might have wondered in regard to her.

"Would the general be interested, do you think?"

"In a game with you?" she asked the lieutenant. "I'm afraid he spends most of his time in his library, so I suspect not, but I can ask if you like."

"I would not have him troubled . . ."

She laid aside her stitching and hurried away before she could listen to the rest of his protest.

She had to get away, to quieten her heart and not let the desire to know what else the captain thought sway her into staying. The enquiry put to the general, she soon returned with his negative, refraining to repeat the exact words of her grandfather's expostulation.

"Might you be so kind as to accompany me, then, Miss Stapleton," Lieutenant Musgrave enquired, his smile warm and inviting. "It has been an age since I played, and I would like the chance to do so, if doing so does not trouble or disturb you too much."

The captain sitting there, watching her, disturbed her. Perhaps this would be a chance to escape his gaze. "Thank you, sir. A game would make a pleasant change."

Lieutenant Musgrave nodded and turned to Becky, who had been sitting and watching proceedings quietly all this time. "Miss Mannering? Have you the happy talent of playing also?"

She blushed and shook her head. "I have never learned."

"Ah, then perhaps you are in need of a tutor." The lieutenant glanced at Theo and smiled before his gaze fixed on Becky. "As I have been instructed that I must keep you under my eye, then perhaps you would be so good as to come with us too."

Theo bit her lip during the interchange. Just what was the lieutenant up to? At times he seemed to possess such engaging manners that she was hard-pressed to know if it was just his way or implied deeper interest. Her heart knotted. What folly to wonder if a man like him could ever have some interest in her. She studied the pair of them, the way the lieutenant seemed oblivious to Becky's open admiration, and the fact that offers like this only encouraged the girl to fall deeper into attraction. How might the captain view such an invitation?

"Coming, Captain?" Lieutenant Musgrave asked and received hasty affirmation.

The billiard room was soon attained, the game commenced, and observations and instructions quickly followed. Theo's lips curved with wryness. How silly to think this would be a simple game.

"Now ladies, I wonder, might I be permitted to assist you?"

She straightened and murmured complaisance—it never hurt to improve her game—even as her skin prickled. However, it wasn't in reaction to the lieutenant's nearness, but more the way the captain's frown had suddenly intensified. She glanced away from where he was positioned on a settee, yet remained all too aware of him, how his gaze seemed to weigh upon her skin.

"Now, if you hold the cue straight, and draw your arm back like so." The lieutenant touched her arm, his breath tickling her cheek, as she sensed his form behind her. "Then with a sharp movement, there!"

The crack of the stick against white ball saw it hit the red and spin it to the side, where it propelled toward the pocket before hitting the corner and rolling away.

"Ah, unlucky."

"Perhaps you miscalculated," the captain said.

"No miscalculation," Lieutenant Musgrave said. "Simply bad luck."

Theo's eyes met the captain's, and she recognized the humor there, present also in the twist of his lips. Yes, she'd thought her game was better before the lieutenant's "help."

"I say, Balfour, are you feeling quite all right?" the lieutenant asked. "You've done nothing but criticize my game the whole time."

"I would have less to comment on if you played better, my friend."

"You just wish you could stand here, teaching two such lovely ladies."

"Perhaps."

Theo's heart curled foolishly, and she averted her gaze to where Becky stood, cue in hand, gazing at the lieutenant with a smile that gave her heart away. Oh dear.

"Miss Mannering. Are you ready to continue?" The lieutenant held up his cue.

"Oh, yes. Yes, please!"

"Right. Well, if you care to shift just the slightest to the left, then I can show you the best way to hold the cue."

Sensing her time with the lieutenant was closed, Theo pressed her stick back in the rack and moved to sit on the only other chair available. The chair next to the captain.

"You play well, Miss Stapleton."

"Thank you," she murmured, "although it seems as if someone feels my game needs a few pointers."

"You would not begrudge a man who seeks to impress a lady, would you?"

She faced him. "Even if he cannot tell when the lady plays better than he?"

He laughed. "Poor chap doesn't realize you are more skilled."

"Well, at least he's found a more grateful recipient of his attentions now."

His shoulders straightened. "You do not wish for his attentions?"

"Not when they seem designed to make me feel inferior."

"It sounds to me as though you have read Lady Wollstonecraft's book." He subtly readjusted his injured leg.

"I will admit that I have. But it surprises me that you should mention it, sir."

"My aunt, the one I would provide as chaperone to Becky, is what some might term a trifle blue."

"How shocking." She smiled, unable to resist the impishness in his eyes. "You do not strike me as being one who sees women as less than men."

"How could I? Not when the Bible makes it plain we are all created in God's image, thus must share an equal value and worth."

"It encourages me to hear you say this. Most enlightened, particularly from one of England's heroes."

He chuckled. "I appreciate such approbation, Miss Stapleton."

"As well you should."

Oh, it was too easy to banter with him. She needed to take heed to herself, to not give in.

From the other end of the room, Becky softly confessed she would like to be shown once again just how to hold the cue.

"Men's superior strength is not a sign of their superiority in mental or moral situations," the captain spoke quietly. "Time at war has shown just how fallible men can be, whereas time spent here has shown just how remarkable some women can be."

Her heart glowed. Oh, she was a fool to sweep his words into her heart. A fool to think he meant her. But after days of keeping him at a distance, her head seemed to be losing its battle with her heart.

"Do you think he stands rather too close?" he asked.

She studied the pair, the way Becky's laughing eyes shone up at the lieutenant's. "She is enjoying his company."

"Rather too much, I fear."

"She will be wise." She hoped.

"Will she? Her mother proved that she was not the best judge of character when it comes to men."

"Yes, but she did not have the advantage of such wise old heads as yours and mine to advise her."

"You do indeed have a wise head upon those shoulders, just as I mentioned a moment ago."

His words released a gush of warmth within. So he *had* meant her. What was the word he'd used?

Remarkable.

Her heart seemed to fill with a hundred points of light, like a starry night in the coldest depths of winter. No man had ever expressed admiration for her before. Well, no man that she regarded highly had done so. And while her head still warned that she was most likely to have her heart broken if she dwelt too long on his words, she couldn't help but wonder what it would be like to venture into the realm of romance.

For years it seemed as if her heart was numb, that she had not realized a darkness veiled the light of her heart and life. She had found a measure of purpose and contentment in her duty, in her quiet focus on her family and village life. And then this man appeared, and it was like the dawn had come. Now a path shimmered before her, filled with possibilities and a future oh so bright. She might have prayed to reconcile these feelings, but how could she ever quench this gnawing desperation? Oh, how she *longed* for her foolish dreams to come true. But simply longing for something was a lesson in destruction she knew by heart, romance being a far-flung star impossible to obtain. It was only a matter of time before the light faded and she tumbled back to the dirt of reality. Romance was not for her. Hadn't the captain made it plain, time and again, he was wedded to his military career and had no plans for marriage or a family?

She inched away, telling herself firmly to guard her emotions. She'd been led by her feelings before and allowed herself to dream of things impossible. That man had laughed and mocked her stained cheek and her pretensions, then gone and married her sister. She could not trust her foolish heart again. She would *not* fall like that again. She would find contentment again one day. She had to.

Chapter 20

The return of Mr. and Mrs. Riley brought the return of bickering and comments that were no doubt designed to bring unease, but which afforded Daniel an unhealthy amount of pleasure. Seraphina and her husband seemed not to know how to deal with him, questioning why he and his friend joined the rest of the family downstairs, which Daniel did not respond to, leaving that to the general who demanded to know what business it was of theirs to dictate where his guests might take their ease.

For himself, Daniel determined that his leg-propped presence would not intrude or impinge on any of Theodosia's comfort, nor lead anyone to question his motives or hers, which was another reason it was good to be downstairs in more public spaces. The general had permitted Daniel's use of a small bookroom, a space off the library, which allowed for a degree of privacy from those visitors who might drop in unannounced but also permitted opportunity for conversation. Indeed, the general had more than once enquired of Daniel and Musgrave whether they knew this soldier or that one and seemed glad to reminisce about his glory days of old.

Lieutenant Musgrave's presence was proving equal parts pleasure and dismay. Daniel enjoyed having his friend with him, feeling at ease with someone who knew him and had experienced similar trials. But the man's presence also brought a degree of concern. Might Musgrave's garrulous nature bring other challenges, especially with the presence of young ladies, one of whom seemed happy to forget her matrimonial bonds as she nagged him to know more? Seraphina's interest vexed Daniel more for what Musgrave might spill than concern that Musgrave would get emotionally entangled. No, it was his friend's effect on the other two younger women with which he was irked. At times Musgrave seemed intent on charming Becky, young though she may be. At other times he sought out the company of Miss Stapleton, which proved more problematic.

Daniel already despised himself for the tentacles of envy that had appeared during that unnerving billiard-room encounter, when his friend had spent time far too close to Theodosia. He'd ground his teeth as the pair of them talked and laughed together. He was not proud of such emotions, for Musgrave's tall, broad-shouldered good looks and handsome features had always appealed to the ladies in a way Daniel's plain features never had. He should be reconciled to this by now. But recognizing he should be reconciled was different from actually feeling it, and led to more of those persistent questions about what he desired for himself and his own future.

Daniel studied Miss Stapleton now, as she and Musgrave helped Becky piece together a dissected map, the contents of which were spread liberally across the oak table in the library. The general was still abed with gout today, and Mrs. Stapleton used the drawing room to entertain her younger daughter. Where that daughter's husband was now was something Daniel neither knew nor cared.

He must look like an old man with his leg propped out on the cushion of a small chair positioned near the fire, a book in his lap. The days remained cool and wet, and outside activities remained unpleasant, not that his injuries would permit him to do much anyway. So staying inside, like the aged uncle he truly was, had become his role.

Compared with the others here, he *was* aged. And it was more than the number of his years or the injuries that had him buttressed here, wondering if he needed a blanket and nightcap to complete the picture. These past two days, ever since the time in the billiard room, he'd known a new sense of unease.

Not just from watching his friend engage in pretty nothings with his niece. Their time together, despite what he'd admitted to Theodosia, he was not overly concerned about. Becky was far too young to truly capture the lieutenant's interest.

But it was what their mild flirtation represented that made him feel his age. Until he met Miss Stapleton, he'd never really engaged in the kind of witty exchanges these two did now. He'd enjoyed that, felt the spark of life within, a quickening of his pulse different from those moments before he faced cannon fire.

And yet, encounters with her felt every bit as filled with potential to destroy him, to destroy all he had known. Perhaps these were the ruminations of a sick man. Perhaps this was what happened when one had too much time to think and had hit one's head. One started to question, to doubt, to wonder, to grow discontented with a chosen path in life.

Theodosia smiled at Musgrave, and Daniel felt another queer sensation cross his chest. How galling. Simply because he wished for her smiles didn't mean he deserved them. For what was the point? He had a job to do, a role to fill. His life was hundreds of miles south, not here. He had nothing to offer a wife, no fancy home, no great income. And staying here, he could see just how accustomed she was to living in this great house, being the lady who near singlehandedly ran an estate such as this. He could offer nothing of great substance or means.

What could he offer, should the most ridiculous of his secret dreams be revealed? A small cottage in Wiltshire, the promise that he would be away for extended periods of time, the fair possibility that he might be maimed or killed. His lips twisted. How could that appeal?

And what alternative could there be? Become a farmer like Adam Edgerton? Perhaps work in a shop? He had little education beyond the basic, so he could not retrain to become a clergyman or legal clerk. And while he might have faith in God and a desire to see others walk in His ways, he did not want to learn and succumb to the rules and laws of the church, not when he'd spent years learning to submit elsewhere.

What else could he do?

Who else could he be?

The thought was almost frightening. For all his life, the army was all he'd wanted. Since his parents' deaths, it was all he'd known. Some might call him courageous—although they might question that now—but he doubted whether he even *could* dare take that step sideways and forgo a future in the armed forces.

Who would he be without the known, without the rules and routines that had served him so well for two decades?

He lowered his gaze, shifting to study the flames burning in the grate. He amazed himself for even thinking like this, amazed himself for daring to contemplate what life could look like if he left the army.

"Captain?"

He blinked, glanced up, saw Miss Stapleton's tentative smile. "Forgive me, ma'am."

"No, forgive me, sir. You looked quite lost in thought."

"I was."

"I realized just how selfish we were being, playing a game that you could not participate in, and I wondered if you might like some company."

He acquiesced, but her nearness only drew further agitation within. Had other men found themselves in a similar quandary, torn between an established life and that which was unknown? He supposed so. But this felt like such a pivotal decision, such a bold move he was not sure he had the heart to make. Especially when he remained uncertain as to just how keen Theodosia might be to explore such things with him.

"Have you finished your reading of *Henry V*? If so, I could retrieve something else for you to read."

"I . . ." He cleared his throat. "I thought you wished for conversation."

"I can do that too." She seated herself in the chair opposite. "What do you wish to converse about?"

He shouldn't do this. Spending time with her would only fuel this agitation and stress. If he was a vain man, he might also think it may fuel expectations in her. And he had no desire to be any more dishonorable than he already felt he was being.

"Apparently nothing," she said, with a teasing glint in her eye. "Very well. I shall return."

"I—" He swallowed. *Really shouldn't, but . . .* "I would be quite happy to talk with you."

Was that relief flitting across her features? Perhaps if he watched and listened, he could discern if there was any encouragement that might guide his next steps.

"Well, that is certainly preferable to being ignored or being forced to converse when one doesn't truly want to. Conversation due to social obligation is never as engaging as when one finds oneself conversing with someone *quite happy* to speak with you."

His heart lightened at the return of her good-humored repartee. "I beg your pardon if I seemed rude before."

"Not rude, although perhaps distracted." She leaned forward. "Are you worried about your niece and friend?"

His gaze shifted to the duo, still chatting.

Becky twirled a strand of her hair around her finger and glanced up at the lieutenant, her gaze one of open admiration.

His heart clenched. If only things could be so straightforward.

"I will admit to you, sir." Theodosia lowered her voice. "I have not seen her so unguarded with a young man before. I hesitate to ask, but has the lieutenant intentions elsewhere?"

"I confess I do not know. You think they are that serious?"

"I cannot say, except that handsome and personable young men of his calibre have rarely come across our path."

Our path. Did she include herself in these estimations?

"It would be best to learn his thoughts toward your niece. She is very young but is not unmarriageable." Her brows rose. "Especially if her guardian approves."

"Her guardian? Oh, I see." He straightened against the cushions. "Such a thought had not occurred to me. She is far too young to hold any lasting interest for him, I should think."

She bit her lip, mottled cheek turned to him as she studied the pair.

"What is it, Miss Stapleton?"

"I . . . I hesitate to mention this, but perhaps it would be best if someone was to hint him away."

"That someone being me?"

"Becky's guardian and the lieutenant's friend, yes. You are best placed, I feel."

"Ah. This was not the topic I had envisaged when you offered to converse before."

"No?" Her head tilted, the questions dancing in her green eyes drawing him in. "And what sort of conversation had you imagined?"

He swallowed. Admit he'd wondered if there was a chance to learn her thoughts about matrimony? To discover her thoughts toward him? Surely a man awarded a medal for valor could be courageous to ask this.

"Aha, whatever conversation you imagined must be most challenging indeed, if you cannot speak of it now. Very well. I shall leave you to your thoughts."

But he didn't want to be left with his thoughts. He wanted to know hers. "Have you—I seem to recall a conversation about this before but cannot remember the whole. I wonder, have you ever . . ."

As he stumbled to a halt, she waited patiently, the little wings of her brows dancing as if in anticipation.

"Forgive me, I express myself so badly. I wonder if you have ever thought about marriage." There! He'd said it. But just as before, her amusement disconcerted.

"Oh, sir, I do not make fun of you, but the question *is* amusing. Rare would be the woman who has never thought of what life would be like if she were married."

"So you have."

"Indeed so." Her gaze strayed from his, to rest on the flickering fire. "But as I think I mentioned before, *thoughts* about matrimony do not equate with wedded bliss. One has to have a gentleman propose, after all."

Her words put him in mind of something she'd shared before about relationships, and God bringing people together. He studied her. His experience with wooing might be at naught, but for all her raillery and cheer, she rarely gave indication of warmer feelings toward him. His stomach clenched. Did that make the question burning in his heart too ridiculous to utter? Would she simply laugh at him? Perhaps it was better to draw back, discretion being the better part of valor, after all. For what could he offer her without being counted as a scoundrel?

"How about you, sir?" she asked, banishing the words he'd tried to formulate.

"Me? No. Never." Until now. Possibly.

Her features stiffened, drained of animation, as she rose. "Excuse me. I must tend the fire."

Theo blinked back tears as she jabbed the poker in and out. This was silly. This was the stuff of fainting misses, of a lass of more tender years. Not how someone of her advanced age should behave. But his words had prodded her heart, like the poker thrust in the fire, stabbing at the emotions until they could not be restrained, as the foolish, silly wisp of hope dwindled quite away.

"Miss Stapleton?" he asked now.

"There," she said, congratulating herself on her steady voice. "I believe that shall be sufficient."

"You have done admirably."

"I have, haven't I?" She dared look at him again, forcing her lips up into a smile. If a man could not overlook her flaws and be conscious of her hard work and talents, then she had no use for him. "I think I shall see how the others are going. I wonder if they might like tea." She replaced the poker, dusted off her hands, and moved away, as standing in his presence, feeling his scrutiny on her, was eating holes in her defenses. No. She must be strong for just a little longer. How soon until they left? Perhaps absence would mend her heart.

"Miss Stapleton—"

She pretended not to hear him, hurrying to the others. "Oh, look, you have almost finished it. Well done, the both of you."

Becky glanced up shyly at the lieutenant. "Lieutenant Musgrave has been telling me about some of the places he has been, and it seems so fascinating."

"I'm sure it does. Perhaps he can continue his tales of travel over tea. I'm sure Mama would be ready to join us too."

"That sounds lovely." Becky glanced up at the lieutenant.

"Wonderful. Well, I shall just go and see where things are up to," Theo said. "You two will be able to manage, especially with Captain Balfour playing chaperone, won't you?"

"Chaperone?" Lieutenant Musgrave said. "I don't think we need a chaperone, Miss Stapleton."

"Don't you?" Her glance fell on Becky's look of surprise. "Forgive me. I'll just be a moment." She hastened from the room, refusing to glance at the captain again. Outside in the passage, she balanced a hand against the wall as she struggled to collect her spinning thoughts. No. She could do this. Just smile and pretend her heart hadn't been touched by one such as he.

One such as he? How galling to know that nobody had truly ruffled her heart until now, and that nobody truly could unless he was known as England's hero. Oh, she might as well be called a wet goose and be done with it!

"Theo?"

Seraphina's concerned voice straightened Theo's spine, affixed a smile to her lips.

"Are you quite all right?"

"Perfectly fine, thank you. I was just coming to find you and see if you'd like tea—"

"Thank you, no. Roger and I plan to visit the village shortly." Seraphina frowned. "Are you sure you are well? You look pale. And your nose is a little red."

"I must be coming down with something," she said, adding quickly, "I shall see about the tea, then perhaps I ought to rest."

It would be a coward's move, but she could surely claim illness. One couldn't be expected to carry on in rude health all her days.

Half an hour later, after Theo's wish to flee had been well and truly impeded by her mother and a sense that one's foolish imagination should really not prevent good manners, she sat opposite the captain in the drawing room, enduring one of the more agonizing moments of her life. She did what she could to promote conversation, to maintain the illusion, but this charade was painful, eating into her heart and composure.

He kept looking at her. What was she to think of that? How could she make him cease? The only way to protect herself was to constantly throw attention onto others.

"So, you plan to return to London," she said to the lieutenant. "And after that, shall you rejoin those at the front?"

He sighed. "One wishes it need not be so, but I fear that will be the case."

"Does your family find that hard?"

"My mother is always disconsolate. Mariah, my younger sister, never wishes to let me go. And I mean that quite literally, as she wraps her arms around me and squeezes, as I imagine a snake might do, from accounts I've heard of from those who have travelled to South America."

Theo shuddered. "I must own that I would never wish to know what it feels like to have a snake squeezing me."

The captain laughed. "Nor I."

She kept her gaze averted, refusing to look at him, and took a careful sip of her tea instead.

"We have sometimes seen adders in the area," Mama said, her gaze on the portrait above the fireplace, "but they seem mostly timid creatures. I had a friend whose poor child was bitten and died, but that was long ago."

Becky inhaled quickly, her fingers at her mouth. "How very sad. Was that near to here?"

"Yes, I believe so. But it was a bite, and there was no squeezing involved, or so I'm given to understand. I should hate to come across a snake that might wish to squeeze one to death." Mama's nose wrinkled as she shivered.

"I should think it most unlikely, ma'am, especially if you are to never leave the country," the captain said kindly.

"Oh no. I could never leave. Why, I don't know if I would want to either. We have very pleasant circumstances here, do we not, Theodosia?"

"Very pleasant." Though that did not rule out a desire to see new places. How could Mama never wish for more?

"And besides, I really could not imagine leaving the poor general, or of course, my darling daughter. Not that I will need to. Theodosia is such a comfort for me, after all." She patted Theo's arm.

Theo wedged up her lips with an iron will, begged her countenance to not betray her.

"Forgive me, madam"—the captain's brows drew together—"but would you not consider moving if, say, the general's or your daughter's circumstances should change?"

"Move where?" Mama asked.

"Why, wherever."

"I see no reason I would want to live elsewhere. Not when we are so comfortable here. Is that not right, my dear?" she asked Theodosia.

"But what if Mr. Bellingham should wish to marry her?" Becky asked. "Would you wish to move then?"

"Thank you, Becky." The captain's expression held sternness. "That will do."

"Oh no, I do not mind answering, sir. If Frederick wished to marry her, then I suppose I could live here. Or there." Mama moved her hands up and down as if weighing items on a scale.

Theo plucked at a loose thread on her gown. *Simply because a man wished to marry did not mean a woman wished to marry him*, she longed to say, but kept such arguments behind her teeth.

"I hesitate to believe a man like Frederick Bellingham would be enough to induce Miss Stapleton to marriage," the captain said.

Her gaze flicked up and met his, and it was as if he could see inside her heart. But no. She couldn't—wouldn't—let him see her pain. Hurt flared into anger. "You cannot know my thoughts."

His mouth fell open.

How glad she was to have flustered him. She had no desire to cause tension, but neither would she let a man charm her, ask her about matrimony, then dare presume she could not know her mind. Such arrogance put her in mind of her grandfather, always presuming he knew what was best for people when he barely took notice of them at all.

"Please accept my apologies." The captain's voice was quiet, his head slightly bowed.

At his look it seemed a bar of cold iron had plunged down inside her chest, into her midsection, and she suddenly hovered dangerously near to tears. After the barest skim of a glance in his direction, she murmured, "Forgive me, I have something of a headache."

"Oh, my dear, should I fetch a powder?" Mama wrung her hands. "I'm sure the doctor would not mind visiting again."

"Thank you, no." She hurried from the room and up the stairs, flicking at the stupid, stubborn tears, before noticing her grandfather standing in his bedchamber door.

"Theo?"

"Oh, Grandfather. I did not see you there. I hope this means that you are feeling better now?"

"Are you well?" He scowled, ignoring her question.

"Oh, 'tis nothing but a headache. I am just going to lie down."

"Hmph."

When it seemed he had no more to say, she begged leave and rushed to her bedchamber. And surrendered to the emotion welling within her for the past hour as her tears finally released.

Chapter 21

Daniel glanced across at his friend and exchanged a silent look as the minister continued on with the sermon. This, his first outing since the accident, had only been enabled by Musgrave's assistance and had been fraught with challenges. Daniel had to work both to maneuver using his new crutch and contrive to avoid the question of his true identity.

Their late arrival due to the carriage's difficulty in traversing heavy mud had forgone some of the inevitable questions, for apart from a few in the know, most people here probably suspected him as some kind of servant. Fortunately, most people would be paying attention to Musgrave and the appearance of Seraphina and her husband, which meant he might slide through the post-service chatter without much talk directed at him.

"And now I must digress for a moment, to speak about some practical applications. In the Bible, God exhorts us to beware the little foxes that can ruin the vineyard." The minister flipped the pages of his Bible. "In other words, beware those little sins that we so easily excuse. Those little darting thoughts we let run free, that we happily ignore thinking they won't matter, the occasional lie here, the envious thought there, the small count of deception there. Beware, for such sins have a way of being found out, and one small fox can soon lead to a ruined vineyard."

Daniel's lips tightened as conviction tensed his stomach. Like a mirror, these verses revealed his all-too-obvious flaws, including the most obvious—his failure to own up to his true identity. *Lord, forgive me. I did not mean things to get quite so out of hand. Please direct my steps and help me put things aright.*

He caught Musgrave's raised brows and offered a wry smile, before returning his attention to the front, relieved to avoid the eye of Miss Stapleton. Her opinion of his cowardice, he did not wish to own.

At the conclusion of the service, he carefully hopped his way outside, his need for Musgrave's assistance making him aware of all the attention being directed at his friend.

The doctor approached, and after a few pertinent questions, pronounced himself happy for Daniel to consider removing to Mannering and to travel further afield—London—in a week's time or so. This news, especially after following a letter from the War Office requesting his attendance in three weeks, once would have brought great joy but now fueled more questions and discontent. For how could he leave when so much remained unresolved?

He nodded to the few men he knew but avoided conversation as he made his slow progression to the carriage.

"Ah, Lieutenant Musgrave! Oh, and Mr. Daniel." A woman's voice carried over the grounds.

Musgrave shot him a quick look, then bowed as the woman drew near. "Lady Bellingham. How good to see you again."

"Oh, sir, before you go, I hoped to introduce you to my husband. Yoo-hoo, Giles!" She waved to a short, wide man of even less hair than what adorned Daniel's head, who swiftly obeyed her summons. There came an exchange of introductions.

Daniel nodded. Just what would the point of all this be?

"Now my dear husband has returned—he had duties in Milfield, you see, and the recent weather has made travel quite the challenge—well, we would be most gratified if you would deign to attend a meal with us," fluttered Lady Bellingham. "If we cannot have the man himself, then it would be good to have one of Captain Balfour's friends."

"I—"

"It will be just a little something. Nothing terribly fancy, only a few courses."

Musgrave cast Daniel a concerned look.

Daniel's eyebrows rose even as his lips flattened.

"I cannot precisely say what my movements will be at this time," Musgrave finally said. "I am sorry."

"Simply name the day. We should be very glad to accommodate you at your convenience. Perhaps this Friday might suffice?"

"Er, much obliged, I'm sure. Thank you for your consideration. Lady Bellingham, did I tell you that my friend here served with us too?" A touch of desperation tinged his words.

"You served at the Peninsular, Mr. Daniel?"

Perhaps he should finally own up. "Yes, ma'am."

"Oh, so you fought with Balfour too!"

"Actually—"

"Well! I thought you just some kind of steward. In that case, Lieutenant, I wish your friend to come as well. If I cannot speak to the great man himself, I suppose it will be somewhat of a substitute to speak to you two."

The inclination to confess frittered away in the light of her condescension. Oh, how great would be her disappointment. But still, his earlier resolve whispered truth be told.

"Lady Bellingham," Daniel began, "I feel that I really must admit—"

"How thankful he is to receive such an invitation." Musgrave smiled wickedly. "You have not received the like for simply an age, have you, my friend?"

"Not since London, that is true. Ma'am, I feel it only fair to say that I am actually—"

"Not partial to seafood," Musgrave said. "So anything of that nature should best be avoided."

Lady Bellingham threw Daniel a puzzled look, which hastened Musgrave to add in a lowered voice, "My friend doesn't like to admit the dramatic effect such things have on his indigestion."

Daniel's jaw dropped, as Lady Bellingham and her husband gazed at him with fascination, as if imagining precisely what dramatic effect would occur should she offer him fish.

"Please excuse us." Daniel departed from the interview before Musgrave could say anything more.

As soon as they were cleared from earshot, he shook his head. "Must you have chosen to speak so?"

"When it became obvious just how little she regards you, well, I was afraid I simply must." Musgrave grinned. "At least this way you may be able to forgo the turtles."

That was something. But still, the ping of conviction from before refused to be silent. "I wished to confess just now, but someone would not permit it."

"I was thinking of what would happen to poor Miss Stapleton should your identity be revealed. This is not exactly the place one would wish to own up to having misled the entire village."

Ah, yes. Of course. He should have realized the same. Perhaps it was just as well he had said nothing now. He supposed he could afford to be patient a little longer.

The Stapleton women drew near.

"Ah, ladies," Daniel said, diverting conversation. "I trust my poor leg has not delayed you."

"I rather think it is the other way around," Miss Stapleton said, before saying that Becky had been invited to dine with the Cleevers, and the Rileys were having luncheon with others, and as such they needn't wait any longer.

Musgrave assisted both ladies into the carriage before turning his attention to Daniel, helping him to ascend and pivot with one heavily strapped leg in the air, then carefully maneuvered inside.

Once they were settled and Robert encouraged to depart, Theodosia gestured to his leg. "I hope such an outing has not proved deleterious to your recovery, sir."

"Thank you. I rather hope for that too."

Her dimples flashed, and his heart knew a corresponding throb as he studied the graceful lines of her face.

"Did I hear talk of an invitation to the Bellinghams?" Mrs. Stapleton asked.

"Yes, ma'am," Musgrave said.

"Elvira has always liked to be first in invitations."

"The first in invitations means one can claim the first in consequence," Theodosia murmured, eyes fixed on the scenery outside.

"My dear, it is not charitable to say such things," Mrs. Stapleton protested.

"Forgive me." Her daughter's gaze returned to Daniel and his friend. "I trust you will enjoy yourself. You need not fear that she has any daughters of marriageable age she will wish to foist onto you."

"I am most relieved to hear you say so." Musgrave shuddered, as if terrified.

"But that is not to say that she won't invite other eligible young ladies to such a party." Mrs. Stapleton rearranged her skirts. "Dear Elvira has always appreciated opportunities to matchmake, whether at a dinner or a ball. Why, one would think her daughter Amelia—just a year or so older than Seraphina—would never have met nor married Mr. Edwards without her plans and ploys. I dare say she likes to think she had a hand in Seraphina's match too."

Her daughter stiffened. "That was all Seraphina's doing."

"Yes, I'm afraid that's true. Seraphina has always had a way of getting what she wants without requiring the assistance of others." Mrs. Stapleton's sigh turned into a smile. "Perhaps it is as well Elvira does not yet know your identity, sir. You would be inundated with such invitations."

"Precisely the reason I am determined to leave as soon as can be, as soon as this blessed leg of mine is mended."

Theodosia's lips thinned. The briefest flash of what looked like dismay smoothed into blandness as her gaze touched his before returning to the window.

His heart caught. Was she dismayed? Or was that his wishful thinking?

"And how long do you think until you leave for London?" Mrs. Stapleton asked.

"A week or so, according to Dr. Linton."

"Does Becky know?" Theodosia's gaze remained averted.

"I will speak to her about it upon her return."

Daniel glanced at Musgrave and, conscious of what had happened back at the church, ventured, "Perhaps we might see where Mannering is up to, and whether it would be possible to remove there for the remainder of our stay."

"Oh, but sir, it would barely be worth the bother," Mrs. Stapleton countered. "And I'm sure you would be far more comfortable at Stapleton Court than in a house still shoring up its foundations."

"Yes indeed, Balfour," Musgrave said, with a slight frown. "I fail to see why you should think such a thing is necessary."

He glanced at Theodosia. Still she offered no protest. "I am sure I have long outstayed my welcome, and now Mr. and Mrs. Riley are here, I should not like to feel I am in the way."

"No, indeed you are not," Mrs. Stapleton objected. "Your company has proved most interesting."

"Thank you, ma'am. But neither should I like anyone's reputation to be compromised by our stay there."

She glanced at her daughter, whose gaze remained fixed on the scenery, even as they entered the gates of Stapleton Court. "Well, I applaud your noble intentions, but I hardly think it can make much difference now."

But it did. And the fact that Theodosia refused to look at him made him wonder if he'd misjudged her and confirmed the fact that she neither felt interest in him nor concern about what their continued stay might mean for her reputation as a lady.

Still, he would not be swayed. A removal to Mannering would mean they would be quite out of harm's way.

Later, when he'd been helped back into his room, where he could finally relax and prop his leg up, not wishing to admit to just how much it ached, he looked at Musgrave. "I'm sorry that moving to Mannering likely won't be as pleasant as here."

"I'm sure." Musgrave offered a searching look.

"What is it? You look rather odd."

"I find it most interesting."

"What?"

"The fact Miss Stapleton knows who you are but makes no push for you to stay."

"Why should she?" he asked as nonchalantly as he could, while his heart burned to hear a rebuttal.

"I just thought . . ."

"Thought what?"

"Oh, never mind. So when would you wish to move to Mannering?"

"As soon as the builders permit it. I shall speak with them tomorrow and determine things, so we can return as soon as possible after that."

For besides not wishing to impair Theodosia's reputation and feeling he had long outstayed his welcome, her lack of response reinforced her lack of interest. With so little encouragement, he was not about to uproot his life's work and career for a young lady who cared not whether he left or stayed.

⁙

He was leaving. The day had been settled, after visits from Mannering's chief builder and begrudging assent from the doctor. Captain Balfour and Lieutenant Musgrave were leaving Stapleton Court tomorrow. Becky had been informed by her uncle of the fact last night, and it seemed her exodus to London would occur the following week, should the captain's leg have healed sufficiently to travel and the weather prove conducive.

Theo drew the curtain aside. A sparrow twittered in the nearby apple tree as it added twigs to rebuild its nest. She'd seen the pale speckled eggs that suggested she'd soon hear the little chirps of tiny birds as they begged for food.

She stroked Maisie, and the cat released a contented humming purr. She'd need to secure the window to ensure the curious feline did not venture outside to harm the little family. She had no wish to see a repeat of last year when Maisie had disrupted a starling's nest, scaring the birds so that the eggs that fell and smashed on the ground remained unhatched, the little lives within never to breathe.

She felt like that. Perhaps it was ungrateful to say so, but she sometimes wondered if her life had stalled. Was she trapped inside this sphere and destined to die without ever having really lived? Was that self-pitying? Her lips quirked, but with no corresponding lift to her heart.

He was leaving. She was staying. And that was that.

Perhaps it was good the captain would leave. Then she wouldn't have to be in this constant state of greedy anticipation to hear his voice, to smell his enticing scent, to see him, to yearn for his smile.

He would leave. She would be sad but then would recover, and that would be all. She had no place in letting the little foxes of ingratitude burrow into her heart. No place.

"But Lord," she whispered, forehead against the window glass, "if You have more for me in this life, then please somehow make it so. And if You do not, then please help me be content. I do not wish to live with this constant seesaw of emotion anymore."

She hoped she had hidden it well. She'd been proud of herself on Sunday when the captain had first mooted the idea of leaving. She'd even managed to convince Mama that his departure would mean nothing to her and expressed gladness that at least it would mean an end to Grandfather's constant sniping about the ingratiating ways of those completely unrelated to them. Mama had been only too happy to agree, and further gentle steering along this path seemed to help Mama forget her original question about the state of Theo's heart.

But to say her heart had been untouched would be a lie. The captain's presence had brought a joy unlike any she'd known before, and she was loath to say goodbye.

She drew in a deep breath, released it. Squared her shoulders and moved downstairs.

"Good morning," Becky greeted Theo as she reached the breakfast room.

There was no sign of Theo's sister and brother-in-law, which released a knot within. She did not want this last day spoiled with complaining and inhospitable comments that expressed her sister's relief at the men's departure. Theo nodded to the gentlemen, taking care to not look at the captain, and moved to seat herself away from him, at the other end of the table, next to Becky.

"How did you sleep?" she asked their youngest guest.

Becky sighed. "Not too well."

"I suppose you were thinking on your going-away," Lieutenant Musgrave said, his face full of sympathy.

"I will miss my friends," Becky said, voice wobbling.

"You will be missed," Theo assured her, with a gentle pat on Becky's arm. But Theo's eyes refused to do what her mind commanded and glanced across in response to the weight of the captain's gaze.

One brow lifted, as if he wished to know if his niece would be the only person whose absence Theo would note.

Such foolishness. She dropped her gaze. Concentrated on her food.

"Well, we are a somber little crowd, are we not?" cried the lieutenant. "We must see what we can do to enliven our last day here."

"Indeed we must," agreed Theo. "What would you suggest?"

"I'm afraid Balfour here still cannot ride, otherwise I would suggest that. Same goes for a picnic, for I fear that would be too much of a strain on his leg."

"Are you to only make suggestions for what I cannot do?" complained the captain good-naturedly.

"What would you wish to do?" she finally asked him, her gaze meeting his, then immediately veering away as her heart gave a tiny, foolish skip. It was only right that she be polite to him, she told herself. Be *polite*. He'd made it clear he wished for nothing more. She forced her attention to return.

"I would wish to enjoy some conversation." His gaze rested on her. "But I fear that those whom I wish to converse with may not wish the same."

No. *No.* He meant nothing by that. Nothing at all.

"Have you spoken to the general?" Becky asked.

His lips pushed to one side, and he shifted focus to his niece. "I will speak to him again before we leave."

"It's a shame you have that dinner at Lady Bellingham's on Friday night," Becky said. "Otherwise—oh! Theo, do you think it might be at all possible for—"

"For a dinner to be held here before your departure? Of course."

"Oh, thank you. I know it seems most presumptuous for me to ask."

"Most presumptuous," Theo teased.

Becky smiled. "But it would be nice to see my friends again."

"I'm sure it would. I will speak to Mother about it this morning." She dared to glance in the captain's general direction again. "Have you decided upon a day to quit the area, sir?"

He nodded. "I received word that I am to present myself to White-hall, and thus must soon return to London. Now my leg is nearly better, I thought next Monday should suffice."

"Monday?" Becky's exclamation echoed the dismay within Theo's heart.

She tamped it down, concentrated on her young guest. "We shall have your dinner on Saturday night, then."

"Thank you," Becky said, tone flat.

Theo knew her lack of enthusiasm stemmed from disappointment about departing so soon, which was reiterated when Becky gave an audible sigh.

The captain lifted both hands as if in surrender. "I know you have no wish to leave, but I assure you that London won't be nearly as dull as you seem to fear."

"I don't think it will be dull," Becky countered. "But it will be dull to not have anyone to share such experiences."

Theo patted her arm but said nothing. That was indeed the point. For what was the point of having grand adventures if there was no one to share such adventures with?

She kept her gaze on her hard-boiled eggs, which reminded her of the nest from earlier, of the broken eggs of yesteryear, whose promise of life had never been fulfilled.

Her heart sorrowed. Was her future destined to remain as lifeless as it had felt before the captain came?

Chapter 22

Sometimes Daniel wished the rest of life could be as straightforward as life within the army. Admittedly, not everything within the military was easy. But it was a blessed sight more so than expecting builders to follow simple instructions, let alone other, more personal matters.

He shoved a piece of veal into his mouth and chewed slowly, as much to aid digestion as to avoid unwanted conversation at the Bellingham's dining table. Military life was also so much easier than this silent expectation that he would know the intricacies of social mores and solecisms, where so many did not say what they truly meant. How he wished he could simply bowl up to a young lady and ask if she wished to further their acquaintance, whether she could see fit to tie her life to his. But such direct speech was not at all the thing, which left him in this muddle of politenesses that never really meant anything.

He was a fool to think on this. He needed to think on his career, on life in London and beyond. But another part of him still questioned if that was enough to satisfy, if perhaps his life was meant for more. A question Lady Bellingham seemed most determined to pursue, at least as far as things went with Musgrave.

The dinner seemed to take an interminable amount of time, all of which he spent ruing that first impulse that had bade him to disguise his identity. Guilt wove with fresh regrets as Lady Bellingham—and her guests—peppered Musgrave with questions about their time at war, occasionally flinging Daniel a question, like one might throw a dog a bone.

He determined to enjoy the meal, and he strove to be polite, but the constant talking about "Balfour" only increased the agitation inside. Musgrave seemed to pick up on this, seemed to take joy in sharing stories that featured himself as the hero, making Daniel fast regret the invitation for his friend to visit.

"And then there was the time he was faced with an enemy cannon, and he simply disregarded it and rode his horse straight at it!"

"No!" gasped the table of diners.

"Yes, indeed." Musgrave tossed Daniel a sly glance. "That was how things went, was it not?"

"Something like that," he muttered, eyeing his friend narrowly. Although perhaps the term *friend* was not justified right now.

"You were there too?" Mrs. Cleever asked.

He was going to have to admit it. He glanced at Mr. Cleever, seated at the other end of the table, who studied him with a frown. Yes, it was time. He hated how such an admission would impact upon the Stapletons, but this farce had gone on long enough. "I was, yes."

Musgrave threw back another glass of wine. "He was there each time Captain Balfour was."

"Indeed?" Lady Bellingham said. "Why did we not know this?"

"Forgive me, ma'am," Daniel said, "but—"

"Cap'n Balfour was there each time because . . . because . . ."

Daniel frowned at Musgrave, but he seemed not to pay heed, lifting his refilled glass.

"Because Captain Balfour *is* he."

The words lingered in the air, directing each face to look at Daniel.

Wonderful. This was not how he wished to speak. But his lie needed confession, needed forgiveness, it weighed so heavily on his heart. He swallowed. Cleared his throat. And finally declared, "It is true, I am Captain Balfour."

"Captain Balfour's steward," Lady Bellingham said, with a frown.

"No. I am Captain Daniel Balfour."

She blinked. "Mister, er, Daniel?"

"Mr. Daniel Balfour, if you prefer not to use my military title."

"But . . . but you do not look like he!"

He raised a brow. "How is he supposed to look?"

As she sputtered and grew pink, he realized the sheer ridiculousness of referring to himself in such a way.

"He cannot help his appearance, ma'am," Musgrave said, as if he was trying to be helpful.

She shook her head, wide eyes fixed on him. "But you said—Miss Stapleton said that you are, that you were—"

"I am Rebecca Mannering's uncle. Clara was my sister. I am very sorry for my deception, but I wished to visit my niece without the fuss and bustle we were subject to in London."

Lady Bellingham gaped at him. "You mean all this time Theodosia Stapleton knew you were Captain Balfour?"

"Well, perhaps not right at the first second."

This was met with a round of gasps and mutters that made his heart sore for poor Theo.

"You, sir, are hardly a gentleman," Frederick muttered.

"And Miss Stapleton is hardly a lady," murmured Mrs. Cleever, her eyes like a cat's. Any moment he expected her to slash her clawlike hands.

"This is most untoward." The squire frowned.

"You have been laughing at us all this time!" his wife added.

Daniel sighed, regret kneading his chest. "I truly am most sorry for the upset I have caused."

"I cannot believe that girl," Mrs. Cleever said. "Always acting so sweet and kind, when really she is no better than a liar."

"I must beg your pardon, but Miss Stapleton was simply following my request. To tell you the truth—"

"Finally." Young Bellingham scowled at him as if he were a cockroach.

"When I was first in the area, I had no inclination for any frivolities. I arrived to learn my only sister had just died," he reminded them. "To have been forced into parties and entertainments would have been neither appropriate nor welcome, and I was very thankful to find what respite I could at Stapleton Court."

Mrs. Cleever sniffed, her eyes tapering further, and he wondered if she might soon hiss.

"Then, when I met with an unfortunate accident at Mannering, I was again able to find help at Stapleton Court, for which I have been immensely thankful for both their generous hospitality and their good intentions to keep my secret."

"But they should have said something!" Lady Bellingham protested. "This is most unbecoming of you. And them."

"Madam," he addressed his hostess, "forgive me, but on our first encounter you were not exactly inclined to believe myself as anything but a servant."

"Because you did not present yourself as anything but one." Her eyes narrowed. "Did you or did you not tell me Captain Balfour was tall and fair?"

He bowed his dark head. "We—I—may have allowed you to believe such a thing, for which I am sorry."

"So you were in cahoots with Miss Stapleton," snapped Mrs. Cleever. "All this time she has known and said nothing."

"She, and the general and Mrs. Stapleton. Oh, and the minister, the doctor, and Mr. Cleever. All sworn to secrecy." He dared not look at the man seated next to his hostess at the far end of the table.

"Mr. Cleever knew?" the solicitor's wife cried, turning to her husband. "And you didn't tell me?" Her voice pitched up into a shriek.

"My dear, it was not my secret to share," Mr. Cleever protested.

"Because it was mine," Daniel said. "I am sorry, and I beg your forgiveness." He glanced around the table. "For forgiveness from you all."

"Indeed you should!"

"Most cavalier behavior!"

"Hardly the act of one thought to be England's hero."

He gathered most did not regard him as such anymore.

He was about to repeat his apologies when the cleared throat of the squire came from the head of the table.

"Upon reflection, I do not see why you should all take this as a personal affront, especially now when the young man has explained his reasons."

"Sir Giles, don't tell me that you knew about this too?" exclaimed his wife.

"I did not. But I can understand his reasoning, and while I don't agree with his methods, I can see why he felt the need for this masquerade."

Daniel glanced at Musgrave, whose face now wore a look of shame. "Perhaps it would be better if we leave—"

"You cannot depart now!" Lady Bellingham said. "Not after all this obfuscation. No, you may *not* leave."

Sir Giles shook his head. "My dear, you cannot force the man to stay."

"By all that is right, I surely can! When I have wished for nothing more than to meet him, and this is how I've been repaid."

"My dear—"

"Such prevarication is not my idea of gentlemanly behavior," the squire's son said with a lifted nose.

"Indeed no," said Mrs. Cleever.

"I imagine it was you who coerced poor Miss Stapleton into your schemes," young Bellingham scoffed.

"The blame is mine." No good would come of admitting she had agreed. Poor Theo. He physically ached to think that his actions would hurt her.

"Scandalous," muttered Mrs. Cleever. "Unprincipled."

"It would appear that some of you are more concerned that you were not first with the news, rather than applauding this young man's brave deeds." The squire sent his wife and her crony a frown. "I should not like to think my actions to protect my family should be so readily dismissed simply because one has a desire to gossip."

"Sir Giles!" Mrs. Cleever exclaimed.

"Husband, that is not necessary—"

Daniel grasped the side of the table and awkwardly pushed to his feet. The conversation stilled, and he glanced around the table, forcing himself to meet each pair of eyes. "I beg your pardon, but it appears that my presence here is not conducive to harmony. I would ask that you would please excuse me. I plan to quit the neighborhood very soon and take Miss Mannering back to London. I am deeply sorry that my actions have led to distress and upset, but I hope I may be forgiven, given that it was made from an impulse to save my niece from unnecessary grief and speculation."

Musgrave rose too. "Thank you, ma'am, for a delicious meal. I must take my leave also. Good night."

A half hour later they were back in Mannering's cold rooms, the small fire Musgrave had lit doing little to take the chill off the air.

"Balfour, please, accept my apologies. I did not mean—"

"Enough. It is done. Something I should have done long ago."

"But—"

"No more, please." Daniel held up a weary hand, his heart too sore, his mind too full of regrets and uncertainties, leaving him no capacity for conversation beyond desultory nothings, comments about the weather, the road, the upcoming trip.

Daniel knew he would need to speak to Theo on the morrow, to somehow warn her and explain what had happened. But while the thought of seeing her would normally boost his spirits, this was one interview which filled him with dread.

Theo paused on the stairs, her ears pricked for the conversation emanating from the drawing room. A restless night had led to a strange sleep that had only been broken by the sound of a horse cantering away, followed not long after by a carriage's arrival. Hettie's disclosure that the departure was Miss Mannering, who had gone for her morning ride, was not unusual. But to have a carriage pull up at such an hour had prompted her dismissal of the maid and determination to learn what had brought its occupants here so early.

She pushed open the drawing room door and was met with five faces: three Bellinghams, Mama, and the general. Oh dear. Whatever this was must be extremely serious, but at least this interview could be conducted without her sister's presence. She curtsied, offered her greetings, then shifted Maisie to take the seat next to her grandfather as he gestured for her to do.

"Theodosia," he said now, "we have been visited so early this morning by people who wish to know the truth of your conduct."

She blinked. "I beg your pardon?"

"Is it true, Miss Stapleton, that you knew Captain Balfour was indeed staying here?" Lady Bellingham asked.

Theo's stomach clenched and she glanced at her mother, who seemed on the verge of tears. Theo sank lower in her chair. How best to proceed? Admit in part, or in all? "May I enquire what has happened?"

"At our dinner last night, Captain Balfour admitted his true identity!" Lady Bellingham sniffed. "You can no doubt imagine my upset when I learned that you had known all this time."

"He said that you knew." Frederick spit the words. "Did you help hide him here, knowing full well who he was?"

"Well, I certainly wouldn't be so foolhardy as to hide someone without knowing who they were," she murmured.

"Have you lost all sense of propriety?" demanded Frederick. "I cannot believe—"

"That is enough," his father said, voice sharp as a knife.

"Indeed," growled Grandfather. "Who are you to preach to my granddaughter about propriety?"

"Sir, I really must protest—"

"That's enough, Elvira," the squire said. "Let the girl speak."

Theo straightened, rested her hands in her lap, her feet to one side, her gaze lowered, the perfect model of submissive womanhood. "I suspected it might be him from the first moment we met. You may recall, Lady Bellingham, that you seemed inclined to ignore him and were very quick to believe a hero to look other than the man did."

"Oh, that is most unjust! Most unkind!"

"I should rather think it unkind to believe a hero must be disposed to look a certain way. I cannot imagine such comments made it easy for him to wish to make himself known to you."

"You blame me for this?" the squire's wife demanded.

"I gather it was rather the idea of being forced to partake in yet another turtle dinner that he objected to."

"He could have simply said!"

"Perhaps." Theo studied the worn carpet.

"Goodness, I did not need to have a turtle dinner," Lady Bellingham said plaintively. "Although I can quite understand it now, seeing as he's apparently allergic to seafood."

"But he always seemed to enjoy Annie's way with salmon," Mama said uncertainly.

"Hmph. It seems the young man is quite adept in deception and ingratiating himself with people. No doubt he would benefit from a greater degree of forthrightness," declared Lady Bellingham.

"Perhaps. Or perhaps he just wished to deal with the grief of learning he had lost his sister." Theo kept her voice even and calm. "I would not imagine many men, no matter how heroic they may be, would be so quick to engage in the kinds of entertainments so many seemed keen to foist on him. To wish to do so at such a time would be quite rightly labeled insensitive and ungentlemanly."

"But my dear, that was at the start. Did you not think it behooved you to own the truth later?"

"No," Theo said bluntly. "I did not think such people here would be offended to the degree they seemed to have been."

Lady Bellingham gasped. "My dear girl!"

Theo's hands trembled, so she tightly clasped her fingers on her lap. "I am sorry that you are upset, but I cannot be sorry that Rebecca was spared some of the speculation and gossip that was inevitable once the captain's whereabouts were publicized."

"Too many gossips," growled the general. "Too much fuss and botheration. People never used to fuss like this back in my day."

The color rose in Lady Bellingham's face, and soon a long exposé of the many outrages the general had inflicted on dear Letitia began, which included the sequestering of poor Theodosia up here for so long without society, without a chance to meet a gentleman to wed.

"But Mama," protested Frederick, "I am, I mean, I was most happy to pursue—"

"Oh, be quiet, son," she snapped. "You and she would never have suited. As this shambles of a situation has proven."

"You mind your tongue about my granddaughter, hear?" Grandfather said.

"Dear Elvira, please," Mama said in a wavering tone, her handkerchief forever at the ready. "You may be sure Theodosia never intended for anyone to be hurt. Quite the contrary, in fact."

The broken note in her mother's voice shafted fresh pain through Theo's heart. She clenched her hands. What wretchedness she had created for her poor Mama. "Lady Bellingham." Theo carefully modulated her voice to avoid the inclination to quaver. "I must beg your pardon if my actions have upset you. I am sorry. Please forgive me."

"Then let there be no more said about it then." Lady Bellingham's tone grew soft and sincere. "If you are prepared to ask forgiveness, then I am prepared to forgive. Now, I think it only fair to warn you that you may well expect to see something of a cold shoulder from some inhabitants in our village who are not so kindly minded as I am. And I certainly don't think you should expect to see many visitors here tonight."

For poor Becky's farewell dinner. Theo's heart clenched.

"I trust you will be able to cling to your principles from now on."

"Thank you, ma'am," Theo said woodenly.

"Well, if that is all, I suppose we shall make our departure," the squire said.

They rose, just as a tap on the door preceded Mr. Siddons.

"What is it?" Grandfather barked.

"Ahem." He glanced significantly at the guests.

"Out with it, man."

"It is the, er, captain, sir. Captain Balfour."

Oh no.

"He desires a word with you all."

Lady Bellingham promptly sat down, as her husband began a fruitless request for them to effect their departure.

"No." She sat upon her dignity as much as if she were the Queen. "I have every intention of staying to hear how this man can attempt to justify himself."

"You do not need to," the squire hissed. "You heard enough from him yesterday."

Theo's heart caught. The poor man, admitting the truth in front of the village notables, taking the brunt of the attack in her absence. How thankful she was for him. But it was no wonder the Bellinghams had visited the Stapleton household so early to learn more.

"Send the man in." The general glared at the Bellingham family. "And you can escort these ones out."

"Oh, but sir—"

"You, madam, are the most meddlesome, interfering person of my acquaintance. Be gone from here, before I tell your husband to drag you out."

"Oh, I never!"

Tears pricked Theo's eyes at the protests, the cries, the noise. Oh, how had a little subterfuge descended into such chaos, where words were being spoken that would likely prove impossible to forget? Regret kneaded her heart, her confession and repentance only going a small way to absolving the guilt staining her soul.

Theo clasped her hands in her lap, barely raising her eyes as they exited, only too conscious of the man who waited on the other side of the door.

Captain Daniel Balfour.

Chapter 23

Daniel rose unsteadily from his perch on the hall's wooden chair, taking care to balance on his crutch and yet not appear weak as the Bellinghams appeared. Some might call him brave, but the expressions on their faces made him wish he had not forgone Musgrave's offer to accompany him inside this morning. Daniel had requested the lieutenant instead remain by the stables, where the intrepid horseman would doubtless be entertained. For this mess was not of Musgrave's making, nor was it his responsibility to supply the remedy.

"You!" the squire's wife exclaimed, before her husband grabbed her arm and led her forcibly away.

Frederick eyed him with disdain, before hissing, "You are responsible for this."

Daniel's jaw clenched. Undoubtedly, he was, whatever this new fracas was, but he'd apologized enough yesterday that he wasn't going to do more today. Not to this young whippersnapper, anyway.

"I would blacken your eye if you weren't injured." Young Bellingham's eyes blazed, as if he thought he actually would. "How could you take advantage of someone like her?"

Daniel did not engage, willing his face to impassivity, and was relieved when the young man's father snapped at him to attend them now.

"You may enter," Mr. Siddons intoned, but with a hint of pity in his eye.

Inside the drawing room he was met with the three Stapletons, but fortunately, not his niece nor the Rileys.

"Ah, the man himself." The general's eyes and voice seemed to be made of flint.

Daniel made his bows and good mornings and glanced at the youngest member of the trio.

She did not return his gaze.

His heart twisted a little more. "I thought my visit was unconscionably early, but it appears I am not the first to visit this day."

"Indeed you are not," grumbled the general.

"I have reason to believe the Bellinghams have forestalled my wish to be the first to share what happened last night, and for that I am sorry. Truly, I beg your forgiveness for what proved to be an ugly situation, and for what I fear will have further consequences."

"Further consequences?" Mrs. Stapleton's eyes darted to her daughter and back. "I don't under—"

The door flung open, and Seraphina entered, followed by the slinking form of her husband.

No. This was not what he wished.

"We heard raised voices," Seraphina said, eyes alight and predatory.

"My dear," her mother protested, "we are in the midst of a private conversation."

"You do not wish me to be here?"

No, he longed to say, but knew no concession would be made for him. He glanced at Theodosia.

Her lips had thinned. Hmm, she never looked at her sister's husband, nor he at her. What *was* their connection?

"Well?" Seraphina propped her hand on her hip, brow crooked. "If there is private conversation, it's because my sister here has never liked me to be part of things." Her gaze fixed on Theodosia. "You have always thought yourself better than me."

"That is not true," she said in a low voice.

"Nevertheless, I'm not leaving. When I enquired of Siddons, he said the Bellinghams were here and most upset about something you had done. And I think as your sister that it's only right and just that I should know of what it is."

"This does not concern you," Theodosia answered. "It is my fault, and not your concern, as it will not affect you at all."

Daniel drew himself up and was about to intervene, when Seraphina laughed. "Your fault? I did not think the great and virtuous Theodosia ever committed a sin. I would dearly love to know what you did wrong. It may give hope for the rest of us mere mortals."

"Mrs. Riley," Daniel's voice burst out. "Your sister has done nothing wrong. The fault is all mine."

"Yours?" She glanced at him, then at her sister, gaze sharp and calculating. Then her eyes enlarged. "Don't tell me you have been forced to offer for her hand! Oh, I knew that all the times she spent in your room smacked of impropriety, but never did I imagine—"

"That is enough!" the general roared. "Sit down! You are making a fool of yourself with your stupid carrying-on. You too," he muttered to the man standing near the window.

A quick glance at Theodosia revealed that she was very pale, her gaze fixed on the floor, motionless, as the cat wove between her legs.

"Oh, my dear girl," Mrs. Stapleton's voice wobbled with the tears shining in her eyes. "I cannot believe you would think such a thing about our dear Theo. She would never be so improper—"

"Your sister has done nothing wrong," the general snapped, "and you should be ashamed of yourself for even thinking such a thing, let alone having the temerity to suggest it."

"Forgive me, sister," Seraphina said with a most unrepentant smirk. "I should have realized that even you were not so desperate as to take up with a servant."

This last was said with a scathing look that made Daniel's blood boil. But another glance at Theodosia's pale cheeks and trembling fingers and his anger found a new cause. "How dare you disparage your sister in such a way?"

Seraphina blinked. "I beg your pardon?"

"Your sister has been the epitome of goodness, which you freely take advantage of, coming here without notice because you have nowhere else to be."

Seraphina's breath drew in. "How dare you speak to me so?"

He glanced at the general, who watched him with lowered brow. No help seemed to come from there. Mrs. Stapleton, too, seemed at a loss, her mouth parted softly.

"I will take full responsibility for what has transpired, which is certainly not what you dared suggest." He returned his attention to the general. "I am sorry, sir. Mrs. Stapleton, I truly had no wish for my subterfuge to cause so much pain."

"Subterfuge?" Seraphina said.

Theodosia raised her chin. "Mr. Daniel is really Captain Daniel Balfour."

"Who?" Seraphina asked.

"Captain Daniel Balfour," Daniel finally owned.

Mr. Riley drew closer to the group. "Weren't you involved in some action in the war?"

Why was the man finally addressing him, after ignoring him these weeks until now? "Yes."

"Oh!" Seraphina eyed him doubtfully, then shrugged. "That is all well and good, but it still doesn't explain what has happened."

"The captain last night admitted to his real name." Theodosia said in a low voice, crossing her hands on her lap. "The Bellinghams were most upset and felt themselves duped and came this morning to say so. They blame me, which is only fair, as I had advised him to keep incognito. I knew that if he did admit to his true identity, he would be inundated with invitations he had no desire for." Her gaze finally shifted to him. "That is the sum of it, yes?"

"Yes. Please, Miss Stapleton, I never meant for you to be caught in the midst of this."

"You cannot blame yourself. It was my suggestion." Her gaze faltered, fell.

"Theodosia lying?" her sister said incredulously. "Will wonders never cease?"

"That's enough from you," her grandfather snapped. "Your sister is sorry, and the captain here is sorry. It seems we have a lot of regret here today."

"Well, I can't say that I do." Seraphina tossed a plump curl over one ear.

"You should," the general huffed. "Coming here without notice, never apologizing for the way you spoke about your sister all those years ago. You have behaved abominably."

Theodosia glanced at her grandfather. "It is forgotten, sir."

"Not by me, it ain't. You"—he stabbed a finger at his younger granddaughter—"will never have the right to sit in judgment on your sister. I heard what you said about her—"

"Grandfather." Theo's cheeks pinked. "Please don't—"

"—and the only reason I said nothing at the time was because I hoped someone as vain as you would get your comeuppance by marrying someone like him." This last was emphasized with a finger at Roger Riley.

"I don't know what you mean." But Seraphina's careless smile and voice held doubt.

"I shall not repeat it here, but let it be enough for you to know you best tread carefully with me."

"I repeat that I do not know what you mean and suspect my dear sister has poisoned you against me. But then, she always has been jealous of me."

Theodosia rose. "I have little wish to hear what else my sister has to say."

"Yes, run away. Go pretend to be virtuous and dutiful. Always the dutiful daughter, aren't you?" Seraphina scoffed.

"One of us had to be."

Theo's insides seemed about ready to perforate her skin with rage. How could her sister berate her—in front of the captain no less? If Theo did not leave, she would say things she would quite likely regret.

"Excuse me." Without looking at anyone else, ignoring her mother's soft plea, she hurried outside to where the friendly cluck of chickens suggested they expected her to feed them, as was her usual chore.

Her usual chore. Her usual duties. The dutiful daughter.

Her hands clenched. Is that how others saw her?

Tears pricked. "I'm sorry, ladies," her voice held a quaver, "but I have nothing for you today."

Nothing to offer. Nothing to give. No one to care about, save for those who depended on her. The dutiful daughter.

She didn't resent this life. She *didn't*. But oh, how she would like the chance to see a little more of the world, to know more than this village that now seemed to despise her, this village that would lay the blame of culpability on her far more quickly than impugn the captain. Blame the woman, excuse the man, that was the way of things here. Not for nothing had she lived here all her life and heard their gossip all her days.

She drew in a shuddery breath. She would not cry. She was braver than this, though her emotions felt as settled as a summer storm.

A footstep crunched on gravel behind her. Oh, she hoped it wasn't the captain. She hoped she would never have to attempt to explain—

She turned. Seraphina. Looking anything but repentant.

"So, here you are." Her sister's eyes narrowed.

"Here I am."

"I will never understand you."

Theo closed the gate to the chicken coop and carefully latched it. "The feeling is quite mutual, I assure you."

"How dare you speak to Grandfather about what you think you heard?"

"About how you called me bran-faced? About how you mocked my skin?" She pointed to her cheek. "I did not need to tell him. You said it often enough that even his aged ears heard you."

Was that a trace of remorse? "That wasn't what he spoke of."

"No? Then I don't know what he refers to."

Her sister's gaze grew piercing, before she glanced away. "You thought I stole Roger from you."

Breath hitched. Dear heavens, she hoped Grandfather had not said that in there.

"I didn't steal him," Seraphina insisted. "Roger never liked you. He never cared for you that way. You know that, don't you?"

"Thank you for making it very plain."

Seraphina sighed. "It doesn't help that you've always been jealous of me. I can't help if I was born with blonde hair and not red. I can't help it if my skin was clear and not marked. And it wasn't my fault that I managed to marry and move away."

"And you always did so well at refraining from pointing out such things to me," Theo said ironically.

"I know you have never appreciated my plain speaking, but I do not say these things because I wish for acrimony between us."

"No? How do you like to justify yourself, then?"

"See? This is what you always do. You always blame me. It is hardly the act of a good Christian."

Theo found a laugh. "You're right. I wish I was a better Christian. If I was, then maybe I would have learned how to forget your many rudenesses by now. But I can't. I may have forgiven you, or maybe I haven't because I cannot seem to forget, because every time I see you, you spout more, and it just brings it all back."

"You talk to me about rudenesses? I—"

"I will speak to you about rudenesses," Theo ruthlessly cut her off. "Like your utter disregard for others. Your constant focus on yourself. When was the last time you wrote to poor Mama and asked about her? Have you even asked about her health while you've been here?"

"Of course, I—"

"Have you given heed to Grandfather, or is he just the old man in whose house you stay? Have you even bothered to have a conversation with him while you've been here? Why *are* you even here? Doesn't your husband have employment anymore? What about your house, Seraphina? When will you move back there?"

Her sister's cheeks flushed to a most unbecoming bright pink. "I do not answer to you."

"No." The new voice spun them both to see their grandfather. "But you will answer to me." The general's eyes sparked dangerously. "I wish to know the truth."

Seraphina ground her teeth.

"I heard you years ago, when you boasted to your friend about how you were so glad to leave this area, laughing at us, laughing at your sister there. You disgusted me, and I was never so glad as when you left."

Seraphina's mouth fell open.

"And now you are back, making trouble again, and I want answers to Theo's questions. Why are you here? What has happened to your house?"

Seraphina paled and shook her head.

"No? Well, if you will not do me the courtesy of an answer, then I will not do you the courtesy of providing a place for you to live anymore."

"Oh, but Grandfather! You cannot mean it."

"I can."

"Oh, but please—"

"Is that it? Nothing else to say? Well, I'm sure you remember where the White Hare is."

"The White Hare? We cannot go there."

"I'm sure their rooms are adequate."

"But everyone will wonder why we're there and not here."

"That might be so. And if anyone has the boldness to ask you, then perhaps you'll feel inclined to tell them what you refuse to tell me."

"Oh, sir, please. Do not make us leave."

"Why not?"

She swallowed. Glanced at Theo. Swallowed again. "We have nowhere else to go," she finally whispered.

"I beg your pardon, child? Speak up."

"My . . . my husband. He lost all our money in a series of bad investments. He, we . . ." She glanced at Theo. "Francis Mannering advised him, and Roger, well, he complied. But then we lost it. Roger, he . . . we lost the house. We have nothing. We need to stay here, as we'd have no money to pay even for the White Hare."

"Roger lost your money?" Grandfather's eyes narrowed. "What about your savings?"

"I . . ." She glanced at Theo again. "I have been a little careless."

"Caring more for appearances than for your future, is that it, hey?" Grandfather sneered.

"I did not realize how bad things had become," Seraphina confessed.

"And I couldn't return things when Roger told me, and now we have nothing." Her bottom lip wobbled.

For the first time in years, the icy walls surrounding Theo's heart concerning her sister thawed a little.

"Nothing?" Grandfather repeated. "Even that which is set aside for your children?"

"That is still in trust, but . . ." Seraphina shook her head again. "I don't know what for." Her gaze shifted to Theo. "I don't even know if we can have children. I want a child so much, and each month I would cry, and now I can't help but be thankful that they will never know what it is to be poor." Seraphina gave a great gulping sob, then silently began to cry.

Compassion surged again, so strong that Theo couldn't help but move close to wrap her arms around Seraphina, even as she marveled at how her sister could still retain her beauty and not even have a red nose when she cried. "You are not poor," she murmured, clutching her sister near. "You have family, and that means you are never poor."

"But I don't want to live here," Seraphina sobbed in her arms. "Grandfather hates me."

"Don't be silly, dearest," Theo said. "Grandfather doesn't hate you." Although she could not say he felt the same about Roger . . .

She smoothed her sister's blonde hair, the hair she had always been so envious of growing up. How silly such things seemed now. One could have all the beauty in the world, but it made little difference without character.

"What am I going to do?"

Theo peeked up and caught her grandfather's scowl. She lifted her brows and held his gaze, silently pleading with him, until he shook his head, resignation in his features, before he pursed his lips and limped away. "I fear, my dear . . ."

"You fear what?" Seraphina pulled back. "What is it?" She glanced over her shoulder. "Oh, has Grandfather given up on us? Do you think he means to send us away? Oh, Theo, what is it that you fear?"

"I fear," Theo said, "that you are going to have to learn how to tend to chickens."

Chapter 24

The past hour had proved one of the most excruciating of his life. Daniel did not recall such times of tension in his household, but perhaps that was because his sister was older and his desire to join the army had stolen focus from much else. By the time he'd joined up, his sister had been married for nearly a year. But never had he witnessed the tension of the past hour.

Theo's departure was swiftly followed by some sharp words by the general, which left Daniel's heart even softer toward the elder grand-daughter. Seraphina's departure had occurred soon after, as the general eased to his feet and told Roger in no uncertain terms what he thought of his ability to control his wife, before telling Letitia to stop her foolish weeping and commanding Daniel not to leave until he returned.

The three of them had sat without a word, although Daniel guessed from the bowed head that at least Mrs. Stapleton joined him in praying silently for those outside.

Dear God, please bring Your peace. And wisdom. And comfort. Please direct our paths and show us what to do.

After what seemed an age, in which Mr. Siddons entered twice and enquired whether they required anything, the general finally limped in, casting Roger a black look that Daniel hoped he'd never receive. A pithy assessment of Roger's character ensued, which was followed by the man's stuttered apologies and assurances, and the general's assertion that he most certainly would ensure that Roger would never be in a position to hurt Seraphina again.

Daniel felt a moment's sorrow for the man who blanched, begged pardon, and was advised in no uncertain terms that he would be better off to go outside and find his wife and beg *her* pardon, and to send Theodosia back inside.

Upon the young man's departure, the general exhaled heavily, and Mrs. Stapleton asked hurriedly if he'd like some tea. Daniel suspected he'd want something stronger and was unsurprised when he refused the offer with an "I'm surrounded by nincompoops and fools."

It was a minute or two more before the door opened and admitted Theodosia. Daniel rose unsteadily, only resuming his seat once she'd settled herself on the sofa next to her mother, across from him, without once looking in his direction.

But he studied her, noting the reddened eyes and nose that spoke of tears and made his heart sore again. How he wished that he could help her, that what he had to say would not simply bring more pain.

"So." The general exhaled, finally glancing at Daniel. "So you finally confessed."

"Something I should have done long ago."

"I don't know what good would have come of that. We all agreed, did we not? No one person can take responsibility."

"I am sorry. And I am most concerned about what consequences may ensue." He dared to glance at Theodosia.

Still no returned gaze.

"Yes," said her mother. "But I'm afraid I don't understand what you mean by consequences."

"He means—" began the general.

"He means," Theodosia interrupted, her face turned to her mother, "that it is likely that we will be ostracized, at least for a time, until people are prepared to forgive."

"That is my fear, yes," Daniel admitted. "Sir, ladies, I truly had no wish for events to descend into shouting matches. I am sick with regret for my role in it all."

Theodosia's lips compressed and she bowed her head.

"Oh, what will this mean for us?" Mrs. Stapleton grasped her daughter's hand. "What will this mean for you, my dear?"

His chest constricted at Theodosia's shake of head, at poor Mrs. Stapleton's fluster, and her daughter's attempt to comfort her. "Mama, would you like me to fetch a cup of tea?"

"Oh my dear, would you?"

She nodded, enquired if either man would wish the same, which Daniel joined the general in declining.

Upon her exit, Daniel turned to her mother. "Mrs. Stapleton, please accept my profound regrets."

"I know you meant it for the best, but I fear for poor Theodosia." She shook her head sadly. "She will never find a husband now. Such a thing will likely taint her forever."

New remorse kneaded his soul.

"Stop being such a watering pot," her father-in-law grumbled. "Things aren't as bad as that."

"Are they not?" she reproached him tearfully. "I worry for her, I truly do. All I want is for dear Theo to be happy, to know the joy of a husband and family as I was blessed to do, and indeed I thought she *was* happy. But then with her sister coming—I'm afraid poor Seraphina has never felt like she can live up to Theo's high standards—"

"Try anyone's high standards," the general muttered.

Mrs. Stapleton sighed. "And now, with dear Rebecca going so soon, and I daresay the loss of your company too, sir, she has been quite morose. It's so much worse than when we thought dear Becky was leaving us before."

He swallowed. "How so, ma'am?"

"Oh, you might not notice if you did not know her well, for she likes to hide her emotions behind a smile and jest. But it's as though the light has left her eyes, and we see an empty shell. And I do not know what to do." Her hands fluttered helplessly.

His stomach knotted. He'd give anything to share another of Theo's quips or smiles.

The door opened, and further revelations were bridled by the reappearance of the subject in question, who moved to give her mother a cup of tea before resuming her seat.

Her reappearance seemed to put the general—who had, these past minutes, been studying Daniel with a deep and profound frown—in mind of his earlier rancor.

"You speak of regrets, Captain Balfour." The general snorted. "You can apologize all you like, express a million regrets from here all the way to the Antipodes, but what are you going to do now?"

"He is leaving, Grandfather." Theo's unsmiling gaze finally connected with Daniel's.

A painful thud resounded through his soul. Did she blame him? Did she despise him? He could not stand for that to be so. "I would not wish to bring any further harm to you all by my association here."

Did she know he meant her, that it was thoughts of her alone that had kept him awake half the night? When daylight came, he had spent some time praying for God's path to be made apparent, yet had no clear direction, save for the urge to attend here as soon as possible. To explain. To make amends, if that was at all possible.

"Harm?" Another snort from the elderly gentleman. "You talk of regretting your role in all of this, but it wouldn't have happened if you hadn't decided to play a meek man's game."

"Grandfather—"

"No." General Contrary held up a hand. "It is time this man took responsibility for his actions."

"Sir, I—"

"Then in that case, Grandfather, you cannot point the finger just at the captain. You said, not ten minutes ago, that we were all responsible, that we all agreed allowing Becky to spend time with her uncle and grieve privately was quite the best thing. I will not let Captain Balfour shoulder the blame for something we all agreed to."

"A courageous man would not let a woman defend him." The general's eyes held hostility—or was it challenge?

"Sir, I have no need for Miss Stapleton's defense. I own my complete culpability."

"That is very noble of you, Captain," Theo said, "but untrue. You may recall that it was the both of us who initially bamboozled the Bellinghams into believing the hero she yearned to meet was not the man whom she met." Her lips lifted. "And amusing it proved too."

"Oh, Theodosia," her mother groaned, "I always knew your levity would lead you astray."

His heart lightened at Theo's smile. Perhaps she did not wish him in Hades as he'd feared. "You are very gracious," Daniel said. "But I really feel that the error was mine, and thus the remedy must be."

"And how precisely do you plan to remedy this debacle?" the general snapped. "Judging from what that dunce Elvira said earlier, I should not be surprised if we see a dozen apologies to tonight's dinner, which shan't bother me too much but will likely distress Letitia and Theo here, not to mention that niece of yours."

"Perhaps it would be best if you left for London today." Theo studied her shoes.

"Leave today? And slink away like the lily-livered man he purports not to be?"

"Grandfather, that is enough! You cannot say such things about Captain Balfour. You may not admire all his actions, but you *cannot* deny his decisiveness and courage in defeating the French and saving his men. Why, I saw you reading about it in the newssheets and commending such a feat. So don't sit there and abuse him now, when we all know how courageous he is!" Her eyes flashed, her cheeks flushed pink, in her brave and kind defense of him.

He experienced another heart pang in recognition of the true beauty of this woman—inside and out—and just what a jewel she had always proved to be. Would always prove to be.

Her sense of humor appealed. Her sense of justice and duty matched his. Her faith and zest and passion for life plucked an answering chord within. He blinked, and in that moment it seemed as if his vision suddenly sharpened. True courage meant trusting God, even though the future was unknown. But one need not fear when trusting God to order one's steps.

Daniel exhaled, peace flooding his soul. It was now abundantly clear what his path should be.

She pushed to her feet, which immediately drew Daniel to carefully rise again, before she offered a curtsy. "Forgive me, Captain. I have been remiss and forgotten I must speak with Annie about tonight's arrangements." She held out a hand. "I wish you safe travels, sir."

He accepted her hand and gently caressed her knuckles.

Her breath caught. Her movements stilled.

"I will not leave you to face the naysayers alone."

She drew her hand back, offering another small smile. "Fie, sir! Would you have me plead to own less than your courage? I would not have you think so ill of me."

"I could never think ill of you, Miss Stapleton," he murmured.

She blushed and shook her head slightly. "I should speak to Cook—"

"Yes, go," her grandfather commanded. "Go, for I have far more to say to this young man here."

She cast him an uncertain glance, then, lips curving wryly, nodded and escaped.

He longed to turn to watch her exit, to see if she'd spare him another glance, but he kept his focus on the old man seated opposite.

"Sir, I must beg—"

"You can do your begging later. Right now, you can sit and listen to what I have to say."

He obeyed. And heard the general utter the most strange, surprising things.

His heart kicked. Yes, there was indeed a way forward after all.

⁂

The very act of maintaining her composure while her heart felt so brittle was wearying to the core. Her bones ached, her limbs grew stiff and sore, as if an escalation in movement would break her. For a moment yesterday she'd dared hope—

Then it had come crashing down.

When his gaze had rested on her, when he'd stroked her hand, she'd fancied she saw tenderness, something reiterated in words. But nothing more had been said, and at the services today he'd barely looked at her, let alone exchanged warm glances.

The absence of his regard, this lack of reassurance, made it impossible to know his thoughts, leaving her with a sense of uncertainty, like a feather on the breeze. And with nothing to pin her hopes to, she was privy to the merciless swooping of those in the village who took exception to the deception they felt the inhabitants of Stapleton Court had played on the village.

Thank heavens for Mr. Crouch's sensitivity in the sermon today, his encouragement to trust God despite challenging circumstances like a lifeline to her soul. *Faith is believing for the future, pressing on, not shrinking back.* His words were true. She could trust God with her future, even one that loomed empty with Becky and the captain leaving tomorrow. Theo had prayed about it through tears last night, had submitted her hopes and dreams to God, as she desperately clung to God's promise to never fail her. But sometimes living in faith and finding contentment felt like battles demanding courage worthy of a certain brave soldier. Especially in the knowledge of what tomorrow's departure would mean. And in the face of the glinting eyes and murmurs that now surrounded the Stapleton party's exit from the church.

Mama, at least, seemed unaware, although—Theo frowned, eyeing her carefully—the quiver in her hand was new. She moved swiftly to her side, placed Mama's hand upon her arm, and rested her hand atop. "Here you are, Mama."

Her mother's expression held a plea, which drew a surge of protectiveness and a gentle pat.

"Ah. Miss Stapleton." Mrs. Cleever's eyes were hard, like polished marble. "I suppose this was just more of your funning?"

"Forgive me, ma'am. Of what circumstance do you speak?"

"Don't play the innocent with me. You must know I refer to the scandalous decision to hide Captain Balfour at Stapleton Court."

"Do you refer to the decision to keep the presence of Captain Balfour a secret to allow time for him to grieve the passing of his sister, or do you refer to the decision—made in consultation with the doctor—to provide a room for the captain to recover while his leg was needing time to mend?"

"I, er, the former, I suppose."

"At such a sad time, I imagine he really appreciated having a space where he could spend time with what little family he has left. Regarding the latter, I believe he was thankful for the opportunity to rest and not have to struggle with stairs or incompetent servants and the like. Stapleton Court also proved to be effective at keeping away unwanted visitors."

In the echo of Theo's words, she realized how Mrs. Cleever would most likely take offense, given that invitations to her had never been in plentiful supply. Theo hadn't meant to say it quite like that.

"Yes. You have done a wonderful job at keeping him to yourself, haven't you?"

"I am unsure what you mean." Those were the polite words to say. She had every understanding about what the barbed words meant, but perhaps Theo had misjudged her, and Mrs. Cleever would be reluctant to own her less-than-charitable thoughts.

"Simply that it is not at all the done thing for a young gentleman to stay in the house where a woman of marriageable age resides."

Or perhaps not. Theo bit back a smile. Apparently her first assumption had been correct.

Mrs. Cleever wore a puzzled frown. "I do not see anything about this situation that is amusing."

"Oh, madam, not amusing. Simply a little diverting."

"What is?"

"Firstly, that you have revised your opinion about my supposed eligibility and now seem to consider me marriageable after all."

This met with a sound of faint protest.

"And secondly, that you would even consider the captain would entertain any interest in me at all. You must comfort yourself that I've not run away to get married. I am not so lost to depravity as that."

Becky moved into view, her downcast face and bevy of equally Friday-faced friends telling the all.

"Ah, you will have to please excuse us, Mrs. Cleever. I see Miss Mannering needs me. Good day to you." She nodded to a sympathetic looking Mrs. Crouch and found a tight smile for Lady Bellingham, which faded the instant Frederick glanced her way. Apparently, she need not worry about him anymore. From the way his gaze passed her without recognition, in what could only be considered the cut direct, it seemed he had well and truly got over his infatuation. Perhaps he'd find a more worthy young lady to give attention to.

She reached Becky's side at the same time as the lieutenant, whose soft enquiry if she was well was followed a moment later by the deeper voice of the captain. As if her head was mastered by an expert puppeteer, Theo's gaze rose to connect with his.

Warmth lay in his eyes, warmth that seemed to leap across and land inside her chest. Her heart thudded at such nonsense, and conscious that others were staring, she forced herself to look away, to pay attention to what Becky was saying.

"Why must I leave?" the girl complained. "It really is most unfair. Why can't I stay here with Theodosia?"

"Becky, my dear, this is not the time," Theo murmured.

"Always been too lax with her," Mrs. Cleever sneered with a loud sniff.

Theo stiffened, but a sharp retort was withheld at the captain's deep voice. "I wonder, Rebecca, if we could perhaps talk of this at home."

Becky seemed set to protest, but a glance at Theo, and Becky's fervor collapsed into a muttered "very well."

The weight of the captain's attention returned to rest on Theo again. "Forgive me, Miss Stapleton, but I wondered if you might be free to attend a small repast at Mannering today. Consider it a chance to see whether you approve the changes made since your last visit. Becky visited yesterday and thought it very fine."

So that was where she'd been all day. "I did not know she had gone."

Another hiss from behind her. "So irresponsible! Gallivanting around the countryside."

"She probably wished to spend some time saying goodbye to the place, as it were."

He'd spoken softly, but she could not be sure that other ears had not heard, that they'd not speculate and gossip. "Thank you for the honor, but—"

"Miss Stapleton," interrupted the lieutenant with a genial smile. "Let this day not be one of buts. Please say you'll come."

"Very well. I can answer for my mother, as we have no previous engagements." She found a smile. "And I believe we shall be able to offer something in the way of food, from all that was prepared last night and yet not eaten."

"A shame things occurred that way due to the small-mindedness of some," the lieutenant muttered.

The small-mindedness of nearly all, save the minister and his wife.

Theo accepted the lieutenant's proffered arm, as he drew her to the carriage. "At least she has had the chance to say goodbye here. And to be fair, 'twas not the first farewell dinner held, so there is that."

"One cannot have too many farewells when one is truly loved," he said.

"I suppose not."

He handed her into the carriage, then gallantly helped her mother in too, while Becky was slowly being escorted by her uncle.

"Mama, I trust you are well." Truly she seemed a little pale.

"Oh, my dear." She held a hand out to her, and Theo clasped it. "How will I ever do without you?"

"Mama, it is Becky who is leaving us. I shall still remain."

"Of course. I was forgetting." She closed her eyes, sinking against the cushions. "I am so very tired."

"Captain Balfour invited us to share a nuncheon at Mannering, but we need not attend if you do not feel well."

"Oh, but we must. I suppose," she added, opening her eyes to glance at Theo. "You would like to, wouldn't you?"

"I do admit to some curiosity as to how the house has fared. I am told Becky thinks it very fine."

"Becky thinks what is fine?" that young damsel said, passing into the carriage and taking the seat opposite.

"Your uncle mentioned you visited Mannering yesterday," Theo said. "If I had known you wished to go, I could have accompanied you."

"I didn't need you to," Becky said, eyes on her twisting hands in her lap. "I wanted to see the place again, before, before . . ." Her voice wobbled.

"We shall see it again today," Theo said, with a new surge of compassion. Was there any point in remonstrating that Becky would have benefited from having an escort? Probably not. Not when Theo decried the use of an escort herself. "Do you approve the changes there?" she asked instead.

"Oh, Theo! I do. I hope you like it too. I think that's what . . ."

Her words trailed off as she shot Theo a wide-eyed glance.

Curious as she may be, Theo refused to bite, simply saying, "If you approve, then we are sure to as well."

"I should think so," Becky said with a small smile.

An hour later, having carefully packed two hampers' worth of food, and the Stapleton party—save for the general, who had declined the invitation, and the Rileys, who had not been invited—were at Mannering's front door.

A *rap rap rap* and Captain Balfour opened the door and swept them inside. "Well, ladies, what do you think?"

Theo's breath caught, and she blinked back a sudden rush of emotion. He had put every one of her suggestions into place. The reception rooms had been switched around, so now the study faced the front, and the drawing room captured the views over the River Till. Furniture was perfectly positioned that the lady of the house could enjoy the space very well. Should Theo have suggested lining the windows with stained glass, she suspected he might have done so also. Such a thought that he cared so much for her opinion, that he was so willing to execute her ideas, was more than a little humbling. It was also a little thrilling. And a little daunting.

If she was given to vanity, it felt a little as though he might actually care.

Chapter 25

A peacock's cry rent the air as Daniel studied her. Did she approve of his changes? "Well, Miss Stapleton? What do you think?"

"Oh, sir." She placed her hand at her throat and surveyed the room with a smile. "I am amazed you have accomplished so much so quickly."

"Once my mind is made up, I like to see things done."

"Well . . ." She traced a hand along an ornate carved picture frame. "It is exactly what I would have done."

"So you approve?"

"Most heartily." She glanced up at him, her half smile revealing a dimple lurking in one cheek. "Of course, anyone who deigns to agree with me, I am most certain to approve."

"Then I hope you approve of me, Miss Stapleton, for I am in complete agreement with you."

She chuckled.

The tension lining his heart eased a fraction at the sound. "It seems too long since I have heard your laughter," he said in a softer voice.

Her gaze was shy as she looked up at him. "I did not know that you paid attention to such things."

"I pay attention to many things, Miss Stapleton."

She bit her lip, as if questioning his words. "I hope you find a buyer who will appreciate the changes you have made."

"I'm sure he will."

"So, have you found a buyer? Does the man have a family as well? It does help to know one's neighbors."

"I cannot be sure as yet just what his situation is," he confessed. "I've a feeling we shall know more soon."

She nodded, glancing at the freshly hung wallpaper. "It will seem strange to have others live here, but I suppose life moves on."

"Yes indeed. Life is too short to spend focused on the past. One must look to the future. Would you not agree?"

Her gaze met his again, and again he knew that throb in his chest. Oh, how he wished she would assent, that she would see a future was still possible.

"'Faith is believing for the future,'" she quoted Mr. Crouch's words from earlier. "I am trying to trust God."

"As am I," he promised.

The golden depths in her green eyes sparkled as she nodded.

Accord wove between them, filling his heart with hope.

"I say, what are you two doing looking so solemn over here?" Musgrave demanded. "Are we going to eat, or are you going to make me starve?"

Theodosia's glance slid to Daniel's friend, but not before he saw the welcome glint of mischief again. "As tempting as it might be to reply with the latter, I think it only fair to see what is in these baskets. Where would you like to eat, sir?" She posed the last question to Daniel.

"Why, in the dining room, of course."

This room, too, had altered its location and now faced a pretty rose garden previously overseen by the morning room. In fact, the only room on this floor not having its position revised was the library, its bookshelves deemed too difficult to replicate elsewhere, having been built to match the perfectly proportioned windows.

The dining room also met with smiles from the Stapleton ladies, as did the abundance of food that soon covered the table.

"One might almost imagine that we are at a picnic," said Musgrave.

"I am glad we are indoors." Mrs. Stapleton peered out the windows. "From the looks of those clouds, it seems we are likely to be in for another storm."

Musgrave shivered. "I never knew such a place for its storms."

"Have you so easily forgotten the storms we faced on the Peninsular?" Daniel asked, as he carved Mrs. Stapleton some cold chicken.

Musgrave immediately told the ladies of an incident in Portugal where they'd been forced to shelter in a small byre. "It stank of cows, and I'm sure you can imagine the mess."

"I'd prefer not to imagine it while I'm eating." Theodosia added a small pastry to her plate.

"Exactly so," Daniel said. "Such conversation is scarcely civil for ladies or, in fact, anyone who wishes to eat with unimpaired appetite. Can't you do any better, my friend?"

Musgrave shot him a considering look and turned to Theodosia. "Which of his many great exploits would you care to hear about? The man is so modest, I bet he has likely never told you the whole, has he?"

"Musgrave," Daniel warned.

His friend ignored him, telling the story of the night when God's prompting had seen Daniel rush into a situation that had resulted in lives saved, the enemy vanquished, and ultimately led to a fancy medal pinned to his chest and all this fuss.

"Such a brave man," Mrs. Stapleton said, with eyes of approval.

"Most courageous," Theodosia murmured, her gaze fusing with his.

In her eyes he saw respect and admiration, hope and regret, feelings he identified with so completely that he longed to have a private moment to share his heart. But now was not the time, not with three interested faces watching her, watching him.

The sound of Musgrave clearing his throat broke the connection, and Daniel bowed his head, his chest whirling with emotion as he prayed for God's blessings on tomorrow's endeavors.

Musgrave turned to Becky, seated beside him. "I do hope you are in better spirits now, Miss Mannering."

"Thank you, sir. I suppose I cannot ever be reconciled to the idea of leaving this area."

"You will find new scenes and people to captivate you," Theodosia said. "You must view this as an adventure."

"Should you like to engage in such adventures, Miss Stapleton?" Musgrave asked, with another sideways glance at Daniel.

She inclined her head, wiped at the corner of her mouth with the linen napkin Becky had somehow found yesterday when she'd been advising on just how the dining room should be set. "Adventures of that sort would be most exciting, should one be so fortunate and blessed to participate." She glanced fondly at her mother, who was studying her too. "But I could never leave my mother."

Daniel drew in a breath, tension spiraling within. That was the most chief of his concerns.

"I don't wish you to sacrifice your future for me, my dear," her mother said.

Theodosia laughed. "I should hardly think that chasing one's own adventures would be considered sacrificial. Indeed, one might consider it most selfish indeed."

Becky laid her utensil to the side of her plate. "Is it selfish to wish to be happy?"

The question seemed to float around the table until it gently rested on Daniel. "I believe perhaps it can be," he said slowly, "when one's pursuit of happiness comes at the expense of others."

"I do not believe happiness need be everything." Theodosia rested her fork on her plate. "Happiness tends to be a momentary thing, too often circumstantial. What brings us happiness can vary."

Becky fluttered her hands. "Oh, like when one has the most perfect gown and you think yourself a picture, then you realize that in certain lights the color does absolutely nothing for your complexion, so what brought joy one moment brings unhappiness the next," said Becky.

"I suspect joy is rather a different commodity to happiness," Theodosia mused. "I see joy more as a bedrock to one's life, always there, connected to one's sense of contentedness and peace."

"That comes from assurance in one's purpose in this life," Daniel interposed.

"And assurance for the next," she replied.

"Salvation brings a sense of joy that those who do not know it can be hard-pressed to find," Daniel said.

"I agree."

Their gazes entwined, and he knew a new certainty that this shared faith was as it ought be.

"I should think that your merry heart would be enough to bring you joy, Miss Stapleton," Musgrave said gallantly.

"Ah, but this merry heart cannot always be merry, so it needs a firmer foundation than my emotions might provide."

Daniel nodded, glancing around at the walls. "Much like this house needed shoring up to stand the tests of time."

"There is little point in having pretty rooms if they are only going to fall," Theodosia agreed.

"A man's heart needs a sure foundation, Lieutenant Musgrave." Mrs. Stapleton leaned back in her chair. "I would hope that one would seek that solid foundation in God's truths."

"Indeed, ma'am," he said seriously. "One should. One does."

"Forgive me, but I do not see how all of this pertains to having adventures," Becky complained.

"We have found ourselves wandering down a path or two, haven't we?" Theodosia said. "Let's just say you are sure to find happiness as you appreciate the new and embrace the unfamiliar." She patted Becky's hand. "It is not everyone who is as fortunate as you, getting to travel and see the delights of London."

Becky's face fell, and it was apparent she took little pleasure in what Theodosia was determined to regard as a treat.

"That's right, dear," Mrs. Stapleton said. "Opportunities do not come to all, and when they do, one should be sure to make the most of it. I was that way when I married my husband and had to leave the known parts of Derbyshire to come here. Though I cannot say it has always been easy, it has been most worthwhile. One never knows what might lie on the other side of an invitation."

"That is very true, ma'am." Musgrave gave Daniel another sidelong look before switching back to Theodosia. "What say you, Miss Stapleton, to the power of an invitation?"

Daniel's breath suspended. That was indeed the question.

Theodosia glanced at Daniel, then back at Musgrave. "It depends on the details of the invitation, sir."

The air in the room filled with a dozen unsaid things.

"Never should I hope to be considered the person who stops a loved one from being willing to accept an opportunity." Mrs. Stapleton clutched her cameo brooch. "Instead, I'd wish to be like my dear parents, who waved me off with a smile. A mother wouldn't like to think she might impair someone's happiness."

Theodosia turned loving eyes upon her mother. "You could never impair my happiness."

Her mother's brow wrinkled, and she glanced at Daniel and the other diners, then rested her attention on her daughter again.

Musgrave chuckled. "Your filial duty does you much credit."

"It is hardly duty when it is born from love." Theodosia still gazed affectionately at her mother. "I have been most blessed with a mother as amiable as mine."

"One should try to have an amiable mother if at all possible," Daniel said.

"Or at least an amiable mother-in-law," Musgrave murmured, studying his salad.

Daniel cleared his throat and turned the subject, doing his best to keep things trotting along until it became clear that his guests had replenished their plates satisfactorily enough and eaten beyond what they might consider full. "I shouldn't wish to be a bad host, but I understand tomorrow will be a big day, so I hope that you have enjoyed your visit here."

Becky sighed, glancing around. "It feels so strange to have things finally looking as they ought, only to leave again." She faced Daniel. "Uncle, must I leave?"

"You know what you have to do," he said.

"Oh, but—" She glanced at Miss Stapleton. "Oh, Theo, is there any way at all that I could stay with you?"

"And end up an old maid like me? I would not wish that on you, child. You were born for greater things than this."

"Greater things than a merry heart, good sense, and wisdom?" Musgrave asked. "I wonder, Miss Stapleton, if you sell short God's plans for you."

She demurred, but the afternoon was growing long and there remained much to be done before tomorrow's adventures.

⁓

"Mama," Theo said the next morning from the door of the drawing room. "Have you seen Becky anywhere?"

"Rebecca? No. I haven't seen her since we helped her finish her packing last night. Why?"

"It's just that the captain said he would be here early, and she seems to be missing."

Her mother's attention wandered back to her stitching. "Perhaps she is talking with Seraphina."

"I thought Becky disliked her."

"Now, now. Your sister is behaving herself and has been quite pleasant these past days."

That was true.

"Becky is probably just taking a final ride."

Theo exhaled. Of course. "That must be it. It is a long drive, so she must have wished for exercise."

"I wonder how long it is precisely until the carriage would reach Langley House?" Mama mused.

"I would think the best part of the day, which is why we should find her before the captain arrives. Excuse me, while I go check the stables." She hurried outside, not trusting the task to Mr. Siddons. That man would neglect to look as carefully as she. But when she reached the stables, Gracie, Theo's mare Becky had been prone to using, nickered in her stables and clearly hadn't been ridden this morning.

"Where is Miss Mannering?" Theo murmured, smoothing down Gracie's mane.

So, not outside. Not upstairs. Not downstairs either, it would seem.

When she returned to the house, the servants had the same response as before. Miss Rebecca Mannering had not been seen since last night when she'd called her goodnights and retired to her room.

"Where could she be?"

Mrs. Brigham bit her lip.

"What is it, Annie?"

She shook her head. "I didn't want to say before, but is it possible, do you think she might have run away?"

"Run away? No," she said firmly, as much to quiet such suspicions as to quell the rapid escalation of her heart. "Becky has too much sense for that."

Mr. Siddons raised a brow, looking like the autocrat she thought he might wish to be.

"You do not agree?"

"She is younger than her years," he said slowly, "and has spent quite some time in recent weeks in the company of Lieutenant Musgrave."

"Surely you're not going to suggest something as nonsensical as her running away with him."

His expression blanked.

Her heart clenched. "You were?"

"I cannot say with any degree of certainty, but I did wonder if I heard carriage wheels this morning."

"What? And you said nothing?"

"'Twas the merest suspicion, miss. I saw nothing, I assure you."

"How can you have said nothing, even if it was just a mere suspicion?"

Her sister descended the stairs to join them in the hall. "Suspicion about what?"

"Oh, Seraphina! You have not seen Becky, have you?"

"Not since yesterday, no."

The library door opened to reveal Grandfather. "Why is there so much caterwauling and carrying-on?"

"We are seeking Becky's whereabouts." Theo's agitation grew, pulsed within her heart. "You have heard nothing untoward, have you?"

"Untoward? Like what?"

"Perhaps Becky has confided in you—"

He uttered a guttural laugh. "That girl always quakes whenever she sees me."

That was true.

"Theodosia?" Mama called from the drawing room. "Have you still not found her?"

Theo shook her head. "I will check her room again."

She dashed upstairs, heart knotting as she noticed details she had not discerned before. The lack of mess. The straightened bedclothes. The lack of the hatbox, although her trunk lay strapped and corded as it had before. She moved to shut the window and noticed a scrap of paper lying on the floor.

She snatched it up, and as she read, her heart sank.

Dear Theo,

Please forgive me. I have no desire to leave, and I know you are too good-hearted to wish me to be unhappy. I trust you will be happy too. Please thank your mother and the general for me. I wish you well.

Rebecca

"No. No, no." She shook her head, unable to believe the words. "She would not have run away. How could she have managed such a thing?"

A cleared throat came behind her, and she pivoted to see Mr. Siddons standing at the door.

"Captain Balfour is here, miss."

What? And she hadn't noticed? She dashed to the window and peered out.

Sure enough, he stood at the carriage, securing the luggage strapped to the back.

What would he say when he learned she had been so careless as to lose his niece?

"Miss?"

"Thank you, Mr. Siddons. I shall go downstairs and speak with him." Dread coiled in her stomach as she hastened down the stairs. Clutching the note in her hand, she moved into the front hall, past the huddled servants and her mother and the general, just as the knocker sounded.

Mr. Siddons hurried to open it, and she straightened, affixing a smile and praying for calm as the butler's greeting was met with the captain's.

"I came to see if Miss Mannering is—"

"Oh, sir!"

His gaze lifted to her, and he smiled.

Her heart gave an answering throb, her gladness at seeing him fading with the knowledge that he soon would not be as happy when she told him the news. She bit her lip.

"Miss Stapleton? Is something the matter?"

She glanced behind her, saw the servants staring, although her mother and the general had disappeared. She drew in a frantic breath, glanced back, met his frown.

"You are most upset. Come, let us talk in the drawing room."

She nodded, emotion cramping her throat, forbidding words. Oh, how wonderful to have him here, to have someone she could rely on, to feel the weight of these burdens need not rest only on her shoulders.

He drew her inside and firmly shut the door.

She crumpled, only to be clasped against his chest a second later, her agitated breathing easing a mite as his heart thumped reassuringly in her ear.

He smoothed a hand down her hair, the act rippling sensation down her spine and tempting her to increase this shocking embrace by nestling yet closer.

She shuddered in a breath and eased back. "I'm so sorry. It's just . . ."

He looked deep into her eyes. "My dear Miss Stapleton, whatever is the matter?"

She shook her head, agitation making it impossible to speak.

"Come." He led her to a settee and encouraged her to sit down, then sat beside her, eyes serious as she struggled to find words. His hands clasped hers gently. "Please tell me what troubles you so."

"It . . . it is Becky. I cannot find her and fear that she has run away."

His brows rose.

"She has—" She gulped. "Oh, read this." She pulled the note from her apron's pocket and handed it to him.

He read it, the crease in his forehead becoming more pronounced. "Where would she go?"

"I do not know. I can hardly believe it. But she has repeatedly said she did not wish to leave with you today."

"But how could she have gone away? Are you sure she has not left for a short time to clear her head?"

"Mr. Siddons said he heard a carriage earlier this morning."

His brows rose. "You think she has had help?"

"What if . . . what if she has run away with . . . with—" She barely dared speak it. Saying it aloud gave the sense it would be true.

"You think she has run away with Musgrave?"

"Was . . . was he at Mannering when you left?"

He frowned. "I spoke to him earlier, but he said he had some things to do before he could accompany us on our journey."

"Oh no." The tremors in her heart matched the rippling sensation as his thumb caressed the back of her hand. Oh, how could she pay attention to such things at a time like this?

"What is it?"

"They—the lieutenant and Becky—have been very close."

"But I cannot think a man of his years and experience would dare risk so much to take up with a girl who just happens to be my niece."

His calm matter-of-factness stole some of the breath from her fears. "You don't think they have run off together?"

"I hardly think Musgrave the sort to run off to Gretna Green."

New dread struck. "They wouldn't need to go there. Anywhere across the border would work if they intend to be married. Anywhere like Coldstream, which is only fourteen miles from here."

His lips pressed together as he gave her a quick, searching look.

"I know it sounds nonsensical, sir, and perhaps you think me foolish, but I cannot but feel a most dreadful unease."

"I could never think you foolish." He drew nearer, possessed himself of both her hands again. "I'm sure she is safe."

"But the border is not so very far after all. They might be getting married as we speak!"

He frowned. "It is not like you to be so worried."

"I know, I know. I don't mean to be a peahen—"

"A peahen is the last thing I think of when I think of you, my dear."

Her cheeks warmed. "It is just that everything has been so topsy-turvy of late, and I hardly know what to think."

Again he gave her that odd look, as if waiting for something more.

Frustration mounted within. Oh, where was his famed decisiveness now? "Sir, you must retrieve them."

As if startled from his lethargy, he gave a short nod. "Of course." Purpose stole across his face, his features seeming to draw in, to sharpen. "What has been done?"

"Grandfather is not well, and my mother is so flustered that I could not speak too openly. But from what I can gather, it seems that someone— perhaps the lieutenant—called for her not an hour ago, and they went off in his curricle."

"And you would have me follow them?"

"As her uncle, it is only proper."

"Of course." He rose, giving her another of those looks weighted with speculation. "I best go and get organized at once." His lips lifted in a rueful smile. "The carriage cannot travel fast weighted down with so much luggage."

"You could use, perhaps, Grandfather's curricle."

"He would not mind?"

"I can ask."

He coughed apologetically. "You must forgive me for pointing out one detail."

"Yes?"

"I cannot help wonder if that niece of mine would prove amenable to any change of plan."

"She can be a trifle headstrong at times." Like the time Becky had locked herself in her room. "What should be done?"

His lips curved in ruefulness. "I hesitate to suggest such a thing, but I am not sure if a curricle will prove the best mode of transportation."

"How so?"

"It's generally only suitable for two, and yet . . ."

"And yet what, sir?"

"Miss Stapleton, I don't suppose you would care to join me on a drive?"

"To Coldstream?"

"I imagine Becky would much prefer to see you than her ogre of an uncle." He smiled. "Your presence always brings a measure of joy."

Her cheeks grew hot again, the warmth in his eyes chasing the tension from within. Perhaps she *should* go and have something of the adventure they had talked about yesterday, even though the cause was so reprehensible.

"If you were to come, then it might make certain explanations easier when we reach the Toll House."

He studied her, brow furrowed as if uncertain she'd agree. But how could she refuse? Not when Becky's reputation demanded such a drive, a drive that would prove Theo's last with him. Her heart panged again. "How long would it take to get there?"

"Truly, you would come?" At her nod, his features eased. "We could be returned by sunset, barring any accidents."

"Of course." Her lips curved. "I suppose I should not ask you to assist me in such a high-handed way without being willing to attend also."

He looked at her keenly. "I would not have you come if you were unwilling."

"Oh, but I am."

He raised a brow.

She blushed. "Willing. To come with you."

His expression warmed. "Then let us tarry no longer. In fact, if you pack a small valise, I shall speak to your mother and beg her permission and seek the general's permission too. I hope they shall take pity on a poor uncle as myself."

"I'm sure you will find Mama at least will not be too hard to convince." Her mother adored the captain. Grandfather, on the other hand . . .

"So go pack, and perhaps find something warmer to wear whilst I seek your mother's blessing for such a venture."

A short while later she was kissing her mother's cheeks, her valise being stored in the curricle Robert had hastily uncovered and hitched up. "I don't expect to be too long, but if anyone enquires where I am, please tell them I am on a drive with the captain."

"Theo?" her grandfather called.

She rushed back up the steps. "Oh, Grandfather, you do not mind us looking for Becky?"

"She needs looking after, as do you my dear. Now go." He gruffly drew her near and kissed her stained cheek, then released her to her mother.

"God bless you, my dear." Mama bestowed another kiss on her cheek. "I think your actions are very wise. One should seek happiness as one can."

Theodosia eyed her mother oddly, then straightened, noting ink-smudged fingers as Mama handed a note to the captain.

Mama gave her a quick glance, then said, "Just a note, should there be any questions."

"That is very kind of you, Mama, but I'm sure it won't be needed."

"One never knows. Now, you best go." She sighed. "Take care of my girl, Captain."

"I always will," he promised, before turning to smile at Theo in such a companionable way she felt a mite of agitation ease. "Shall we go?"

"Yes."

He handed her into the curricle, and they rushed off, soon passing the stone pillars that marked the entry to Stapleton Court.

Chapter 26

Daniel snapped the reins, now that the town was behind them and they approached a straight stretch. He could never claim to have the skills of the Corinthians, men like Nicholas Stamford, the Earl of Hawkesbury's son, whose exploits on the battlefield were matched by a certain sophistication Daniel ascribed to members of that class. He glanced across at Theodosia. She possessed a quiet elegance that some might consider as of that class too.

"I see your driving has improved," she noted. "But it might prove even better if you kept your eyes on the road."

He laughed and obeyed. "I'm glad you noticed."

Hedges flashed past, stands of trees, farms, and the long, broad brown hill known as Humbleton.

He risked her displeasure by sneaking another peek at her. "Are you warm enough?"

"Yes, thank you."

"Not daunted?"

"How can I be when with you?"

He chuckled. "You say the kindest things, dear heart."

She blushed and pulled the lap robe higher. "Remember when we read *Henry IV*?" She pointed to a stone marker in a field on the right. "That is the Bendor Stone, which some think to be the battle stone associated with the Battle of Holmedon Hill."

He slowed a little, saw a nondescript stone propped up in a green field with a few uninterested sheep. A wry chuckle escaped.

"What is so amusing?"

He shook his head. "It astounds me that we are so determined to lay our lives down to possess land or fight for a cause, and yet here, hundreds of years later, it's so peaceful."

"Yet without the fighting, that peace may not happen. Which makes it worth it, does it not?"

"I should like to think that our cause in the Peninsular was most worthwhile."

"Saving lives from a dictator most certainly counts as worthwhile."

His heart grew soft at her approval.

They talked little as they completed the next miles, but though his tongue was still, his mind turned quickly. Her willingness to join him on this mad endeavor was one thing. Would she acquiesce to what he posed next? He exhaled, conscious of a drumming pulse, and prayed.

She shivered.

He inched a fraction closer. "This air has a nip, doesn't it?"

"I wasn't expecting to be travelling today," she reminded.

"I am very glad that you agreed."

"Poor Becky. I hope the woman you have arranged as Becky's companion will be kindly and of good cheer."

"I think she will prove most appropriate."

"Hmm. But 'appropriate' does not always lend itself to endearment."

"In this case, I'm confident Becky will find the woman I have chosen to be most endearing."

"Well, if you are, then I will trust you."

"I'm very glad you trust me, Miss Stapleton. I should be most heartwrecked if you did not."

"Especially as I've willingly placed my life in your hands today."

"Exactly so. Why, for all you know, I could be driving you to the border for nefarious reasons myself," he dared.

"Saving dear Becky from social ruin is worth it. Oh, look! Here is an inn. Perhaps we should see if they have stopped here."

He obeyed her implied request and stopped at the Akeld Arms, where quick enquiry of a coaching boy was met with a negative of sighting them. Daniel tossed the boy a coin and resumed their journey.

"It was perhaps a little close to Wooler to expect anyone to change vehicles there," she said with a heavy sigh.

"One would hardly need the horses to be changed so soon," he agreed.

"I suppose you are right, and they must have travelled further. Do you think they stopped at Milfield?"

"To reach the border is only fourteen miles. With good horses, one shouldn't have to change before that, I would think."

"I have never contemplated all that would be necessary if one was to elope."

He smiled. "I can't help but be relieved."

"I still cannot believe the lieutenant was so utterly unscrupulous as to persuade poor Becky to agree to such a deed."

"A man will do a lot to win a wife," he said.

"But by so dishonorable means? I should think you, sir, would not wish for Becky to be so stained with disgrace."

"I should most certainly not wish any such a thing for my niece."

"And for any other females of your acquaintance, I should hope."

The horses slowed as they rounded a bend. "I agree that in most cases that would be so, but I cannot agree in all."

"But just imagine the scandal, and how people would talk!"

"Which would only matter if one cared about the nattering of others," he countered. "You, I am persuaded, would not be as concerned as some about the opinions of people like Mrs. Cleever."

"Because I know most of the village gossip anyway. But that is beside the point. One simply cannot cast one's reputation aside as if it is no very great thing."

"A reputation built on the judgments of others for whom you have no care?"

There was a pause, then she said quietly, "I might wish to not have to care, but I find I care all the same."

And that honesty was why he loved her.

"Perhaps it is different for a man. Your reputation need not damage you in the way a lady's does."

"I must disagree. I have spoken to you before about James Langley, my friend with the castle by the sea. His reputation was such that few men wished to work with him, and it was only by God's grace that he changed and became quite a different man. A man's reputation means he can be known as a crook, a sad dog, or a cur."

"Or a rum 'un, or a trump, or a Trojan."

He laughed. "Where did you learn such language?"

"My grandfather was never moderate in his language, and I may have overheard others describing you like so."

"As the sad dog or the Trojan?"

"I believe they thought the latter."

"And you?"

"You wish to know my thoughts on you?"

He refocused on the road. "It does sound rather vain of me, does it not?"

"Most peacock-worthy, if you are expecting a favorable answer."

He glanced quickly at her, caught her smile. Felt his heart ease. "I see."

Nothing more was said for a minute or two, then she clasped her hands. "I suppose it does sound ungracious to not answer your question, sir. If you must know, I . . . I would consider you a most kind and benevolent and courageous man. Although, apparently, a little addicted to pride and vanity."

A chuckle escaped. "Well, 'tis kind of you to say so."

"I was trying very hard to be kind," she said meekly.

"Would you care to know my thoughts concerning you?"

"Not at this time, no."

"At some time soon?"

"Sir, I really think your attention should be focused on retrieving your niece from an escapade most scandalous."

"Then after she and Musgrave are found? May I be permitted to tell you my thoughts?"

He glanced at her profile.

Amusement faded from her face as her lips pressed together. "For what purpose, sir? You are leaving. I am staying. There can be no good to come from words that might as well be said in jest."

"Miss Stapleton, please, I do not—"

"Sir, I am a little weary, and do not have the heart to play."

He knew remorse. These past few days had been fraught with emotional upheaval, and he was creating even more. "Here. Rest against me if you wish."

She made a slight protest, but soon the invitation to lean against his shoulder proved impossible to ignore, and she sank against him and closed her eyes.

And Daniel continued to pray.

The rocking of the curricle ceased, though her head felt as though she'd travelled many miles further than such weariness warranted. She caught a tang of musk, that scent that had lately infused her dreams, and her eyes drifted open. Where—?

"Oh!" She straightened, skin prickling at having rested against Captain Balfour's shoulder in such an unladylike fashion. She smoothed down her sleeve, tidied her hair. Saw that the curricle was rolling past a coaching yard. "Are we there?"

"In Cornhill, yes."

A turn in the road revealed a stone bridge of several arches, which led across the river to another stone structure on the right, a cottage of proportioned windows and three chimneys.

"That is Scotland, across the River Tweed." He pointed to a stone structure. "And that is the Toll House, or the marriage house."

"And you think we'll find them there?"

"We shall see."

Nerves pattered in her veins as the horses crossed the bridge and slowed before the white-painted gate. She was now in Scotland.

Scotland!

"What is it, lass?"

"We talked of having adventures just yesterday, and to think that I am now here. I can hardly believe it."

"Aye. I can scarce believe it myself."

She adjusted her bonnet, swiped hair from her forehead. "Do I look presentable?"

"You look ever sweet and bonny, my dear."

A wrenching in her midsection drew fresh determination to tamp down these feelings. He was simply being kind. That was all. There was no need to read anything more into his sweet words. But there had been so many sweet words this day.

"We best see if they are here."

"Of course."

A boy came to hold the horses, and they soon entered the Toll House, moving into a dim room and encountering several seated persons, including a man who eyed them narrowly, then demanded they pay the toll.

Captain Balfour explained that they had no intention of travelling further.

"But cross the bridge ye div, and there's no comin' back from that."

The captain paid the ninepence demanded, lifting a brow at Theo as he did.

She shrugged, the amusement at the tollkeeper's parsimonious ways fading in recollection of the purpose of their visit. "Sir, please, we wish to know if a young couple came to be married in the last few hours."

He glanced at her, then at the captain, rubbing his grizzled jaw.

"Sir?" the captain asked.

"Nae, no young people have been here today—"

"Yesterday? It would likely have been very late."

"Nae. Not yesterday neither. No young people have crossed—"

"Oh, where can they be?" She turned to the captain.

"—save yerselves, of course." The tollkeeper glanced at the captain. "I gather you div not find that which ye seek?"

A strange look crossed the captain's face, then he turned to her, eyeing her in a way that made her heart flutter, and her pulse race faster in her veins. "But I did."

"I beg your pardon, sir?"

The captain smiled, the depths of his eyes warming as he drew even closer.

Her breath constricted as he possessed her hands.

"I have found what I'm searching for."

"Sir, I—"

"You would not let me tell you my thoughts before, but I cannot wait a second longer. For I find myself unable to think of anything but whether what you once said still holds true."

She held in a smile, thinking of all she'd said to him over the past weeks. "And which of those many things might that have been?"

"About how God can miraculously work in relationships, and they can overcome obstacles." He swallowed. "If the right woman meets the right man, that is."

Her breath caught. *No. Surely he didn't mean—*

"Would you really be willing to consider a man who might not have a grand house or income but would love you fiercely all his days?"

Yes, her heart cried.

"Would you be willing to trust God and this man with your future?"

If "this man" meant the one standing before her, then yes, a thousand times.

A cough from the Scotsman drew reminder of the reason for their flight.

"But what about Becky?" she felt obliged to say.

"Neither she nor Musgrave are here, and after travelling all this way, I suddenly find I have little care to chase them further."

"You cannot say that. She is your niece!"

"That is so. And because she is not here, I fear this may have proved a wild goose chase."

A mite of concern eased. "Truly?"

He nodded. "And truly, I find my interest in her future far less interesting than another's."

"But—"

"Your future, my dearest, I confess to having a great deal of interest in."

She swallowed. Did he mean to suggest—?

"As I be sayin'," interrupted the Scotsman, "there be no young people here today save yerselves. So, do ye want to get married or nae?"

"Married? Oh, but we're not—I mean, we are—" She faltered, cheeks heating at the smile on the captain's face.

"Are we not?" he said softly.

"But you do not—that is, you do not feel that way about me," she stammered.

He lifted her hand and pressed her fingers to his lips. "Surely you cannot still think so." He turned her hand over and kissed her palm. "Dearest heart."

"But . . ." She glanced at the Scotsman watching them with an approving smile.

"The more important question, my dear, is whether you feel the same."

"The same as what?"

"Whether you feel as I do, that life, that a future, would be unbearable without you in it."

Breath caught at his tender look, his sweet words . . .

"I feel it only right to tell you, fair Theodosia, that if you should refuse me, I have every intention of throwing myself back into the campaign, for life would truly be unbearable if you said no."

A chuckle escaped despite herself. "You would resort to blackmail?"

"I would resort to anything if it made you understand how much I care."

Her cheeks warmed again. "You cannot mean such things."

"I assure you that I do."

Life without him in it? She had thought she had reconciled her heart to his absence. Could he really be suggesting that she might not need to say farewell to him after all? "Is this a dream?" she whispered.

"It could be." He gently pressed her hands. "If you say yes."

Her heart squeezed with emotion. How could she return to what she'd known without his sweet tenderness, his kindly humor, his lively spirits? "I . . . I never dared to think . . ." She glanced helplessly at the Scotsman, who watched them with avid interest. Oh, what was she doing here? How unbelievable was such a thing?

The captain seemed to sense her agitation at the audience, and said, "Could we have a private room, please?"

"But ye be not wed!"

Theo's cheeks heated, as the captain assured that he only wished to speak with her.

"Well, of course, sir—if ye pay for the privilege, and leave the door open. We be civilized folk 'ere."

The captain pulled a coin from his coat pocket, handed it over, and they were escorted to another sparsely furnished room.

The Scotsman gave a knowing smile and pulled the door to just ajar.

This was zany. This could not be real. She moved to the window, her agitation such she scarcely knew to sit or stand. She resorted to pacing in front of the meagre fire, only stopping when the captain moved before her and held her hands.

"Dearest Theodosia, I cannot remain silent. You should know that I adore you, and nothing would bring me greater joy than to see you made happy all your days. And I dare to hope, dare to dream, you might find such blissfulness with me."

"You truly wish to marry me?"

"You. Only you." He pressed a kiss to her knuckles. "I know I am no great prize and lack the income for someone used to the likes of Stapleton Court, but if you're prepared to overlook that, I promise I will love you all my days." His mobile lips tweaked to a quarter-moon. "I find myself quite astonished that, until I knew you, I never realized how much I missed having you in my life. And then we met, and I found my days were lit with a sunshine I had never known. If you were to reject me, I suspect I would never feel entirely happy again."

Her heart tingled with a fizzing delight that nearly stole coherent thought. And the ability to stand. She drew her hands away and sank into a nearby wooden chair. "I do not know what to say."

"I understand this is a shock, and quite likely you never dreamed of marrying like this, but I wish you would consider it. For I love you. I love your faith, your kindness, your generous nature, your wisdom, and your wit." The captain drew near. "I knew from the first moment I saw you that I found you attractive. And then I learned your mind was as sharp as your face fair, and your heart was as kind and good as anyone I ever met, and I realized I loved you. I will do all in my power to see you happy all your days."

Such tender words were almost overwhelming in their intensity. She drew in a deep breath. Shivered with pleasure as he recaptured her hand and pressed it to his lips.

"Let me see if I can claim another's words. Ah. You know I have been reading the Bard and admire Henry the soldier, so let me say this:

'A good heart . . . is the sun and the moon; or
rather the sun and not the moon, for it shines bright
and never changes but keeps his course truly. If
thou would have such a one, take me. And take me,
take a soldier. Take a soldier . . .'"

Tears blurred her eyes. Oh, how these words spoke to his character. This man might have his flaws, but he possessed a good heart. Could she ask for anything more?

"I'm sorry if the abruptness of my declaration has startled you. But please, would you consider my proposal in the light of this." He pulled out an envelope, the one which bore her mother's handwriting.

"What is it?"

"Please, just read."

And so she did.

Dearest Theodosia,

Please do not be alarmed by what has occurred. Dear Daniel has explained matters fully to me, sharing that his affections have long been engaged by you. What a wise man he is, for what man could not recognize that you are such a special treasure?

I know these events may seem shocking, but if you do hold him in regard, I urge you to consider his proposal with favor, without considering any obligation you may feel to me or your grandfather. Daniel has promised I can live with you both, if you so choose, or not, if you prefer, so I shall be well. And now, as Seraphina seems settled with us here, my care and that of your grandfather's need not be yours to bear. As you well know, your grandfather has had his wishes pandered to for so long I cannot think he would ever consider your happiness above his own, so you must choose your own path. It is not selfish, and I assure you no one else will be harmed.

So, darling daughter, whom I suspect holds a great deal of affection for the dear captain, please consider his suit favorably. For your mother's sake, as well as your own.

Your loving Mama

She glanced up, saw the regard in his eyes. "Did you ask her to write such things?"

Surprised hurt filled his features. "I have no idea what she wrote," he said quietly.

Chagrin bloomed. "Forgive me."

"Always."

She studied him, saw the man behind the uniform, *knew* this man would always hold his word, would always forgive, always protect, always serve.

Always love.

And now, with her mother's blessing, why did she still hesitate?

"Darling Theo, when you look at me so, it fills my heart with misgiving. If your mother's words were not of approval, then tell me so at once. But if she does view this as a good match, then say you'll marry me. Please."

"She approves," she said, knowing an almost overpowering sense of shyness.

"Then my heart clings to hope that you will too."

Could this be truly happening?

"If you'd prefer to wait, to be married by Mr. Crouch in front of your friends and neighbors and not have such a scandal attached to your name, then I can wait. It may be quite some time. I must return to London and cannot stay for banns reading now." His lips tweaked ruefully. "I fear it only fair to tell you that my visit to Whitehall may see my immediate return to war, and I might not return this way again for quite some time."

And he could die. And this grasp at happiness would be forever lost.

"My dear." He stroked her blemished cheek. "Do not look forlorn."

But she could not help the wild imaginings, the practical consider-ations. "What about Becky?"

"I had thought of a most suitable companion for her, someone with a joyous heart and hair the color of fire, but if she says nay, then my aunt Louisa will have to do."

She could keep the companion she so enjoyed? "And you would truly allow my mother to live with us?"

"I quite like your mother."

"Where would we live?"

"That, too, could be your choice. I have my parents' small cottage in Wiltshire, or we could rent or even buy a small place somewhere else. I've heard that a recently refurbished manor could be available soon. If one wanted to continue to live in the neighborhood."

Heat radiated through her chest, stealing her breath. So he truly *had* remodeled Mannering with her in mind? That would mean his hopes for a future with her extended far beyond the whim of a day or so. But to live at Mannering and be forced to endure the stings and sneers of those she'd always thought were her friends? "I—"

A knock interrupted her, and the door swung wider to reveal the man from before. "Excuse me for bothering thee, but if ye have anything fur-ther to say, ye may want to get it said in a hurry. For unless my ears be deceiving me, I hear the jangle of another carriage approaching."

Her breath caught. She turned to the captain. "Do you think it is Becky?"

"I rather doubt it. Actually, about that—" He moved to the window, peered past the ruffled curtain. Drew in a breath.

"Is it my grandfather?"

"There be a carriage pulling in!" called another man.

"I'm afraid so, yes." The captain grasped her hand. "And—"

"Oh!" Panic whirled around her and within. "He has come after us! He will wish to take me back! He won't bother trying to understand we thought Becky was here."

"Probably not." He smiled.

"Why are you smiling? What should we do?"

"Well, we could ask this kind gentleman to marry us without delay, then no one will be able to drag you away."

"Aye, that would be true," agreed the Scotsman.

"Oh, but . . ." She glanced between them. *Lord God, what should I do?*

"I love you, Theodosia."

She touched her mottled cheek. "You do not mind this?"

His hand covered hers. "Your cheek looks as if it retains the sweet kiss of a rose. How can I mind that? I love *you*, Theodosia," he repeated. "I always will, whatever you decide."

His words, the truth of them, eased the sharp edges of her panic. "You do?"

"I do."

The words rang around the bedchamber, echoing around the chamber of her heart, as a sense of utter rightness filled the room. "Yes."

His lips pulled to one side. "Is that an answer?"

"Yes. Yes, it is a yes." She turned to the tollkeeper. "Please. And hurry."

"Verra well." In a manner surprisingly quick for a big man, he bustled them out to the big room and hastily retrieved book and ink. "What do they call ye, my man?"

"My name is Daniel John Balfour." He threaded his fingers with hers.

"And where div ye come frae?"

"I come from a village called Melksham, in Wiltshire."

"Weel! I am not familiar with that, but I'll take yer word for it."

Silence filled the room, save for the scraping of his pen against the page of what looked to be a register.

"And noo, me bonnie lass, what's yer name?"

Her chest was tight, but the way the captain regarded her so tenderly only magnified the certainty within her heart. "My name is Theodosia Grace Stapleton, from the parish of Wooler."

"We be near neighbors, then." He led them through the vows, much the same as she'd heard in church.

They repeated the Scotsman's words, promising "to have and to hold, from this day forward, for better, for worse, in sickness and in health, till death us do part."

She then repeated the words appropriate for this location. "And I take all these folks to witness that I declare and acknowledge Daniel John Balfour to be my good man."

Daniel smiled, and the moment swirled with hope and certainty. This was right, this was good, this was—

"You do what?" a voice cried from the door.

Chapter 27

The door pushed wide with a thunderous crack, revealing Frederick Bellingham's equally thunderous face as he advanced into the room. "Stop!"

"Nae, man, ye cannae interrupt the most important part," complained the border priest. "Me man 'ere nae got to kiss the bride."

So true. Daniel had been longing to know the sweetness of her mouth for weeks now.

"No, he does not!" The squire's son advanced into the room, cheeks of puce. "How dare you?"

"How dare ye?" the Scotsman bristled. "This be me own establishment, and all. Now, pay the toll, ye wee grumble-gizzard."

"You—" The stripling ignored him, pointing at Theo. Words seemed to fail him, as he opened his mouth and closed it several times before audibly grinding his teeth at Daniel.

"What do you think you're doing, Frederick?" she asked.

"I came to save you from making the worst mistake. Theo, please, come home with me—"

Her brows rose.

"—and your grandfather."

"He is here?" She glanced quickly up at Daniel.

He nodded, the alarm in her eyes vibrating in his heart. Had General Contrary changed his mind?

"He insisted on coming with me when I heard what was going on." Frederick took a step toward Daniel. "How dare you think to marry her?"

Daniel moved forward to shield her. "I dare because I love her."

"And I love him." Theodosia moved beside him, tightened her clasp of his hand.

"You do?" Daniel turned to her.

"You know I do."

"Well, I hoped."

She leaned close. "It seems I will have to make sure you know my heart for the rest of my days."

"I am very willing to be obliged."

"I'm glad." She placed a hand on his chest, ignoring the huff from the younger man.

"Well?" A new voice swung their attention to the door.

"Grandfather!"

Daniel caught her tremble and wrapped his arm around her waist, bracing for what was about to happen, even as another part of him marveled at how perfectly she fit.

The Scotsman made a noise of disgust. "Am I to be interrupted again? Where be my ninepence?"

"What ninepence?"

There followed a sharp quarrel about the legality of paying the toll when one planned to return immediately to England, which the canny Scot won, pocketing the coin the general flung at him with a nod. "Aye. Cannae have an ill-willie Sassenach cause a carfuffle now, can we?"

"A what?" Frederick demanded.

"Hush." The general frowned at Daniel. "Well, sir? What has happened here?"

"Not nearly enough," the Scotsman said, winking at Daniel. "Go on, man, kiss yer bride," he entreated.

So Daniel did.

He had known moments of hard-won victory. Moments of pride and humbling joy. But this moment, when he bent and closed his eyes and felt the sweet brush of her lips with his, seemed to light a million stars in the heavenlies.

She feted him with her kiss, and he slipped his arms around her and drew her even closer.

Someone somewhere was saying something, but he cared not. Her kiss. Her love. He needed God and nothing else but his new wife's sweet love.

Eventually he drew back for breath, saw the unsteady rise and fall of her chest, and from the stars in her eyes, knew she felt as he did.

"That's it, then?" the general demanded. "The deed be done and they are truly wed?"

"Aye, as true and as legal as in any English church." The Scotsman winked. "Just one more act needed to seal the deal, as it were."

Daniel cleared his throat.

His wife's stricken swain shook his head. "I cannot believe you would hive off in such a fashion, Theo!"

"A brave lassie, she be," the Scotsman said with a grin.

"A Trojan, indeed," Daniel murmured, squeezing her hand.

Her silvery laugh floated on the air.

"You are sure about this, Theo? Nobody need know, and you could return with me now," young Bellingham implored.

"Thank you for your concern, but I'm extremely sure."

"But he's a soldier!"

"One of England's finest, or so everyone has been saying for months."

"You *are* sure about him?" The general spoke with lowered brow.

"I wouldn't have married him if I wasn't." She drew close to Daniel again. "Really, Grandfather, you cannot think I would marry someone without being sure of him? I am neither a green girl nor a fool. Besides, imagine the scandal if I returned from such a shocking adventure unwed." She mock-gasped. "Can you imagine what Mrs. Cleever might say?"

Her grandfather nodded. "Which is why I came to make sure you followed through."

"What?" Frederick turned startled eyes to the general. "I thought you came to stop the wedding."

The general shrugged. "I cannot be responsible for what you might've thought."

Theo stilled, gaze shifting from her grandfather to Daniel then back again. "How did—? We came to stop Becky."

"Ah." The general blew out a breath. Looked at Daniel. "You haven't told her yet?"

"Told me what?" She faced him, questioningly.

His stomach tightened. "What I tried to say before about Becky."

"Do you think she will dislike our union?" Theo quavered.

"Oh no. I know that she approves."

She blinked. "She knew you were going to propose?"

"Actually . . ."

"Did she tell you this before she ran away?"

"About that—"

"For a girl who claims not to be green, you can be awfully blind." The general emphasized his acerbity with a snort.

"I beg your pardon?" His new wife looked at Daniel. "What is he talking about?"

He sighed. "Becky didn't run away."

"How do you know that? We chased her up here—"

"You thought she was missing, but in actual fact, she was not."

"I don't understand. You thought she was missing too. Didn't you?"

He shook his head.

"Och, the lad be in trouble with his new bride already!" the Scotsman said with far too much glee.

"Then Becky isn't missing?"

"She appeared not an hour after you left," her grandfather said. "Just like I told her to."

"You what?"

Theo's high-pitched ascending note drew a gasp from young Bellingham and further mirth from the tollbooth officer.

Daniel frowned. "Thank you, sir. I don't know that we'll require your services anymore."

"Nae?" The Scotsman rubbed his jaw again. "Weel, that be half a guinea then, me man, that's me usual charge."

Daniel paid the man, who chuckled, reiterating with a wink that they'd paid for the use of the bedchamber, before wishing them well and retreating to another room, leaving Daniel to turn to his disgruntled bride. "Theo, darling, I hope you don't judge me too harshly—"

"Put the blame on me, lad. Put the blame on me," the general said.

"Grandfather, whatever do you mean?"

⤳⤳

Theo listened as between them her grandfather and her new husband shared about the general's plan. Everyone she'd thought she knew—Mama, Becky, the lieutenant—actually had conspired against her?

The knowledge was so galling she could not look at either man who claimed to have her interests at heart. How could they have treated her so?

"You had to be *forced* to marry me?" she whispered, inching away from Daniel and placing her hand on her mouth.

"Ah, don't blame him, lass," her grandfather said. "We knew how you felt about the man—"

Heat tingled through her skin. Oh dear heavens. How obvious had she been?

"—and circumstances would never allow for a traditional wedding." He cast a withering look at Frederick. "So this was the best way." His bearded cheeks lifted as he offered a rare smile. "And my being here lends countenance to it all. Now we can just say you were lately married, not how you were married."

She glanced at Frederick, who wore his own look of disbelief. The knowledge he was witness to her grandfather's machinations and her own mortification caused her to whirl away from them and move to the other room, wrapping her arms around her.

"Young Bellingham is witness that the marriage is legal too. And I'm sure he won't want it spread around that he lost out to the better man."

She closed her eyes, barely hearing Frederick's mumbled assent or his muttered farewell. Her heart swelled with a dozen conflicting emotions: anger at being manipulated, shame at being meekly led, uncertainty about what she had just done.

"Now, Theo." Her grandfather patted her shoulder, and she had to fight the inclination to jerk away. "You have a good man here. I'm sorry you did not like the method, but I cannot be sorry about the outcome. You will be happy, I know."

It was a good thing *he* knew, because she was feeling uncertain about so many things right now. Tension rooted her stock-still, the click of the door closing giving a measure of relief. What had she done? Who had she entrusted her life to?

"Theo, dear heart." The heat of Daniel's presence drew behind her. "You cannot think I'm such a ninny that I would need persuasion to marry the most wonderful woman in the world."

"How can I believe anything you say?"

"Because." He placed his hands on her hips and gently turned her to face him, his eyes intent and true. "Because you *know* me, and you know my heart is yours, as I am."

Moisture blurred his features and she blinked hard.

"Oh, my love." He drew a finger to wipe away spilled tears. "Do not cry. Truly, the reason I wished to marry you in this manner was because I wanted to protect you, especially after the trouble my actions caused you. I love you, and at the risk of sounding presumptuous, hoped you might be kindly disposed to me. And this presented a chance to wed without the watchful stares of those who may not wish us well."

"You were not coerced?"

"Indeed not. I wanted to be married to you. It was my chief desire. I confess I do not know exactly what the future holds, but who among us do? That is God's privilege."

True.

"But for those of us who claim faith in Him, we can be assured He is guiding our steps, that He can be trusted. And I know that you, like me, are trusting Him with your future."

A future with Daniel in it. Her heart throbbed painfully. Imagine a future without him in it? No. No. She'd been imagining that for too long. And she didn't have to now. For she had just promised herself to a future *with* Daniel in it. Together. Forever. Oh, how wonderful.

"I love you, Theo." He drew closer, traced a finger down her marred cheek, his eyes intent on her. "Let me show you just how much you mean to me."

And he drew her nearer still, breath warm against her skin as his lips traced her stain, then he touched his lips to hers, and kissed her once again.

Her eyes closed as his mouth softly pressed against hers before his lips firmed to cling more insistently. Under his tenderness the frost of hurt and confusion melted away, and she sank into his embrace, letting him hold her. Her heart was a flame, kindled by the sweetness of his lips, the gentle caress of his hands, the breath they exchanged and shared. And as he murmured sweet sayings to her, as he spoke of devotion and promise and care, and he kissed her again and again and again, she soon grew convinced that this man had needed no coercion, nor any persuasion, and had simply done what he'd said before. He'd married the woman he wanted as opportunity had presented itself.

And seeing she was so glad he had, she found she could not blame him at all.

Somehow the promise of a mere few hours across the border had turned into several days. She soon discovered Captain Daniel Balfour was every bit a man of his word and was taking his role of proving his love to her very seriously. She'd also discovered Mama had packed a small bag of clothes for Theo, items that Theo had blushed over, but which had been received most appreciatively by her new husband. She didn't even know that Mama had kept the items destined for her trousseau. Seeing clothing her mother had labored over stitching half Theo's lifetime ago seemed so poignant and strange.

How funny to think she had once dreamed and believed a gentleman might wish to wed her, only for no such man to appear for so long. For her to think she cared for a man only to see him marry her younger sister. To see those around her betrothed, wedded, and enjoying hopeful families of their own, while she'd been left wondering what was wrong with her. To learn that nobody but the man considered England's hero could be the first—the only—to truly raise a flutter in her breast. Yet how wonderfully heartwarming it was to know Daniel seemed—for some reason—to think the exact thing about her.

She still didn't fully believe it, so he tried to convince her, and really was most thorough in some of his efforts to show his love . . .

"Are you ready, my love?" He stole her attention from the carriage window.

"I suppose so." She clasped his hand and gently squeezed. "Though I am not at all certain about the reception we shall meet."

"I do hope you're not going to concern yourself with what the likes of Lady Bellingham thinks of as proper."

He kissed her hand, and the tingles leapt up her skin. "I'm afraid nobody thinks running off to Scotland to get married is proper."

"Then let's not tell them that. We can follow your grandfather's advice and have a wedding in London. Three weeks of banns reading, correct?"

"Yes, but—"

"Would that make you feel more comfortable with things?"

"Yes. But doing so just to suit some conventions is not really what I wish to do."

"Then we could simply ignore people's speculations, seeing as we are married after all, and immediately head south, taking my niece and your mother with us."

"But would that not smack of running away?"

"You need simply tell me what it is you wish to do."

Her heart burned. For so long she had been at the mercy of others and their decisions. To know she now actually had a choice almost overwhelmed her.

"My dear?"

The carriage slowed and turned into the gates of Stapleton Court. While she didn't expect to have to do any explaining today—all the family and staff were fully apprised of the situation—it would only be a matter of time before such explanations became necessary.

She exhaled. "I cannot believe that I've had so much time to consider this, and yet I still can't decide what is best to do."

"We could defer to your mother."

"Yes. Mama might offer wise counsel." Her lips twisted. "I'm rather of the impression that Grandfather would say other people's opinions should be condemned to Hades."

"I'm of the impression he'd word it rather more strongly than that," Daniel murmured.

She chuckled. "Oh, I wish you would not constantly make me laugh."

"Why? Nothing enchants me more than hearing that little burbling sound, like a little cheerful waterfall one discovers on a hot and thirsty walk. You are like that to me." Eyes tender with sincerity, he drew her close once more.

Another moment passed before she finally pulled away, breathless. "I'm all rumpled now."

"You simply look like you have been thoroughly kissed."

"What?" She patted her hair, straightened her bonnet.

"My dear, you look beautiful." He drew his knuckles gently down her cheek before cupping her chin loosely. "I find you most appealing." His lips found her skin again.

Well, he'd certainly given that impression in this past week.

The horses slowed and Stapleton Court came into view. Arrangements beyond spending a night or so here remained to be sorted, and tension rose higher in her chest. But at the squeeze of his hand on hers she felt calm again. How different things seemed, knowing she was beloved, and that this brave man would both stand beside her and protect and guide her. Her shoulders eased.

"Are you ready, Mrs. Balfour?"

"To face the general and Mama?"

"And dear Becky. I hope she has forgiven me for using her name in vain."

"She is hardly the Almighty, so she should not take things too close to heart. I should hope she does not see our escapade as one to emulate."

"Not everyone can make their perfect match in a run across the border. Only the most adventuresome, the most courageous, and most blessed."

"Most blessed, indeed," she murmured, smiling at him in sweet contentment.

For how else could she have married this man, except that God had brought them together to walk this untrodden path into the dawn of a new day, a new life, and God's glorious light and future.

Acknowledgments

Thank You, God, for Jesus Christ, and the promises found in the Bible, that mean we can trust You to direct our paths (Prov. 3:5–6; 16:9), and that You are able to do exceedingly abundantly above all we can ask or imagine (Eph. 3:20). Thank You for the hope, joy, peace, and purpose this brings.

Huge thanks to my husband, Joshua, for believing in and supporting my writing dream. Thank you, Caitlin, Jackson, Asher, and Tim, for understanding why your mum talks as if imaginary people and problems are real. Thank you to my extended family and friends, especially my parents, Kay and David Weaver, my sister, Roslyn Howe, and my mother-in-law, Lynne Miller, for your prayers and constant encouragement.

Thanks to my agent, Tamela Hancock Murray, and the team at Kregel Publications, for allowing me to write books that can be considered unapologetically Christian. Thanks to my editors, Janyre, Christina, and Lindsay, for helping me to shape this story into what it is today, and to the wonderful designers who make such beautiful covers that always get high praise.

Thanks, also, to the authors and bloggers and influencers who have endorsed and supported and opened doors along the way. You are truly appreciated.

And thank *you*, wonderful readers, for choosing to read this book (and hopefully others of mine too!). Thank you for buying my books and sharing the love with others through your kind reviews and your encouraging messages and emails.

I hope you enjoyed Daniel and Theodosia's story. God bless you.

Author's Note

Thank you for reading *Dawn's Untrodden Green*, a book I hope Georgette Heyer fans love reading as much as I relished writing. I trust you enjoy the sparkle and banter of this story, with its nods to both Shakespeare and Heyer. After the heavy topics discussed in the previous Regency Wallflowers books, I found it a little necessary to return to something more lighthearted in tone!

Persuasion, one of my favorite books by Jane Austen, has a dutiful daughter not unlike Theodosia, who often takes time from the stresses of life to pause for "solitude and reflection." I liken this to the selah moments in the book of Psalms, where readers are encouraged to pause and reflect and think, tasks we don't often manage in our busy, modern lives. But there is value in being still, in waiting on God, listening, trusting, and filtering life's challenges through God's promises. Both Daniel and Theo believe they know what God has in store for them and struggle to trust for the unknown. Theo has wisely learned contentment yet struggles to believe God might have more blessings in store. There is a tension, isn't there, between counting our blessings and being thankful for what we have, and daring to believe God might do "exceedingly abundantly above all we can ask or think"? I like how Daniel tugs at Theo's secret hopes and dreams, while she helps him realize that a man can plan his way, but it's ultimately God who directs our steps, which encourages us all to trust God and His timing, even when the future seems unknown.

AUTHOR'S NOTE

Regency-era elopements fascinate me, and I focused on the aftermath of an elopement in *The Making of Mrs. Hale*. But while many focus attention on Gretna Green, any village across the Scottish border from England would have had a marriage house for those desperate to wed. Such marriages didn't need to be conducted by a blacksmith either. Coldstream, situated on the border and famous as the birthplace for Britain's oldest regular regiment, the Coldstream Guards, had its Toll House double as a marriage house, where couples could legally be married without parental consent, prior public notice, or residential requirements, which saw thousands of couples marry in the eighteenth and nineteenth centuries—including several earls and lords chancellor. I found some very entertaining anecdotes on the Northumberland & Durham Family History Society and Border Ramblings websites, which flavor the scenes in this book.

For more behind-the-book details, sneak peeks of my Regency and contemporary books, and to sign up for my newsletter, please visit www.carolynmillerauthor.com. You can also follow me on Facebook, Instagram, and Pinterest to learn more about my bookish news.

Finally, thank you, lovely readers, for all your wonderful support! I truly appreciate you.

EARLIER BOOKS IN THIS SERIES

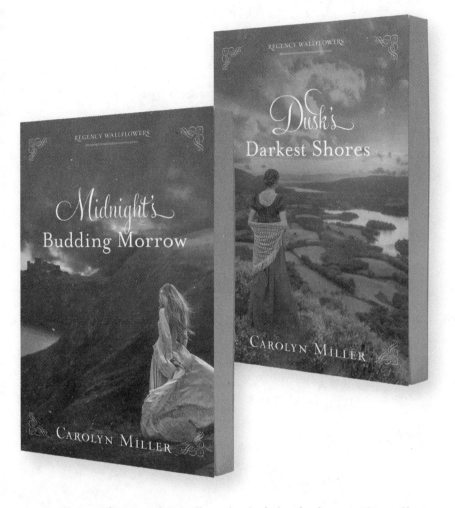

"Best-selling author Carolyn Miller is back with a fresh series that will not only thrill readers eager for more of her work, but bring in new fans looking for beautiful writing, fascinating research, deftly woven love stories, and real faith lived out in the Regency period."

—*Midwest Book Review*

KREGEL
PUBLICATIONS

REGENCY BRIDES
A LEGACY *of* GRACE

Clean and wholesome romance you'll swoon over!

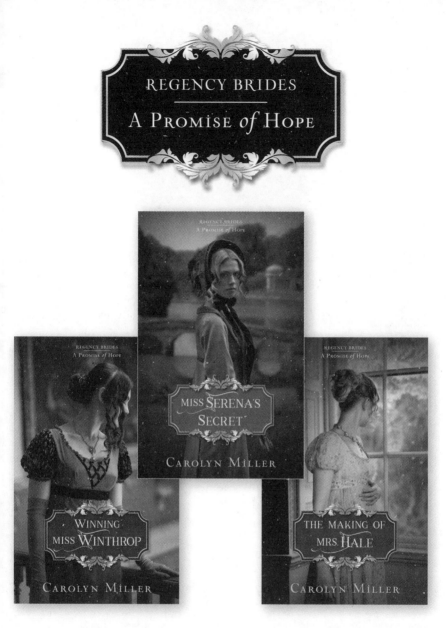

REGENCY BRIDES
DAUGHTERS *of* AYNSLEY

"Miller's inclusion of faith issues with an authentic portrayal of Regency society will continue to delight her growing fan base."
—Publishers Weekly